MW01127060

triscelle publishing

presents

CRONE OF WAR

MORRIGAN'S BROOD Book II

By

heather poinsett dunbar

and

christopher dunbar

map of story locations

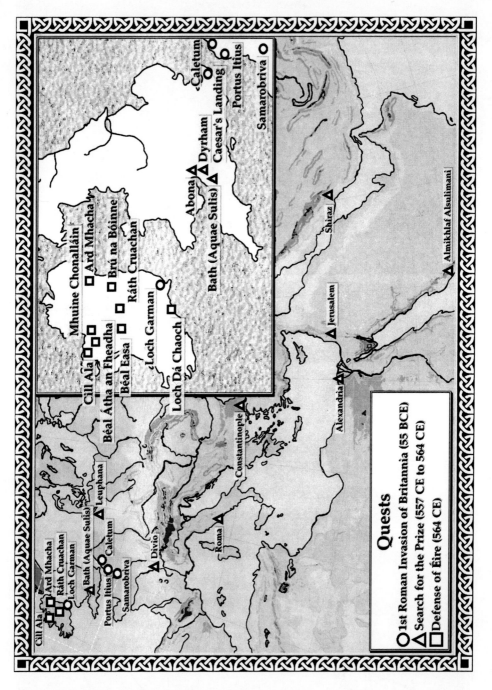

Map details are on the next page. The same map is used for both Morrigan's Brood and Crone of War; some locations may only appear in one book.

map guide

Western European Story Locations

Ancient Name	Ancient Kingdom	Modern Name	Modern Country
Kingdoms of Éire (circa 55 BCE through 564 CE)			
Ard Mhacha	Ulaid (Ulster)	Armagh	Northern Ireland
Béal Átha an Fheadha	Connachta (Connacht)	Ballina	Ireland
Cill Ala	Connachta (Connacht)	Killala	Ireland
Loch Dá Chaoch	Laigin (Leinster)	Waterford	Ireland
Loch Garman	Laigin (Leinster)	Wexford	Ireland
Mhuine Chonalláin	Connachta (Connacht)	Bonniconlon	Ireland
Brú na Bóinne	Mide (Meath)	Palace of the Boyne	Ireland
Ráth Cruachan	Connachta (Connacht)	Roscommon	Ireland
Kingdoms of Britain (circa 55 BCE through 564 CE)			
Abona	Britannia	Sea Mills (Bristol)	England
Bath (Aquae Sulis)	Britannia	Bath	England
(Caesar's Landing)	Britannia (Cantiaci)	Walmer	England
Dyrham	Britannia	Dyrham (Bath)	England
Rome, Gaul, and the Frankish Kingdoms (circa 55 BCE through 564 CE)			
Caletum	Austrasia (Francia)	Calais	France
Divio	Burgundia (Francia)	Dijon	France
Leuphana	Saxony (Old Saxony)	Lüneburg	Germany
Portus Itius	Gallia Lugdunensis	Wissant	France
Samarobriva	Gallia Lugdunensis	Amiens	France
Roma (Rome)	Roman Empire	Rome	Italy

Eastern European, Asian, and African Story Locations (circa 564 CE)

Ancient	Modern
Alexandria, *Dioecesis Aegypti* (Byzantium)	
	Al Iskandariyya, Egypt
Almikhlaf Alsulimani, Hejaz	
	Jizan, Saudi Arabia
Constantinople, *Dioecesis Thraciae* (Byzantium)	
	Istanbul, Turkey
Jerusalem, *Dioecesis Palaestina Prima* (Byzantium)	
	Jerusalem, Israel
Shiraz, Sassanid Persian Empire	
	Shiraz, Iran

Dedication and Copyright Page

For John J. Haas

August, 2012

Crone of War

Morrigan's Brood Book II

Reprint ISBN-10: 1-937341-10-0
Reprint ISBN-13: 978-1-937341-10-7
Original ISBN-10: 0-692-00992-2
Original ISBN-13: 978-0-692-00992-5
by Heather Poinsett Dunbar
and Christopher Dunbar
Published by Triscelle Publishing
Edited by Sarah E. Aalderink
Cover art, map, and website by Khanada Taylor
Triscelle Publishing Logo by Dayna Hartley
Proofread by Jillian Rosenburg
Original Print and Copyright: July, 2010

Printed by permission in the United States of America, the United Kingdom, or Australia. See back page for printing information. For any issues with print or binding quality, please contact the company through which the purchase was made and give the code number on this book.

Visit our website and find us on WordPress, Goodreads, Shelfari, Facebook, the Library Thing, LinkedIn, Twitter, and many other places on the Net.

www.triscellepublishing.com
triscellepublishing.wordpress.com

Also available in several eBook formats

acknowledgments

Heather's Acknowledgments

Once again, I thank my husband for all his hard work in creating plots and characters with me. There are also big thank you's to our editor, Sarah (Sally), whose encouragement is one of the reasons that there is a Morrigan's Brood series; Khanada, who has done so much more for us than merely maintain the website – she encouraged and inspired us with breathtaking cover and interior art; Jillian, who joined our merry team in searching for and correcting the layout goofs on the final draft; and Dayna, who worked on the logo for us.

There is also much love and thanks to my and the hub's ever-growing circle of friends and coworkers, especially Irene, Christi, Christine, Annette, Shelley, the FList, the Fanggang, The Writer's Cabal (Vampire Division), otherwise known as Heidi, Khanada, Tracy Angelina, Jill, Ruth, and Kara. I must also thank our parents, who have offered so much.

Christopher's Acknowledgments

I would like to thank my wife for continuing to urge me on to work with her on more novels, and I would like to echo her sentiments. In addition, I would like to thank her parents and mine for being so supportive during these hard times between jobs.

Lines of Blood-Drinkers

Algul – An Arabic blood-drinker, created by their God of War, Verethragna. Their known abilities include the power to create visual hallucinations in both mortals and other immortals. However, their vulnerability lies in strong smells. Their numbers are small, due to a genocidal war between themselves and the remnants of the Ekimmu.

Deargh Du – An ancient line of blood-drinkers from Éire (Ireland) that trace their ancestry to the Goddess Morrigan. Their true talents lie in their magical skills and their fae-like beauty, known as glamoury. They can fly, create glowing light, heal mortals as well as other immortals, and draw down darkness and shadow. Their major weakness is the metal gold. After the creation of the Ekimmu Cruitne, the Deargh Du withdrew back to their native land and ceased interacting with other blood-drinking races.

Ekimmu – A group of blood-drinkers originating in Assyria from Zaltu, God of Strife. They grew in strength and power, eventually dominating the Middle East. However, other races, such as their enemies the Algul and the Lamia, began to hunt them down, decimating their population.

Ekimmu Cruitne – The Ekimmu, fleeing a genocidal war, removed themselves to the northern regions of Alba (Scotland). After meeting some of the Deargh Du, who traveled with the Scoti tribe, an Ekimmu and a Deargh Du conspired to tip the balance by creating a new being. Morrigan, in her rage, sought to confine them to their lands. Ekimmu Cruitne are struck by illness whenever they try to cross the ocean. Their greatest talent is their olfactory sense, making them excellent trackers. They can also heal others, fly, read minds, and enjoy manipulating games of chance. In addition, they can create the sensation of pleasure as well as harm in themselves and their victims.

Lamia – According to legend, Lamia was a Queen of Libya who seduced Zeus. In retribution, Hera killed all of her children. Heartbroken, Lamia began feeding on the people of Greece, and before long, she had many new immortal children. The Lamia infiltrated Roman society, and soon Rome became their seat of power. The Lamia's skills lie in mind-bending, or manipulation. They even have an ability to enter dreams and manipulate the dreamer.

Ouphe – An ancient Saxon line of blood-drinkers that moved into Britannia during the Saxon conquest. Their strength is in their monstrous lycanthropic nature; many blood-drinking races can die from the wounds given by an Ouphe. Yet, the Ouphe are severely affected by silver. Their origin is a mystery.

<u>Strigoi</u> – A line of blood-drinkers that began from a cursed Greek beauty named Iris. Aphrodite's curse did not grant Iris and her victim's immortality until later. Yet, they only survive fifty years after their transformation. The Strigoi are telepathic and unleash uncontrollable madness upon mortals and immortals alike. Affected mortals tear at their eyes and puncture their eardrums to escape the onslaught of sights and sounds. Despite their talents, Strigoi are physically weak, stunted, and are the ugliest of the blood-drinkers.

<u>Sugnwr Gwaed</u> – A British group of blood-drinkers created by Cernunnos, the Horned God of animals, wilderness, and the wild hunt. Their strengths include enhanced communication with animals and their talent for vocal persuasion. They can convince their victims of almost anything. They also fly, like the other Celtic lines, and have an aptitude for healing others.

<u>Chiang-shih</u> – A Chinese line of blood-drinkers that originated from Shenlong, a dragon god. Shenlong created the Chaing-Shih to protect His earthly treasures from greedy mortals. While the Chiang-shihh can control storms like Shenlong, they can only fly when the moon is full and have difficulty crossing water. Little else is known about them, as they chose not to interact with most of the western lines. Their true talents lie in their medical knowledge and their gifts.

<u>Pacu Pati</u> – Blood-drinkers from India that originated from Kali. The Pacu Pati tend to cloister themselves with their new families of other Pacu Pati and do not meet with the other lines. When other lines have witnessed the celebrations of the cycles of life and death, they tend to misunderstand the celebrations, and a lack of a common language generally adds to the confusion.

Other lines will be revealed in future works.

character and pronunciation guide

Marcus Galerius Primus Helvetticus   Marcus

Life as a Deargh Du for Marcus is a lonely one, as he has never met one of his own kind. Still, this former Roman general manages to find friends, but most of them are mortals. While he enjoys Berti's antics, there is something the Briton keeps hidden about himself. Oh, and that Maél Muire? There is just something about her...

Mandubratius   Awvarwy (a-war-wee)

With the Great Prize close at hand, this Briton turned Lamia must slosh through the wilderness of a foreign land to seek this most valuable treasure. Leadership of the Lamia is not enough to sate his thirst for power. Mandubratius must place this artifact on the statue of Mars himself and usher in a new age for the Lamia.

Maél Muire Ní Conghal Uí Máine   Maél Muire (mal mure)

Upon the departure of her uncle Cennedi, Maél Muire is given the mantle of power over her clan, but she must earn the respect of her neighbors. Even now, after the death of her latest betrothed, her neighboring chieftains vie for her hand in marriage. Will she choose for the sake of love or politics? Only the Goddess knows.

Claudius Metrius Sertorius   Claudius

Leadership is a difficult mantle for Claudius to carry. While he enjoyed serving as a lieutenant under Marcus when he was a mortal, Claudius never quite enjoyed being in charge after his departure. Now the Sugnwr Gwaed look up to him... sigh.

Arwin Mac Alpin   Mac Alpin

Wine, women, gambling, and spilled blood are Mac Alpin's motivations in his life as an Ekimmu Cruitne... especially gambling against mortals and other blood-drinker lines. Ah... Marcus and Claudius... how he loves draining them of silver.

Bertius Lancastrius   Berti

To most who see this dashing Briton, he appears the fool, dressed in foppish fine linens and reeking of exotic aromas. Still, a few have seen this dandy dispatch marauders with precision, lightning speed, and grace... hardly the earmarks of a fop. So, who is this Briton really, and why has he befriended the outcast Roman Deargh Du?

Tertia Amata Antonia   Amata

What a small price she has paid, in retrospect, to become the leader of the Lamia. She conspired with Mandubratius to murder their Sponsor, Felician, she let Mandubratius 'rape' her on the floor the Lamia Senate, and now she allows Marcus, who she knows is a Deargh Du, to hunt down Mandubratius. Power at a good price.

Sáerlaith Ní Adhamdh   Sáerlaith (saer-la)

Far removed from the events taking place around Connacht, Sáerlaith must spend her nights waiting for word about the Lamia encroachment in Éire. With her friends Ruarí and Caoimhín further south, she must alone contend with the politicians of Ard Mhacha. She wishes she could leave, but her duty is to stay, and so she shall.

Ruarí Mac Flan   Ruarí (*ro-ree*)

Troubled is the mind of this elder Deargh Du, who has witnessed many atrocities in his lifetime, though none more heinous than the Roman assault on the defenseless druids of the grove of Loch Garman. If only he knew how twisted fate could be.

Téa Uí Cennedi Uí Máine (*tay-a*)   Talia de Burgundy

What luck! What fortune has blessed Talia de Burgundy! Soon, she can throw off the shackles of this marriage to that tiresome, near-sighted Cennedi, and then with her fellow Lamia, drive the Franks out of Burgundy, thus regaining her birthright!

Connor Mac Turrlough Uí Niall   Connor

After his son's mysterious, brutal death, Connor, with firm encouragement from his mother, seeks out his son's betrothed for his own wife. With his eyes set upon Maél Muire, Connor searches for how best to court her, but he soon finds competition.

Cennedi Mac Lubdan Uí Máine   Cennedi (*kenn-edi*)

From chieftain and husband to slave, Cennedi finds his life as a Lamia to be an abomination. Every time he gives into his thirst for blood, he silently curses his wife... his Sponsor, for changing him. How he misses his niece, Maél Muire.

Sive Uí Fergus Uí Máine   Aunt Sive (*se-ve*)

How much Sive worries about her niece, Maél Muire, who has never before had so much responsibility thrust upon her. Such pain she sees in her niece's eyes with all of the death she has experienced, and yet, she holds much love for her clanspeople.

Seosaimhín Uí Turrlough Uí Niall   Seosaimhín (*sho-siv-een*)

So, you wish to read more about us, learn our innermost secrets, but the mists lead both ways. I see you where you sit. This night, the white crow Nagirrom will signal my arrival as I take you with me through the mist and reward you for your curiosity.

Other Character Name Pronunciations

Name	Pronunciation	Name	Pronunciation
Adhamdh	*ad-am*	Lileas	*lil-ee*
Bearach	*ba-rax*	Lughna	*loo-na*
Caile	*kay-la*	Máire	*moya*
Cailin	*kay-lin*	Maon	*may-own*
Caoimhín	*kev-een*	Niamh	*neev*
Dechtire	*dec-tir-a*	Nuadin	*noo-ah-den*
Emer	*eem-ir*	Oisín	*osh-een*
Etain	*ey-taw-in*	Seanán	*shaw-nawn*
Gaelen	*ga-len*	Ségnet	*seg-net*
Ioin	*oh-een*	Sheevan	*she-va*

Irish Story Location Pronunciations

Location	Pronunciation	Location	Pronunciation
Ard Mhacha	*ord wa-hcah*	Cill Ala	*kill-la-la*
Béal Átha an Fheadha	*beh-lo-ina*	Loch Dá Chaoch	*lo-hc daoh-hco*
Béal Easa	*bell-assa*	Mhuine Chonalláin	*moonie hahn-alon*
Brú na Bóinne	*bruna bun-ee-ay*	Ráth Cruachan	*raw kroo-uh-ckahn*

gods and goddesses of the series

Irish Pantheon – Tuatha dé Danann (People of Dana)	
Aine (*An-ya*)	*Goddess of love and fertility*
Aongas Og (*An-gus Og*)	*God of love and youth*
Brigid (*Bri-jid*)	*Goddess of healing, writing, water, and cats*
Dagda (*Dah-dah*)	*The 'good' God of many skills*
Dana (*Day-na*)	*The Mother Goddess*
Lugh (*Loo*)	*Multi-skilled God of battle, light, writing, and the harvest*
Medb (*May-v*)	*Goddess of sovereignty*
Manannán Mac Lir (*Mannan-awan Mac Lir*)	*Guide to the Otherworld and God of the wind, travels, sea, and sailing*
Morrigan (*Mor-ee-gan*)	*Goddess of death, battle, blood, and rebirth*
Nuada (*Nu-a-da*)	*God of healing and weaponry*
British Pantheon	
Cernunnos	*God of animals, wilderness, fertility, and the Wild Hunt*
Greek / Roman Pantheon	
Aphrodite (*af-rə-dy-tee*) / Venus (*ˈwɛnʊs*)	*Goddess of love, beauty, and sexuality / Goddess of love, beauty, and fertility*
Ares (*áreːs*) / Mars (*Mārs*)	*God of War and Manly Virtues / God of War; part of the Archaic Triad*
Hera (*Hēra*) / Juno (*ˈjuːnoː*)	*Queen of the Gods and Goddess of marriage, women and birth / Patron Goddess of Rome and Goddess of women; part of the Capitoline Triad*
Zeus (*Zews*) / Jupiter (*Joo-pi-ter*)	*King of the Gods and God of the sky, thunder, lightning, law, order, and justice / King of the Gods and God of the sky and thunder; part of the Capitoline Triad; Patron Deity of Rome*
Arabic (Zoroastrian) Pantheon	
Verethragna	*God of war and sexual potency*
Assyrian Pantheon	
Zaltu (*Zal-too*)	*God of strife*
Hindu Pantheon	
Kali (*Kālī*)	*Goddess of time and change; "She who destroys"; "Redeemer of the Universe"*
Chinese Pantheon	
Shenlong (*shén lóng*)	*A dragon god in Chinese mythology known as the "Master of Storms"*

pROLogue

Dearest friend,

I hope your journey is going well and that you will return to Éire soon.

A strange experience occurred a few nights ago, and the shock of the entire encounter still resonates in my brain. I performed a ritual to part the mists, and then I found myself someplace else.

Marcus, it was so beautiful. The moon seemed ready to swallow the land, and the sweetest of smells wafted with the winds. The stars seemed to be within arm's reach. Then I knew that I had departed our world and arrived in the Otherworld. Manannán Mac Lir must have allowed my entry into these realms. I considered seeking His guidance, but then a series of images overwhelmed me, causing me to forget myself.

Then all turned to bright sunshine, and I found myself face to face with the One-Eyed Seer. I stared into Her dark eye and felt so insignificant and unworthy. After all, here I stood, a silly, mortal woman, demanding Her attention.

I began to lower my eyes, trembling with excitement and a little fear, but as my eyes started for the ground, I realized that I had witnessed a gleam of respect in Her eye.

I could feel Her power as She spoke. She informed me of a secret that I must keep.

I've never felt such warmth, and then She bade me farewell.

I'm so upset that I didn't have the chance to spend more time with Her. This will probably be the only opportunity I will have while walking this world to see Her.

I wish you were here so we could speak together again. Writing lacks the flavor of the incident that night.

There are strange things happening here, Marcus, things that I cannot discuss now. Return soon to Éire, my friend. You are missed.

Maél Muire paused in her writing before tearing apart the scroll. Her writing seemed ridiculous. She paused before rubbing her hands together, wishing she could make sense of her meeting with the One-Eyed Seer. No words would ever describe the event to her satisfaction.

She stared at another scroll and opened it, resolving to begin anew. This time, she would stick to more comfortable matters.

---

chapter one

The Red Sea

Sitara paced the deck of the trireme, watching the flotilla of eleven boats behind her. The dusk skies made the water turn gold, red, and some of the most beautiful colors she had ever seen. She could hear the rowers grunt with their labor as the ship moved with a skilled refinement that reminded her of a graceful bird, spreading multiple wings to stroke through the winds of clear water that reflected the skies. It seemed fitting for this graceful bird to be destined for Alexandria. Father had often said that the buildings of white limestone could not be described.

At that moment, her mother placed a hand on her arm, and Sitara jumped in surprise.

"What do you think of on this night?" Devayani asked her daughter.

"The sea is…" Sitara murmured before pausing. "I am speechless. It is more beautiful than anything I have seen in such a long time."

"Yes, it is an awesome sight." Her mother turned to stare at the waters. "And you will be able to see it at our new home in Alexandria."

Sitara smiled at her mother. "Is this as picturesque as your family's home in Varanasi?"

"My child, nothing can match that," Devayani replied before wrapping an arm around Sitara. "Not even your grandfather's home in Shiraz. Of course you know better than to tell your father such a thing." She chuckled. "Speaking of your father, you must help me. The sea does little good for Vivika."

"She is still seasick?" Sitara asked, while playing with the edge of her indigo silk shawl.

"Yes, and Sarid and Nadeem have been fishing most of the afternoon. We have fish to cook."

Sitara watched her mother shudder.

"I hope these are large enough to cook," she whispered to her mother.

"They are, unfortunately."

Sitara giggled, before following her mother into the lower level of the ship, past the crew of oarsmen as they ceased their shift for the night. Every night, a smaller group of sailors would allow the ships to continue traversing the dark seas. Sitara and her mother then left rowing desk as they moved into the room that served as the kitchen.

"I cannot wait to get to Alexandria," Nadeem muttered between bites of fish.

"Anything would be better than the food in Rome," commented Sitara.

"I know," replied their father. "It's such a pity that the city lingers in its death. However, Alexandria offers a place on the route to Constantinople. Pass me the dates, Sarid."

Without warning, a series of whooshing noises and screams echoed through the room.

Berti started to pace the small room, bothered by the cramped quarters. "Do you ever feel as though you may never escape this?"

Marcus yawned before sitting up in the small bunk, effectively banging his forehead against the upper bed. "The ever so pleasant experience of feeding on rats because I do not want to exhaust the crews? Or do you mean these lovely quarters?" He smirked and then inhaled. "Someone is cooking stinky fish."

"Does the increase of your senses ever become a distraction?" Berti asked, while sitting on the floor.

"Some…" Marcus closed his eyes for a moment. He then rolled out of bed and stood up. "I hear something."

"Oh, I am sure you do," chortled Berti as he rolled his eyes a bit and laughed. "This is the wondrous display of talents that you master, correct?" He then stood up as Marcus turned back to face him.

At that moment, the sound of splitting wood echoed around the two of them as a huge ballista spear cracked through the deck in between them.

Berti blinked, and began coughing as bits of splintered wood ended up in his open mouth. He and Marcus tilted their heads to the side to study the spear for a moment.

"I will take back my stupid question about heightened senses making one distracted," Berti replied, still spitting up wood dust.

"We had better find out what this mess is about," stated Marcus, before opening the hatch to the upper deck. Sharp screams of crewmen in pain increased in volume as they saw a large group of marauding boats surrounding the flotilla of merchant vessels.

Berti drew his sword.

"Those pirates are too far away for swords," Marcus reasoned before tossing Berti a bow and a quiver of arrows. "However, I am going to get in a bit closer."

The Deargh Du then drew one of his gladii from his belt scabbard and took to the air, disappearing into the dark skies.

Berti turned, pulled out an arrow, nocked it, and drew back the string, aiming for one of the figures on the nearing boat. In an instant, the pirate clutched at his eye and fell overboard.

Sitara threw a knife at the marauder as he neared her mother. The man held up his arm to deflect the blade, but it sliced into his wrist. She heard the screams of her mother and sister as they searched for her, Nadeem, and Sarid.

She grabbed another blade she found on the deck when a hand encircled her wrist and forced Sitara to the ground. She cried out in pain as a sword point drew blood.

"Look for the other merchants, and do not destroy the ships, you fools," yelled her captor as he ground her head into the deck with a stinky foot. "I bet you are worth quite a bit, either to your family or on the open market," her captor whispered in her ear.

Sitara stretched for another knife when blackness surrounded them again. She then stabbed the pirate's other foot and pushed her way out from under him. Sitara ran through the door before falling to the floor as she tripped over scattered wood and the lifeless bodies of the crew.

"Stupid whore," the pirate cursed as he spat at her. He then flipped her over and thrust his sword at her neck. Sitara closed her eyes in the hopes that her death would be quick and merciful, but instead if dying, she heard a soft cry, and then she looked up to see her attacker collapse by her side with an arrow protruding from his skull.

One of the Briton merchants smiled at her for a second before offering her his hand.

As Marcus faced off against a marauder, the screams and cries of women and children echoed around him, and he knew he needed to rush to their aid. Instead of fighting the marauder, Marcus pushed him from the merchant ship to splash in the dark waters many yards from the sides.

When he arrived where the pirates attacked the women and children, the scent of spilled blood inflamed his nostrils. He grabbed a drunken pirate as the man cruelly cut into the stomach of a pleading child who sat crying next to his father. The very sight disgusted him, and he could almost see himself as a mortal dispatching a weeping Helvetian child as she crouched over her dead mother.

He pushed the pirate to the ground, wishing he could think of an appropriate torture, when the sobs of other women and children filled his ears in a harrowing song of death and destruction. Soon a raging fire began to consume him within.

He could see his swords flying and decapitating the struggling pirate and then continuing on to other marauders. His gladii and body danced with a speed and precision he had not felt before, dodging weapons and the enemy, almost lost in his body as if someone else controlled him. In this hyperactive state, he could only hear vague screams as he moved from one boat to the next, dispatching the enemy. Soon, a growing need for blood clouded his mind, but Marcus pressed on.

A slight sting at his back made Marcus slow to a somewhat normal speed before whirling around to face a trio of pirates. What he first took to be a sting began burning at his back, and he could feel blood dripping from the wound. Ignoring the pain, Marcus quickly dispatched the one to his left with a thrust, and then he kicked the marauder to his right into the one at the center, leaving one pirate behind.

The quickness of this warrior surprised him, but Marcus could hear others regroup. The mortal managed to avoid his blade and even matched his speed at some points, as Marcus could not seem to dredge the speed he had exhibited earlier. He soon found himself pushed against the edge of the boat. The wind and the blood-coated deck made his footing shaky as the nameless thief pushed Marcus against the side. Then the pirate started yelling at him in some unrecognizable tongue.

"I am certain you do think I am that. However I wish that you would stab yourself," Marcus yelled at the warrior. "Do it and die!"

A sudden ache burned through his body and moved up to his temples. Then the pirate's eyes seemed blank as he raised his sword, took a few stumbling steps away from Marcus, and in one single thrust, shoved his blade through his chest. Marcus watched in disbelief as the pirate's body collapsed to the deck.

"By Morrigan's strength," Marcus whispered in awe. He had never done such a thing before. Only the Lamia wielded the talent of manipulation.

Marcus took a steady breath and closed his eyes, feeling the strange ache pass. He then ran a trembling hand over his forehead as he began to feel normal again. Marcus opened his eyes and looked over the dead body that lay at his feet.

Behind him, he could hear the remaining pirates run for their boats, leaving the surviving crew and merchants behind. The greedy marauders attempted to take some of the merchant ships, only to see their victims destroy their own ships in a strange victory to prevent the pirates from taking the treasures within.

Marcus snarled, blinded by red, as an arm grabbed his. He tried to swing his sword, but the appendage stopped the arc of his blade, which rest at his victim's neck.

"Marcus!" Berti yelled as his eyes met Marcus' gaze. "Please, allow us through." Marcus raised his gladius and wiped the blood drenching his face. He then notice a young woman, who had wrapped her arms around Berti, press her face into his neck in an attempt to avoid looking at the surrounding death. Vitae covered her clothing, and he could see that she gripped a knife in her hand in a vice of tightened, pale fingers, as if the knife would remain in her palm forever.

Marcus nodded as though mute, but Berti murmured words to the young woman in Latin. "Over, it is all over. Those pirates will be lucky if they can make it to shore," murmured Berti. "We will find your family, Sitara. Marcus, it is over, you know."

Berti's eyes met his for a moment, before he whispered in Gaelic, "May Morrigan release you from Her sway." Berti then returned his attention to the shaking woman, who regarded Marcus with her blue eyes for a moment, asking horrible questions with her silent stare.

Sitara shuddered as she walked amidst the dead. The now-hallowed boards of the ship creaked with her steps and those of the survivors behind her. She closed her eyes and uttered a soft cry at the sight of the broken and battered forms lie scattered aboard the trireme.

The man who had saved her life walked but a few steps behind her. He had the strange, pale skin of the Northerners that moved through Rome in coarse skins and furs, though sometimes they dressed in colorfully patterned linens. They wore some gold and silver, but they never seemed gaudy. This man she had met before, and he possessed pretty eyes and golden hair.

The other merchant, the tall one named Marcus, followed behind them with a slow and strange grace. He had the most entrancing silver eyes that she could ever remember seeing, which seemed to be a strange contrast with his dark hair. As they walked, she could hear him sheath his short swords. The sight of the sheathed blades caused Sitara to relax her hand, and she felt the dagger slip from her fingers.

"So many losses," Marcus murmured, sounding almost angry, but then a loud crack rattled permeated the trireme.

"This boat will not last much longer," stated Berti as he gazed upon the other denizens who jumped or swam to the remaining triremes and some smaller ships, leaving behind their luxurious trade goods.

Sitara ignored him and began to look over the corpses. So far, she had not found any of her family members. "Mother? Father? Sarid? Nadeem? Vivika?" she yelled.

The two men moved away from her as she continued to call for her family, hopeful they would come forth from their hiding places or call for her from one of the surviving triremes or quadriremes. Soon, however, she heard her name, but it was not a family member who called her.

She spun around to face the two merchants who stared back at her. Their eyes flashed from the lights of the surrounding fires. Berti then walked towards her as Marcus lingered behind before turning away.

Berti took her hand. "I have found your father, Sitara," he whispered, "and perhaps some of your brothers and sister."

"You are wrong," she cried as she pulled her arm back, unwilling to believe. She then took another few steps closer to a set of corpses and inhaled a steady breath before leaning forward and uttering a soft cry.

"No," she groaned and then began sobbing. All she could hear were the strange muttering of the men and the crew as she wailed.

Her black hair whipped in the wind, blocking out the rest of the world as she knelt down and traced the face of her mother. Her father's body laid face down a few feet away, surrounded by a pool of blood that stained the surrounding deck. A few feet away, Nadeem and Sarid's heads stared at her with death-filled eyes, and Sitara could see that one of Sarid's arms rested around Vivika in a protective gesture.

She stared at the forms, waiting for a sign of peace, but only the heavy weight of death surrounded her, much like a cumbersome shroud.

"We need to leave, now," Berti whispered in her ear. Before she could argue with him, he lifted her and pulled her, running towards the deck of another ship and across a series of planks between the ships. The two merchants followed her. As soon as they reached the other ship, Sitara turned and watched as before her eyes, the trireme capsized, plunging beneath the waves.

Sitara sat on the wooden deck of the ship, watching the moonlit waves ebb against the boat. The surviving merchants and crew cowered in fear as if expecting another attack, all but the two pale men from the North.

They spoke in their musical tongue in low voices as they glanced around the quadrireme, but soon they began watching her with wary eyes as if to see whether her emotions still ruled her judgment.

Sitara stared at them for a moment, until Berti walked to her side and sat down. At the same moment, she saw Marcus walking towards the captain.

"What is happening?" she asked Berti in Latin.

"Most of the merchants do not want to continue by boat," answered Berti, "but Marcus thinks that the pirates will stay away from this flotilla, since there were not many left." After speaking, he chuckled a little.

"What is so funny?" she whispered.

"I mean no disrespect," the merchant answered in a soothing tone, before studying her for a moment with his sea-colored eyes. "I am laughing because I pity the captain. My friend is very stubborn about things being a certain way."

"And what do you wish the captain to do?" Sitara asked.

"Travel by sea is the quickest," Berti replied, "and we must hurry to Alexandria. Therefore, Marcus will insist that the captain venture on. What will you do when we get to Alexandria? Do you have family there?"

Sitara shook her head. "My family is in the ocean. Now they travel to be reborn." She bit back her tears, still mourning their loss. "You saved my life... therefore, I am in your debt. I will travel with you as your servant."

The merchant shook his head. "Sitara, I do not want a servant. Besides, we must go quickly. I have to know that a new traveling companion can keep up with us."

"I have spent many years with my father and brothers in the caravan. I know what it means when one must make haste."

"Will you continue with us after we find the treasure?" Berti asked, smiling for a moment.

"Treasure?" Sitara queried as she raised her left eyebrow.

"Yes. We are searching on behalf of a Hibernian princess," he explained. "She wishes us to find a piece of a Roman statue."

"Which part?" Sitara queried. "Was it broken?"

"Yes," Berti answered. "It is ehm… the specific part is…" The moonlight revealed his face as it took on a red tinge, "... the phallus," he snickered.

"Oh!" Sitara exclaimed, smiling at the blushing Briton, forgetting all the death for a moment. "Is it made of gold, or is it jewel-encrusted?"

"No. It is old, marble, and is more of a spiritual treasure than a monetary one. We believe it may be in Alexandria, or at least that is what the shah had said." Berti then wiped his face, removing traces of black stains and blood onto his sleeve.

Marcus's dour face soon came into view as the Briton walked up to them. "No luck for us," the other merchant grumbled, while holding a bowl of water. He then sat down across from her. "The captain wants to go ashore and stay put."

Sitara glanced at the other merchant. While soot and dried blood covered his features, Sitara felt something oddly entrancing about this man's pale features.

"Sitara, though you have heard me use his name, this is Marcus."

"Sitara," Marcus greeted as he handed her the bowl. "I am sorry about your family."

She took the bowl and nodded her head. "Thank you," she said as she handed the vessel to Berti. "You first."

Berti shook his head and countered, "I said that I did not want a servant, Sitara," before pushing the bowl back toward her.

She cupped some water in her hands and splashed her face, hoping it would remove the filth. Marcus handed her some clean, soft wool, and so she wiped away the water with it.

"I heard you desire to travel with us," Marcus intoned as he stared at her with eyes that seemed to glow.

Sitara cleared her throat. "I thought you were speaking to the captain."

"Marcus has excellent hearing," stated Berti. "His skills at eavesdropping are second to none."

The sarcastic barb made the other merchant laugh.

"I must repay my life boon back to Berti," she explained.

"I understand," Marcus acknowledged, while holding up his hands. He even possessed lovely fingers. Such beauty made her almost uncomfortable. "But, you must be able to keep up with us." Marcus then took the proffered bowl from her arms and began to clean off his own face. His pale skin soon gleamed.

"I know," she answered. "I told Berti that I have traveled with my family. I will not slow you down." She returned his ready stare, but she soon felt herself become dizzy in those eyes.

Marcus broke eye contact, and then Sitara turned back to Berti, whose gaze seemed less captivating. Berti regarded her with a friendly grin as if he could not be certain about how to deal with this new twist in his life.

"We will eventually go back to Éire," Berti stated, while taking the bowl from Marcus. "Do you know where Éire is?" Sitara looked on as Berti splashed water on his face. With all of the blood and grime that had covered their faces, she shuddered to think about the sludge and filth in the bowl. Men seemed to care little about cleanliness.

"North," she answered, "near Britannia."

Berti said something in that strange language again and grinned.

"Sorry," he said. "I forgot you did not know Gaelic. You are correct."

"You are willing to travel to Éire?" Marcus asked her. "It is very cold and wet."

"I am sure I can get used to that," she answered.

The two men shrugged while glancing at one another. Then Berti announced, "Then you can join us on our journey. While Éire and Britannia are dank and wet, they both share a beautiful wildness that I find invigorating."

"The sun rises soon," observed Marcus before standing up. "Goodnight, Sitara, Berti." He gave them both a strange, all-knowing smile before walking away.

"He goes to sleep now?" Sitara asked Berti in a half-whisper.

"Marcus keeps strange hours," Berti whispered back.

Sitara nodded her head, wanting nothing more to do other than sleep. Perhaps this was only a dream that would disappear as soon as she closed her eyes and rested.

"I think there are some storage holds in the lower decks. You need some time to yourself to sleep and to mourn." Berti took Sitara's arm and led her toward the hatch and ladder to the lower decks.

Marcus grabbed Berti's arm as he passed by the hammock. "Berti, we must talk," he whispered Gaelic, hoping not to wake Sitara in the hammock on the other side of the hold.

"I tried, Marcus," Berti explained, anticipating his question. "She wants to repay her debt. Plus she's pretty. If we left her on her own, she'd be in danger."

Marcus smiled for a moment. "I think you just like her, Bertius, though she is indeed a pretty woman, with that dark hair and her sea-colored eyes."

He heard an impatient sigh.

"That has nothing to do with it," Berti argued. "This strange land is not a place to leave Sitara."

"I apologize," Marcus offered. "You are right. These lands are not safe for a lady. I think she should join us." Marcus sat up. "Now to change topics, I have a question for you."

"What is it?"

"I fought one pirate who started yelling at me, and I yelled back. I told him to kill himself. He then stabbed himself to the hilt," Marcus intoned before biting his lower lip. "Have you ever heard of a Deargh Du doing such a thing?"

"You what?" Berti shrieked. "Marcus, that is impossible."

Sitara stirred in her slumber.

"Hush," Marcus whispered. "She has tossed and turned most of the day, but I did, Berti. I convinced a mortal to kill himself."

"Are you sure?" Berti's eyes revealed his disbelief.

"I am certain," Marcus answered. "What do you think this means?"

"I do not know, Marcus. I would say that you need to practice this newfound talent, except–"

"Except what?" Marcus interjected.

"Except you will not make me do humiliating things like kissing a dog or some horrible yet entertaining act to you," Berti demanded.

Marcus covered his mouth to keep from laughing loudly. "I promise. No dog kisses." He then became calm again. "Yet, I do wish I knew what to do about this strange, new skill of mine."

Almikhlaf Alsulimani

"So, you are sure you want to join me today?" Berti inquired as he strode through the alleys of the village.

Sitara followed him until he motioned for her to walk closer, and so she soon matched his strides.

"You do not need to walk behind me," he commented, while shading his eyes from the bright sun with his hand. The welcome feeling of the cobbled roads against his feet made him wonder why he wished to set foot on another boat again, but the noxious fumes of animal dung that wafted towards them favored boat travel.

"So, where is our traveling companion?" Sitara asked as she looked at the small bazaar set out a quarter mile from the harbor.

"Marcus?" Berti replied and then laughed. "He is doing what he does every day. Sleeping."

"Well," Sitara murmured, before turning her bright blue eyes toward him, "is that not unusual for a person to prefer the night to the day?"

"Oh no, not for Marcus," Berti mumbled, trying to think of the correct way to address this question. Maybe he should attempt to direct the conversation into Gaelic, since she insisted on learning it, 'to help matters', she had said, but he decided against it and continued in Latin.

"Marcus likes to spend his evenings gaming and carousing with disreputable women. He must sleep during the day to continue his nighttime activities," he explained, attempting to maintain a serious tone and not laugh at the lie. The cobblestones soon gave way to planks as they walked on the docks, where several ships of varying descriptions were moored.

"Oh, really?" He watched Sitara arch her brows. "And yet you do not join him, Berti?" A prim smile settled on her lips.

"No, no," he insisted, while holding up a hand. "I prefer to spend my evening in the study of… ancient languages."

Sitara's smile broadened. "Have you been studying them long?" she asked in Greek.

"I have assaulted the Greek language for many years," he answered, giving her what he hoped to be a serious stare before feeling his face stretch into an open grin. Sitara chuckled a gleeful giggle.

"Are you always this much fun?" she asked.

"Possibly," he answered, before taking her arm and leading her towards a small trireme. Soon they encountered several men standing around the gangplank. Berti cleared his throat as he neared the best dressed of them.

"Are you Ahab, the captain of this ship?" Berti addressed in Greek.

The man tilted his head a bit and nodded.

"I have need of your sailing abilities. We were in the flotilla that those pirates attacked a few nights ago."

"I thought the merchants decided to take the land route," chided the captain, who began rubbing his beard.

"All but me, my partner, and my friend," Berti replied. "We must get to Alexandria with all due haste."

"My ship does not come cheaply," the captain answered. "I am one of the few that survived pirate attacks, and with the recent activity, it would take a great deal of money for me to disembark."

"Let me look over the boat first and make sure it will meet our needs," Berti demanded. In response to his query, the captain nodded his head, and so Berti walked past the captain to inspect the ship and make sure that there would be space for the goods and for Marcus during daylight hours. Sitara followed

Upon stepping on a loose board, he caught sight of a bit of fright in Sitara's eyes. Berti left her on the top deck to inspect the lower decks and found several rooms for the crew. There also appeared to be ample space in the spare holds for travelers and their goods. He then returned to the deck and met up with Sitara, before returning to Captain Ahab.

"This trireme could suit our needs," he commented, not in the mood to begin another endless bargaining session that the residents of these parts seemed to enjoy. "Would one hundred silver pieces change your mind?" Berti asked, while removing a bag from his belt. He hoped that by naming a high price that these negotiations would finish sooner

"We can hire him for much cheaper," Sitara whispered in his ear.

"One-fifty!" shouted the greedy captain with a grin that revealed a love for the game. Berti cursed himself for starting so high.

"Eighty!" Sitara yelled back.

"One hundred and twenty five, because your woman is most entertaining," replied the captain.

"One hundred and my partner and I will assist in the defense of the trireme, or we walk," challenged Berti, while tying the coin purse back onto his belt.

The captain screwed up his face in contemplation, but he finally relented. "Fine, but you must give me an advance to stock supplies and pay my men."

Berti poured twenty-five coins into Ahab's open palm. "When will we depart?"

"Tonight, if the weather allows it," replied Ahab.

Berti nodded and then walked away.

"Do you always carry so much money?" Sitara whispered, walking next to him.

"Sometimes," he answered. "I know that I can protect whatever is on me. Now, let us return to the inn and pack our supplies."

"On the ship, you will sleep in the bed this time," Sitara said, giving him what sounded to be a demand. "You should not have placed me in the bed while I was sleeping last night. I am here to help you."

"My father always taught me that it was age before beauty and women before men," Berti answered. "That is how the tribes in Alba, Éire, and Britannia treat women, for the most part, because otherwise, they may beat us." He smiled at her.

"Why is that?" Sitara asked, looking at him as though it were a strange idea.

"I believe it has to do with the fact that we come from a people who venerate goddesses as well as gods. The deities of Éire are called Tuatha dé Danann. It means the 'people of Dana'. Dana is a goddess."

"I thought they worshipped the same god that they do in Rome," stated his companion.

"Some do," replied Berti, "and we who follow the older religions do not slight them for it, unless they try to force their beliefs on us."

"Do they?" Sitara asked. "My father always tried to get my mother to change her faith, yet he could not."

Berti nodded his head. "Most of the druids hide within villages. Many people in secret still seek their advice, as they are very wise men and women."

"Will I ever meet one?" she asked.

"If you continue traveling with us to Éire, I am certain of it," Berti answered.

"Marcus," Berti murmured as he shook the Deargh Du. "Marcus, wake up! I have found a ship."

"Mmmm?" The elder blood-drinker turned to face him, his eyes still half-closed from sleep.

"I have found a ship, and we leave tonight. I trust that your things are packed. I also bought some extra items in the bazaar that I thought we could sell in Alexandria."

Marcus nodded and sat up. "Of course, a soldier is always prepared to go into battle." He yawned and then stretched his arms overhead. "What extra items?"

"Oh… a dozen Kashmir sheep," answered Berti.

"Sheep?"

"Well, you did mention that you were tired of feeding on rats, and I heard a rumor that wool is a rarity in this part of the world, especially in Alexandria," stated Berti.

"I see. I certainly hope that there is room for all your pets." Marcus began to chuckle. He then rolled out of bed and began to gather his things. "You certainly seem happy," he remarked, while holding a few scrolls, his gladii, and a few other accompaniments. He then found a bag and tossed in the scrolls. "It must be due to a certain person who received a free trip from you." He paused. "Is she still troubled with the deaths of her family?"

"She seems a little better," Berti answered. "I think she has such beautiful eyes and her body is…" He paused, forgetting the direction of the conversation. "She also wonders how you can sleep so soundly during the day."

Marcus frowned for a moment. "How did you explain it?"

"I told her you spent your evenings drinking and whoring," Berti answered.

"Lovely," Marcus grumbled. "Do I need to slur my speech and start finding companionship in every port? Must you make me out to be such an irredeemable louse?"

"She thought it was funny." Berti chuckled as he held up a hand. "However, I am sure she will help you write your little missives to Éire."

Marcus nodded, before handing the bag to Berti. He then pulled on his belt and attached his gladii and their scabbards to his belt. "I see. So, this allows to you make yourself look better," he suggested. "You are worried that I will allow my glamoury to ensnare her. She is a lovely young woman, but I barely know her. She has attached herself to you, so why should I bother?"

"You have used it before on mortals," Berti noted. "Not that I have minded. After all, it has assisted us many times. You do not seem to realize the profound effect you have on some people." His joviality ceased as he grew serious. The elder Deargh Du nodded his head.

"You are right. I will curb the glamoury, and if she asks, I will tell Sitara that you are a manly paragon of virtue who never imbibes to excess and cares little for the frivolous beauties that ply their trade in these villages." Marcus then opened the door.

"I am in your debt," Berti confirmed as he passed through the door and walked out of the inn following Marcus. Sitara awaited them on the trireme.

Red Sea

Sitara tossed and turned in the hammock, as the visions of her family had returned, crying in their death throes. Unable to sleep, she kicked her legs over the side of the hammock and slid onto her feet. Sitara then squatted next to Berti's sleeping form.

"Berti," she whispered, while leaning over the man, who insisted on sleeping the deck. "I cannot sleep," she whispered to him. She then closed her eyes, wanting just to curl up against his shoulder and cry. However, embarrassment at herself encouraged her to cease such insane thoughts. "Berti?" Sitara whispered again, "do you have any idea when we are going to get to–"

A steady snore answered her question. The man could sleep through almost anything. The storms and the noise of the raucous crew during the nearly three fortnights at sea never seemed to have an effect on Berti.

She tried awaking him once more. "Berti?" This time, she even tried placing a hand on his shoulder and shaking him a bit, but he just rolled in his sleep and snored even louder.

She stood up and rubbed her sore knees, astonished how he remained so comfortable. Still, this was her duty... she owed him for saving her life. "Next time, I get the floor," she muttered, before creeping to the hatch, opening it, and slipping out.

Sitara walked around the crew's quarters, noting that only four of them remained out this night. She then ambled to the main deck and gazed at the placid sea, which reflected the brilliant light of the moon and stars. The silence seemed to stretch on for miles across the quiet waves. After a few moments of silent contemplation, Sitara leaned over the rail for a moment, studying her face. She smiled at herself and imagined seeing her family with her in the reflection.

A soft bleat made her look up from her reverie, and then another bleat echoed through the lower levels. Sitara grinned, recalling how much she enjoyed looking after the sheep, despite their odor. Their gentle faces would turn toward her whenever she joined them, and they would rub against her hands, hoping for a scratch or a treat.

Sitara decided to check on the sheep, so she shuffled over to the trapdoor of the hold, opened it, and then stepped onto the ladder, which took her to the lower deck. Soon, her eyes adjusted to the lack of light, and she could make out the shape of the twelve sheep in their makeshift pens as they shifted about.

One of them bleated again, drawing her attention, but then she noticed a man-like figure kneeling next to that sheep. She could see the dark-haired man rub his pale right hand across the sheep's back in a soothing manner. However, the visage of the figure remained hidden as it leaned into the sheep. Sitara tilted her head to her right side as she realized who it might be.

"Marcus?" Sitara queried in a whispered voice, before taking a few steps towards the left side of the sheep. "I did not know that you–"

Marcus looked up at her, and a pair of glowing green eyes dazzled Sitara for a moment, until she witnessed his blood-drenched lips and elongated teeth.

The dread epiphany melded with a joyous realization. The divine avatar of Shiva had arrived... He must be Shiva. After all, Marcus radiated beauty as did the god, Shiva. Then again, he may be the male avatar of Kali, who shared the duties of destruction and creation with Shiva. All that mattered now was that her family awaited her to join them in new lives.

Sitara trembled and fell to her knees. "I am ready to begin again, Shining One. I embrace the dance of my destruction and new life." She lowered her head, closed her eyes, and smiled, wishing to end her days in peace.

She heard another soft bleat, the creaks of the deck planks as he stood, and then footsteps as he approached her. Sitara held her breath, waiting for the end, and the beginning, but instead of a killing blow, a hand slid under her chin and tilted her face upwards.

"Sitara." The soft voice purred her name like a satisfied tiger. "Who do you believe I am? Open your eyes."

Sitara opened her eyes. Marcus stared back at her with his normal silver eyes and natural features. The blood on his lips had disappeared, although a small fleck of redness remained on his chin, but he soon swiped it away. He almost appeared embarrassed.

"You are an avatar of Shiva or Kali," she answered, fearful he merely played with her.

"No," he answered. "I am no god or goddess." His eyes met hers, and he pulled Sitara to her feet. "Have you ever heard of the Deargh Du of Éire?" he asked.

Sitara shook her head. "Do you mean that you will not kill me?"

He shook his head. "No, I will not. Allow me to explain. I am Deargh Du, one of the Children of Morrigan. She is the goddess of death, battle, and rebirth. Morrigan is quite similar to Kali."

"Why do you feed from the sheep?" Sitara asked. "Why not feed from me?"

"The sheep keep me from feeding too much on the crew," he replied as he sat down on a bale of hay. "I do not want to slow their progress, not to mention that the sheep are an improvement over the rats and mice I have fed upon of late."

"Rats?" Sitara asked, trying to disguise her disgust.

Marcus laughed, his chortles a strange, beautiful music to her ears. "I usually feed from humans, but my kind does not kill unless it is necessary. After all, we need mortals to continue our lives. We need to get to Alexandria in haste, so I do not wish to overtax the crew with my needs."

"Is this why you spend your days sleeping?" she asked. "Berti told me you drank too much."

Marcus' right eyebrow arched. "I spend my days sleeping because I cannot abide the sun, much like the Pacu Pati, Ekimmu, and Algul of your homeland. The Deargh Du, like them, are beings of the night."

"Those beings are but tales," Sitara deadpanned, recalling the horrible stories her father's father once told her of monsters in the night.

Marcus took her hand and placed it on the left side of his face. "I am no mere legend. I exist." His warm skin started to cool beneath her fingers. Uncomfortable with touching him, she pulled back her hand slowly.

"Is Berti?" she asked.

"Oh no, no, no." Marcus laughed again. "Berti is mortal."

Sitara smiled. "So, why are we traveling to Alexandria? Please tell me the truth."

"We are looking for a lost treasure of another kind of blood-drinker. The Lamia consider it a holy relic Mars, the God of War to them."

"So, he was telling the truth about that," Sitara surmised aloud.

"Oh yes," replied Marcus. "The Deargh Du council needs it to keep the Lamia at bay, I suppose," he answered before sighing. "It is a very complicated tale."

"I cannot sleep," Sitara told him. "You could tell it to me. Perhaps it will keep my dreams away."

"You keep seeing your family," Marcus observed. His smile faded. "I understand."

"Yes," Sitara admitted, before sitting on the deck. "Tell me this complicated tale about the Lamia."

"The Deargh Du fear an invasion of Éire," Marcus began to explain. "Many immortal invaders stalk Éire, Britannia, and Alba. In fact, I was in Britannia fighting another line of blood-drinkers called the Ouphe when the Deargh Du sent Berti to find me."

"Why did they select you for this duty?" Sitara queried.

"I am an outcast in their eyes." He gave her a most sardonic smile. "The Deargh Du do not care for me because I am, was… a Roman invader to their home. I must be an abomination in their eyes, at least I am treated as such."

"That is a pity." Sitara leaned forward and placed a hand on his arm. "All this time I thought you were a Briton. Do you miss their company?"

Her pale-faced companion barked a quick laugh. "Perhaps I would, if I ever knew them. I do miss Éire, though. I miss the rain, the cold nights, and the mortals there."

She watched Marcus close his eyes. When he opened them, they were blue, yet something more. Then Marcus started to speak again.

"However, the Deargh Du deserve some of their righteous indignation,"

Marcus answered. "I assisted in the destruction of many people."

"So, are they who you write to?"

"Write? Oh, my correspondence." Marcus' frown faded into a smile. "I met a young druid some time ago, and we converse about my travels. Perhaps you could assist me with that. I believe that Maél Muire must find my writings to be quite dull."

Sitara giggled. "I am sure she finds them fascinating. Are you working on one now?"

"Yes," he affirmed.

"Then read it to me, and I will tell you what I think. Say it in Gaelic, since I need to learn more about the language you and Berti chatter in." Sitara stood up and headed toward the ladder. "But we must do it outside in the fresh air. It will keep my mind off my sorrows."

"Sitara, you survived because it was not yet your time to die," he stated as he stood and waited for her to climb out of the hold.

"I know," she murmured, "but I still have my time to grieve."

Outside Jerusalem – Monastery of Martyrius

"Hush, or you will give us away," Lucretia whispered as she stared at Assim and witnessed the reflection of her red eyes in his. She then turned back to stare at the Christian monks who held out cups for alms. The monastery of Martyrius was almost complete, and yet they still needed funds to finish their grand works and their mission to Jesus. She remembered doing the same thing when she was a mortal, yet that life seemed so far away from this one. Those days occurred long before she met a strange yet beautiful green-eyed Briton calling himself 'Mandubratius'. Her sponsor's appearance varied greatly from the short Persian with dark flashing eyes standing with her in this monastery.

"But I hunger," Assim muttered, interrupting Lucretia's musing on the past. "Why can we not feed now?"

Lucretia faced him before pushing Assim into a dark corner of the monastery. He still acted like a mortal prince in ragged clothing. "We wait because I say so. You obviously do not understand our relationship, Assim. I sponsored you, so I am the master. You obey my orders as I obey the orders of my elders." She then grabbed his neck and pushed him to the wall. "Never, ever question my orders," she hissed before releasing him.

Assim dropped to the ground, clutching his throat.

"But why do we need to accomplish this mission?" he queried again, trying her patience. "Why must we follow this Deargh Du, Marcus?"

"If you must know, we are following this Marcus because my sponsor, Mandubratius, wishes to kill him. I am to follow Marcus wherever he goes and make sure Mandubratius has his chance. I shall contact Mandubratius' sister-in-darkness, Amata, when the time is right. Mandubratius and Marcus both search for the Phallus Maximus. I have to make sure Marcus reaches wherever Mandubratius is, but I do not know where Mandubratius is now."

"Why?" He straightened up and leaned over her shoulder, trying to get a better look at the mortals. "Why did we not follow them on a ship?"

Lucretia walked into the monastery church, when the smell of incense overwhelmed her. "It would be foolish to follow them in the same flotilla," she whispered. "Do you know what the other option was to that, Assim?"

He shook his head side to side, causing his dark hair to gleam in the candlelight. She then noticed many pilgrims, monks, and priests watching them. In an attempt to blend in, she dropped to her knees, again remembering her days of prayer in a church such as this.

Lucretia turned her eyes to the blackened relic of some sainted martyr surrounded by gold and jewels. "Kneel," she whispered to Assim, who knelt next to her with some reluctance. "We would travel underwater," Lucretia stated, answering her own question. "Do you know what it is like to feed off fish and other water animals?" Lucretia shuddered and almost gagged at the unpleasant memory. "Such nasty blood," she whispered. "This is why we travel by land."

She then made the sign of the cross and folded her hands together. "Follow my motions, the others are staring," she told Assim. He began to copy her movements.

"I do not like this place," he muttered.

"Monasteries and churches offer free lodging to pilgrims, so we can easily be lost in the crowd of worshipping faithful," Lucretia murmured. "Also, there are caves here, caves that lead into a necropolis. It is a safe sleeping place for you and me, because we cannot afford luxuries such as a soft bed now. I had attempted to get alms from pilgrims, but they have nothing left to give."

"I need to feed again," he begged, before grabbing her arm.

"You have become too needy," she replied, pushing off his grip. "That is why you only feed from me. I cannot trust you yet."

Lucretia began to mutter a prayer to sound authentic to the passing pilgrims. "We will feed tomorrow night. You have fed enough tonight, Assim."

"You still tell me nothing about this strange, new world of the night," he hissed between clenched teeth.

"I will explain to you all the different kinds of blood-drinkers before we sleep. Now be quiet, Assim."

Assim sighed. "I hunger, Lucretia, despite your refusals, I must find blood soon."

Lucretia pulled on his arm to hold him down, but this action seemed to draw more attention. "Then, it is time for us to retire. I am exhausted. I cannot be fed from again now." She arose and dragged Assim with her out onto the monastery grounds, before looking for the ancient mausoleum.

Assim grumbled as he began to walk through the maze of caverns that led to the outskirts of the monastery. He continued out of the shadows toward the well-lit building covered with jewels and crosses. These religious buildings were almost as beautiful as the Zoroastrian friezes in Persia. As he entered the church, the whispers of the praying mortals became louder.

His mouth began to water as he neared a group of praying monks rise from the stone ground. Assim crept among the last of them and pulled one back into the shadows, preparing to feast, Lucretia's wishes be damned.

Assim closed his eyes, concentrating his will on making the monk submit, when he felt a growing pain as his teeth extended. He then tipped the monk's head to the left side as he prepared to feed.

"Help me!" the monk yelled as he scampered away from Assim. "Demon!"

The twenty monks grabbed weapons and holy water and began to surround Assim.

He crouched into a little ball as they swarmed in, fearful that they would harm him. His growing hunger made his movements slow.

As a church bell sounded the hour, the entire church shook with each peal, but as soon as the bells ceased thrumming, their Latin voices swelled. The sweet-smelling incense made him begin coughing, which seemed to embolden the remaining monks and clerics who surrounded him, believing him to be weakened, praying that their god would make the demon depart before they dispatched him to hell. Soon the priests began throwing water on him, and he blinked as the water got in his eyes and hair.

"Stop that!" he yelled.

The priests continued dousing him with water, praying that their god would cleanse him of the demons that were hounding his soul. They even pushed a cross in front of him and waited for him to scream in fear.

"You idiot!" a shrill, female voice echoed in the small room.

The monks and priests ducked away in fear as Lucretia rushed towards them, revealing her red eyes and a sword, which glowed in the candlelight.

The men cowered as the sword sliced through the air, decapitating the holy men who stood with meager weapons in their hands. Mortal blood splashed Assim's clothing, and he quivered, hearing their inhuman screams. He found himself covering his ears to deafen the noise.

"Now you see why I cannot trust you to even feed yourself," Lucretia nagged, while tugging his arm. She then turned and faced a young monk holding a crucifix. Assim watched in shock as the monk placed the crucifix on Lucretia's forehead.

"Be gone, ancient demon of old. Go back to the place you came from with your little apprentice. The Lord Jesus Christ commands it!"

Lucretia tipped her face to look at the monk. Bemusement shone in her eyes.

Assim covered his face with his hands, expecting his sponsor to tear the foolish young man in half. Through his hands, he watched Lucretia smile at the monk and grab the crucifix. She then kissed the figure of their god.

"Thank you," she said, before taking the crucifix. She then grabbed Assim's right ear and snarled an order. "Let's go, you wretched piece of refuse. I will not forget your disobedience!" she shouted as she tugged him away from the shaking hermit.

"If you ignore my orders again, I will behead you myself, or I will let one of them do it. Disrupting my sleep…" Her words faded into another language that he could not understand.

As he followed Lucretia out, Assim caught a glimpse of the young man as he passed out amidst the dead bodies of his fellow monks.

"Do you know how hard it is to sleep on top of a skeleton?" Lucretia growled at him. "Now we will have to move deeper into the graves. It will stink of old death, and yet…" she said, as she pulled on his arm. He stopped and stared into her hate-filled red eyes. He remembered hearing ancient tales of Lamia and wondered how closely Lucretia resembled their great mother. "… it still is not enough of a punishment for you," seethed Lucretia. Her dark hair grew dishevel. "If I could, I would make you sleep in the desert! We will have to join the skeletons in stone coffins, now."

chapter two

Béal Átha an Fheadha

aél Muire continued to cleanse out the dun with herbs, which offered protection from unseen forces, as the servants swept out the offensive thrushes.

"Maél Muire?"

"By Brigid's mercy!" Maél Muire exclaimed as her concentration on the purification waned, causing the burning herbs to singe her fingers. She then dropped the herbs and raced for one of the buckets of water, plunging her hand into the cold water.

"I am so sorry," Flanna apologized before covering her mouth.

Maél Muire removed her digits from the icy liquid. "I will survive, Flanna."

Basala, Druce, and Dougal followed her.

"Maél Muire, do you know when they will return?" asked Flanna.

As Maél Muire turned to face them, their eyes revealed their overwhelming concerns. After all, without a chieftain's leadership, they were open to attack from all sides. She shook her head before saying, "I know as much as you do. Give me a day to think this over. Perhaps they will send instructions to us." However, she did not know whether to hope for that or not.

At that moment, Bearach walked through the great hall and admitted, "I still cannot understand how they could leave without my knowing, Maél Muire."

Maél Muire bit her lower lip before speaking. "I know, Bearach. Perhaps you fell asleep. The chieftain's hours have been long and strange in the past few weeks."

"Perhaps," he mumbled as he scratched his red-tinged beard.

She shrugged and wiped the sweat off her forehead as the herb smoke seeped into every corner of the dun. "We should continue cleaning in preparation for the new chieftain. Tell the guards to continue their watch." She shuddered a bit, unsure of what awaited in the ensuing darkness.

Bearach nodded and left the great hall.

"What shall we do?" Basala asked.

The three other servants followed Maél Muire. Behind them, she looked on as Druce closed the door of the dun and then stood in front of it.

"Do whatever the chieftain would ask you to do at this time," Maél Muire suggested before shrugging.

Heather Poinsett Dunbar & Christopher Dunbar

"Then I would ask you what you would like for dinner," Basala stated.

Maél Muire bit her lip, unused to such treatment. "I have no preferences, something simple. After this afternoon's events, I have no appetite, and I am fairly certain you four wish for something simple as well."

"You look weary," Flanna said while patting her shoulder. "Go rest. There are some clean blankets in your old room. We will take care of things here."

"Yes," Maél Muire agreed. "I am exhausted."

When Maél Muire arrived at her old room, she sat down on the bed of furs and blankets, listening to the sounds of the others as they finished cleaning out the stink. Soon she rolled onto her side and pulled up her legs. As she closed her eyes and drifted off to sleep, Maél Muire could hear Basala and Flanna starting the meal.

The massive unkindness of ravens flew together and cawed to each other. They then dove as a group, headfirst into a grove.

The ravens swarmed, forming an undulating sphere.

"Wake up, Maél Muire."

Maél Muire rubbed her eyes before rolling onto her back. Her aunt's candlelit face reflected back to her.

"What is it?" Maél Muire queried Sive, as her aunt pulled her up to her feet, though her aunt's tangled hair and tired eyes revealed her state of mind.

"You have guests, and as the acting chieftain, you must see to your duties." Aunt Sive set aside the candle and grabbed a bowl. "Now, wash your hands and feet."

"Acting chieftain?" Maél Muire asked as she cupped the water into her hands and splashed her face. "What are you talking about?"

"You missed the meeting this afternoon. The clan decided that until Cennedi returns, sends word, or dies, you will act in his stead," her aunt explained, before handing her a clean léine.

"Who suggested such a thing?" Maél Muire asked with a laugh. "I am not a leader of men. I am not even a warrior."

Sive rolled her eyes. "We have all seen you knock down men at celebrations for believing that you could not. Besides, a chieftain should be more than a mere warrior. He or she needs a brain between his ears, which you possess, most of the time." Her aunt chuckled. "Do not worry, this is just temporary."

Maél Muire grabbed a bronze mirror and unfastened her unruly plaits. She shook out her hair and pulled a bone comb through it.

"Or at least that is what Connor suggested," her aunt muttered under her breath.

"What?" Maél Muire almost dropped her bag of rouge.

"He said that he would honor the ties between his clan and ours." Her aunt's stare bore into her eyes. "After all, you are his son's widow." Sive then pulled back and added, "Do not forget your father's torc. I know you hide it."

Maél Muire nodded and began to pull on her jewelry. A few moments later, she stepped out of her room and moved into the great hall.

Oisín, her uncle's harker, cleared his throat before announcing, "I present the acting chieftain, Maél Muire Ní Conghal Uí Máine."

Her servants and guards strode in closer to her guests, six cloaked figures. Five of them wore gray cloaks, while one wore a dark green cloak. All stood at least six feet tall. She attempted to ascertain the features of the strangers in her midst, but the cowls of their capes hid their faces.

It seemed rather odd, even impolite, to continue to conceal themselves, but Maél Muire decided to wait for her guests to identify themselves. To break her unease, she motioned for the servants to begin to setting out the meal and pouring the mead. She then nodded toward them and then to her aunt and uncle.

One of the figures in gray glided to Oisín's and whispered into his ear. The harker then walked over to her and whispered, "He wishes that I do not introduce his party at this moment. However, he asks if the chieftain could dismiss the non-essential people of the staff because of the nature of their visit. They would be most grateful."

Maél Muire studied the faceless men or women who watched her, unsure of how a proper chieftain should act in this strange situation. However, her suspicion settled when she witnessed her uncle and aunt nod to her.

"I will do so," she announced in a calm yet authoritative voice before nodding to the gray figure as he or she rejoined the ranks of the party. "Please take a seat," she bade as she motioned to her guests to the chairs at the dining table. Then she announced, "Everyone is dismissed for the evening... everyone but the guards and Bearach. I wish the guards to remain outside and continue holding the dun. Make sure we are not disturbed." They nodded and departed. "Bearach, please join us."

"Thank you, chieftain."

The gray-robed figure that had addressed Oisín bowed and removed his or her cloak, revealing a masculine face. His long, nut-colored hair curled as it settled down his back. He held the bearing of one familiar with combat. His léine displayed expressive needlework of ravens. "I am Lughna, guard and protector."

Maél Muire tried not to stare at Lughna as she bowed her head in greeting.

"I would like to introduce the rest of my party," he requested while motioning to his right."

"This is Niamh." The figure to Lughna's right removed her cloak, revealing brown eyes and long black hair. "This is Lileas." Lughna motioned to the figure to Niamh's right. Lileas removed her green cloak, revealing the druid's cloak of six colors. Her gray eyes reminded Maél Muire of the curling smoke from the hearth fire. Her golden hair lay in plaits.

"To Lileas' right is Ségnet." The woman revealed her bright red hair and smiled. Her cloak fell to the floor, showing a yellow léine of linen.

"I believe you already know Caoimhín," Lughna said, while motioning to the Deargh Du near Ségnet. Caoimhín removed his cloak, revealing druid's garb.

Maél Muire smiled at him and regarded the remaining cloaked figure.

Lughna cleared his throat, allowing a great reverence to permeate his voice. "And last is our leader, who speaks for Her. This is Ruarí."

Maél Muire nodded her head before announcing, "Welcome brood of Morrigan. My home is honored with your presence." As soon as she finished speaking, however, Maél Muire noted the looks of surprise on the faces of the guests. Even her aunt and uncle exchanged glances.

Ruarí smiled for a moment. He appeared to be the eldest of the party, in many ways. He then glided towards her, shedding his plain, green cloak along the way, revealing the robes of an arch druid.

"How did you know that we were all Deargh Du?" he asked. Despite his age, even he reflected a brilliance that a mortal could not ignore. His eyes searched her for an obvious answer. Maél Muire could sense a cloaking of beauty amongst the Deargh Du, but soon, the glamoury faded. "Have we ever met, my child?"

"I do not believe so," she answered.

"Perhaps in some other life," Ruarí suggested as he grinned at her for a moment. "Now tell me, how did you guess our identity?"

"I have met Caoimhín once before," Maél Muire revealed, "at my aunt and uncle's home. I also have an affinity through my family's teachings to those who walk with the Goddess on the ancient path. It is hard not to recognize beauty when I have seen it once before. Please sit."

The other Deargh Du began to sit at the low table.

The arch druid smiled and patted her hand before sitting at her left side. "Chieftain, I have come to this village for reasons that I am certain you are quite aware of," he intoned before pausing. "My bard disappeared several weeks ago when he came here with Caoimhín. At first, we dismissed it as a mere dalliance. I know my bard, and the beauty of the Otherworld can ensnare him, if he parts the mists. However, I hear his words on the western winds. I feel he has gone to the Otherworld permanently. Someone assisted him in this act, and I am here to learn what and who dispatched him. We can only hope that it is not the Lamia."

"There was one here. At least that is what She told me," Maél Muire explained before taking a deep breath. "He searches for a hidden treasure. He asked me to go on a vision quest to find it."

"A treasure," Ruarí whispered. "Tell me, who is this Lamia?"

"His name is Mandubratius," Maél Muire replied.

The arch druid's cold hand latched onto her arm. "Mandubratius? Describe him."

"He is tall, but," she paused to take a breath, "not as tall as you Deargh Du. He has black hair and green eyes. He seems to be a Briton, to my eyes."

"Aye, he is," Ruarí confirmed. "He is a Briton, a son of a chieftain who believed that he had been wronged when the clansman chose his uncle to be chieftain over him. He went to Rome and met Julius Caesar. Together, they planned to return to Britannia to invade it," Ruarí amended before pausing. "Or at least, that is what our spies say. He and his sister-in-darkness rule the Lamia in Rome. What happened in your vision quest?" Ruarí asked, before taking a sip of mead.

"Morrigan came to me in the guise of the One-eyed Crone and revealed Mandubratius' cruel nature. She then gave me a simple riddle to tell him."

"What was the riddle?" the arch druid asked.

"Tell him to search for it in the place where the fae run and play. It is near where the winter sun strikes the ground on the morning of the shortest day, where the Tuatha dé Danann met the great Míl's clan."

"Brú na Bóinne," stated Lileas.

The arch druid frowned for a moment as though somewhat piqued that he had not replied as quickly as she did.

"What is the treasure and where is it?" he asked, after turning back to Maél Muire.

"The One-eyed Crone did not reveal that to me," she answered.

The arch druid frowned again. Disappointment marked his features.

"We are very grateful for this knowledge," he mumbled, sounding troubled. "Thank you for sending word to Caoimhín regarding your interactions with this Mandubratius." As he arose from the bench the others followed.

"Wait." Maél Muire stood up and walked over to Ruarí. She then pulled on her sleeve, baring her right arm. "Do you require nourishment?"

The arch druid turned his weary eyes back to her. She looked over at her aunt and uncle as they quickly bared arms, bowing to the six Deargh Du. Bearach glanced her way, and she nodded her head. He then shifted up the left sleeve of his léine.

Maél Muire took a deep breath as the arch druid turned her arm to look at the underside. His eyes met hers, and she lost all comprehension as his orbs glowed an unearthly green. A sharp sting brought her back to reality, as Ruarí's eyes remained locked with hers.

Maél Muire could hear what sounded like noises of pleasure echoing around her, yet she remained silent as a pressuring suction enveloped her arm. She continued studying the arch druid's eyes as the sounds of bliss continued.

Despite the withdrawal of her essence, she did not feel weak. In fact, she felt a burgeoning strength growing within her. She started to smile and felt a strange peace enter her heart.

Ruarí released her arm and placed his hands on her shoulders. She leaned into his embrace for a moment.

"Odd," he muttered in her ear.

"What?" she inquired while pulling back. She witnessed a funny smile spread over his beautiful face. "Does my blood taste different?"

"Of course not, though your vitae is delicious, yet, you do not require healing." He motioned to Bearach, Sive, and Fergus. "See, almost all mortals need some form of restoration after we feed." Bearach lay on the floor exhausted, as Caoimhín and Ségnet started to heal him.

"You must have a very strong constitution, physically and spiritually," Ruarí added, while picking up his green cloak. He then motioned to the other Deargh Du.

"Where are you going?" Maél Muire inquired.

"Some of us will follow Mandubratius," Ruarí answered. "Others will go to Ard Mhacha." The other Deargh Du pulled over the cowls of their capes, hiding their radiant faces again.

"Many blessings of the Gods and Goddesses on your home, young Chieftain." Ruarí and the others bowed towards Maél Muire. "It was an honor and a pleasure to meet with you. Continue on your path of Morrigan, and do not forget to honor the Tuaths."

"Goodnight, and have a peaceful journey," she bade them.

Red Sea

"What are you two doing awake at this hour?" Marcus asked as he walked onto the upper deck. Berti and Sitara sat on the floor, chewing on what smelled like rotting meat when they weren't talking of the limestone city of Alexandria. Marcus looked at the horizon. While the luminous stars and the moon lit the dark skies, the seas remained a barrier to fresh supplies. The obsessive draw of distant blood made him close his eyes in silent yearning for the ancient city with the western hill known as the acropolis, the site of the Serapeum, a temple dedicated to an Egyptian snake deity, which also served as a center of learning. Marcus grumbled and shook his head. What was he thinking? The Roman monks and soldiers destroyed the Serapeum, leaving only one thing behind, the oddly named Pompey's Pillar.

"I cannot sleep," Sitara replied before crossing her legs. "My stomach is hurting. The cook is not good," she whispered.

Marcus shrugged. "It smells perfectly wretched. However, it is sure to be better than the time I had to eat grass as a mortal."

"It tastes worse than wretched," stated Berti. "I wonder whether they are trying to poison us." He grinned at Sitara.

Marcus sniffed again. "No, it is only rotten."

"I suppose that is meant to be a relief to us," answered Berti.

Marcus sat down next to him, trying to ignore the rancid smell that permeated the air. Soon a light breeze pushed the stink out, leaving the smell of salt-laden waters behind.

"You were in the military, were you not?" Sitara asked.

Marcus nodded and looked over at Berti. The mortal shrugged his shoulders. "Did Berti tell you, or did you divine that yourself?"

"A woman knows some things by intuition," Sitara answered and then laughed. "And you tend to march a bit when you walk."

"Not to mention, you give orders like a general, or whatever you were as a mortal," added Berti.

"Old habits die hard, I suppose," replied Marcus, while staring at the stars. "I did not interrupt anything, did I?"

Sitara raised her eyebrows for a moment and grinned, leaving the truth unsaid. "Berti just finished telling me about Alexandria. Have you ever been?"

"Several times," Marcus answered.

"So what is Alexandria like?"

"Berti could tell you better than I," Marcus suggested. "Last time I was there… it was nearly ninety years ago. I will tell you what I remember. It was a beautiful city with a library that held all the knowledge of the world. It was a true shame that they burned it down." He felt his face tighten in indignation.

"Why did they burn it?" Sitara asked, her voice quavering.

"Parts of it burned once before in the time of Cleopatra when Rome took over Egypt. It was pure stupidity on the part of the soldiers and Rome in general. No offense, Marcus." Berti seemed to give up on the meat and tossed it overboard.

Marcus smirked. "None taken. I never went there as a mortal. The true burning of the library was not the fault of the Roman military. Christians, such as the saintly Bishop Theophilius, destroyed the library because it contained many texts and scrolls about homosexuality and herbalism," Marcus replied.

"They proclaimed it to be nothing more than evil witchcraft. Now, many die from the plague that might have been prevented because of the knowledge that was in those scrolls."

"That is a pity that texts which could have helped cure diseases were destroyed," Sitara murmured before pushing her bowl away.

"Yes it was," Berti agreed. Marcus noticed an odd seriousness darken Berti's face, before a silence settled between the three of them.

"How many Deargh Du are there?" Sitara asked before looking at Marcus and then Berti.

"I have yet to meet another," Marcus answered. "I have no idea of the numbers of their population."

"I do not know the exact number. I've met perhaps a dozen," Berti answered with a shrug. "In truth, I know more of the other races."

"Tell us about them," asked Sitara while stretching her arms overhead. She then leaned against Berti's shoulder.

"The Sugnwr Gwaed are based in Britannia. They are not bad to deal with, in general, but one must be prepared to hear a tale or two."

"Many Sugnwr Gwaed love the sounds of their own voices," Marcus chimed in. "My old lieutenant is one of their leaders. He always enjoyed talking."

"And they are dangerous to talk to?" Sitara asked.

"Only if you have a limited amount of patience. They do not kill for pleasure, most of the time. Their voices are beautiful, and they enjoy seeing the effects of their fae-voices on mortals," Berti stated.

"Then there are the Ekimmu Cruitne," Marcus continued. "They are excellent warriors." He leaned in closer to Sitara, lowering his voice for emphasis. "But gods, they are ones for games, and woe to he or she who thinks they can trick them."

"Yes, and they will cheat you out of money during such games," Berti added. "Never, ever gamble with one."

"I promise," Sitara answered. A grin lit her features. "Tell us of the Pacu Pati. My mother used to whisper warnings to us about them."

"Very, very odd," muttered Marcus. "They tend to hide, these days. In the past, they liked to pretend to be avatars of Shiva and Kali. I once witnessed a blood dance." He shuddered a bit at the memory. "Maybe they believe themselves to be avatars. I could not understand their transformation. They seemed almost to lose control. They had destroyed every living thing in a mile radius, including animals, plants, and mortals, of course, but they did not even feed on them... they just did it for the thrill of the slaughter. I could never understand that. The Pacu Pati seem to ignore the aspect of destruction that involves creation." He stopped, realizing the subject was causing some unease. "I should tell no more of that nightmare. Even the Lamia are grateful that the Pacu Pati are hiding."

"They sound horrible," murmured Sitara as she wrapped an arm around Berti. "What about the Lamia?"

"Not as bad as the Pacu Pati or as insane as the Strigoi in the east," stated Marcus.

"They are just numerous and rather annoying," grumbled Berti. "They believe that a new empire of Rome is waiting to be built."

Marcus smirked. "The Lamia control the new power structure there, already with bloodied hands in their politics and the Church. It's just a different god this time instead of many."

"And the Deargh Du," Sitara asked, "what are they like?" she asked Berti.

"They are both feared and respected. Feared by those who could not understand how a line received blessings from a goddess instead of curses, but respected by most. Many say that they are the most eye-filling of the blood-drinkers." Berti raised a pouch of mead towards Marcus.

"Fae blood," Marcus added, grinning at his companions. "That and glamoury. You two smell... ill. Go and lie down. I need to write, anyway." He then pulled out a bag and removed vellum, a quill, and a bottle of ink.

"Oh, the wise druid he corresponds with," Berti stated.

"She is just a friend of mine who wished to read about my travels. Her name is Maél Muire."

Sitara grinned as she teased, "A lover in Éire?"

"Maél Muire is not my lover. She is engaged to some chieftain's son, who still sleeps with whatever women cross his path," he answered, before pausing to swallow his anger and turn away from Berti's and Sitara's stares. Marcus could not be certain why this stranger's infidelity enraged him. After all, who was he to judge a mortal's actions? "She is just someone who wants to see the world but cannot. I found her to be quite extraordinary, and I thought it was a shame she could not travel, and so we exchange letters."

"An extraordinary girl," Sitara observed while pursing her lips. "Is she attractive?"

"No... I mean, yes." Marcus sighed. "Looks have nothing to do with this, Sitara... she looks quite ordinary, though I thought she had pretty red tresses. However, her eyes are her best feature. They remind me of the radiant, green bounty of Éire before my transformation. On the other hand, perhaps my own memory of the grass and trees is different from the reality, yet her eyes are magic."

He could see Berti and Sitara smirk at each other, and then Berti began to chant, "Marcus misses his Maél–"

"Berti, go to sleep, or I will toss you overboard," Marcus warned, while trying to keep his laughter quiet.

"Goodnight," both mortals rejoined, giggling, before trotting towards the bedroom.

"Goodnight." He turned back to the star-filled skies and started writing. "I am most happy to see two out of the three of us enjoying this voyage," he whispered to the night sky.

"Your favorite dish, Sitara," Berti announced as he placed a clay dish in front of Sitara.

"Oh, lemon chicken," she replied. "You are too kind." She glanced in the direction of the cook. "When I checked with him, he said it was only going to be chicken. I am supposed to be assisting you and catering to your needs," she teased, giving him a bit of a grin, "not the opposite."

"So I talked him into throwing some fresh lemons into the chicken," Berti answered. "It makes us both happy, alright? So, where is Marcus?" Berti asked while glancing about the ship from his vantage point.

"Still working on his love letters and journal," stated Sitara in between bites of chicken. "You know, I wish I could read. Do women in Éire read?" Berti could see a nervous glint in Sitara's eyes.

"Most women in Éire are as well educated as the men."

"Really?" Sitara put down her chicken. "So why is that?"

Berti laughed and then covered his mouth. "Because, someone must keep the house and lands while the men go fight each other over the cattle they raided from one another."

Sitara choked on the wine she was drinking, sputtering her laughter.

Why did every woman seem more beautiful with the sound of merriment on her lips?

Berti leaned in closer. "I will teach you if you want."

"To read, or did you have something else in mind?" Sitara murmured before grabbing him by the shoulders, forcing him against the hull of the ship, and kissing him.

Eastern Shore of the Nile near Henen-nesut (Herakleopolis Magna), Ægypt

"Are we there yet?"

Lucretia tugged at Assim's hand as he began to slow down. "Every night for the past week you've asked the same question." She stopped running and sniffed the air. "People are nearby, and I am ravenous."

"But you promised to explain further," complained Assim, "and yet you still have not."

"Explain what?" she demanded while turning her red-eyed glaze on him. Assim felt his heart leap in his throat. Lucretia frightened him when she revealed her true nature. After that one evening of absolute ecstasy, she had allowed him nothing more. His frustration always peaked when he awoke to the dying sun. After digging his way out of the sand, he would find her braving its red rays as she held the Christian crucifix and watched the stars become bright.

"Everything," answered Assim, "why you clutch that piece of carved wood, for example." He nodded toward the bag that held her crucifix. "What you meant by the different kinds of blood-drinkers, and why you made me into this? And why you do not even want me anymore."

Lucretia sighed. "That is many questions, and I still hunger. I hold this crucifix because it reminds me of my past, and a Lamia must keep a tie or two with the past, or they will become lost forever. Mandubratius taught me that. Before I began this life, I was a nun, Assim." She smirked as she faced him. "I worshipped this man, this son of a god." She pulled the crucifix from the bag.

"Mandubratius pulled me from my convent one night, and he gave me no choice in the matter. He wanted me, so he took me. That was all there was to it. He promised me power in exchange for my obedience. It was that or death. Unlike a good Christian martyr, I begged for my life. He took my life and gave me a new one." She shrugged, while staring into the small pain-stricken figure on the cross. "I suppose it is kind of funny. Jesus Christ promised me life after death, and now I have it." She then placed the crucifix back in her sack.

"As for your other questions, there are many kinds of blood-drinkers. There are us, the Lamia, the supreme line. There are the Algul, which of course you know all about. Then there are the Bruxsa, the Ekimmu, although they have almost disappeared from the earth." She took a breath and continued. "There is a group from Germania called the Ouphe, and there is a group from Egypt called the Sekhmetites." She paused again in the midst of her list. "Then there are the cursed Strigoi and the Celtic lines, the Deargh Du, Ekimmu Cruitne, and the British ones, although I have forgotten their unpronounceable name... all with their own gifts."

"And we have the most gifts," Assim ascertained.

"Of course," replied Lucretia, as if he were an idiot for asking such a thing. "That is why we are trying to get the other lines to recognize us and yield to us as the proper leaders in our dark world. Now," she said as she stared at Assim with a fanged smile. "It is time to feed." She gathered herself, preparing to start running again.

"Wait," he said, while placing a hand on her shoulder. "You did not answer my last question."

Lucretia ran her tongue across her teeth. "You wish to know why I chose you." She tilted her head and stared at him with red eyes. "I told you once before."

"Tell me again," Assim requested.

"I chose you because you are useful to me," Lucretia purred before leaning closer and running her right index finger across his lips and down to his chin. "I chose you because I needed information. However, if you cease to be useful, I will have to destroy you, by sword, fire, or sun." She then gave Assim a small, tight grin. "What I create, I can destroy."

Assim closed his eyes as she ran her fingertip down his throat.

"Soon, I promise you," she whispered, while pressing her mouth close to his ear, "as soon as we have time to relax and not worry about that grove dweller, Marcus, and his mortal friends."

She brushed her fangs against his skin from his neck up to his ear, causing Assim to close his eyes and swoon in delight.

"Soon," she purred before pulling away. Then, she started to run.

He followed in the wake of dust and sand she left behind her.

Alexandria

Lucretia noticed Assim smile as they came upon the city. "It is more beautiful than I remembered. I have always believed Alexandria to be elusive and mysterious, like many women," said the former shah.

Even though the city gleamed white under the moon and torch lights, Lucretia shrugged at his comment. To her, Alexandria could never compare to Rome, even in its dilapidated state. However, this city did offer some semblance of civilization. "Do you know where this merchant lives?" she asked Assim.

Assim stared back at her. "It has been a great many years since I visited here. I only remember that Thabit Hamadi has a store in the Brucheum, and he mentioned returning here as soon as he left Shiraz."

Lucretia sighed before closing her eyes for a moment in disgust. The lights from the lit torches of the city brightened the horizon and beckoned to her. "I suppose someone must know who this Thabit is and where we can find him." She offered Assim a hand and a small smile. "I can tell you are hungry. After we find Thabit, we can find a meal."

"I hunger for more than that," Assim flirted, smiling at her as he licked his lips.

Lucretia felt impatience tap her remaining strength as Assim started to annoy her yet again. She hoped that his presence would be useful again... perhaps he could speak to the merchant so they could be one step closer to finding Mandubratius and bringing Marcus to her master.

"There is little time for that now," she hissed. "Now, you must talk to the locals. You do know the language spoken here, correct?"

Assim laughed. "Only a few words of it. You are older than I, surely you must understand it?"

Lucretia pulled him toward the first inn she saw. "My knowledge of languages is limited. Almost everyone speaks Latin or Greek, so why should I bother learning anything else?"

Assim stared at her for a moment. "Why must I ask them?"

She dragged him with her into the inn. "It does not matter. Ask them now. You have a greater chance of understanding them."

They moved into the inn and walked past the long row of tables.

A tall man saw them and clapped his hands, beginning to speak in a language that she could not follow.

Assim laughed and replied something back to the man.

"Alright, in Latin then," the man said. "As I was saying, I am Edfu, the proprietor of the best inn." He waved his arms around. "I have the best of everything in all of Alexandria... the best wines, the best beers, the best roast lamb. Whatever you desire, we have or can make. Now, what would you like? You two almost look as though you may fall asleep while standing. I have a spare room upstairs if you need accommodations."

Assim opened his mouth to answer, before Lucretia shook her head at him.

"We may need accommodations later. However, we require information first. We are searching for a merchant named Thabit Hamadi."

"Oh, that swindler?" the innkeeper spat and made a face. "Everyone here knows Thabit the Cheap. If you are selling anything, I may be interested, and I will give you a much better price."

"Thank you, Edfu." Lucretia smirked at the innkeeper. "We may be selling something later. However, we are in the market for an artifact Thabit owns."

"An artifact? Perhaps I can–"

Lucretia stared at Edfu while interrupting him. "I want to speak to Thabit," she demanded, as she concentrated on unlocking his brain and manipulating his will.

"Yes of course." Edfu glanced away from her in a nervous manner. "He is nearly one mile away to the north from here on the right side of the road."

Lucretia nodded. "We shall return, Edfu. Thank you for the information."

Edfu nodded as if distracted before tending to some other customers.

"What did you do to him?" Assim asked Lucretia as they stopped at a decrepit storefront. He felt as if Lucretia continued to keep him in a weakened, ignorant state, but why? Did she fear him for some reason? Why didn't she teach him?

"It is just a little mind trick, simple manipulation," Lucretia answered, shrugging in a nonchalant manner.

"Will you teach me that soon?" Assim asked.

"Perhaps," she muttered, before walking into the shop. "Although, you should already have some inkling of how to use it yourself. Though, there is much I cannot teach, you must know."

A young man wandered downstairs, shaking his head and yelling.

Lucretia looked at Assim. "What is he saying?"

"They are closed." He began explaining in halting Egyptian that they were there to see Thabit. "This is Thabit's apprentice, Sudi," he explained to Lucretia. "He says Thabit is occupied with other matters and will see us tomorrow."

"We don't have time for this," grumbled Lucretia. "What if the others arrive tomorrow? They will find their way over here. I want to know before they learn. It will keep us a step ahead of that grove dweller. Ask him about the Phallus Maximus," she demanded. "Use your will against his, Assim."

Assim paused for a moment, hoping he would be able to explain in Egyptian what they were seeking.

"Well, go on!" Lucretia stared at him, impatience marking her face.

"I am thinking," Assim replied, his words sibilant, revealing his frustration at his task. He began to speak again in unsure Egyptian before pausing.

"What is it?" Lucretia demanded with impatience.

"I cannot remember the word for 'phallus'." Assim felt his facial muscles tighten in irritation. He then glanced back at the apprentice, who gave him an expectant look. Assim held his hands up for a moment and then made a pantomiming gesture to his nether regions.

The apprentice's eyes widened, and he began yelling and motioning back at Assim with his hands.

"What's he saying?" Lucretia asked.

"Something about an insult. Let me try to calm him down."

Assim tried talking to the enraged apprentice again, but nothing seemed to help. The apprentice began hitting Assim over the head.

"Damn it, why is he hitting me?" Assim asked. "I tried explaining that I do not know Egyptian very well and asked for his patience."

"Maybe you asked for something else instead," suggested Lucretia with a snicker.

"But why is he still hitting me?" The hits had become punches and kicks. Assim made a face as the apprentice kicked him in the groin.

"By Jupiter," he whispered. Assim lost his senses and growled. He then grabbed Sudi, forced his neck to one side, and drained the apprentice, who cried in pain. The apprentice screamed as his life force flooded from his body.

"You fool!" Lucretia yelled before pushing Assim to the side, away from the now dead apprentice.

There was thumping on the stairs as someone came down the steps.

Assim wiped the blood away from his lips as Thabit came into view.

"What? Your majesty, why are you here? You have…" the Egyptian stared at Sudi. "You killed Sudi. I am going to call for the night guard! I was going to retire in a few months and enjoy living for a change instead of bowing to men of power."

"Thabit wait," Assim requested while holding up his hands. He then wiped the blood from his face. "He attacked us when we arrived."

"Nonsense!" Thabit yelled, while staring at Assim. "I heard you two arguing." He turned to look at Lucretia. "Who is this slut? Surely not one of your wives." Thabit hiccupped and then covered his mouth. The scent of wine revealed his inebriation.

Lucretia's eyes began to glow. "Thabit, be at peace. We merely want to question you about something Assim sold to you when you were in Shiraz."

"Monster," Thabit accused while backing away from Lucretia. "You are one… you are both unholy creatures of the night. You think I have never heard of Sekhmet's minions? Help, night guard!" he yelled.

"What's he raving about?" Assim asked. Thabit began running toward the door and managed to get it open, but Lucretia grabbed him and pulled him back inside.

"I am no Sekhmetite," Lucretia whispered in his ear. "Stop screaming. We only want to ask you about the Phallus Maximus."

"Night guards, I am being attacked!" Thabit yelled.

Lucretia covered Thabit's mouth. "Be silent," she hissed in an attempt to regain control of the situation, but Thabit continued to scream.

Assim watched in horror as she twisted Thabit's neck. The sickening sound of breaking bones echoed in his ears.

"Ignorant ass," Lucretia spat as she dropped the lifeless body. "It is so hard to get them to listen when they are drunk. Hurry, go find his records." She began pulling Thabit's body toward the back of the shop. "I will take care of this. Hurry! I hear footsteps."

"Why do you think it is gone?" asked Assim.

"My master searches for it. Why would it be here if he is not?"

Assim shrugged before walking upstairs to search the records. He picked up an open book and began scanning the entries. He then found his name and an entry underneath it.

"He traded it for some caskets of rare silk," he informed his sponsor after walking back down to the shop, just as Lucretia carried out the dead apprentice.

"Who to?" Lucretia asked.

"It does not give an exact location. It merely says somewhere in Britannia."

The sounds of approaching mortals startled Assim, and Lucretia dropped the body. She then motioned for Assim to leave the book, and so he followed her out the back door into the city, just as the night guard kicked in the front.

Qeb and Tarik of the night watch surveyed the shop, searching for the killers.

"Unbelievable!" Tarik exclaimed as he shook his head. "I have never seen anything like this before." He turned to the captain of the night watch and asked, "What do you think happened?"

"I would say that Thabit's back door dealings got the best of him," answered Qeb. "However, whoever we scared will be back for the rest of his goods soon."

Qeb turned to the rest of the night guards and began issuing orders. "I want guards watching the back and front of this store until we find the murderer. Even Thabit the Cheap and his apprentice did not deserve this."

The trireme sailed into Alexandria's port as the wind raised a cloud of dust that grew around the torch-lit city.

"Is it all you remember?" Berti asked.

"You ask me that as though I have spent the last six hundred years in some backward part of Éire," Marcus answered. "I was here less than a century ago, you realize." He was tired of the blue seas, yet only sand and grit greeted him here, as well as the smells of rotting meat and the dank smell of illness coming from the city and its bazaar.

"I am sure it has changed since your last visit." Berti coughed. "Damn dust."

Only Sitara enjoyed their arrival. She watched as if fascinated with the city. "I am so excited to get off this boat!" Sitara exclaimed. "Do we leave the sheep here for now?"

"Yes, we'll take them to the bazaar tomorrow," Berti replied.

Marcus sighed as they moved into the bazaar. "Hopefully, we can find this Thabit, whatever his name is, soon, although my hope is almost gone." Marcus felt as though he would spend the rest of his nights searching for the Phallus Maximus without smelling the groves of Éire.

"Oh, cheer up," Berti grumbled. "I am sure we will find the phallus soon enough, and then we will return home. You and I will meet up some rainy night when it feels like Éire will disappear into the sea, and you will say how much you miss the desert."

Marcus made a grumbling noise under his breath. Berti opened his mouth to say something, when Marcus interrupted, "Let me guess," replied Marcus. "You are hungry and you want wine, so you and Sitara are going to an inn."

"I didn't know your kind read minds," Berti replied with a bare trace of a smile.

"Call it intuition," teased Marcus. "I am off to find some disease-free food." He shook his head. "My apologies if I have become unbearable." He walked away, heading towards the Brucheum, the old Greek and Roman quarter of Alexandria, where the wealthy resided. As Marcus walked away, he could still hear Sitara and Berti talking.

He heard Sitara comment, "Marcus seems rather ill at ease to me."

"I know," Berti agreed. "That happens to Deargh Du after so long feeding primarily on animals."

"What do you mean?" she asked. Marcus hid at the periphery of the bazaar so he could still here the conversation but not be seen.

"Deargh Du are not meant to feed on animals. If they do it for too long, they become detached from humanity. There is a growing insanity from it," he whispered. "The crew grew weak from his feeding, so he stopped a week ago."

"How distasteful that must be for him," Sitara replied. "I had been wondering why he had been so cranky the past few days. I just thought he wanted to go home."

"The Deargh Du prefer the cold and the wet, and I must admit I miss it too. Yet, I think for him, Britannia is the closest place that he calls home. Éire means isolation from the others. However, they all feel a connection there that becomes lost in the rest of the world." Berti pointed her to an inn in the bazaar. "We can eat and ask around for this Thabit."

Sitara nodded her head as they entered the inn. "I know how he must feel, as I have no home either."

He patted her arm. "Home does not need to be a literal place, but you already know that."

Soon they walked into the inn. "Two portions and your best wine," Berti called over the innkeeper, "and an answer to our question. We are searching for a merchant named Thabit Hamadi."

"Oh yes, Thabit the Cheap," answered the young man. "He is across the street from us."

Berti grinned. "You have dinner," he said to Sitara. "I will return in a few minutes. Marcus heard the sound of a few coins hitting a hard, wooden surface.

"Oh no you don't," Sitara argued as she followed him. "My dinner can wait."

Marcus changed his mind about going to the Brucheum and decided instead to join the others at the front of Thabit's shop.

"Hello?" Berti called as they walked into the store.

"Thabit Hamadi! We are here to look at your best wares," Marcus added.

"The place looks deserted. Perhaps we can come back tomorrow morning," Sitara suggested.

"Nonsense! I am sure he will see us tonight. After all, this is a chance to make a profit," Marcus touted with a chuckle. "Thabit? We are here to buy an ancient relic," he added, but then the stench hit Marcus' nose while he strolled through the front room of the store.

"Something is very wrong here," Berti announced.

"I smell death. Recent death," Marcus warned Berti.

"Oh, you smell death everywhere," replied Berti.

"What is that noise?" Sitara asked in a whisper.

Marcus heard the sound of rapid footsteps echo through the shop. He then shushed them both. "Hide and start searching for Thabit or anything that might indicate where the phallus might be. I will find out what is going on."

Marcus walked out of the shop and came face to face with one of the night guards. He watched as another of them ran through the square. Marcus chuckled a bit as he realized how little the town had changed in the last century. An inept mob of men, who called themselves the night guard, still ruled the streets after dusk.

"Halt."

A torch passed close to his face, and he met the guard's eyes.

"Yes?" Marcus asked, while crossing his arms over his chest.

"What were you doing in that shop?"

"I saw something in the window of interest to me," explained Marcus. "I entered the store and found no one inside, so I left." He inhaled for a moment, relishing the scent of a healthy mortal. He had not get his fill earlier. Marcus stared back into the face of the guard and realized that his eyes reflected back to him as a glowing green.

The guard stared at him a moment before drawing his sword.

Marcus snarled and then grabbed the guard, pulling him into the dark stoop of the front door. He opened the door and pulled him inside, willing him silent. He shut the door and began to glance about the room. He noticed that Berti and Sitara continuing their search. Marcus could concentrate on nothing but the smell of blood, and so he pulled the guard's neck to one side and bit into the man's throat. Sweet release from hunger filled him, and his senses reeled as he regained his strength and mind.

He could soon feel eyes on him, and he turned his head to see Sitara watching him. Marcus released the guard, licked his lips, and let the unconscious body fall to the floor.

She looked at him, still struck by his actions.

Marcus decided to break the spell. "You had better hurry," he warned. He watched Sitara as she sorted through some of the vellum scrolls. "I thought you could not read."

"I am learning," she countered, while giving him a wary grin. "Berti offered to teach me."

"What is it?" Berti asked as he stumbled down the stairs carrying an armful of papers.

"We are not going to be alone for long. Guards are searching through the town. I just had to take care of one outside the front door."

"Crieche," whispered Berti under his breath. "We will go back to the docks, hurry." He then dropped the paperwork on the stairs and leapt down to the first level.

"What about those other papers?" Marcus asked as he glanced back at the paper littering the stairs.

"Do not worry about it. It is old, several years old. Apparently, Thabit the Cheap is as retentive about records as you are. Is there anyone guarding the back door?"

"Not that I saw," Sitara commented.

Berti opened the door cautiously and stuck his head out, but the sound of a blade slicing through the air made him back away. Berti reacted by grabbing a dagger from a nearby table and throwing it at a shadowy figure, which collapsed to the ground.

"It is safe now," muttered Berti before taking Sitara's arm. "Let's go." He handed half of the papers to Sitara.

Marcus began to follow them out, when a blue stone with a small carving caught his eye. He picked up the lapis and found it attached to a short, silver necklace that bore several other pieces of lapis. The center stone sported an odd carving in the center.

"Marcus," Sitara called to him, "hurry, I can hear the guards."

Marcus grabbed the necklace and ran out the back door. He then grabbed the two mortals and took to the air, unwilling to fight his way through the streets. Of course, had he not fed, they would have had to fight their way out.

Berti laughed and cheered, while Sitara shuddered and then wrapped her arms around him. Soon the three of them landed next to the trireme.

"We have got to do that again!" Berti demanded. "I almost forgot you could do that."

Sitara clutched at his arm. Her eyes were squinted shut. "Is this ground?" she asked.

"Yes," Marcus answered.

Sitara let go of Marcus and took a few shaky steps.

"Could you carry us like that the rest of the journey instead of us traveling on ships and in carts?" Berti asked.

"No," snapped Marcus. "I am not carrying two people over oceans and across the alps. I am a Deargh Du, not a pack mule."

Rome

Konstantine wandered into the great house as the sun's rising arc turned the skies purple and red. The excruciating return from Shiraz had exhausted him, and he wanted to remain in the temple for the rest of his nights, desiring never to see a rat again. Soon, however, his joy drained from is being as he recalled that the temple also contained his sponsor, Amata the trickster.

At that very moment, he saw Amata stare down at him from the staircase. "Konstantine? Why are you back here? I thought you were in Shiraz."

"Sandstorm," he answered with a shrug. "Lucretia thought it best to continue on her own."

"I see," remarked Amata. A frown creased her features as she walked downstairs, tracing her fingers over the multi-colored tiles. Piles of incense dust littered the marble floors. "So, what happened during your journey? Where are Lucretia and the others?"

"The grove dweller almost found us. However, I think the smell of the caravan confused him. Perhaps the legendary olfactory senses of the Deargh Du are mere legends."

"I see." Amata nodded. "So, you believe he is just looking for Mandubratius?"

"That was all I could gather," replied Konstantine. "I am very tired, Domina. Can we continue this tonight?"

Amata frowned again. "Yes, of course. I have another task for you, now that you have returned. We can discuss it after sunset."

Konstantine closed his eyes. "Whatever," he muttered to himself. He then walked away from her. All the empty promises of power in the past hundred years rang in his ears.

Konstantine woke up in the early hours of the morn the next day. After feeding from a slave, he knocked on Amata's door.

"Come in," she called.

Konstantine opened the door and walked in.

Amata, clothed in a dress of the finest linen, gave him a small smile before waving him closer. He could not help but stare at her, as her well-defined nipples grew hard through the white cloth. Of course she already knew he would stare, since she knew how to manipulate men.

"I have another task for you. You must leave for Britannia."

Konstantine glanced away from her breasts to her face. "Britannia? Why?"

"In case Marcus does not find Mandubratius, he will return to Britannia. I have heard rumors that my brother searches in Bath."

"Bath?"

"When did you get into this annoying habit of repeating the last word of each of my sentences?" Amata asked. Her red eyes glimmered, reflecting the light of the candles.

"My apologies," answered Konstantine. "It is just that—"

"Yes, I know," Amata interrupted him. "Britannia is the Sugnwr Gwaed stronghold." As she tilted her head, a sensuous smile play at her lips. "While you are there, I wish you to learn about this Marcus." A frown creased her beautiful features. "You will let me know if he arrives in Britannia, and you will let me know Marcus' whereabouts so I can speak with him."

Amata turned away, as if she were dismissing a slave. "You're free to go, Konstantine." Her face revealed a hidden fury. "I have secured passage for you on a ship that leaves with the dawn. I would hurry, if I were you. You know, I am still your sponsor. Do not ever forget that you are alive because I allow it."

Konstantine backed slowly out of her room. He then closed the door and began walking through the winding halls.

Perhaps I could join Mandubratius' forces. Amata's orders seem so pointless and tiresome.

chapter three

Alexandria

 omeone will take the sword," the Goddess whispered. "Someone will take it and avenge the wrongs done outside of the Otherworld." She turned Her unwavering, black eyes to Her children and the gathered forces of mortals.

"Which of you dares to come forth?" Morrigan queried.

He stood, as the others watched him with deriding eyes. Yet, another joined him. Her mortal heartbeat shook the ancient walls.

"My brood," The Great Queen whispered, "you make me so proud."

Marcus found himself most disappointed when Berti woke him up.

"Wake up, I have some exciting news!"

"You found the Phallus Maximus?"

"Well…" Berti began before pausing, "almost." He whirled Sitara around the room. "We discovered where it is now. Britannia."

"Are there any specifics other than just Britannia?"

Berti shrugged in a nonchalant manner. "Thabit was cheap and not wordy. He just wrote that he unloaded the unholy, ugly object on a merchant who was returning to his home in Britannia."

"So, some merchant carries it now?" Marcus inquired as he sat up. "Did you and Sitara find a name?"

"Yes, I have a name. Artus de, well, the rest was smudged."

"And how, pray, do we reach Britannia, Berti?" Marcus chuckled softly.

"Well, you could fly us," Berti suggested.

"No, I won't," Marcus countered while grinning at him.

"I thought you might say that. I have booked passage for us on a ship, but I have some bad news."

"And what is the bad news?" Marcus queried.

"Well, we have a bit of a trip on our hands. We have to sail to Rome, travel on land to the northern coast, and then we will sail to Britannia."

"Most ships have a straightforward passage."

"Well, until we reach Rome, we are kind of low on funds. I bought what we could afford."

"How low are our reserves?" Sitara asked.

"Well, we have not sold much," replied Berti. "Also, the Deargh Du council

---

did not give us much to begin with. Sáerlaith said that reserves were needed for the possibility of a future battle with the Lamia."

"Berti, I thought you were keeping track of our resources," Marcus complained before closing his eyes. "You know I cannot touch gold, and so I trusted you to take care of our money."

"Well, I have been, but you try surviving after giving gifts away, bribing local officials, and paying for messengers to go to Éire to deliver your letters," argued Berti. "Do not look so upset. We will get to Britannia, but we have to go to Rome first."

Marcus closed his eyes in frustration for a moment. "How long will it take us to reach there?"

Berti smiled and scratched the top of his head. "The ship's captain said it would take three months."

"Unless the winds are against us," added Sitara. "It is a smaller vessel, unable to make the direct route. I am sure you two would understand what would happen then."

"Three months?" Marcus tried to rein in his annoyance at the idea of feeding on ill-smelling sailors and rats for three months. "When do we leave?"

"Tomorrow at dawn," answered Berti. Marcus watched Berti's arm loop around Sitara's waist for a moment. "The ship is called 'Pearl of the Ocean'. While you get your rest, we will need to purchase some other supplies."

Marcus nodded his head before sliding back into the inn's dirty bed, trying to return to his strange dream. Thankfully, Morrigan's words still lingered in his mind.

Brú na Bóinne

Mandubratius dodged the other Lamia and mortals as they continued digging at the grounds surrounding Brú na Bóinne. They had almost missed the overgrown Sidhe monument. He soon found himself tripping over a lamp, and then cursed it in frustration.

"Watch your step!" a mortal grave digger yelled at him as he stepped on the man's back. Mandubratius kicked the mortal with his foot and felt the mortal collapse.

Damn their weak eyesight.

"Mandubratius? Where are you going?" Teá called after him, while dodging a few candles set aside for the mortals. The lights reflected her golden tresses. Despite her beauty, Teá seemed to be a waste of his energy.

Mandubratius waved Teá off.

By Mars, the woman is annoying.

When she complained about the accommodations, the digging, not wanting to get ragged nails, and whining about how much she feared the forested areas around the ancient mound, all Mandubratius could think about was beating her in front of everyone, just to make an example of her.

The ancient forest surrounded a smaller circle of new growth that encircled the Sidhe mound, Sí an Bhrú, and the ancient Bóinne River flowed past the forests. The Lamia had never cared for the wilderness in these distant lands. He and a few others had explored the surrounding forests and discovered a few large stone buildings suitable for their sleeping needs, yet only he had ventured into the ancient mound itself, after breaking the seal to the entrance.

While beautiful carvings of spirals and triscelles decorated the interior and exterior stones, he found little else there other than mud and an unsettling sensation that remained with him. He hated to admit that he found the fae mound to be frightening, but a strange and magical sensation lingered in these surroundings. Still, Mandubratius managed to shake away those concerns as he stepped back into the forest and closed his eyes for a moment. Perhaps a decent meal hid itself in these sylvan paths.

After a few moments of standing with his eyes closed, seeking the wind for the spoor of his next meal, he heard leaves crunch under his feet, and so he opened his eyes and looked down, but nothing seemed amiss. However, when he looked back up, an old hag stared him in the face. She had appeared without a sound. She gazed at him with an anomalous smile.

"Mandubratius of the Trinovantes," stated said in perfect British.

Mandubratius tried to regain his composure and began to stare into her glassy eyes. "Who are you?" he asked. "How do you know such things?"

The shrew smiled. "We are She who seeks you." She then placed her left hand on his shoulder. "We seek to tell you many things."

"And your name, old crone?" he asked.

The woman laughed. "Our name is the wind, the moon, the sound of the babbling brook, so many names for us. You need not worry about such trivialities." She then placed a dirty finger over his lips, never revealing a trace of fear. "Our purpose is to warn that you should not be here, for what you seek is where you have been," she added.

"Impossible," he stated. After all, Maél Muire would not lie... not while under his influence. "I was told that the treasure lay buried somewhere in Brú na Bóinne near Sí an Bhrú. She would not be false to me," he stated. At least, he felt certain of the validity of Maél Muire's words. He had searched her thoughts and found her truthful. He had controlled her, had he not? He then looked back to the old woman and studied her as she tilted her head to one side and smiled a toothy grin.

"Lied to you, the diminutive of Mary did not, but the Goddess lied to you, She did. The Goddess lies, Mandubratius." The crone put a hand on his arm. "The Goddess would not show, and instead said these words. 'Tell him to search for it in the place where the fae run and play. It is near where the winter sun strikes the ground on the morning of the shortest day, where the Tuatha dé Danann met the great Míl's clan.'"

A flush of anger burned through his being. "She lied to me," he hissed, while clenching his fists in rage. He began to pull away from the strange woman. "That little lying, manipulative–"

"Shhhh," the crone murmured, while placing her hands on his again. "Shhhh, master of darkness and drinker of blood, she did not wrong you. Tricked she was, only to tell what the Goddess told her. Maél Muire believed this to be truth." The hag smiled at him again, capturing him with her odd eyes. "Do not judge her too harshly."

"Then tell me, crone," Mandubratius commanded, while staring into her eyes, willing out the truth, "where is the Phallus Maximus?"

"As was said in our first telling, it is where you have been. For you to find it, you must go back."

"Fine, continue these riddles." Mandubratius closed his eyes for a moment, remembering the ancient druids of his village, and then he resumed his glare at the strange woman. "Then tell me when I was there."

The old woman smirked at him. Her hands gripped his arm and became like claws on his skin as her eyes clouded over. "We cannot always see. From the west says the wind, and south says the birds. The owl cries a fortnight."

"Connacht?" he whispered.

She ignored his query, still lost in her trance.

"Before the sun rises again, find you another one who seeks you. He is of the druid's arch. A powerful one is he. Of the fae they say. As Deargh Du as any, and he is not alone. Not alone is he."

"Where is this Deargh Du?" he asked.

The crone laughed. "Where laughter abounds and consumption consumes, you impatient Briton."

"How do you know this, and why do you tell me?" Mandubratius asked, shaking her a bit. The old woman's eyes focused back on him.

She then pulled away. "The Goddess the Deargh Du worship, I do not. See them suffer, we shall, and see that warrior of Rome behind you, we do."

Mandubratius turned around to look to see if anyone had followed him, but no Lamia stood behind him. He then turned back to the crone, only to find that she had disappeared into the endless black of the night. Mandubratius shuddered and then headed back for the teams of mortals and his own warriors. When he arrived, he waved his assistants forth.

"Dismiss the diggers," he stated to Wicus and the two other Lamia. "We need to leave for the local inn, now."

Ruarí sat at a table in the inn, holding onto his mead and attempting to feign some interest in it. He and his party had spent most of their evening searching for the elusive Mandubratius. Someone had disturbed the grounds at Brú na Bóinne, but none remained. Neither mortals nor blood-drinkers remained near the Fae portal. In addition, the mortals here at the inn and in the village knew nothing about the happenings at the ancient holy mound. Ségnet and Lileas had remained at Brú na Bóinne to sanctify the land, and Lughna had left the inn to empty his bladder of ale.

It was time to search in a wider arc around Brú na Bóinne, and as soon as Lughna returned from his piss, they could meet up with the others. Feeling rested and desiring to make haste, Ruarí nodded to the innkeeper and asked, "What do I owe you?"

No words came from the owner. In fact, all conversations at the inn had ceased. Before Ruarí could get up to investigate, a hand clamped down on shoulder, and he could smell a Lamia's death-laced breath as words poured into his ear.

"You would not happen to be looking for Mandubratius, would you?"

"You," accused Ruarí. His ire grew at the audaciousness of this young, Briton upstart. He turned to face this despoiler of the sacred.

Hands grabbed him and forced what felt like a golden bit into his mouth. Ruarí screamed as his mouth and lips sizzled, burning from gold's poisonous embrace. Someone then wrapped a collar around his neck as two sets of arms held him in place. An unseen Lamia latched golden shackles onto his wrists, which caused searing pain.

He cried out to the other inn patrons who watched the spectacle in silence, but no one intervened. Then a hand pulled the silver torc off his neck before several Lamia dragged him into the moonlight. Afterwards, a light netting of gold settled over his arms and back, and then he collapsed. The Lamia then pushed him into a large sack and carried him away.

Lughna? Did the Lamia kill them all?

The painful burn became a deep throb, and an overwhelming weakness made him shudder and close his eyes.

Phantom Queen, protect us all.

Outside Ráth Cruachan

Ruarí groaned as someone kicked him off the cart and onto the ground. He had lost count of the number of days and nights that had passed, but he could sense that they were arriving near the sacred home of Morrigan in Connacht near Ráth Cruachan. The magic in the air made his senses reel. He could hear the soft echo of the fae whispering to each other as he fell onto the hard dirt.

Two sets of arms carried him into a place with cool air and dropped him on the floor. They tossed him out of the bag and onto the cold, hard stone ground of the cave. The golden manacles continued to burn his wrists as they moved with him.

Blazing torches made his eyes ache, so he closed his eyes and began blinking. Despite his fuzzy vision, Ruarí slowly began to regain some focus.

Soon, a pair of hands slid around his head and removed the gag from his mouth. The wounds on his lips and tongue tingled as they began to heal.

"Mmmph?" he muttered, attempting to ignore the burns from the golden cloth.

A set of hands turned him with a light touch, and then a face peered at him with a smile and green eyes.

"I hope your mouth heals soon," the Lamia stated in a gentle purr, yet much malice laced them. "I had no idea that gold would do such damage to your beautiful face. We must talk, Ruarí Mac Flan."

Ruarí's eyes began to close when he could no longer concentrate on the Lamia and his words. Soon gray and then blackness overwhelmed him.

"Wrap iron chains around him to keep him from slouching on the rack," Mandubratius heard Wicus order the mortals as he watched his minions wheel the stand around to get the bindings in place. The wheels squeaked on the ancient torture rack.

Mandubratius looked over the Deargh Du, noting that the arch druid's eyes began to flutter. Mandubratius backed up and motioned another Lamia to check on their captive. The Deargh Du's face appeared diseased, and red blisters and burns encircled the blood-drinker's wrists and ankles, as new golden manacles encircled his lower legs.

"Let's have a look at your tongue and see if it has grown back," stated Calleo before opening the Deargh Du's mouth.

"Watch out," Mandubratius warned, noting that the Deargh Du's eyes glowed green. He then witnessed the arch druid bite down on Calleo's hand and begin to sup greedily on the blood that flowed forth. Calleo closed his eyes as though lost in a spell.

Mandubratius hit Calleo, knocking him into the wall across the room. He then stared at Ruarí as the Deargh Du licked his lips, revealing a healed tongue and mouth. Mandubratius considered that feeding the arch druid once in awhile to keep him healed and conscious would be in order.

"Why am I here?" the arch druid demanded in a harsh-sounding voice, like the raspy sound of dried leaves shaking against each other on the branch.

"You are here because of me, Ruarí," Mandubratius answered him. "I am here from Rome to question you about a lost treasure. Perhaps you have heard of it? The Phallus Maximus has been missing for almost eight hundred years."

"We have nothing from Rome or Greece," replied Ruarí. "I cannot think of anything we have that you could possibly want. We are the Goddess' hands here on earth, Her balancers of wrong and right, the keepers of darkness and light."

Mandubratius rolled his eyes a bit at the speech. He then picked up a sword and tested the balance of the blade before slicing into the arch druid's stomach.

"For some reason, Ruarí, I am not sure whether I believe you," Mandubratius taunted as e wiped the Deargh Du's blood from the blade onto his fingers and licked. He closed his eyes, tasting the golden kiss of honey-drenched loveliness. When the allure drifted away, it reminded him that he remained in a cold cave. He then sliced again at the Deargh Du's stomach. "Tell me, Ruarí... where is our precious treasure?"

"I know not of what you speak, Lamia," Ruarí answered.

"Well, I am sorry, but I just do not believe you. I mean, after all, there was a British merchant who came here with goods from the east. We found him, and he divulged his secret. However, he could not remember any details about whom he sold it to or whether it was stolen from his cart." Mandubratius sighed. "Let's go over this again, Ruarí. We will continue until we reach a consensus on this story of yours."

Mandubratius sliced through the Deargh Du's stomach once again.

Ruarí winced as the shallow cut bubbled forth more vitae and then began to heal.

"I understand that you have not been properly motivated to tell us all about the artifact we are seeking, Ruarí," Mandubratius stated while pacing in front of the rack. He could see Ruarí watch him move back and forth, until he stopped by the left side of the arch druid.

"I know the truth lies somewhere in here," Mandubratius deadpanned as he tapped the side of Ruarí's head. "Now, I will use the best motivations that I have available." He held up one of several nine-inch spikes in his hand and handed it to a mortal servant.

"Are you certain you have nothing to tell me, Arch Druid?" he asked Ruarí one last time.

"I know not of what you seek," answered the Deargh Du.

Mandubratius turned and nodded to the mortal henchman, who then placed the first nail at the arch druid's left arm. There was a mighty swing of a hammer, and then the sound of shattering bone echoed through the cave.

Mandubratius felt himself cringe a bit as blood splashed over Ruarí, the gathered Lamia, the mortals, and himself.

"Oh, that must not be very comfortable," he stated. "Are you sure that you do not wish to tell me anything about the artifact?"

The arch druid shuddered before turning to stare at his left wrist. A wordless cry from his form echoed through the cave.

"Normally, I am sure that this would not hurt so much, Arch Druid, but there are flecks of gold in the iron. It now is in your blood, causing you a great deal of pain, I imagine." Mandubratius turned to face Ruarí. "Please speak and tell me what you know, Ruarí. I hate to see a fellow blood-drinker in pain."

The arch druid shook his head, and his hoarse voice whimpered, "I know not of what you speak, Mandubratius."

"You know my name?" Mandubratius grinned at the ancient Deargh Du. "I am flattered that such a grand personage here in Éire knows of me. Unfortunately, I see that I have not motivated you well enough." He handed the mortal henchman more spikes and motioned for him to continue nailing. Mandubratius then stepped aside, licking his lips as the taste of Deargh Du blood cascaded into his mouth.

Before long, the mortals completed the crucifixion.

Mandubratius stared at the Deargh Du as the other blood-drinker met his stare.

"Looking at you," Mandubratius began to explain, "reminds me of the Appian Way. All those poor, tortured souls who rebelled against Rome. Some lived for days in the hot sun, Arch Druid. I can almost smell the rot." Mandubratius shook his head and clucked a bit. "You still have not said a word. One would think with this motivation, you would have told me anything to make it stop. Alas, I must now resort to this crude, yet simple punishment unless..." he murmured before pausing, "unless you tell me what I wish to know."

The arch druid hissed, dropped his head, and whispered, "I know not of what you speak."

"Very well," Mandubratius answered, before pointing to another mortal. "Start setting up the mirrors and the tripods." Mandubratius turned back to Ruarí and said, "I am certain you know that the sun has risen. Our kinds know these things instinctively."

He heard the tripods wheeled about as the mirrors were tipped. Wicus then handed him a cloak, which he donned. The mortals adjusted the mirrors until a beam of light appeared above the arch druid's head.

"Since you will not tell me what I want to hear, I am afraid I am going to have to induce more pain upon you," Mandubratius stated, before moving to Ruarí's right side. "Now, this will hurt me as much as I am sure it will hurt you. I prefer people to talk so we do not have to resort to such barbaric implements, but you leave me no choice."

Mandubratius pulled down the cowl and hood of the cloak before motioning the mortals to move light to Ruarí's left hand.

The arch druid started screaming in pain as the small beam of light moved to his forearm, burning his arm and singeing his limb down to the bone. His left hand turned to ash and fell to the ground.

Mandubratius waved to the mortals and the light disappeared.

"Again, tell me the story," he bade Ruarí. "This will be all over, I promise. Tell me, and I will give you blood. Do not make me do this to you, Ruarí. Unlike these others, I respect your position."

Ruarí whimpered for a moment and began to stare at Mandubratius as if gathering his thoughts. After a moment, he replied in a sibilant hiss, "May Morrigan feast upon your bones."

"That is not what I want to hear," Mandubratius spat. "Start the light again," he ordered the mortal underlings. "Start at the mid chest and go down from there. I am afraid we will have to keep at this until sunset, if you continue to say nothing of use, Ruarí. If you keep your silence, I will have to come up with something else to make you talk."

Béal Átha an Fheadha

Oisín cleared his throat as Maél Muire checked on the young calves. "Chieftain, your judgment is needed."

Maél Muire stood up before dusting off her muddy hands on her blue cloak. "What is it this time, Oisín?" She laughed, thinking of her last decision regarding the ownership of a pair of hens, and shook her hair out, allowing the plaits to settle down her back.

"Two important personages have arrived," he answered in a half whisper.

Maél Muire began to lead the way back to the dun.

Flanna waited for her outside the main door, holding a bucket of water and a clean cloak. After a quick wash of her hands and feet, Maél Muire heard Oisín announce her from inside, and then she walked into the great hall.

"Chieftains," she called, upon seeing Mac Turrlough and Seanán. Their servants, clansmen, and warriors milled about the great hall. Maél Muire could nearly detect a smell of rising anger, as she observed the elder and younger chieftain staring at each other, too distracted to call their clansmen to silence in respect of her.

"Silence," she ordered, and the gathered people grew silent. "I am called for judgment in a grievance between the two of you," she surmised aloud.

"Your father and uncle always assisted in local judgments," intoned Mac Turrlough. "Instead of turning to the King of Connacht, we turn to other local chieftains. You are the neighboring clan between us, and we both thought you would be a fair judge." He stared at her a moment, as if to remind her of the expected fidelity to him. After all, she had inherited his son's property.

"No extra grain or cattle fees that way," Seanán stated. Maél Muire noticed that a smirk graced his features, revealing his own expectations.

"And what problem has befallen two friends and neighbors?" Maél Muire queried, after taking a seat in the chieftain's chair. "Chieftain," she acknowledged, motioning to Mac Turrlough. "I will listen to your disputed claim first."

"Something is killing our sheep," stated Mac Turrlough as he scratched at his graying beard. "Our herds that border Seanán's lands are disappearing at night. Then in the morrow, we find them dead. I know he's having my property killed at night."

"Why would I be killing our sheep as well?" Seanán snarled in reply.

She faced Seanán and held up her right hand. "Calm down and tell me your side, Chieftain."

"We have the same problem. We have lost a great many sheep between us."

"Your sheepdogs and the shepherds, are any of them untrustworthy?" she asked.

"We have already considered such issues," Mac Turrlough grumbled, while giving her an impatient glare.

Maél Muire inhaled and closed her eyes. "I would like to see a dead sheep from each of you. Perhaps the wounds will reveal how they died. I trust that you each brought a sheep from home?" She then opened her eyes and crossed her arms over her chest, hoping this would give her time to think of other questions.

They both nodded mutely, giving each other distrusting glares. The two parties then began to head outside, and she followed, wrapping the cloak around herself as an incoming afternoon storm prepared to send rain and winds to them.

Maél Muire walked over to the first carcass and tried not to inhale the sharp fumes of rotting meat. She shooed away the black flies that gathered near two strange circular wounds on the sheep's neck. A quick study of the other sheep revealed a shared, desiccated appearance.

"Are these the only wounds?" she asked, while glancing from one chieftain to another. She then opened the sheep's right eye and studied the sunken orb.

"Yes, only one set of wounds on mine as well," stated Mac Turrlough.

"Druce?" Maél Muire called to her butcher, "I want to you to remove the heads of this and the other sheep. I believe they have been exsanguinated."

Druce walked to the back of the dun and returned with a pair of large knives.

Maél Muire took a few steps back to allow him room.

A few minutes later, both heads lay on the ground, and Mac Turrlough knelt down to investigate. "No blood," he confirmed.

"I believe this to be the work on an unknown creature," Maél Muire surmised aloud, knowing who might be feeding upon her neighbors' livestock. She had to wonder why her clan managed to escape the feeding. Perhaps they should consider themselves lucky that the Lamia had limited themselves to feeding on sheep.

"Let us go inside the dun, just the three of us," Maél Muire suggested, while gesturing for the other two chieftains to follow her. Upon arriving at the door, she held it open until the other two chieftains walked inside. The door closed behind her. "This creature would be as large as a man with the jaws of a wolf or mighty hunting cat," she stated as she walked to the table within the great hall.

"Well, that does not even address the issue of the lost sheep," Seanán replied in a curt tone.

"I agree. I want some form of compensation," Mac Turrlough added. "Who is to say that he," continued Mac Turrlough, while pointing at Seanán, "did not send some beast after my sheep and killed one of his own in order to throw off suspicion?"

Maél Muire pulled the sword from her belt, turned, and slammed the flat of the blade against the top of the table.

"If one of you makes war on the other, my clan will side with the wronged chieftain," she growled. "My judgment is that this is not the fault of either of you."

Seanán lowered his head a bit. "Then, what do you suggest we do?" he asked.

"I suggest you track the beast," Maél Muire answered.

"Chieftain, might I ask where your clan's sheep graze?" Mac Turrlough asked.

"I do not care for your insinuation," answered Maél Muire. "However, I will tell you that our sheep graze on the southern edge of our lands, far away from where your lands and Seanán's lands lie."

"I apologize, then. Thank you for your judgment, Chieftain Maél Muire." Mac Turrlough gave her a brief nod, opened the door, and allowed it to shut behind him.

Seanán watched Maél Muire shrug as the elder chieftain left the dun. Upon Mac Turrlough's departure, her servants returned and began to hustle through the great hall, cleaning and preparing for the evening meal. He smiled a bit at Maél Muire and took a few steps closer to her as she started to leave for the kitchen area.

"Madam Chieftain," he called to her, "might I have a word with you?"

Maél Muire regarded him for a moment with her moss-colored eyes. "Of course, Chieftain," she acknowledged as she tilted her head a bit to one side. People walked in between them, carrying meat and ground flour. Soon, Bearach walked in and fixed a stern set of blue eyes on him.

"What is the nature of the business between us?" Maél Muire asked with a small smile. Her pink lips curved in a most attractive manner.

"It is personal, Chieftain," Seanán replied, hearing his voice purr like a satisfied cat's.

"Oh, very well, if we must speak." She turned and nodded to her uncle's armsman, who then clapped his hands. The servants filed out in an obedient manner, yet he witnessed the knowing grins on their faces. At last, Bearach exited the dun, closing the door behind him.

"Do you wish to discuss the ruling?" Maél Muire asked.

"I would never insult an equal by questioning her ruling," Seanán acquiesced with smile, before making a slight bow to her. "Your judgment is binding, and I stand by it." He then met her eyes and straightened his back.

"Are you patronizing me, Seanán?" Maél Muire demanded as she took a few steps closer to him. Her voice grew lower.

"Not at all, Chieftain Maél Muire. I merely wish to ask you a question, after I praise your decision. Mac Turrlough is a fine chieftain, but he seems to believe I am in need of his advice. I listen, but I seldom follow through, and I believe you saw through his calm exterior to the ire within. So, I compliment your womanly intuition and wise judgment."

He watched as Maél Muire pulled a small dagger from her belt and drew closer. She played with the dagger across his léine.

"Excellent," she murmured. "It would be rather rude of you to patronize me, and I do not tolerate rudeness." Maél Muire then raised her eyes to his, and he could see playfulness dance within them for a moment, revealing her mischief.

"Now," she purred, "if you wish to dispense with your glowing compliments, Seanán, and get to the proverbial point," she accentuated as she gently pressed the tip of the dagger to his shoulder, "I would be quite pleased. Just because we enjoyed each other once, many years ago, does not give you the right to patronize me as one might a child."

Seanán squirmed a bit at the brief flicker of pain, but thankfully, Maél Muire sheathed the dagger before walking to the chieftain's chair. He eyed her as she crossed her right leg over her left and slouched a bit. She then grinned, and appeared to wait for him to speak.

"I would like to dine with you tonight," he announced as he strolled closer to the chieftain's chair.

"You go through this attempt at flattery to ask me to dine with you, Seanán?" Maél Muire rose from her chair and took a few steps towards him. "You need not stammer a reply," she cooed as she gave him that strange twist of a smile. "I accept. Few men have the courage to sup with me, and I never have been able to understand why. I do not think I am that frightening. I may be tall, but I do not think I am so intimidating."

Seanán grinned. Maél Muire would be a bit too much for most men to handle. Even her use of her dagger to make her point would have driven off most men.

"Where should I have my harker find you when it is time for supper?" she queried.

Seanán lowered his head for a moment before raising it. "I have not thought far enough in advance," he stated with a large smile. "I had not counted on your agreeing."

"Then you shall be my guest. Oisín!" she yelled, calling for the harker. The front door opened as the servant rushed inside the great hall.

"Set up the guest quarters for Seanán, Oisín, and see to the needs of his party."

Seanán attempted to stammer his thanks, but was interrupted.

"Oisín will call for you when it is time," Maél Muire stated as she started to saunter towards the back of the dun. "Until then, stay there," she said with a smile. "I need a bath."

Seanán paced the guest room several times before stopping in front of the basin of water. He then splashed the water over his face and examined his nails by the light of the dying sun in hopes that they would not be ragged. A loud knock interrupted him, and so he raced to the door.

Oisín nodded and gave him a polite bow. "The Chieftain awaits you. Follow me."

Seanán walked toward the hall and hearth, but the dark room revealed nothing to his eyes.

"Chieftain?" Oisín queried as he turned to face Seanán. Then the harker gave him a smile as he pulled open a door to another room. Sweet smelling smoke filtered through the open entrance. Seanán closed his eyes for a moment as he neared the room. The scents of mutton, apples, and mead wafted to his nose, and he inhaled before opening his eyes and walking inside. He soon heard the door close behind him.

"Chieftain," he called before studying the table laid out in front of him. He waited until she caught his eyes. Maél Muire, dressed in a thin, linen léine, walked over to him. The sheer material, which revealed her nipples and russet nether regions, flowed over her form like the soft, gentle waves of a calm sea.

She took his hands and pulled him closer towards her. She then led him behind the table towards a bed of furs and blankets.

"I do not know about you," Maél Muire purred, "but I am not quite hungry yet. Perhaps we should work up an appetite?" She began to unfastened his belt as she manhandled him closer to the bed.

Seanán inhaled a sharp breath as her lips brushed against his. He pulled her closer to him as their kisses grew frenzied. She shivered as the cool night air moved through the room from the slits in the wood. The sweet taste of mead honeyed her lips and tongue. Seanán laced his fingers through her hair.

She pulled back and stumbled, as if a bit surprised by the kiss.

Seanán took her hand as she tottered and finally sank to the bed, illuminated by the light of the crescent moon. He sat down next to her without a word.

He slid her arms up over her head and unfastened her belt before removing her léine. As he stroked his fingertips down her arm, she snorted and began to giggle. He could not help but be stunned by the sounds of her laughter, as his light caresses seemed to tickle her. What power he felt.

"Banbh," he snickered, while leaning in to kiss her neck. "I never thought I would miss the sound of you snorting."

"And I told you never to call me that again." She paused for a moment and stopped laughing.

He smiled, before tracing his right index fingertip down the cleft between her breasts and circled her bellybutton.

She snorted a giggle again. "You are not supposed to call me that. I am the chieftain now, and I really do dislike being referred to as 'piglet'."

"Why, you never told me not to call you piglet," he teased. "I think you secretly enjoy that nickname."

"I know I have told you many times not to call me that, and I just told you a few moments ago." Her face turned up in a beautiful twist of a smile. Maél Muire then pulled off his léine and traced her fingers over the muscles of his skin. She began kissing and nibbled her way down his stomach. Once she reached his groin, she began to run her fingers over his shaft.

Soon he felt her rub some scentless oil on his erection, and she began to stroke him with vigor. Seanán hissed as she squeezed the head during her downward strokes. He then rubbed himself to get some of that oil on his fingers and began to run his fingers up her stomach to her breasts, stroking her rose-hued nipples with her oil, which had mixed with her sweat.

Seanán wrapped himself around her, as his kisses traveled down her body. He inhaled the sweet scent of a lavender infusion that cascaded around her. He then wrapped one of her legs around himself and felt Maél Muire shudder as he moved against her. She then wrapped her other leg around him, and he settled on top of her, pushing into her heat, driving into her again and again.

Maél Muire clutched at him as she closed her eyes. Soon his breath caught in his throat as an overwhelming pressure swallowed him whole. She whimpered as Seanán felt a shattering release engulf his body. His muscles tensed, and he could thrust no more. All he could feel was each spasm of essence into her. He soon collapsed on Maél Muire's body with his ear resting between her breasts. He could hear her racing heart as it slowed in time with his. Seanán then leaned up on his elbows to look into her eyes.

"I love you," he whispered.

"I love you too," she sighed, while running a hand through his hair.

Seanán kissed her again and began to pull away. "Have you worked up an appetite?"

"No. Please," she whispered, "stay with me awhile. I have been alone for so long."

"As you wish," he offered, before lying next to her on his right side. He then ran his left fingers over her right nipple and then slid the digit to her left breast. "Hmmm, that was quite a welcome," he murmured, before leaning in for another kiss. The taste of honey still laced her breath.

She smiled as she ran a finger across his lips. "I can welcome you many more times if you want. In fact, I wish you had come home sooner." Maél Muire leaned forward and captured his lips in a kiss. She then pulled back and murmured, "I am hungry now."

"I came home when I could, Maél Muire," he explained as he ran his fingers over her hair and frowned slightly. "You have the oddest color of hair. It reminds me of dried blood. I have seen that hue too much in the last few years. However, just this once, I am grateful to see it."

Maél Muire smirked. "Morrigan's hair, as your mother had said once before. How is she, by the by?"

"She is doing well and told me to give you greetings." He grinned as pulled away and planted his feet. He then walked over, with her following, to the table to sit down, and they both started eating. He picked up a portion of the mutton and started to chew.

As he watched her take few bites, he found it astonishing how the lamp light made her hair shimmer, almost like fire, and her nipples continued to stand erect. Her green eyes exuded a warm playfulness, and her quivering lips promised more sensuous delight.

She handed him a goblet of mead, and then he took a long sip, but he continued to study her naked form. Soon his erection returned, and all he could think about was entering her again. So he decided to push aside the food and remove the bowl from her hands.

"Dinner can wait again," he whispered into her ear.

Maél Muire leaned in for another kiss and then pulled back as Seanán's hands wrapped around her waist. He watched her grow serious, preparing to turn back into the leader of her clan. Seanán withdrew his hands as she stepped away from him.

"Goodnight, Seanán."

"What do you mean by 'goodnight', Lady Chieftain? Why not lie with me tonight? I could make love to you all night" He then stood and took a few steps closer to her.

"Shhhh," Maél Muire whispered, while placing a finger over his lips. "Be happy that you got as much as you did." She then handed him his clothing, which she had already gathered up. "Sleep well."

He could feel himself pouting a bit, but Maél Muire just smiled at him while crossing her arms over her breasts. Seanán opened the door and walked out of the room, naked, and ignored the stares and snickers of the shocked servants. Seanán stepped into the guest quarters and closed the door behind him, still hearing the whispers of servants.

Women. Could one never fathom them?

Mhuine Chonalláin

Connor walked through the grove and then glanced over his shoulder at the noises that echoed around him. Snapping branches, the calls of birds, and the footsteps of the wild animals grew silent as he neared her house. The stench of death and decay grew stronger with each step. He felt a sudden compulsion to run in the other direction, away from the growing darkness, but instead he steadied his racing heart and took a ragged breath. Only the sound of a cawing crow broke the silence.

"So, you finally decide to come for a visit?" whispered a familiar voice as a hand grasped his shoulder. He tried to control his fear as his mother's gnarled digits encircled his arm. "What is it?" she asked. "You look upset."

"I am upset," he replied, after turning to face her. Her soot-covered face stared back at him, expressing too many things to count. "Maél Muire favors another over me. Your plan is not working, mother. I know you have experience in these matters, so help me."

Seosaimhín closed her eyes and then released his arm. "We see her with that other," she acknowledged while nodding her head. She then opened her eyes and stared at him. "Have you seen the dark one she consorts with, the one who hides in the night?"

Connor raised a brow. Once again his mother resorted to nonsensical riddles. "No, I do not think so," he replied with a sigh. "Is this the being who is supposed to assist me while I assist him?"

"Yes," Seosaimhín replied with vehemence. "Fine, remain calm, child. We will tell Maél Muire that fate draws her in a different direction. My sources say she is to be my student, and your life is tied to hers. Wait for us, and we shall return with her."

Béal Átha an Fheadha

Maél Muire leaned forward as she placed her scythe and knife on her ceremonial cloth. She then leaned in to place her hands over the periwinkle flowers and closed her eyes, searching for the right blossoms by scent. How wonderful she felt as the cool night breeze lifted her hair.

She soon heard footsteps and wrinkled her nose at a cloying scent, which prevented her from seeking the right blossoms. "You are spoiling my concentration," she muttered, before opening her eyes, only to find a stranger staring down at her.

"And you are spoiling our plans, young Maél Muire," a dirt-smudged woman spat as she grabbed her hand. Maél Muire grimaced at the pressure the old woman's hands exuded. She was stronger than she seemed and smelled of death and decay.

Maél Muire drew her sword with her free hand and held it above the crone's arm that held hers at bay. "What plans do you speak of, crone? Speak honestly. Release me and I will give you the respect your age deserves."

"I am here to tell you to give up on your young love. You and he are not meant to be together in this life," the crone answered. Her fingers snaked around Maél Muire's wrist. "Perhaps in the next, you and he may meet again. In the meantime, you should be looking towards my son, the chieftain of Mhuine Chonalláin. Your life and his are irrevocably entwined. Your notions regarding Druidism are weak at best," she hissed. "Your great aunt and uncle are poor teachers, and so you will join me to learn what power you can wield."

"I know what power lies beyond the mists," Maél Muire rejoined as she pulled her hand away, now that the crone's grip had loosened. "I will continue my studies with my family." She ignored her desire to run and hide.

"Stop playing the young, stubborn fool. We may influence fate, but we can never change it. You will marry my son. The entrails do not lie."

"I do not know of what you speak." Maél Muire then turned away and ran from the grove, not stopping until she threw open the door to her aunt and uncle's home and slammed it shut behind her, gasping for breath.

"Where's the periwinkle?" Uncle Fergus inquired, while giving her a strange look. "What happened? Settle down."

"She is out there waiting!" Maél Muire yelled as she raced around him.

"Who?"Uncle Fergus asked with a laugh. "You act as though you have seen the washer at the ford."

"Mac Turrlough's mother," she hissed, still trying to catch her breath. "She says that I need to forget Seanán and your teachings. She says that we are–"

"Seosaimhín?" her aunt queried as she walked out of the storage room and dusted off her arms. "I am surprised she had not shown herself to you sooner." She sighed and sat down. "Sit down, Maél Muire. Do not worry. She will not come in here. Seosaimhín does not want to see me." Her face turned up in a sad smile.

"Why is that? She certainly seems to dislike you both," Maél Muire observed before sitting down and pulling her knees up to her chest.

Sive chuckled. "There is a very good reason for that. You see, she taught me almost all that I know."

"What?" Maél Muire exclaimed with a humorless laugh. "You… you… learned our faith from others at Tara and in Britannia. Aunt, she's not healthy in the mind or the soul."

Sive nodded her head. "She was not always that way, Maél Muire. Seosaimhín came from an ancient line of gifted druids who knew all the secrets of the elements, understood the paths of the gods and goddesses, and had the strength needed to contact and use the powers of both." Her aunt then took a deep breath. "They said that she could draw down the mists before she even took her first steps into womanhood, yet she fell from that grace and the balance. One night, she and her beloved were cutting down sacred mistletoe for Meán Geimhridh."

"The winter solstice," Maél Muire whispered, nodding her head a bit.

"Yes, and she and her husband traveled deep into old groves without fear. However, this time they happened onto an ancient transformation rite, the transformation process that overwhelms a mortal when they become Deargh Du."

"They say that it tests the strength, the mind, and the soul of the mortal who dares to take the challenge of Morrigan," her uncle added. "They say their first night is full of tests, magic, and even insanity. The newborn Deargh Du may attack their friends and loved ones without thought."

"Seosaimhín and her husband, Finian, were trapped. The Deargh Du attacked them, and his mother-in-darkness could not get there fast enough.

Finian died in Seosaimhín's arms. She swore off the balance and turned towards the darkness. Her hatred of Deargh Du and Morrigan overwhelmed her... changed her, and in her rage she lost sight," Sive added. "All of her students left, fearful of the changes within her. I traveled to Tara to get away from her." Her aunt shifted before stretching her bare feet. "With distance, I realized that she only sought to destroy herself. So, your uncle and I returned to the grove of my family."

"And what am I to do about this plan of hers? I am going to marry Seanán, I hope, and I do not want to be her student," Maél Muire muttered. "Something about your old teacher turns my heart cold."

"She is old and misguided," Sive suggested. "Just ignore her words and know you are safe on your own path. Leave her if she makes you uncomfortable, but leave her in peace."

"If one is not balanced in the head, one cannot find balance in life. Treat her with respect, but do not forget to take precautions after crossing her path," Fergus added. "She still possesses gifts. The darkness offers great powers to those who adhere to its path."

"Perhaps I will never see her again," Maél Muire mused. At least she hoped that they would never meet again.

"I would not count on that," Aunt Sive warned.

Rome

Lucretia arrived at the back door of her old home and knocked on the frame. After several attempts to gain passage, she began banging on the door.

"Password?" a breathless voice answered. A mortal heartbeat raced inside.

"Roma vitrix," Lucretia answered, and then the door opened. Lucretia grabbed the servant and began drinking from her. After months of feeding from sailors, she needed a good meal. Her fury subsided as the tastes enveloped her, and she became lost in the silky, red rivers of vitae.

"Lucretia."

The voice startled her out of her reverie. Lucretia looked up and saw Amata watching her from the hall. She began walking forward.

"You look and smell like-- " Amata accused.

"I know," Lucretia responded, before staring down at the men's clothing she had been wearing for months. She then dropped the corpse of the serving girl.

Amata stared at her. "Was the trip that bad?"

Lucretia shrugged and wiped away her reddened lips. "Months of feeding on the most vile sailors," she answered.

"Why are you here?"

"Your friend Marcus arrived here. They are on their way to Britannia, and they need to meet up with a caravan and probably get gold from you."

"I see," Amata answered. "You came here to report to me."

Lucretia nodded her head.

"Excellent. Welcome home to Rome. Go upstairs, find fresh clothing, and bathe. Then, meet me in my chambers. Oh, and do something with that body." Amata then walked away.

"There, you look so much better," Amata purred in a haughty manner. The very sight of it made Lucretia squirm with indignation.

"And smell better?" Lucretia could feel her blood begin to boil, especially since Amata's blue eyes revealed great pleasure.

"You look upset," replied Amata. "I thought you would be happy to be home, at least for a visit."

Lucretia was about to reply when she heard a soft knocking on the door. A heartbeat drowned out all of the other noises.

"Domina?" a voice called from beyond the door.

"Yes, come in, Julia," Amata called.

Julia walked in and then glanced over at Lucretia before addressing Amata. "Domina, there is a man downstairs to see you."

"His name?"

"Marcus," Julia answered.

Amata chuckled and then covered her mouth with her hand. "Bring him upstairs," she told Julia. "Now, Lucretia, go into my bedchamber." She gestured for Lucretia to leave with a condescending wave of her hand. "I will call for you in a few moments."

Lucretia stared at Amata for a few breaths before stalking away, as her bitter hatred still burned within.

Amata smiled and arose from her seat as Marcus walked in. She sauntered over to embrace him and then watched as he pulled away and accepted a chaste kiss.

"It does me good to see you," she purred as she ran a hand across his beard, which felt rough against her fingertips.

"You flatter me," Marcus answered as he gave her that same sensuous smile she remembered from his last visit.

"How did you end up back here?" she asked, before taking a seat again. His clothes looked worn and dirty, but he appeared the same as he had when he had left, except for the beard. His silver eyes gleamed in the light from the candles. "Please sit," she requested, while motioning to the chair across from her.

"It's a long story," Marcus commented as he took the offered seat.

"I do hope it is an exciting one."

Marcus smiled again. "I wish it was," he answered. "We went to Shiraz and ascertained that Mandubratius had left for Alexandria. We now believe he is searching for the Phallus Maximus in Britannia."

"I see," Amata acknowledged as she pulled at the corners of her dress. "And you have just arrived today."

"Yes," answered Marcus. "I need to ask a favor of you."

Amata felt warmth move over her cold body. "And what is this favor?"

"We feel that it would be easier to join with a caravan and receive compensation by guarding the caravan. Berti and I traveled in this manner when we went to Shiraz."

"I see," Amata purred, feeling her lips curl into a smile. "Oh my, forgive my manners." She stood, handed a goblet to Marcus, and poured a cup of donor's blood from a large jug.

"Thank you." His fingers moved over hers, and she felt warmth move through her again, even though his fingers felt cold.

"Yes, I know of a caravan that may need such protection," she answered. "I have 300 soldiers that need to join our battalion in Britannia. One of our most trusted associates, the Legate Patroclus Statilius Messalinus, leads them. This is great timing for you and your friends. The trip will be by cart. We have many supplies and trade goods that must go to Britannia. Are you interested in this guard duty?"

"Yes, we would appreciate this chance to reach Britannia," Marcus answered.

"However, I have one small request," she purred, as she placed a hand on his arm.

He looked up at her and stated, "I am at your command."

Amata faced the bed chamber and called, "Lucretia!"

Lucretia then walked in from Amata's bedchamber to stare at her.

"Yes, Domina?" Lucretia's voice betrayed her confusion.

"Marcus, this is Lucretia. I wish her to join you on your journey to find Mandubratius. She will be your assistant when you provide protection for our caravan, as well as when you are our commander over Hibernia."

Amata stared at Lucretia, daring her to say anything contrary.

Marcus nodded and bowed. "That is an excellent plan."

"Perhaps you and your traveling companions would like to stay with us until the caravan leaves?" Amata asked.

"I will have to check with Berti and Sitara. She joined us near Alexandria and is invaluable to us now. Plus, Berti needs mortal companionship, Domina."

"I see." Amata smirked. "Go find them, and we will prepare rooms for them. They will have my protection."

Marcus nodded, inclining his head in a bow, before leaving the room.

Amata smiled and nodded to Lucretia. "All is set then. Prepare for your journey. I will follow you. I do not want to miss Marcus' death. Try to not annoy Patroclus too much."

She left Lucretia and walked out of her chambers, seeing a deep frown settle on Lucretia's face. All was going to plan. The best thing to do was to confuse everyone and then become the victor or heroine by default.

"Forget it, I would sooner stay here," Berti pouted.

"I have a feeling that Amata's requests are never an option," answered Marcus. "You'll be safe... she promised."

"No offense to Amata, but a promise from her is probably not worth the breath to voice it," argued Berti.

"Who is Amata?" Sitara asked while raising a brow.

"You and Sitara both have my protection, Berti." Marcus turned and addressed Sitara. "Amata is a sister-in-darkness to Mandubratius, the leader of the Lamia who is searching for the Phallus Maximus. I mean... damn it." He sat down on the bed. "If we want to ever get to Britannia, we have to make some sacrifices."

"Like that horrible beard, I hope," Berti mumbled under his breath.

"Excuse me?" Marcus challenged.

Berti coughed in an attempt to hide his laughter. "Just some dust in my throat from all that incense. So, why exactly do we have to take this Lamia?"

"I convinced Amata that I would take over the fight in Éire for the Lamia as her commander. She wants this Lucretia to assist me." He shrugged. "Other than that, I could not tell, but it has me worried."

"Why?" asked Sitara.

"As you say, it is intuition. However, at the very least, you will get a good meal, a bath, and fresh clothing."

"At the very least," grumbled Berti, "we better not end up as a meal."

As soon as Lucretia entered her quarters, Assim sniffed air and stated, "You smell funny."

"I took a bath," Lucretia countered. "I am leaving my dirty rags behind. I have yet to tell Amata about you, but I am sure you will be welcome to stay at the temple. You are not going to be able to travel with me anymore."

"What?" Assim snarled.

She stared at him, fascinated by his fury. She could not help but be surprised to see his eyes turn red. Then again, why did he complain? He would be able to enjoy life within the confines of the temple, while she had to travel on dusty roads with a grove-dweller and his mortal friends. Mandubratius would have killed her had he ever witnessed her behave in such a fashion.

Instead of killing Assim, she turned and slapped him, pleased to see him cower. Assim held his cheek as he looked up at her with fear instead of fury in his eyes. "Much better," she hissed. "You will never question me in such a manner again. My sponsor would have done away with me for less. Amata ordered me to travel with Marcus and his companions."

"You are my sponsor," answered Assim. "Why do you want to leave me behind?"

"You have outgrown your usefulness to me at this time," Lucretia replied. "However, instead of destroying you, I wish for you to remain in the temple of Mars to learn who you are."

"Do not leave me behind, I beg of you," Assim murmured, while clutching her leg in a manner that reminded her of a two-year-old mortal child.

"You will do as I wish, Assim. Don't make me tell you this again."

"I can be useful to you!" He pursed his lips for a moment. "How can you trust this Deargh Du? You will be alone, surrounded by his friends. You deserve protection."

Lucretia stared at him. "There will be other Lamia with us."

"They will be more concerned with their own protection. Please, allow me to join you."

Lucretia sighed and rubbed her forehead in frustration.

Perhaps Assim could be useful.

"Alright, you can travel with us. However, you will need to shave and find your own way with the caravan at night, or something." She hated relenting to his wishes. Assim would try to take advantage of any privilege she gave him. "You must behave and remember who and what you are."

Assim kissed her right hand. She wanted to yank it away, but she let him continue kissing her palm.

"Lucretia," he whispered. "Can we?"

She shook her head. "We do not have time for physical enjoyment." She did not add the part about his stench. "Remain here until I come back for you."

Marcus took Sitara's arm as they walked through the corridors of the old temple. Whispers echoed in the hallways as they passed many Lamia.

"I believe I heard the words 'great' and 'dinner'," hissed Berti.

Marcus stared at the pale faces in the hallway, and all became silent. The burning ash falling from incense censers echoed in the silent temple halls. The Lamia stared at him for a moment, but then they turned away, all but one. As the Lamia ambled through the small piles of ash, dust rose in the great corridor.

Lucretia, the only remaining Lamia who stared at them, crossed her arms and asked, "Who are they?"

"My mortal traveling companions," answered Marcus. "Do you have a problem with them? If you do, you may as well say your peace." He stared into her dark, brown eyes, although he could still see through his periphery Berti placing a hand on his sword's hilt.

"I have no problem with the arrangement," Lucretia intoned with a smile, revealing her teeth. "Amata wished me to tell you that she is making arrangements as we speak. The caravan will leave at dawn." She turned on her heel with a chuckle. "If you wish for refreshments, they are in your rooms." She ran away, leaving behind a few puffs of floating dust from the incense.

"She seems like a pleasant sort," grumbled Sitara, while coughing and waving her arms at the flying ash. "And by that, I mean I really dislike her."

"Definitely trustworthy," added Berti, while turning away from the floating ash. "I would be willing to put my life in her hands."

Marcus sighed before gesturing for them to follow him into the room. "I am certain, if warranted, I could take care of Lucretia. However, she may have an insight into Mandubratius."

Berti raised a questioning brow. "So you think she would be an asset to our little team."

"She may make things go faster if she wants Mandubratius dead, just as Amata does. However, we will remain silent on these plans."

"In case Amata has plans of her own," Sitara stated before sitting down on the bed.

Berti sat down in a chair and sighed. "Do you think she has a plan or two up her sleeve, Marcus?"

"Amata is what she is. The Lamia never leave things to chance. There is always a plan and a contingency plan or two in place. She wants to be their leader." He picked up the jug and poured himself a cup of the lukewarm blood. "She would be foolish to not have many plans in mind."

"I thought you said she had left for the caravan's departure point already," Marcus grumbled at Berti, mildly concerned about Lucretia's absence, though he felt more concerned that they leave before the sun rose.

"That is what she said," answered Berti. "Maybe something will keep her from joining us."

"Highly doubtful," Marcus replied. He watched the caravan wagons prepare to begin their journey. Soon, however, the cloying scent of roses overwhelmed him, and he held his nose.

"Phew," Sitara coughed before backing away as Lucretia arrived. Some Lamia marched up to them and opened the door to their cart.

"You know, you do not need to wear that rose oil all the time. We're heading north, not into the east with the Algul," suggested Marcus as he grimaced at the strong smell.

Lucretia walked closer to them so they could speak more privately, he resumed.

"When the mortals think it is too much, think how those with stronger senses have to compensate for your overwhelming stench," he added.

"It is far better than how you smell," Lucretia challenged as she sniffed him. "How long has it been since you had a proper bath or a shave?" She stalked away with a hiss towards a series of other carts that carried the night guard.

Marcus watched Berti join the rest of the mortal guards, leaving only Sitara.

"You have driven a cart before, correct?" he asked Sitara.

She gave him a grin. "A few times... do not worry," Sitara boasted before hopping into the front seat and grabbing the reins of the oxen.

Marcus stepped into cart and closed the door. He then slid into the hidden compartment. Despite the padding, he felt a jolt of movement as the caravan started to lumber forward.

chapter four

Outside Divio

s Lucretia ran ahead of the glittering caravan, she felt a presence follow her. "Why are you following me?" she demanded after stopping and staring at Marcus as he glowed under the starlit sky. His pale, silver eyes entranced her for a moment, and she wondered how any blood-drinker could make himself look so disarming. Perhaps all the Deargh Du did this trick to make themselves seem harmless and beautiful.

The Deargh Du interloper smirked at her for a moment with a calculating stare. "Patroclus sent me on a scouting errand, and to be honest, I am hunting. I could smell and hear something ahead of us." He paused as they both heard a sound. Marcus picked up a squeaking rat and turned it over, revealing its furry underbelly. Lucretia nearly gagged as he started to feed from it, greedily draining its blood. He then tossed aside the carcass.

"You are the only one of my kind who will take a rat as opposed to a mortal," Lucretia observed as she tilted her head to one side.

Marcus sniffed a bit before looking back at the caravan as it stopped on its path toward the Alps. "Your friends do not seem to know the meaning of moderation. We will be lucky if one-quarter of the mortals on this caravan survive, the way the others feed upon them."

"They will all survive," stated Lucretia. "You are an odd Lamia. So, when were you sponsored?"

"Almost six hundred years ago," he answered. "Is there any particular reason why you are scouting ahead, Lucretia?"

"It was my turn, but mostly because I wanted to get away from Assim, the one I sponsored. He has a habit of being annoying, and he asks too many questions while demanding attention and affection," she muttered.

"Assim?" Marcus asked, while raising a brow. "You transformed the Shah Assim from Shiraz? So, you were the one following us."

Lucretia looked around at the upcoming mountains and shrugged. "Yes I did. I needed his assistance at the time, and of course I followed you. Amata always sends spies. So, why do you not sponsor your slaves?" she asked.

"First off, they are not my slaves, and second, they prefer mortality for the time being," Marcus answered. She watched his eyes as they scanned the skies for a moment and then returned to her. His stare encompassed her being for a few seconds, but then she at last found her voice.

"Have you sponsored anyone before?" Lucretia asked.

"No," Marcus replied.

Lucretia gasped. "But you are almost six hundred years old." This fact surprised her.

Marcus laughed outright. "If I sponsor someone, I must make sure that I can handle the responsibility of being around for them in case I am needed. I mean," he said, pausing for a moment, "you already are tired of Assim. How long did you know him before you sponsored him?"

Lucretia sniffed a bit. How dare he judge her? He was not even Lamia. She crossed her arms over her chest and pouted, "That is not your business! I do not answer to you... only to Mandubratius!"

"And Amata, don't forget her," Marcus teased and began laughing.

"Must you be so smug?" she muttered, wondering why it was men, Lamia or mortal, who always seemed to find such satisfaction in being correct. She then looked over the starlit horizon, hoping to find an answer to such a query. "You have to answer to her as well."

"Yes, but I somehow sense it is more of an issue for you than for me." At that moment, Marcus looked over his shoulder and became agitated.

"What is it?"

He held up a hand, while continuing to scan the grounds surrounding the caravan. "Nothing," he muttered. "Let us continue this conversation while we act as scouts." He then held up his right hand again and sniffed.

"What is it?" she whispered, impatient with this game.

He held up two fingers and pointed toward the north.

"What are you doing?" she asked, while staring at him again.

"Do you not even recognize Roman military signals?" Marcus asked in a whisper.

"No," she answered with a pout. "It just looks like you are wiggling your fingers at me!" It soon dawned on her that she had seen these hand signals amongst the Lamia in the caravan earlier. "I cannot believe they were talking behind my back!"

Marcus shushed her and looked to the north again.

"Stop telling me to be–"

Lucretia squeaked as Marcus clamped her mouth shut with his hands.

"Listen to me," he whispered in her ear. "I sense two mortals to the north, and I can hear them speaking of a rich caravan."

"Rich caravan?" she muttered as his hands continued to grip her mouth.

"You heard me," he whispered in her ear. "Now listen, no more questions. You will go to the north," he ordered, before turning her face to the north, "in that direction. I will circle around to the west and double back on them. Do not do anything until I signal you to do so. Do you understand?" He then turned her back to face him. As she stared up into his silver eyes, Lucretia nodded her head. He then released her and disappeared to the west.

As Marcus stalked the two closest Goth scouts, he heard one mutter, "I have not seen such a rich caravan."

"I have heard this one carries so much gold that we could buy an entire kingdom," remarked the other Goth.

Marcus moved behind a rock and continued to eavesdrop on their conversation.

"Do you really think Euric could manage an attack on a caravan this size?"

There was a brief pause. "His plan is very good, and we are to wait at the pass–"

A scream and the sound of a pain-stricken gargle made Marcus race out of hiding to find a dead man lying on the grass, his throat torn out and his wasted blood coating the blades of grass, turning them black as night. Lucretia fed off the other, while tipping his pale face to one side. The mortal moaned in pain and debilitating fear as death drew near and soon overwhelmed him.

Marcus growled and then grabbed the now dead victim.

"My apologies. I thought you were full from feeding off rats," Lucretia offered as her red eyes met his.

He slapped Lucretia with the back of his right hand, causing her to land ten feet away and several of her broken teeth to scatter. Her blood and her victim's blood drenched his hand. Marcus then leapt onto her and grabbed Lucretia by the collar of her armor before she could run. "You are an absolute fool," he snarled, while giving her a bit of a shake.

Assim strained his neck to watch them. His sponsor and the Deargh Du continued their argument, but then he saw Marcus effortlessly slap Lucretia to the ground. He inhaled as Marcus shook Lucretia, enraged with her. He could not decide whether to assist her or allow Marcus the upper hand. However, he did enjoy watching Lucretia's frightened eyes. Her fear grew palpable on the shifting mountain winds.

Pain and hatred radiated through Lucretia as she stared up at Marcus, who seemed to want to lecture her.

"Until you interrupted them, they were discussing their plans of attack. Now we do not know where they plan to attack the caravan! Not only that, but you are little more than a monster wrapped in a pretty body. We were like

Heather Poinsett Dunbar & Christopher Dunbar

them once. Do you not remember waking up with a husband and leading a peaceful life with children and the lot, where the worst problem was a wolf killing your livestock?" Marcus asked through his snarling visage.

Lucretia growled in an attempt to exert her superiority. "I have never had to toil in the earth with the excrement of animals, nor would I ever imagine a mortal wishing to do the same. When I take a life, I am relieving them of their earthly boundaries so they do not have to worry about their miserable, little existence. Now release me, you bastard son of a whore."

He dropped her to the ground and then leaned over her. His soft whisper sent a chill through her body. "How would you like to be the victim?" Marcus asked.

Lucretia inhaled, resolved to keep her fear hidden. He would not see her cower.

"That is absurd," she stated. "I am the victim of no one!"

"We shall see," echoed a voice to her right. A brief flurry of movement in front of her made her turn to look for Marcus. Yet, he had disappeared into the mountains, but then a solid blow from her right side sent her flying in the opposite direction. She and a heavy object continued moving across the clearing. Lucretia felt weightless for a moment, and then a sharp pain radiated through the right side of her throat. She whimpered as her life force started to drain out of her body.

She landed on the hard ground and could not draw a breath as Marcus pinned her against the dirt, restraining any movements. Lucretia moaned softly and closed her eyes as he continued to feed. Every moment of his fierce and brutal attack drifted by in agony as her fear built.

Marcus soon pulled away, licking his lips. He then leaned down to whisper into her right ear. "I have left you just enough blood to be able to move, Lucretia. I think you understand my objections to your feeding practices now."

Lucretia blinked as a great blanket of weakness settled over her. She reached for Marcus, slowly, and placed her hands on the sides of his neck.

"Now," she whispered, as she could not seem to speak at a louder volume. "Let me have some of your strength."

Marcus pulled out of her grasp. "I am sorry, Lucretia, but I do not allow others to feed from me."

"Then you will leave me here?" She hated to hear herself whimper again.

"I would not do that, as I have some mercies," he teased, smiling that annoying, all-knowing smirk. "I will teach you another lesson. Where there are no mortals or blood-drinkers from which to feed, there are always animals." He then pointed to her left, where a grazing deer watched them with large, lucid eyes. After a few moments, the doe took a few steps forward.

Lucretia gagged at the thought of the deer blood, though she watched the wild animal walk closer. "I cannot possibly–" she argued.

"Nonsense," Marcus chided as his arms slid around her. He then lifted her off the ground, and together they approached the deer. "When one must survive, one does so."

Lucretia shuddered at the thought of feeding from a wild animal. Her surprise grew as the deer came closer, looked up at Marcus, and then knelt down, turning its neck to the right.

Lucretia tried to make her body obey her orders to pull away from this disgusting meal. After all, the deer probably had worms, and she could see vermin crawling in its fur. Yet, Lucretia could not find any strength to resist. Finally, she gave in to her undeniable thirst.

She bit into the doe's neck and felt her strength grow. The taste differed a bit from mortal blood, as a thin, gamy flavor infused the vitae.

Too soon, Marcus pulled her head away from the deer. "You have had enough," he murmured before placing her on the ground. She shook her head a bit, trying to clear the fog that remained.

Lucretia looked up and watched Marcus rub the deer's neck as though it were some favored pet. He leaned in and whispered something to the doe, something that sounded like harsh gibberish.

Marcus gave the deer a final pat and then turned back to Lucretia, who managed to stand up on her unsteady feet. "Please, do not let me see you kill any more mortals for food," he stated. "It is pointless to kill a mortal if you do not need to." He then looked up at the skyline. "We should return to the caravan. The others need to learn about this new threat." He turned away and left her behind.

Lucretia shook a bit, as a confusing mixture of hatred and fear pulsed through her.

Something bad should happen to that bastard, something very bad.

"He is more powerful than Amata could ever hope to be," she whispered to herself, but her words died on the winds. Mandubratius could kill him, at least she hoped he could.

Marcus cleared his throat outside the legate's cart, remembering how once he had been a young mortal soldier, waiting for instructions from his elders.

The cart door opened, and he saw a bleeding mortal slave cover the wounds on his wrist. The slave then motioned Marcus into the tent.

Patroclus nodded to him. "Marcus, you have a report to give me, correct?"

"Legate, I encountered two Goth scouts," Marcus recounted. "I heard them speaking of an ambush against this caravan."

"I see. Where and when will this ambush take place?" Patroclus asked while rubbing his chin. His blue eyes glowed like fading red embers.

"They never had a chance to discuss that," answered Marcus, after meeting the Lamia's eyes. "Someone ended their lives."

"Who?" Patroclus asked as he ran a hand over his pale, blonde hair.

The cart door opened again, and Lucretia walked inside.

Marcus glanced in Lucretia's direction and said nothing more.

Patroclus seemed to study Lucretia for a moment. Marcus watched a smile twitch at Patroclus' face. "I see. Well, at least we know what to expect from the Goths, and I presume Franks will be with them. I will inform the day watch."

Patroclus turned back to Marcus. "You have earned your refreshment tonight, Marcus. Outside, I have three mortal slaves. You may feed from whomever you prefer."

"No," Marcus demurred for a moment, noticing Lucretia lick her lips in eager anticipation. "I have fed enough in the field. Goodnight."

He walked out, but he could still hear Lucretia ask for sustenance as he wandered towards the cart where Berti and Sitara slept.

"Do not steal my food." A harsh sound of a leather and metal meeting human skin made Marcus turn back towards the other tents, in time to see one mortal beating another with a cat-o-nine tails.

Without any forethought, Marcus grabbed the man holding the whip and pushed him away from the unfortunate, tied slave.

"What could he have possibly done to deserve this treatment?" demanded Marcus as he grabbed whip from the surprised mortal's hand.

"He already had a meal," grumbled the slave master.

"And whatever sustenance he had disappeared after my kind fed from him." Marcus then glanced over at the slave, who attempted to turn his head to look at him, despite the bindings that held him in place. Marcus witnessed a flash of pale, gray eyes.

"I will buy the slave," he hissed, before tossing coins at the infuriated slave master. Something about seeing a person trapped in the whims of someone with a greater power made rage boil within him. It seemed an odd reaction for someone who in another lifetime owned many slaves. "Unfasten his bindings."

The slave master salivated has he picked up the coins. He then removed the slave's bindings.

"Follow me," Marcus ordered the slave.

After a lingering glance at the slave master, the slave followed Marcus.

"I thought you would be asleep by now," Marcus chided as he sat down in between the beds and stared over at Sitara. A tiny, lit oil lamp hung between the two small beds, casting a soft glow around the gilded interior of the cart.

The slave glowered at him before glancing at Sitara and Berti. "Are you planning on feeding from me now? If so, I hope you choke on it."

Marcus laughed and sat down on a bed. "If I wanted to feed on a mortal, I would have chosen someone who has not lost as much blood as you have. Sit. These are my traveling companions, Berti and Sitara."

The slave sat down and gaped a bit as though confused. "Why was I purchased?"

"I was a slave to someone's whims, once upon a time," Marcus answered, deciding to say nothing more on the matter. "So, what is your name?"

Sitara and Berti smiled at the stranger.

"You are the strange Lamia everyone speaks of," the slave ascertained. "The one who travels with the Briton and the lady of the east. I am Leandros... Leandros Galerius."

Marcus sat up a bit. "Galerius, you say."

"Yes, what of it?" Leandros asked, while staring back at him.

Berti snickered. "I have to say it." Before Marcus could silence him, the Briton announced, "Leandros, meet your forbearer, Marcus Galerius Primus Helvetticus."

Marcus felt a little embarrassment, but Leandros seemed surprised to find long-lost kin in his midst, though perhaps that was disbelief.

"Oh, you have a scroll, Marcus," Berti added. "A messenger brought it this afternoon, and he will come back tomorrow for a reply." He then tossed the scroll to Marcus before turning to Sitara. "And you said you were hungry. What would you like?"

"Some of that bread, and maybe some pomegranate. Just get me a variety of things," Sitara answered. "Thank you."

Berti chuckled, before grumbling under his breath.

"What?" Sitara asked in a sharp tone.

"I said, 'you are welcome'." Berti then walked to the cart door, opened it, and slammed it shut after leaving.

"You seem to be in bad mood," Marcus commented as Sitara stretched out on her bed, revealing her swollen ankles and feet. "What is wrong?"

Sitara grumbled. "I will apologize later. I am just tired, and I have no idea what is wrong with me."

"Are you ill?" Leandros asked.

"No," she snapped. "I am just tired and hungry. I will be fine tomorrow. So, what does your note say?" Her voice grew tempered.

"Let us see." Marcus opened the vellum scroll and summarized. "Maél Muire says that her wedding is off and her betrothed is dead. What a relief that must be for her."

"Indeed," muttered Sitara. "Perhaps, she wants a proposal from you." Her even tone dripped with sarcasm, before she leaned back onto her side.

"Highly unlikely," Marcus surmised with a smirk. "An old friend has returned from the battlefields in the north. I can read between the lines," he said. "Besides that, she is now acting as the chieftain of her tribe. I think she may be too busy to think of marriage, at the moment."

Sitara raised her eyebrows, and Marcus could see her blue eyes sparkle a bit. "A woman leader?"

"There is no such thing," Leandros muttered, but he soon looked a bit frightened, perhaps believing his tongue revealed too much.

"Obviously, you have not met the women of Éire," Marcus explained, but then he grew silent, worried that Leandros might reveal too much of his identity to the other slaves.

"So, what will you write in reply?" asked Sitara.

At that moment, Berti walked in and announced, "I found some leftovers for you. I managed to get past the hungry Lamia with nary a scrape."

"Thank you." Sitara gave him a small smile as she sat up. "I really do appreciate your doing this." She then started in on the bread and stew. "Now, what will you write her?" she asked in between bites.

"I will write Maél Muire that we are doing well, that we will be in Britannia soon, that I hope to visit her village again soon, and that perhaps you three will join me," Marcus answered, before shrugging. "How is that?"

"You should tell her more about the mountains and the beautiful water," stated Sitara, who then twisted around before placing her feet in Berti's lap. "Would you, please?" she asked as she gave Berti a wide grin.

Berti laughed and started to rub her ankles before moving down to her feet. "And will I get a rub in return?"

"We shall see," teased Sitara, though she continued to eat.

"Mountains and water," stated Marcus. He looked over Leandros and inclined his neck toward the outside. "I will start working on it now. Leandros, I need a pair of mortal eyes to tell me what this place looks like during the day." He then reached for the cart door and stepped outside. Leandros soon followed. As soon as the door closed, Marcus heard a series of giggles from within.

Berti pulled the chestnut gelding to a halt before staring at the long line of fifty carts in the caravan. The warming rays of the mid-afternoon sun made the transport shine like a golden convoy carrying the Tuaths. Within each transport, four Lamia slept under the floorboards within cushioned, hidden compartments. He scanned the caravan before he yawned, but soon his eyes settled on their cart, and he decided to trot over to Sitara.

"What's wrong?" he asked, as she looked pale and ill. "No one fed on you, did they?"

Sitara turned her body and stopped the oxen, before retching over the side of the cart. She soon began to dry heave. Berti jumped off his horse and grabbed her before she could fall, and then he pulled Sitara to the ground.

"What's wrong?" he asked again, "are you sick?" By Airmid and Brigid's healing graces, he would rather be ill himself.

"I do not know," she muttered. "My stomach hurts."

Berti called Leandros over. "Could you continue driving the cart once I have her settled inside?" He did not even wait for an answer before stepping into the cart with her and setting her on one of the beds above the secret compartment. He then handed her a flask of water. "Keep sipping on it," he ordered before leaning over to kiss her forehead.

Sitara gave him a weak grin before taking a few gulps of water. He then heard a commotion from the back. Berti dashed out of the cart and scrambled onto his horse. Berti looked over the caravan and started to add up the carts. Soon he noticed that two were missing. He then galloped to the front of the caravan and met one of the guards. "What happened?" he asked as he approached.

"What do you mean by that?" the guard queried.

"Two carts are missing from the end of the caravan," Berti answered. "I was assisting a driver when I heard noise. I trotted to the back of the caravan when I noticed that two carts were gone."

The guard stared at him for a moment. "It must be the Visigoth raiders that they spoke of last night. I do not know who I should be more concerned about, our cargo or the raiders." The guard then chuckled.

"I will inform the Lamia," murmured Berti, "although, I am certain that those two carts will be fine on their own."

Thorismund drove one of the carts into his camp and pulled it to a halt. He then jumped down and rubbed his hands together. "Look at the wheels!" he said to his men. Just the wheels alone sparkled like the sunlight pouring through the eternal oaks.

Amalaric cleared his throat and argued, "I still think that this was a foolish undertaking. Now they will expect us." He stepped off the other cart and added, "You should have listened to Euric and the others."

"I wanted to see the wealth within this caravan," Thorismund countered. "I wish to make sure that we receive our fair share, Amalaric."

"Now," continued Thorismund, "you and Theudis will start with this cart." He placed his hand on the cart as the nine others watched the two men climbed into the gilded transport and began looking over the inside of the carts, guessing at the price they could demand for such glory.

Thorismund heard Amalaric and Theudis opening up various compartments, but then there were soft whispers, words he could vaguely hear, but not understand.

His two men came back out a few minutes later, and their eyes appeared larger with what he presumed to be greed.

"We must attack at night. They are but weak mercenaries, and these carts carry gold, silver, spices and gems," Amalaric explained. "It must be a massive attack with all our forces. They are but weak mercenaries, but we cannot underestimate their resourcefulness. Tell the leaders." Amalaric finished his sentence before closing his eyes. "The wealth will be beyond our dreams."

Thorismund felt his spirits lift. "I will go inform them myself, Amalaric. Keep an eye on the men here."

Marcus heard the compartment open and blinked at the interruption of sleep.

"Careful of the light," he muttered as the heat increased from the beams of light that infiltrated from the door of the cart.

"I'm always careful," Berti whispered upon opening the hidden compartment. "Two of the carts are missing," Berti stated. "I have a feeling some of the Visigoths grew anxious to get a peek inside the transports."

Marcus grinned back at Berti. "I do hope they are not greedy enough to open the hidden storage. Has someone informed Patroclus?"

"He is being informed as we speak," Berti answered, revealing a grin. "I just thought you would like to know. Sleep well."

Berti lowered the lid on the compartment and shifted the floorboards about again.

Marcus closed his eyes before drifting back into another dream of soft green grass, red fires at Samhain, and cool rain that filled the star-drenched skies of Éire with black clouds.

Marcus gently pushed back on the arm of the female slave he had been feeding upon. "Thank you," he said, while attempting to meet her gaze.

The slave backed away from him with a strange combination of fear and fascination in her brown eyes.

Patroclus raised a curious brow. "Do you always thank slaves?"

Marcus shrugged. "Sometimes it is easier to deal with slaves with a gentle hand as opposed to harsh words and whips."

"Yes, sometimes that is true."

Soon the sound of wagons rolling into the encampment interrupted their conversation.

Patroclus grinned. "It appears that our missing supplies have returned."

At that moment, Lucretia stumbled through the milling servants. Her red eyes revealed her ire. "Who is in those carts? Where did they come from, Patroclus?"

Patroclus cleared his throat. "Those were the two carts stolen by Visigoths and Franks during the day, Lucretia." Marcus caught a glimmer of a sardonic smile growing on the legate's face.

"The Visigoths stole two of our carts? Why wasn't I notified?" Lucretia demanded as she paced in front of the legate.

Patroclus cleared his throat again. His hidden laughter seemed obvious to anyone there, with the exception of Lucretia, who appeared oblivious to any clever or hidden insults.

"You were asleep, Lucretia, and did not want to be disturbed, remember?" Patroclus gave her a cloying smile.

"Well? Is anything missing?" she asked with an impatient sneer.

Marcus cleared his throat this time and then stepped from the shadows while pointing in the direction of the carts. "They are just now arriving, Lucretia. We have not had a chance to ask them."

"Where did you come from?" Lucretia queried, while fixing him with a brown-eyed glare.

"Patroclus and I were speaking before you interrupted us," he replied.

Lucretia raised a brow at both of them. "Well, go find out! Marcus, you wait," she added.

Marcus watched Patroclus smirking and shaking his head as he left.

"Your man was on the watch duty during the day, was he not?" Lucretia asked. Her words grew soft, yet querulous and full of angry energy.

"Yes," Marcus acknowledged before studying his nails. "He woke me up and told me what happened after he had informed the head guard. He,

Patroclus, and I believed that the wagon would return at nightfall, safe and sound. So, there was no need to wake you or the others."

Lucretia stared at him. "Very well, carry on," she choked out.

Marcus gave her an overly dramatic salute before spinning around and marching off, trying not to chuckle. Her anger was palpable on the night winds.

He walked toward the returned carts and heard Lucretia muttering to herself in abject irritation with him and the other Lamia. He then strolled over to the two carts.

"… and one thousand men on horseback will attack tonight," stated one of the Lamia soldiers.

"I see," commented Patroclus.

"Do they know what we are?" Marcus asked the gathered party.

The other Lamia laughed at the question. "No. They just think we carry enough gold to buy this cold, barren land," stated one of the other soldiers.

Marcus chuckled. "If you think this is cold, wait until you get to your post in Britannia."

"Do not remind me of that frigid place," added Patroclus. "I hear the blood sours as you go further north."

"Returning to the unpleasant task in our immediate path, you will prepare for this attack and not leave it to less capable hands, correct?" Marcus reasoned, nodding toward Lucretia as she neared.

"Of course," Patroclus acknowledged before walking to a centurion. "Centurion, dispatch runners to each cart to warn them of a combined Visigoth and Frankish attack." As the centurion went to his task, Patroclus snapped his fingers at the mortal slaves and his staff. "Bring my table, chairs, lantern, and map." They responded quickly, bringing everything Patroclus had ordered. The legate then set the map on the table and secured it with some stones he found on the ground. Then the two Romans sat at the table.

"This is our route through the mountains, correct?" Marcus asked as he ran his finger along a valley, trying to repress an authoritarian tone of voice.

Patroclus nodded as his staff gathered around them. Lucretia joined them and took the other chair.

"We should concentrate on looking for the widest areas on our path, since they will be attacking on horseback," commented Patroclus.

"Why should we bother with this? We should attack them now!" Lucretia demanded.

"A frightened foe can be twice as dangerous as a prepared one, Lucretia," commented Patroclus. "It would be best if we surprise them when they think they have the upper hand."

"This clearing in the trail here," commented another Lamia. "It is about a day's journey, and they could surround–"

"I still feel that our best advantage is to take out their entire camp and be proactive," Lucretia pouted a bit.

"Lucretia, this plan is proactive," Patroclus grumbled. "All those who have fought in battles with or against Rome, raise your hands."

Marcus noticed the entire Legate's staff raise their hands, along with Patroclus and himself.

"Lucretia, you are in charge of making sure we reach our final destination with our supplies. That is your duty. Yet, you do not know much about warfare," stated one of the staff members. "In fact, you were a nun, correct?"

"In the interest of self-preservation, I think we would rather use tactics we are familiar with," Marcus suggested, as he tried to hide his smile. The rest of the Lamia chuckled, while nodding their heads.

"Yes, perhaps you should concentrate on our next step," Patroclus suggested in a patronizing tone, "and assess how this attack will alter our arrival time in Britannia."

Lucretia frowned while raising a brow. Her eyes gleamed for a moment as she studied the men there. She then turned on her heel and strode off.

Patroclus sighed before rolling his eyes. "Now, without further interruption, we can plan for a little surprise for this band of barbarians."

Thorismund trotted his mount over to Euric. "Amalaric and Theudis said that this caravan would bring us wealth beyond our dreams."

"Yes, yes, you have said this every hour," commented Euric. "But I still have my doubts…" Euric stopped talking as the sight of the caravan came into view.

Thorismund watched as the elder leaned forward, licking his lips in anticipation. The glittering caravan came to a stop at the clearing. Only a few sad-looking drivers remained, sitting in the carts.

No mercenary warriors acted as guards. In fact, the caravan seemed silent.

Euric motioned to his lieutenants, and then the gathered force of one thousand warriors readied for a quick attack. The pack of Goths and Franks eased their horses into a gallop as they surrounded the caravan.

Without warning, horns trumpeted. Thorismund turned his mount around and watched in confusion as a mass of soldiers appeared from their hiding places, dressed in the ancient uniforms of Rome that Thorismund remembered the storytellers describe in their tales of long ago victory.

Thorismund witnessed the pack of soldiers with their weapons drawn rush in closer. He turned back to see his compatriots killing the cart drivers, but he finally noticed the chains attached to the drivers' legs.

"This is a tra–" he began to call out, before turning to Euric and noticing that he was gone. Thorismund avoided a spear from one of the soldiers and sliced at him with his sword. He turned back and noticed that all his friends either lay on the ground dead in a wide, swept slaughter or…

Thorismund gagged as he watched their killers bite into his warriors' throats and arms in an orgiastic feeding. He shuddered a bit, considering that no soldiers of Rome did this. Then a dark-haired woman crept slowly through the path of blood-red destruction, an angel amongst the devils. She smiled at him with elongated teeth. Before Thorismund could think, he found himself on the ground and in her arms. The red destruction turned gray, and his moment of distress became a pleasuring numbness.

Marcus watched the thin circle of Lamia surround the large mass of marauding barbarians. He blinked as the brutal efficiency of the Lamia soldiers as they swept over the mortal raiders like a deadly swarm.

"Almost breathtaking, is it not?" Patroclus smirked and added, "We are such a better army as Lamia than we ever could have been as mortals."

The remains of the Visigoths and Franks lay scattered about the caravan. The soldiers began to drag bodies away from the road.

"Should we burn the bodies?" he asked Patroclus.

"That would be the right thing to do, but I am afraid that we have no time for that," Patroclus surmised while shrugging. "We must make haste to our departure point."

Marcus watched the legate leave, but then a hand gripped his shoulder and shook him for a moment.

"Marcus, Sitara is hurt. She came out to help us when they attacked the cart," Leandros said as he grabbed his arm, pulling him toward the cart. Marcus followed, and when they arrived, he could see Sitara sitting outside with a spearhead embedded in her shoulder.

"I broke off the shaft," Berti explained before pausing. "Well, do something!" he cried before pacing about, his face displaying a combination of confusion and fear.

Marcus looked at her wound before ripping off the shoulder of her léine.

"I need a donation," Marcus demanded as he grabbed Berti's wrist, "if you're willing."

"What?" Sitara asked as she faced them. "You are not going to feed off Berti. Just pull it out and it will heal on its own."

Marcus shook his head. "Do you smell it?" he asked as he leaned over her shoulder.

"Smell what?" Sitara and Berti asked in unison.

"Rot and disease is what I smell. Someone might have left this spear in the mud before battle. Gods only know what the Visigoths did with it before tonight. If we take out the spearhead and leave you to heal on your own, we will be sawing off your decaying arm in a few nights."

Sitara blanched.

Berti stuck his arm in front of Marcus. "Deargh Du have fed from me before," he assured Sitara in Gaelic, while glancing at Leandros. "I can say that it is not an unpleasant experience. In fact, the process is a little exciting."

Marcus looked over at Leandros. "Speak to no one of this," he stated, before turning Berti's wrist over. When Marcus leaned in to bite, he felt Berti wince a bit as his fore teeth impacted Berti's skin.

Berti leaned up against the side of the cart as Marcus continued to feed.

After a few moments of drinking, Marcus pulled back.

Berti slumped against the cart, slid down into a sitting position, and giggled.

"What is he laughing about?" Sitara asked.

"Lack of blood makes some mortals light-headed, plus sometimes it is an effect of my feeding off him," Marcus reasoned while shrugging. "Are you ready?"

Sitara nodded her head.

"Try not to move," he advised before grabbing the embedded spearhead and pulling it out in one swift motion.

Sitara cried out in pain as he covered the wound with his mouth and extracted the diseased blood, which began to flow from the wound. Marcus then turned aside and spat it out.

Marcus tensed his face as he placed his hands over the wound and then saw Sitara close her eyes as his healing warmth passed to her. The sudden drain of power made him blink his eyes, and then Marcus went to his knees.

Sitara stared at him and then at her shoulder.

"It should heal fine now," he announced before standing up again.

Berti sighed. "I am famished. I need food." He then took Sitara's arm.

Marcus followed them.

Leandros met his gait and whispered, "You are not Lamia."

"I do not know what you are speaking about. I'm Lamia," Marcus answered, before pulling Leandros to the side. "We will speak of this later."

"No, I need to understand. The Lamia do not heal others," stated Leandros. "What are you?" he asked.

Marcus glanced around and stared down at Leandros. "I am Deargh Du, not Lamia."

"What does that mean?"

"It just means that I am a different kind of blood-drinker, but no one here must know."

Leandros nodded his head. "I do not plan to tell them. You are different from them. However, they do notice your peculiarities. Even the mortals can tell you and the others are dissimilar in many ways."

"How do I know we can trust one another?" Marcus asked.

Leandros laughed. "I suppose we must. Even if I had freedom, they would just capture me again, and that female Lamia…" He shuddered a bit.

"Lucretia?" Marcus queried.

"Yes. She has toyed with many of us," Leandros answered. "If she learns the truth, I may end up dead with you."

"Alright, we will keep this between us," Marcus said. "When we get to Britannia, we can decide what to do next."

Assim watched Lucretia wandered towards one of the carts and sit down as the cart prepared to roll. He joined her and then removed his helmet. Now that he saw her flustered state, he felt it would be a good time to confront her with the truth.

"I saw you," he accused. "You were weak with our enemy. The Lamia are supposed to be strong, are we not? That's what you said." The remembrance of her weakness still made his mind ache with worry. Lucretia was more powerful than Assim, and yet Marcus defeated Lucretia with such graceful ease.

"I am on the wrong side," he muttered. "You made me weak. He made you drink from a beast," Assim hissed. "How could you not stand up to Marcus and punish him for such an insult?" Assim then turned away to stare at the canvas-covered walls of the cart. "It was an effrontery to all Lamia, and you let him get away it!" he continued.

Lucretia turned her rage-filled red eyes on him, and he felt himself fall backwards to the rear of the cart as she backhanded him. Assim rubbed his stinging cheek as he lay in the cart.

Lucretia then drew her blade and kneeled on his chest with the tip of her sword resting against his throat. She then leaned over his head, and the point of the blade stung as it grazed the skin of Assim's neck.

"Now listen to what I have to say, Assim Ibn Kalil," she hissed with vehemence.

He tried to move away, but he could find no strength as he stared into her red, glowing eyes.

Lucretia's entire body shuddered with anger as she continued. "What you witnessed," she growled, "was not for your eyes. It was a personal exchange. Amata instructed me to allow for such interactions. It helps us learn more about him and the rest of the Deargh Du."

Assim stared at the gleaming blade as it neared his face. "I beg your forgiveness for my lack of vision."

"I forgive you for having too much vision," Lucretia answered. She then withdrew her blade and sheathed it. "Now, not a word of this to anyone," she whispered.

Béal Átha an Fheadha

"Are you sure they're asleep?" Maél Muire asked as she snuck a look around the food preparation area.

"Of course," Seanán murmured into her ear.

Maél Muire snorted and giggled again as his warm breath tickled her left ear. She then pushed away from his grasp.

"Hush, Banbh, or you will wake everyone. Think of your reputation." A mischievous smile spread over his face as he followed her into a dark corner.

"Yes, my reputation is already in tatters, thanks to you. Everyone seems to suspect that you and I will marry soon and that I am a most disrespectful girl for allowing you to visit me without a suitable matron to watch over us. My aunt Sive does not count, apparently," Maél Muire murmured as his arms moved around her.

"If you do not wish them to talk, perhaps we should announce our betrothal," Seanán replied.

A sound nearby echoed through the silent dun as Seanán's mouth slid down her throat and his hands stroked her hips.

"What was that?" she whispered.

Seanán chuckled. "I do believe you have already seen–"

"The noise," she muttered, as she pushed away from him.

"Take my word for it, no one sees us, Maél Muire, and if they do, who cares?"

Seanán closed in and nuzzled her neck. She closed her eyes for a moment as he ran his fingers over the plaits in her hair, and then his left hand caressed her thigh.

She forgot all of her misgivings as he pushed her to the wall and lifted her léine over her head.

Maél Muire wrapped her legs around Seanán's waist as he pushed into her moistened cavity. She closed her eyes and moaned as they began moving together. She leaned back against the wall as pleasure coursed through her body.

"Marry me," Seanán suggested as he ran a finger over her lips.

"It's almost time for the solstice," she muttered.

"So?"

"The traditional time for us to marry would be on Beltane, next summer."

She watched Seanán's expression change from exhaustion to anger.

"I am not going to wait until Beltane, Maél Muire." He then pulled away from her. She sunk on her weary legs and watched him pace.

"I am just saying that it–" Maél Muire began to explain before Seanán interrupted.

"Traditions were meant to be changed when necessary," he muttered, while crossing his arms over his chest. "We both know that, especially when the Christians took the ancient holy days and used them for their religion. We continue to celebrate those days, keeping the true meanings in our heart. Why do we need to wait?"

Maél Muire stared at the ground for a moment, not really remembering her reason for a Beltane wedding in the first place.

"Silence from you?" Seanán muttered. "Well, there is a first time for everything. Soraidh."

Maél Muire watched him leave the room. Soon after the large front door slammed shut, she heard the sound of hoof beats as Seanán's horse galloped into the distance.

"I just wanted to wait until it seemed right," Maél Muire whispered to the empty room. The romantic idea of a Beltane wedding feast seemed unlikely at this point. Not only that, but Seanán appeared to be frustrated with her. Loneliness made her feel cold, so she pulled down her léine.

Perhaps a gift of some hares, apples, and quails to his clan would settle things between them. She would send the gifts over tomorrow, hoping that it would bring some peace in time for the summer solstice celebrations.

Maél Muire sat down at the small table and felt the stickiness between her legs. So far, she had been safe, but how long would it be until she was with child? She remembered seeing many young, unmarried girls of the village leave to seek out her aunt and uncle with guilty eyes, their sin written in worried tears on their faces. Would she join them?

Maél Muire rested her hand against her head. It was a coward's way out. The term 'bastard' was a new one to Éire. Before the great conversion to Romanized religion, children were cherished, whether they were the child of one night of passion or a relationship between a husband and wife. This was Seanán, not a dishonorable man who only wished for nothing more than his own pleasure.

I love him, and I should marry him. Traditions have their place, but this is more important.

She walked to the hearth to watch the fire spark. Maél Muire soon closed her eyes for a moment, feeling the warm air of summer drift through the slats in the dun. After a few minutes of relaxation, Maél Muire concluded that she needed to take a bath in the cold river and think things through.

"And he has not said a word to me since," Maél Muire grumbled. "I suppose I forgot how stubborn he is."

Caile took a sip of her ale and stated, "He is probably busy preparing for The Seilg."

"Oh right, I forgot about that." Maél Muire rubbed her forehead and then stared at her cousin. "You are supposed to offer me some sort of advice, Caile. You are getting married in a few weeks, so you should know how a man's mind works. At least you would know better than I would. He has not spoken to me since then, and I doubt he will take part in The Seilg at all."

Caile shrugged. "I just know a man does little thinking with his mind. You should go to visit him instead of sending gifts to his clan."

"Caile, I cannot look like I spend all my time mooning over Seanán. The rumors here are bad enough. If I did, I'd look like a silly girl, not a chieftain."

"And that is why you ignore all invitations to visit your own family now?" Caile asked with a sharp voice. "You have not even helped me with my own wedding preparations, and yet you want to whine to me about how Seanán ignores you."

"I am sorry," Maél Muire offered. "I have been called to answer disputes in the village and pass judgment. I want to prove that I am just as worthy as any man, though after the last few days, I am much too tired to do anything. I promise that I will help you finish your dress after the Solstice celebrations." She placed a hand on Caile's arm. "You must think me a very small-minded and selfish woman."

Caile shook her head. "Selfless is more like it. You now think only of the clan. The chieftain, your uncle, never did as much."

"I know. I just want to know that I can do everything a male chieftain can. In order to do that, I have to do more than my uncle."

Caile nodded her head, causing her brunette plaits to swing. "So, will you join us and try to watch the preparations for The Seilg?"

Maél Muire felt her face heat in a sudden flush. "I should watch over the arrangements for the feast and games here. We are hosting the festivities for all the clans in the Moy Valley. Besides, Caile, it is not our place to watch the men. It is a very important and ancient spiritual quest that we have no part in–"

"It is a chance to see them running around naked," Caile interrupted with a healthy chuckle. "In a few weeks, I will have to be an honorable married woman and will no longer have time for such silliness. Now will be my last chance to see them."

Maél Muire bit her lip, not wanting to admit that she had already seen Seanán naked.

"Dullard," Caile muttered. "I suppose that you will consider us who do try to find them beneath you."

"No, I just don't think you will be able to find them. No one who has looked for them has ever seen the rites."

"There is always a first time," Caile muttered before standing up. "I should go. You know how my mother likes to worry." She then embraced Maél Muire.

"I swear that I will help you soon."

"You better," Caile advised in a playfully stern tone before pulling away and walking toward the door. "I will see you in two days. Soraidh."

"Soraidh," Maél Muire called back before staring at the fire in the hearth. She then turned as she heard a raven's caw on the wind.

chapter five

The dun echoed with the chatter of women and girls. The squeals from their prattle started to set Maél Muire's teeth on edge.

Is it too wrong to hope for a moment of silence to contemplate all the mistakes made in the last few days?

Sive interrupted her thoughts by pulling Maél Muire toward the large circle of women gathered around the hearth. "Chieftain, you need to fulfill your duties here," she murmured into Maél Muire's ear. "Many of our neighbors are here. Besides that, I need your assistance tonight in a spiritual matter, but now, greet your guests."

Maél Muire turned around and, after feeling the weight and strain of a smile settle on her face, announced, "I welcome all to Meán Samhraidh. The white horse and bonfires are all set up in the grove. We will have to decorate the trees tomorrow, but so far, we are ahead of schedule in our preparations. I thank you all and hope my home will give you many happy memories. If there is anything you need, just ask."

Maél Muire tried to soften her smile for a moment as she took her seat in her uncle's chair and began swinging her bare feet, impatient that her chance of a quiet evening had faded. Now, happy young girls who awaited gifts from their ardent young admirers surrounded her. As usual, she would be waiting to the side, a twenty-five-year-old old maid.

The older women chuckled as though they were sharing a fantastic secret and began to throw herbs into the fire.

"So, who is going on The Seilg?" a young girl, not even past her sixteenth year, asked before giggling, though she managed to cover her mouth with her hands.

"Sheevan, that is a secret," Caile shushed, while putting a finger to her lips. "It is bad luck to say who participates."

"Daughter, that is old nonsense."

Maél Muire stared for a moment at her aunt Eithnè. "And you," Eithnè indicated, nodding to Maél Muire, "shame on you for spending all your time decorating when we are supposed to do that tonight." Eithnè smirked. "I would think you were waiting for the king of the fae underneath the elders to whisk you away from us. After all, we should all have that opportunity to join in this timeless celebration."

The room exploded with loud talk as the women started on their second cups of mead.

"Perhaps we should all go and wait out the fae king in the grove," stated a crone. "He would certainly keep us entertained for the night."

"I'd rather go look for The Seilg," Caile proclaimed, though her face seemed flushed with embarrassment. "It is my last time to have a chance for that."

Maél Muire watched the older women shake their heads, but she caught a smile or two on their faces again.

Sive leaned toward the fire and tossed in figwort, before whispering something under her breath.

"Chieftain, have a drink."

Maél Muire looked up at Basala. The servant grinned as she passed her a cup of mead.

Maél Muire took the cup and swallowed a few gulps, but she managed to catch many other guests watching her and smiling. She then pulled on her aunt's sleeve as she walked by. "Why does everyone giggle and smile every time they look at me?"

Sive smiled as she threw in lavender, leaving her question unanswered for the moment. Her aunt then dusted off her hands and sighed at the smoldering fire. "They smile because they find everything amusing now, Maél Muire," Sive added before addressing the gathered women. "What shall we ask Patroness Aine for tonight, ladies?"

Maél Muire glanced up as several women answered in a loud chorus.

"Bring us love, prosperity, and healing."

Caile giggled. "And send for more mead, Maél Muire, before Sive puts on the special Cnáib gallowgrass."

"And spiced wine."

"Ale too," another matriarch requested while raising up her cup.

Soon liquor moved around the circle again. Basala, Laetitia, and Flanna poured for the women already too shaken to fill their own cups.

After a few moments observing the growing merriment, Maél Muire felt an elbow in her ribs. "This is why they were giggling," Sive whispered before opening a large bag and tossing its contents, leaves and flowers, into the fire.

There was a collective sigh as the smoke moved through the dun. As the smoke dispersed over the congregation, a series of giggles and loud laughter echoed through the room.

Sive smirked as she pulled Maél Muire to her feet, and then she clapped her hands. "All single girls move to the front. Sing the song, sing the song!"

"Yes, sing the song," the betrothed and married women trilled as they began to toss small bags to their unmarried kin.

"Just because you are the chieftain does not mean that you do not have to sing," Caile snickered before tossing a bag of seeds to Maél Muire.

She sighed and then joined the other young women who were carrying the bags. The Cnáib gallowgrass, or hemp as Uncle Fergus called it, always gave her a headache after the euphoria.

She inhaled and began to giggle, as her earlier worries seemed to disappear as the sharp scent of the burning gallowgrass swarmed her senses. She and the other girls joined arms and started singing as they tossed the hemp seeds around the hearth.

"Cnáib, Cnáib that I throw, now tell me who will come to me and sow."

As the girls twirled around the room, Maél Muire knew what would come next. Tradition held that a loud fight would start when the girls would begin flinging the Cnáib seeds at their elders. Any moment now, someone would throw the first handful, and a mock battle would begin. Just then, a smattering of elderberries hit her in the chest as the married and engaged women giggled before rolling on the floor.

"That hurt," she cried in jest before grabbing a handful of seeds and throwing them at the instigators. Hemp seeds and berries scattered across the room, hitting the clean walls. Maél Muire stared at her léine, noticing that the purple elderberries had stained the front and sides of her clothing.

Suddenly, as the wind from the windows blew the smoke of the hemp around the room, everyone grew silent and watch the light of the hearth flicker. The servants then closed the windows, and soon a hearty round of nervous giggles echoed in the hall.

"Perhaps that was the fae king calling us to meet him in our dreams," Maél Muire suggested as she yawned and stretched. "Aunt, tell us about Lugh again. You know the song almost as good as Uisdean."

As the women warriors began to pick off the stuck hemp seeds from their sticky clothing, Maél Muire sunk into the Chieftain's chair as the unsettling laughter died down. A drowsy blanket of peace settled around her. She yawned as soft songs retelling Lugh Lamfada's glories floated on the air.

She closed her eyes as the women moved off into guest quarters or slept in front of the glowing hearth. Maél Muire then gestured for her family's servants to begin passing blankets and furs around the great room. She closed her eyes once more and yawned, ready to fall asleep in the comfortable chair. She barely noticed when someone placed a bear fur over her sleeping form.

Fergus breathed in the scented air as the herbs began to simmer and the smoke and scents from the herbs surrounded those sitting around the fire.

"Welcome to The Seilg, the ancient hunt," Fergus announced as he scanned the twenty faces surrounding the fire. "So, why are you here?"

"To make sure Biana knows I can provide for her."

Several chuckles and guffaws echoed into the night. Fergus allowed himself a small smile.

"Yes, it is that and much more." He glanced around at the fire-lit faces before asking, "Any other ideas?"

"To follow the ancient rite. It was the way of our forefathers and the Tuatha dé Danann to initiate betrothal," Devan answered.

Fergus nodded his head. "An excellent point. However, I have always believed that it was what you made of it. It is a way to connect with our ancestry, but it is also a wonderful way to show love and commitment by proving that you can provide for your future family."

There was another fit of laughter as the smoke blew over a young man to his right.

"Hush, Kern," a darkened figure whispered as he crept closer, "or you will get a bath earlier than you expected. We are the guests of the Chieftain here, so behave yourself," Seanán chided his clansman. "Thank you for allowing us to take part in the rites here, Fergus."

Fergus glanced at Seanán for a moment and then smiled. "The job of hosting Meán Samhraidh passes to a different clan each year. You will just have to outdo us for the next year's celebration." Fergus then sat down with the others. "Where was I? Oh yes, the first Seilg. Lugh, God of All Skills, was lonely. He spent His days lighting the sky for mortal man, yet He longed for companionship. He starved for it. One morning, He saw the most beautiful creature in the world... Aine, the Queen of the fae Sidhe race and Goddess of Love. Aine is all things beautiful and graceful. Her hair is gold, and Her eyes are like iridescent pearls. No words can describe Her."

Fergus sighed before taking a breath, noting the hunters' quiet, expectation.

"As Aine walked through the forest, Her court of fae followed Her, along with many Gods, enraptured mortals, and others of the Sidhe race. Lugh was so stunned at seeing Her, He stopped, and the world became dark for a moment. Aine, surprised at the darkness, turned to the sky, and their eyes met. She then left Her followers behind and soared toward Lugh, but the Lord of Light was too stupefied to think of anything coherent to say."

The gathered men snickered again in a nervous fashion, perhaps recalling their own bouts with speechlessness.

"Aine smiled as She greeted Him and asked why She had never seen Him at Tara. Lugh finally found His voice and said that He usually had to cast the spells that would light the world in the morning. Then He spent the rest of His day hunting. Aine grinned and offered Him Her hand. She told Him that the preparations for Meán Samhraidh had begun at Tara, and She hoped that She would see Him there. After all, it was a day of celebration. She soon left His side, and Lugh watched as Aine rejoined Her train and sauntered back into the forest."

Fergus coughed into his hand and rubbed his eyes, as the winds had shifted, and the Sponnc now blew into his face. He arose from his seat before ambling toward the opposite end of the campfire. The twenty warriors followed his movements with their eyes.

"Lugh knew that to win Aine, He needed to give Her a gift. Unfortunately, He had no idea what to give the Goddess of Love and Desire. There was so much that others had already offered Her. How could He show that He could give more? He asked Levarcham and Lot, the ladies of strength and prowess, for advice. Meán Samhraidh was but a few days away, and the more Lugh thought about it, the more concerned He became. After all, so many would offer their love and fidelity to Aine that day."

Fergus paused for a moment, trying to remember the rest of the story that Uisdean had told him earlier, before the had bard lost his voice that morning. Uisdean still could not speak louder than a whisper, despite all of the herbal concoctions that Sive made him drink earlier. Uisdean had mumbled the story of the first Seilg, but he began snoring at one point. Fergus had shaken Uisdean awake to remind him about Meán Samhraidh and The Seilg. The tale was a mishmash of other stories, who knew how truthful it was, but Fergus considered the lesson behind the tale much more important.

"And what happened next?" Pailte queried.

The twenty or so young men began shifting about, trying to get closer to the small bonfire. It was a cold night, and the warmth of the fire and the effects of the herbs were becoming apparent.

"Can it wait a bit, I have to take a piss," Eilban muttered, drawing chuckles from everyone.

"What herbs did you throw in here?" Aisling asked as he opened the pot to get a better whiff.

Fergus bit his lip and tried to recall the rest of the story, but the Sponnc made linear thought difficult, and all these questions and disruptions added to his confusion.

"Stop it," Seanán warned before pushing Aisling away from the fire. "It is Sponnc. If you smell too much of it, you will be too ill to participate in The Seilg."

"Really?" Aisling asked as he pushed away from the pot.

"Thank you, Seanán," Fergus said, giving him a small smile. Finally, the rest of the story came into focus. "Meán Samhraidh was but a few days away. It was the middle of summer, a few months after the coupling during Beltane, and a few months before the festival of Samhain. Levarcham and Lot told Lugh that Aine could be won by a feat of bravery, and to do that He would have to put aside His gifts and talents and take a risk. So Lugh left His special armor, His magic, and all His fearsome weapons behind, save a single knife, in the early morn of Meán Samhraidh. He traveled deep into the forest, away

Heather Poinsett Dunbar & Christopher Dunbar

from the hill of Tara, toward the Boyne."

Fergus heard his own laughter along with the young men as they all moved aside from the smoke of the Sponnc. "After a few hours, Lugh found His prize, the dreaded boar of the Boyne. Even the fae avoided this boar. His nasty temperament was legendary, as was his bloodlust. However, the boar was a shrewd and crafty beast. Lugh spent most of the morning chasing him."

Fergus took a sip of mead before continuing the tale. "Finally, the boar tried to quench its thirst. It searched for Lugh, and after seeing that the hunter was nowhere to be found, it cautiously waded into the cold water of the Boyne." Fergus watched the men grin and quaff the ale and mead in their mugs before he continued. He then picked up his own cup and gulped down his remaining mead.

"And then what happened?" Aisling asked, grinning.

"Lugh surprised the boar, leaping on the creature from an overhanging rock. He wrestled with the infuriated boar for an hour, and then finally, Lugh drove His knife into the boar's neck, killing the beast. He then gathered up the boar and took it to great mother Dana's house in the land of the Tuaths, on the hill of Tara." Fergus had to clear his throat, and then the chuckles began again.

"How much longer is this going to take?" Eilban grumbled.

"Just go behind the trees, you will not miss much," Fergus groaned, before rolling his eyes. After a few moments, he continued the story. "As Lugh approached the beautiful house of Dana, He could smell fatted calf, apples, and fermented cider. The sweet aroma of honey clung to the air. Lugh walked into the home of the Tuatha dé Danann, and then all talk and feasting stopped."

The chuckles had stopped, and all the eyes had turned to him once again as they waited patiently for him to continue.

"Lugh said nothing as He moved through the guests. The gods and goddesses of other lands moved aside, even the fearsome Lord of Sidhe Hosts and Morrigan Herself moved away, as He finally reached Aine. He then threw down the boar in front of Her and waited for Her to say something. Aine said nothing, but She took His hand and led Him away to Her home in the mist-covered trees in the east."

Fergus paused again and chuckled as the young men awaited him to carry on with the tale.

"After their evening of sweet delights, Aine whispered to Lugh how much the boar meant to Her. Others wishing Her company had tried bestowing gifts that were beautiful, but useless. He had shown selflessness and that He cared enough to provide for Her needs."

Fergus tossed more fennel into the fire. "And that, lads, is the story of the first Seilg. Despite the fact that our land has changed, Lugh's story still holds true for us. Love is more than the beauty of the flowers and Lugh's sunshine.

It means making sacrifices for your love, providing for her as she nurtures you, as the bible and our own stories say."

The twenty pairs of bloodshot eyes turned to him and nodded.

"Now, pass me some of that ale," Fergus called as he held out his cup. Devan poured him a cup of the black, frothy liquid.

"That is one of the reasons why I got married," Fergus stated, recognizing a slight slur in his voice. "It was the best decision I ever made."

"And what did you give your wife on Meán Samhraidh?" Seanán asked, while leaning forward to inhale the Sponnc and apparently forgetting his own earlier warnings to Aisling.

"Ah, ah, ah, be careful," Fergus warned as he pushed him back. "Smell too much Sponnc, and you will see a thousand Boar of the Boyne. I presented my wife with a beautiful buck. She still has the hide, and it's over…" he drawled before pausing, "almost forty years old. Now, it is time to prepare for the hunt. It's nearly dawn."

"Wake up, Maél Muire," whispered a voice as a hand squeezed her shoulder.

Maél Muire grumbled and woke up in her uncle's chair. "What is it?" she growled.

Caile frowned at her. "We are going to find The Seilg. It is almost time for the river bath." Several giggles echoed in the darkness.

"You will never find The Seilg, you know." Maél Muire smirked. "There are guards in all the directions, especially in the early morning." She yawned, covered her mouth, and then stood up to go lay down in her room. "You should go back to sleep. We do have a lot of decorating to do."

"You are no fun, Maél Muire," Caile teased. She giggled before tossing some Cnáib seeds at Maél Muire before she and the other girls ran out the door.

Maél Muire sighed and then headed for the comforts of her room.

Fergus stared into the dying embers of the fire. Except for the sounds of the whispering river and the wind catching the leaves, all remained silent. After the embers of the fire died, the wind carried away the sponnc and hemp ash. He looked on as the silent hunting party stared at the fire, but all would glance into the forest whenever a twig snapped.

Fergus considered reassuring them that no one would find them. After all, no one interrupted The Seilg. He opened his mouth to speak, but then he closed it again when he realized that he did not want to break the silence.

Then a pair of male corncrakes sung to each other in a duel over a mate.

Their chirps disrupted the deafening quiet, and everyone shuddered, as if trying to free themselves from the insights of the herbs.

Fergus finally found his voice. "It is time. Go prepare yourselves physically for today." He then gestured toward the river. "There are bags of salt by the shore."

The twenty men stood up and stumbled their way over to the cold river. A few seconds later, he heard a series of running footsteps.

Fergus crept to the edge of the forest by the river and watched as a pack of guards, married men who had been through The Seilg before, snuck up behind the dazed participants and pushed them into the river. Their shouts of surprise echoed into the forest. Fergus snickered as the participants grabbed the bags of salt and tried to throw salt at the escaping guards.

He then heard a girlish squeal, and so he turned around. Soon sounds of a scuffle broke out amongst the squealing, and Fergus ran to investigate. When he stepped into a clearing, he came face to face with one of the guards, who had captured several of the unmarried women who appeared to be spying on The Seilg.

"Shame on you, girls. Go back to the village," he ordered, before shaking his head at the foursome. "Or better yet," he said, after turning back to the guards, "make sure they go back."

The guards began to drag and carry the women back to the village.

A rustling of trees echoed, and then one of the remaining guards grabbed another intruder. The young woman slipped past them, but ended up sliding in the mud and falling flat on her face. One of the guards sat down on her backside to keep her from escaping. Fergus strode over to get a closer look.

"Caile?" he asked, as he stared at the prone figure covered in mud. The woman began flailing her arms about.

"Tell him to get off me," Caile pleaded as she spat mud out of the corner of her mouth. "I just wanted to take a bath!"

"I see," Fergus mused as he watched the guard drag her away. "You are nearly married, correct? You are far too old to be sneaking into The Seilg."

Caile made a grumbling noise as she stopped resisting.

The twenty hunters returned, dressed in tunics of doeskin and hunting brócs.

"Just as Lugh had but one weapon, so shall you. You may use it to carve other weapons, but no swords, no arrows, no shields. Nothing but a knife or what you make yourself from using the knife."

The men carefully selected their weaponry.

"You are not to hunt in the grove or wander into the village until after you are finished. The Seilg ends at noon, so you have seven hours. You may hunt in groups, but each person must bring back his own kill. You can help each other, but you cannot hunt for another. May God and our ancestral spirits protect you." He then stepped over to Aisling and pointed to the west. "Take that path." One by one, he pointed off various directions for the hunters to take, until just one hunter remained.

"I thought you and Maél Muire had a disagreement, or do you hunt for someone else?" he inquired, while raising a brow at Seanán.

Seanán's lips curled up into a secretive smile. "You should not ask such things," he replied.

Fergus chuckled for a moment. "You two are made for one another... you are both very stubborn. Go to the east and walk in Lugh's path. Here," Fergus called before tossing Seanán an amulet. "I carried it with me during my Seilg. Good luck."

He watched Seanán glance at the amulet in his hand. He then placed it around his neck and nodded.

"See you at noon, and thanks," Seanán offered with a smile. He waved at Fergus before walking toward the east.

The early morning breeze gently rustled the tree leaves. Seanán walked into the forest before closing his eyes for a moment, holding onto his makeshift spear. He had found a large, sturdy branch and tied his knife to its tip.

After a moment of concentration, he stared at the ground. A trail of dew made the grasses shimmer with an almost luminous glow, but then he saw that a series of animal prints dotted the muddy ground. Seanán knelt for a closer look and then ran a finger over the tracks.

Fresh. A bear has walked by, not too long ago.

He followed the tracks with his eyes and noticed that they led away from the forest toward the river Moy. He closed his eyes for a moment as he heard a rustling sound. He then faced the forest and saw in the distance a proud stag staring at him with defiance gleaming in its brown eyes. Seanán stood up and murmured, "No, not today," before walking into the darkened shadows of the forest. He saw the stag watch him leave before it lowered its head to graze on the wet grass.

Seanán followed the trail for a while before stopping to stare at his spear. He realized that he needed more than a simple spear to take out his quarry. Seanán stared up at a tall tree. Its canopy shaded out most of the sun, but he could make out a few shapes. A large branch dangled at a precarious angle from the middle of the tree.

He removed the knife from the spear and placed it in between his teeth as he began to ascend the tree.

Maél Muire heard an irritating voice say, "It is time to wake up," just before feeling a rude shake. As Maél Muire began to wake, she blinked at the sunlight as it peered through the slats. Despite the blinding light, Maél Muire discerned Aunt Sive grinning at her.

Maél Muire brushed the hair away from her face and muttered, "Good morning to you too, aunt. Caile woke me earlier. Did she get caught?"

Sive smiled. "Yes, she did. She and several others tried to find The Seilg. Not very smart on her part, but I suppose curiosity got the best of Caile." Her aunt then pushed open the door.

Maél Muire noticed that the doors of the dun were open, and a large group of women carrying decorations and dishes of food exited the house.

"You got to miss most of the food preparation," Sive explained with a chuckle, before pulling Maél Muire to her feet. "Basala!" she called out for the servant, who soon joined them. "Surely, we can find something more suitable for the chieftain, other than this dirty léine. All the clans will be here in an hour to begin celebrating."

Basala giggled before bringing a hand to her mouth. "Yes, of course," she murmured from behind her hand. She then walked towards the far side of the dun and disappeared for a moment, but Basala soon returned holding a nondescript bundle. "I will help you."

Maél Muire caught a bit of a smile on her aunt's face before the elder woman left the room, moving to the exterior of the dun.

"What's going on, Basala?" Maél Muire asked as she turned to face her servant.

"Nothing at all, aside from preparations for this day's events that you asked for," Basala answered, while opening and shaking out the bundle of clothes.

Maél Muire stared at the new clothing on her bed and then noticed a dark green overdress resplendent with knotwork patterns in blue and red and a linen léine resting on her bedding.

"This is not mine," she observed as she regarded Basala. She then picked up the overdress before continuing. "I do not own... we do not get material like this, Basala, and I certainly know I cannot sew this well. Some of this is linen. Is this my aunt Teá's?" she queried.

Basala closed the door before shaking her head. "No. It belonged to your mother."

Maél Muire ran her fingers over the material as Basala began to pace.

"You of course do not remember, but I used to work for your mother. Aife could sew the most beautiful dresses. I remember watching her embroider your father's léines with beautiful, intricate patterns and vibrant colors. She traded many cattle to get material such as this. Then after she passed," Basala sighed before continuing her tale, "your father grieved, and it was as if the lands grieved with him. Then the clan lost a lot of cattle and sheep to storms. It was a lean year for all."

Basala sat down on a footstool. "Then like the great cycle, things improved." She smiled. "Your mother gave me a few dresses before she died. She said that she wanted you to have them. Sive and I think they should be yours now. I have others stored away in the cupboard."

Basala stood up and smiled. "After all, no chieftain would wear such a thing as this," she commented before plucking at the léine Maél Muire wore. "The great Queen Medb would sooner appear naked than show up at the great feasts in your léine. This is yet another test for you as the hosting chieftain." Basala then moved toward the door.

"Thank you," Maél Muire murmured before getting up to embrace her and kiss Basala on her brow.

Seanán ran his thumb over the tip of the long point at the end of the pike he had carved. He then dusted the wood shavings from his legs and stood up. He had about four more hours until midday, yet he needed one more weapon.

Soon, soft footsteps echoed in his ears, and Seanán crept behind the large tree, before extracting the knife from his spear. He became silent and still as a small hare wiggled through the tall grasses. The brown hare wiggled its nose, trying to pick up the scents of danger. It then stepped over the wood shavings, sniffing at them.

Seanán leapt from behind the tree and grabbed the hare. It uttered a soft squeak before its blood covered his hands.

Seanán wiped the sweat from his brow and began to dress the hare. Its hide would make an excellent sling. He then gathered up the remaining carcass, thinking that perhaps it could work as bait. Soon, he resumed his bear hunt.

As Maél Muire walked out of the dun, a dirty figure traipsed across her path, causing her to laugh.

"What is so funny?" Caile growled.

"You still have mud in your hair," Maél Muire teased as she pulled on a dirty plait.

"I realize that, but I could not use the river because of The Seilg," Caile grumbled as she crossed her arms over her chest. "Oh is that new?" she soon asked as she gazed at Maél Muire's dress.

"For me, yes. It belonged to my mother. Apparently, I have to impress the other chieftains today."

"So, is Seanán coming?"

Maél Muire felt her face cramp into a frown. "I do not know or care," she answered.

Caile snickered. "How foolish of me to ask, when you so obviously do not care whether he is here or not."

"Of course I will be polite to his family and clan, but I will ignore him."

"Of course," Caile replied. "Oh look, I believe that is his family there. Yes, there is Brigid." Maél Muire began walking toward the clearing. "Oh, and here comes the rest of the clan," Caile continued.

Maél Muire felt her face clench in a smile as she moved past Caile to begin her hosting duties.

As Seanán crept toward the river, the splashing water echoed through the glen. He hoped the noise covered up the sounds of his footsteps on the smooth stones. He finally saw the shaggy fur of the brown bear in the distance as it tried to catch a slippery salmon with its right paw. He then noticed a sloping cliff of rocks that jutted out over the water a short distance from the bear. Seanán backtracked into the forest, carrying the spear and the pike, and then crept around the opposite side of the bear. As soon as he crawled up the cliff, he could see the bear catch a fish and take a bite, too busy to notice him.

Seanán picked up a pebble and placed it in the sling. He then raised his arm. The sling gathered momentum as he swung it around over his head. Then he let loose one of the thongs of hare skin at the right time, and the pebble flew across the rocks to hit the water near the bear, splashing it.

The bear let out a low growl and turned to sniff the air. Then the bear turned back to his own prey and began eating again.

Seanán picked up another rock and lifted it into the sling, swung it, and let it loose. This time, the small rock hit the bear in the left shoulder.

The bear growled and stood up on its hind legs, searching for the scents on the wind.

Seanán glanced down at the hare carcass and then back at the bear. It turned around, faced him, and growled again before getting back down on its four feet.

The bear stared at Seanán, not with defiance, but with pure anger, which made Seanán shiver.

He could almost hear the bear's voice in his mind, daring him to make a move. Seanán then picked up another rock before he had a chance to change his mind. The sling released the rock after a few rotations over his head and hit the bear over his right eye.

The bear growled and began to run toward him.

Seanán had a few precious seconds left, and he hoped that all would go to plan. He grabbed the pike, backed himself against the river ledge, and waited.

"It is so good to see you again," Brigid greeted as she leaned forward to kiss Maél Muire on her cheeks. "You and yours have done a wonderful job of decorating. I am sorry I did not have the chance to reciprocate your lovely gifts."

"I am honored you are pleased with them," Maél Muire replied. She then paused for a moment, hoping she did not sound too desperate. "Where is Seanán?"

"Oh, he had an emergency to deal with at home," Brigid answered.

"I see." Maél Muire felt her face turn down a bit in a frown. "Go help yourself to the ale and wine. I have to play host."

Brigid nodded and then meandered through the guests.

Maél Muire looked over the gathered chieftains and began to walk over toward them. The men smiled as she glided into their circle.

"Ah, here comes the prettiest chieftain in Éire."

She gave them all a small grin. "Well, that's quite a compliment from you, Malachi, especially since you used to hold that title."

The men chuckled and grinned.

"Well, don't just stand there," she added. "We have ale, wine, and mead. It is time to celebrate our peace and prosperity." She then waved them toward the direction of the refreshments. "Enjoy. Just do not fight each other over my hero's portion," she teased while patting the sword at her hip.

The chieftains rushed past her like a horde of ravenous wolves. She snorted and laughed, before covering her mouth with her hand.

"So, is that why you were called 'Banbh'?"

Maél Muire faced Mac Turrlough, stopped laughing, and asked, "Excuse me?"

"I do not think I have ever heard you laugh before. It's," he commented before stopping and smiling, "quite amusing."

Maél Muire felt her face tighten into a set smile. "I am glad to see you again, Mac–"

Mac Turrlough interrupted her, "Call me Connor, remember?" He drifted in closer and gave her a small smile. "You should remember that this is a time of joy for a blissful summer. Let's get some wine. I need to talk to you about business. I wish to hire the services of your bull, since mine passed on this past spring."

"Oh, our black bull," Maél Muire answered. "I am sure he will enjoy visiting your cows. What will I get in trade?" She did not expect much.

"I have a few sheep, some sows, and piglets, a few cattle if he impregnates the ones going into heat."

Maél Muire stared at him for a moment. The offered trade seemed a bit too generous. Most chieftains would 'borrow' the bull and return it in the middle of the night or use the excuse that the bull had wandered away on his own. Her clan even used those tactics.

Why is he being so fair?

"Alright," she answered before smiling at him.

"We can finalize this later," Mac Turrlough suggested as he returned her smile. "I think it's time for breakfast." He then took her arm and led her toward the tables.

The smells of the roasting meat made her stomach growl.

The bear rushed toward Seanán as he backed further into the curves of the wall. The ledge shook when the bear leapt onto it and began to run toward him. Seanán steadied himself as the bear lumbered closer to the pike. He then heard a loud growl as the bear ran into the pike, lodging it deep into his chest.

The pike shattered from the weight of the bear, but not before its paw scratched him. As they fell down together, Seanán felt warm blood trickle over his body. He then heard the bear uttered a soft growl before turning his fearful eyes to Seanán.

"I am sorry," Seanán whispered. "Your gifts are appreciated, and I will honor your spirit."

The bear heaved a soft sigh and then closed its eyes.

Seanán slid out from under the massive weight of the bear and wiped its blood off his forehead. He then ran a careful hand over the deep scratches in his chest, but there was little time left to tend to his wounds. He gathered the broken pieces of the pike and removed the knife from his spear.

Seanán pulled off his tunic and cut it into strips of doeskin, which he used to tie up the branches into a makeshift sled, before pushing the bear's huge form onto it. He hoped his sled would last until he reached the village. Soon he heard a loud horn blare from the west, signifying the end of The Seilg.

Several people covered their ears as the horn blew. One after another, a few of the hunters returned, carrying their game into the village. Each hunter handed his carcasses to Sirac and some of the married women. The butcher and his assistants would then quickly remove the head of the prey and hand it back to the hunter.

There were cheers and shouts as a hunter returned with his quarry, and a few sounds of disappointment when a hunter walked in without anything. Then the loud laughter echoed through the village when a luckless hunter received the traditional bowl of a cow turd. Soon, however, a silence came over the raucous crowd.

Maél Muire stood up from the chieftain's place of honor and stared at the last hunter in the distance, who pulled a litter behind him.

"Seanán?" she murmured.

"It's a bear!" someone shouted.

"The last man to bring back a bear from The Seilg was the High King Cormac," another person shouted.

According to legend, Cormac, king of Connacht, had brought to his beloved a humongous bear that his clan had fed on until the next spring.

Several men ran out to help with the litter, but after the hunter waved them away, they moved back.

"This is my burden to carry," a voice echoed in the distance.

"It is him," she whispered. Maél Muire continued to stare as Seanán pulled the great bear into the village.

The butcher shook his head and chuckled. She heard him mutter something to Seanán before he and several women began sawing at the bear's massive head.

They passed the huge head back to Seanán, and then the hunters lined up in order of their arrival.

One by one, the hunter walked up to his intended and recited, "'I have prayed and walked in the legendary Lugh's path. I will honor you and provide for your family. I hope you will accept my proposal.'"

There were squeals of delight, tears of joy, and confusion. One girl even gave an unsuccessful hunter a kick in his shin when he presented her with the bowl of turd.

Maél Muire felt her heart sink as Seanán looked past her for a moment, but then he began walking to her. He stopped in front of her and gave her the bear's head.

"You look nice," he murmured.

"You are bleeding," she whispered, before leaning forward to run her hand over the wounds on his chest.

"I know. I have walked in Lugh's path. You know I can provide for us, and I love you. Marry me."

Maél Muire hefted the bear's head onto the table before leaning in and brushing her lips over his. All the other noise seemed to wane as she kissed him and then pulled back. "You fool," she whispered into his ear. "I would have said yes to a boar or stag."

He pulled her into a crushing embrace. "Tomorrow," he whispered. "No more of the waiting."

"I need two weeks to prepare," she countered before chuckling.

"Your uncle was right. You are as stubborn as I am." Seanán uttered a soft moan.

"What is it?"

"I feel…" he whispered while pulling back. His eyes revealed pain.

She took his hand. "I will take care of you." Maél Muire then gestured for Sive and Brigid to help.

Connor watched the three women drag the semi-lucid warrior towards the dun. Seanán followed them with a silly grin as though almost oblivious to his wounds. He wrapped his arms around Maél Muire's neck and leaned into her hair as Seanán's mother and Sive opened the doors and dragged him in. The doors closed as soon as Seanán walked through.

Connor put down his mead and frowned a moment, considering how this chasing game had grown old. He soon noticed Bearach and the other warriors of Béal Átha an Fheadha loitering about and looking over the prizes. Perhaps they would know the location of Cennedi and Teá. After all, Teá had promised her assistance in this matter.

"A bear that size," Brigid grumbled at her son. "Who do you think you are? Cu Chulainn? Finn Mac Cumhail? You are lucky you are not dead. Maél Muire, hand your aunt the needle."

Maél Muire passed the bone needle to Sive and went back to wiping Seanán's forehead with a cool, wet cloth.

Sive threaded the needle and handed it back to Brigid.

"The stag told me to take the bear," Seanán explained with a snicker.

"And you always listen to animals," Sive chided. "Here, drink more of this, or else you will be feeling a lot of pain."

"I do not care. It was worth it." Seanán grinned at Maél Muire. "We are going to be married in two weeks."

"Two weeks? I see he wore you down," Brigid observed as she chuckled.

"Yes, well, I would have said yes too if someone had presented me a bear's head," Sive added while patting his hand. "Close your eyes, Seanán."

Maél Muire watched him stiffen in pain as the needle moved back and forth through the cuts.

"We are done," Brigid announced after a few minutes. "He is a tough lad."

"We should probably leave now," Sive advised as she took Brigid's arm. "They need time to talk." The two older women then left the room.

Maél Muire sighed as she ran her fingertips over Seanán's hair. "Why a bear?" she asked.

"Because I knew you could never say no to something like that," Seanán murmured while sitting up.

"Careful," she murmured. "You might break the stitches."

"I do not care," he whispered, before pulling her closer to him.

She snorted and giggled as he kissed her.

"I think your aunt threw something else into that horrible brew she made me drink," Seanán murmured as he pulled her onto his lap.

"Or maybe I did." Maél Muire giggled again as he shook his head at her.

"Well then, I will just have to get even with you," Seanán answered.

She could not help squealing as he began to tickle her.

Mhuine Chonalláin

Teá watched as Mac Turrlough paced through the length of the hall. She felt her mouth curve into a smile as Mandubratius slinked into place on the other side of the room. She moistened her lower lip and closed her eyes, trying to keep her hunger in check. Teá then cleared her throat.

"Where have you been?" Connor demanded as he stared at her. "Your plan is failing, Teá."

Teá chuckled before staring into the chieftain's blue eyes, though she had no idea what made him so anxious. "What is so urgent, Connor?" she purred as she glided closer and took his hand.

"Seanán and Maél Muire are courting," stated Connor. "Today was Meán Samhraidh, and he brought her a bear. You know of course what that means."

Teá stroked his hand. "Calm down, Connor, be at peace. There is a simple solution to this problem," she said mid-laugh. "Kill him."

Connor closed his eyes. "I do not want his murder to come back to me. Why would she marry me if his death is on my hands?"

Teá chuckled as she noticed Mandubratius creep closer to the chieftain. "I know someone who would be willing to do this just for the fun of it, Connor."

"Who?" he asked.

Teá looked past Connor's shoulder and grinned.

The chieftain turned his eyes to the left, and the he slowly turned to his left as if he comprehended that death leaned over him.

"Me," Mandubratius whispered before revealing his teeth in a fanged smile.

Connor stumbled away from Mandubratius and turned back to Teá, who also revealed her. Connor then drew his blade.

"Whatever is the matter, Mac Turrlough? Do you not like this arrangement?" Teá teased as she and Mandubratius stalked closer to him.

"Deargh Du," he whimpered before crouching on his knees.

"Poor Connor," Teá mocked throatily. "We will not kill you. Mandubratius and I only wish to assist you."

The chieftain ceased cowering and allowed Mandubratius to help him to his feet. "Why would a stranger care about our plans, Teá?" Connor queried.

"I have an interest in our shared friend, Maél Muire, chieftain," remarked Mandubratius. "She has talents, worthy talents that I wish to exploit. Not many can call down the One-eyed Crone. If she joins us, you may have her property to do with as you please. However, I have found that it is best to sponsor those who ask for such gifts. Force is such a nasty thing."

Teá attempted to hide her disappointment from Mandubratius.

Lovely. Now my niece will have power over me once again.

"If you and I take care of her lover, she will become consumed with revenge upon the mysterious killer," Mandubratius proposed. "That is where I come in. Her desperation will drive her mad and to my side."

"And upon who will you blame the death?" Teá queried, hoping he would forget about Maél Muire and this stupid plan. After all, Maél Muire did not deserve such gifts.

"I will blame the death on a member of the arch druid's retinue that he mentioned during torture. Caoimhín," he replied.

Teá watched her sponsor smile.

"She will come over to me," Mandubratius murmured.

Teá could not help but notice that his eyes glowed red, for a moment.

Béal Átha an Fheadha

"I can stay if you need me," Maél Muire cooed as she ran a hand over Seanán's brow. The velvet caress of her hand made him want to pull her into the blankets with him.

Maél Muire seemed oblivious to the effect her touch had on him and continued talking. "I need to pick up that salve and a few other things for you, though I am sure you will be fine on your own. Everyone left for a day and night of rest."

"Hmmm," Seanán mumbled as he stretched on the bed and began to scratch at his wounds. "Make sure you know for sure before you start anything."

"Stop that," Maél Muire growled. "I have told you not to scratch the healing scars."

"If you stop nagging me, I will stop," Seanán replied. He could not help but laugh at her frustration.

"Your mother said you were stubborn. Somehow I forgot that when you were gone," Maél Muire pouted in a most sensuous manner before standing up. "I still do not like the look of your stitches, and you have probably been picking at them when my back was turned. I need to get some herbs from my aunt and uncle for that."

"Allow a man some form of satisfaction," he replied. "You are thinking about how we can enjoy ourselves." Seanán pulled her close, and then she slid under the covers with him. "You would much rather spend time making love to me than picking herbs or fetching salves." He brushed his lips against hers and then rolled her onto her back, crushing her against him.

"You are incorrigible, Seanán," Maél Muire whispered. "You need to rest."

He could feel himself swelling against the soft material of her léine. "I am tired of resting. I want to have fun with you." However, he pulled away as a sharp pain moved through his body. Seanán could hear an impatient longing in his voice, but the soon pain grew stronger. "You are probably right. Go get the herbs you need."

Maél Muire sat up and smiled at him. "I will be back as soon as I can."

He reached for her hand and brought it to his lips. "I love you, you know, mhuirnín. I swear by the depth of the sea and height of the stars that I will always love you, even though I am too tired to prove it."

"And I love you too, mighty bear hunter." She leaned in for a kiss. "And I swear by the sun, moon, and stars that I will love you, no matter how annoying you are."

He then watched her graceful form leave the room and heard her footfalls echo down the hallway as she left. Seanán soon closed his eyes and waited for sleep to overtake him.

"You remember the plan as we discussed it outside?" Mandubratius whispered. He saw Teá and Connor nod their heads in response. "And you have the claws, Chieftain?"

Connor smiled and nodded his head.

Mandubratius had to admit he liked the perversity of Connor Mac Turrlough's plan. It would be a shame to kill him later. "Let me go first."

He walked into the room in silence and sat down next to Seanán's head. Mandubratius leaned forward and smiled, while running his fingertips along Seanán's neck. He felt a strong pulse, though the mortal seemed weak from his injuries.

Good. It will be easier to trick him.

Mandubratius could feel his lips tug in a smirk as he began to whisper into Seanán's ear. "It's me, Maél Muire. Rest. Keep your eyes closed, chroí."

"Maél Muire, you've returned," Seanán whispered.

"Yes, I have," Mandubratius replied, "and I've missed you."

"I think you need to take our friend home," Mandubratius stated as he looked over at his child, who helped Mac Turrlough pick up the pieces of the dead chieftain's flayed skin. Connor bore a wild look to his eyes. It was the same madness Mandubratius had seen reflected from other warriors in the heat of battle. Mandubratius then drew a small blade and stabbed it into the young Chieftain's body. It would give Maél Muire a false clue as to who had committed this rash deed.

"But I want to see her find him," Teá pouted.

"And I told you no, Teá," Mandubratius growled, tired of her whining.

Teá pouted again and then took Mac Turrlough's arm. "Fine," she hissed. "Come, Connor. I need to take you home. Perhaps I can find some food, and you can take a bath along the way."

The bloody elder chieftain nodded his head. "Yes, a bath would be good."

It is strange how mortals deal with their wickedness.

Mac Turrlough stared into the distance, lost in another world, perhaps.

"Remember," Mandubratius reminded as he stared at Connor and got his attention, "in a short time, all he had can be yours, if you play the game well. Perhaps you can seize control of his lands in the confusion." Mandubratius then kneeled down beside Seanán's body and dipped his fingers into the congealing blood. He caught a glimpse of Mac Turrlough shaking his head.

Teá soon left the room. Her telltale presence lingered for a moment and then disappeared into the dark night.

Mandubratius brought his fingers to his mouth and closed his eyes. The blood was cold, but still palatable. He opened his eyes, stood up, and heard the sound of his boots sticking to the drying blood as he walked around the room, but soon an idea flashed into his mind, and he kneeled back down to the drying blood.

Teá bit her lip as hunger overwhelmed her. She grabbed Connor before he reached his horse and turned his neck to one side. His movements were sluggish as she began to drink from him. He moaned with pleasure as she licked his wounds, removing every little trace of blood from his neck. She then pushed him away with a groan.

Mac Turrlough staggered and collapsed on the grass.

Teá sighed and pulled him back up onto his horse.

"Why?" he asked.

"I was starving," she whispered, but she was surprised when he latched onto her arm and stared at her with hunger.

"I want more. Feed from me again. Make me one of you. I could care less about Maél Muire's cattle and Seanán's land."

Teá heard herself begin to laugh. She let go of Connor and wrapped her arms around herself. Without anyone to hold him, he fell to his knees. She steadied herself against an oak before whispering, "I cannot do that now, Mac Turrlough, although the idea of you as one of us is an entertaining one."

She knew that Mandubratius would leave her behind soon enough in favor for Maél Muire... her own husband taunted her with that truth. Perhaps it would be best for her to ally herself with Connor, but until then, she would play the dutiful child to Mandubratius. A kiss on Teá's hand broke her concentration.

"If you do as we wish, I will make you one of us, Connor," she offered while running a hand over his light-brown hair. "I can give you the power of the ancient immortals, the blood of the strongest line of the world, the Lamia line."

Connor stared into her eyes and stated, "I will do whatever you wish."

"Then you will take Seanán's place in my niece's heart. I know she already has yours in some way, so you will not have to pretend. Propose to her, soon. A woman is weakest when she is convinced that she has no one to love." She then stroked his stubble-covered cheek with her hand.

"What does your... why did he choose me for this?" Connor asked.

Teá saw her reflection smile back at her from his eyes. "I cannot claim to understand Mandubratius. He has a few strong goals. He is obsessed with finding this lost treasure, and for some reason, he has deluded himself into believing that Maél Muire has invaluable magical skill that she will use to help him..." Teá bit her lip as she realized she had said too much to him. She then stared at him and whispered, "Forget I said that."

Connor's eyes became as dark as a starless night.

"Go home and remember that she will be weak after this," Teá added. "You can be all that she needs then." She watched Mac Turrlough smile, seeming to grow younger with the thought she planted.

Why was it that almost every man wanted Maél Muire for one reason or another? She was not pretty, and her personality was on the dull side. Teá heaved a sigh as the mortal chieftain mounted his horse and galloped away.

Men are fools.

A scent soon drifted on the wind, and she felt her lips curl into a grin. Even Macha, the fleet of foot, would have trouble keeping up with her tonight. She dashed toward the potential victim, her footsteps silent as her form remained hidden in darkness.

Maél Muire picked up the bags of herbs and placed them in her sack, just as Taliesin wound his way around her feet. His green eyes watched her with bemused interest as she tripped over him.

"Silly cat," she muttered, before leaning over to pet the cat.

"'Silly cat' is right," grumbled Sive. "I wish he would kill the mice." She began humming again.

"Like most cats, he will do as he wishes in his own time," Fergus commented with a smirk before picking up the gray cat. Soon loud purrs echoed in the small house.

"Sleep well, soon to be Maél Muire Uí Seanán. You will continue to clean the grove with us, I hope?" her uncle asked as he crossed his arms over his chest. "After all, who else will do it after we pass on? The village will rely on you to take care of their 'other' spiritual needs."

"As if I would refuse." Maél Muire felt a smile tug at the corners of her mouth. She then leaned forward and planted a kiss on his cheek.

"Tell Seanán that he had better take care of himself if you are to watch over both his clan and yours. No more chasing after bears." He chuckled and turned away before walking back to his bedroom. Fergus rubbed Taliesin's forehead on his way out. "Soraidh, and pleasant dreams."

"He will miss you, you know," Sive muttered in an undertone.

"I am not going anywhere, only ten furlongs away," Maél Muire countered.

"Yes, but Brigid has her children to carry on our ways. We do not have that luxury. We only have this one silly cat."

Taliesin cooed before leaping onto the table. He allowed Maél Muire to scratch his chin and head.

"You and Fergus spoil him something awful," Sive sighed. "Go on and scoot, old man."

A cawing of a raven nearby startled everyone, including the cat, who turned away and hissed, revealing the white corners of his eyes.

"What is the matter with him?" Maél Muire asked before staring at her aunt's troubled face.

After a few moments, Taliesin lay down and began cleaning his feet. As the caw echoed in the house again, his ears swiveled as he appeared to try to pinpoint the origin of the sound. Then the cat raced off through an open window.

"I guess he caught the scent of prey."

Maél Muire heard his feet scurry as he ran into the grove.

"No, it's something else. We all know animals, and in particular, cats, are gifted and can see more than what we see. He knows more than what he is saying. He is quite perceptive about the world of spirits," Sive stated as she hung up a handful of lavender to dry. She then leaned over and stared at the open window for a moment before tilting her head.

"He always gets this way if something is passing through from the world of the Sidhe, or maybe if someone is going there," she muttered. Her eyes darkened as she shook her head. "I am sorry, Maél Muire. Something has kept me from being myself tonight. Your uncle has had a horrible headache since this afternoon, yet he cannot rest because something is on the wind. I too sense something." She paused. "As you walk home, ask Morrigan to protect you and your home and then ask for her sister, Brigid, to light your path."

Maél Muire shook her head. "I hear nothing on the wind, nothing but my own joy."

"Just be careful," her aunt before turning to stare at the moon. "Do not let one of the fair folk tempt you tonight. Perhaps that is why everything feels so odd now. Goodnight." Sive then kissed her brow.

An eerie silence surrounded the dun as Maél Muire walked to the front door and dropped her bag of supplies. She could feel her heart leap into her throat as a raven screeched from the dun.

The clouds covering the moon shifted, and a deafening silence greeted her as she pushed the door open, only to be buffeted as she sensed something fly past her. She jumped again at the sound of flapping wings.

Maél Muire turned to see the raven take off into the night sky. She returned her gaze to the door and took a cautious step into the dark dun. Maél Muire's eyes adjusted to the low light as she shuffled toward the hearth. She grabbed a stoker and stirred the ashes and embers, which soon glowed as if revived.

"Seanán?" she called for him while chuckling nervously. She then pulled off her belt and kicked off her léine before running toward the back bedroom, planning to jump under the warm furs and blankets with him. Once she kicked the door open, she noticed that a single candle sputtered in the room, illuminating the horror before her.

She raced to the bed and cried out at the bloody mess on top of the furs and woolen blankets. She kneeled down and clutched her chest. She could see Seanán's mouth open in a final, agonizing scream. His skin resembled a disgusting battle or hunting trophy. Flayed skin and organs lay on the floor along with an Uí Briúin dagger.

Maél Muire closed her eyes and screamed in fury as hot sweat drenched her body. She then clambered to her feet and yelled, "I will not be trifled with!"

After inhaling a breath, she turned around the room, facing each of the four walls, and began to speak. As she spoke, she could hear her voice shake in fury, and each sentence became louder than the prior one.

"I may die before we meet again, but I will find you and rip you to pieces. I curse you to the height of the stars and the width of the sea. May you never feel peace, happiness, and well-being ever again. I hope the raven-feeder tears you to pieces in the Otherworld!" Her voice shrilled in a scream. "Run, like the frightened coward that you are!"

Maél Muire could feel her voice crack. She collapsed to her knees feeling drained. She then ran a hand over Seanán's arm, feeling nothing but sticky, cold blood. "I will say goodbye later," she whispered to the bloody form, before swallowing her pain and tears. She then headed for the hall, dressed, grabbed her sword, and then sheathed it in her belt.

Once outside of the dun, she strode into the barn, grabbed a bridle, hid it behind her back, and whistled for Biast.

The mare flicked her ears and wandered over in hopes of a treat.

Instead of feeding her, Maél Muire wrapped the reins around the horse's neck and placed the bit in Biast's mouth before jumping onto the horse. She then nudged the mare past the walls of the dun before noticing a cloaked figure watching her from the edge of the woods. The stranger's face hid with the assistance of a deep cowl.

"Show yourself!" she ordered the stranger as she drew her blade. She then gave Biast a nudge, and the mare trotted forward toward the stranger without hesitation. "Come forward and reveal who you are!"

The featureless being remained still and silent for a moment, as if frozen in time, but then it turned with a preternatural grace and took off in a dead run.

Maél Muire kicked Biast into a gallop and then growled a wordless challenge to the stranger.

The thunderous sound of hoof beats echoed behind him, and he could hear Maél Muire mutter a tirade of curses, including 'You are nothing much' and 'You are a coward, and may the ravens pick their teeth clean with your bones', upon him under her breath as she and her horse grunted with exertion.

He smirked as he decided to slow down a bit, upon sensing her approach, glad that his curiosity emboldened him. He pulled back a few small branches and loosed them. Glee filled his heart upon hearing them land against his intended target. Mandubratius then increased his speed as the forest cleared into a field. After the play-fight during their first meeting, he wanted to see what Maél Muire could do when he provoked her.

He felt a smile tug at his lips as he heard no cries of pain or wailing on the wind. Where other women would be tearing out their hair, she continued to chase after him. However, surprise greeted him as he heard a growl and then the strange singsong noise of a blade slicing through the air caught his attention. At that moment, pain sliced through his shoulder. He uttered a soft moan as he noticed her sword peeking through his chest.

The game had gone far enough, he realized, as blood dripped from his arm. He grunted as he pulled out the sword from his shoulder. He sped up and dashed toward another forested glen. Mandubratius then ran around a tree, grabbed a long branch, and pulled it around the tree, hoping it would not break.

Soon the sound of galloping hoof beats moved closer. Finally, the chestnut mare and her rider came into view.

Mandubratius let go and watched the tree branch snap back into place, knocking Maél Muire off her horse. The impact of the branch had thrown the young woman ten feet away from the tree.

The horse whickered softly and then walked over to her rider to sniff the body and then nudge her.

Mandubratius watched Maél Muire for a moment. There was no movement. He crept closer, trying to hear a heartbeat, wondering whether she had broken any bones from the fall. He then threw Maél Muire's sword into the ground near her body. A sudden gasp of air made him back into the enclosure of trees.

He watched her as she sat up to caught her breath. She then rolled forward and started to keen in grief. Maél Muire pounded the sod with her fists, howling in frustration. He could not help but stare as she began to shake, while covering her face with her hands. Her earlier bravado disappeared in a deluge of tears, and Mandubratius felt a moment of pity for her. He then turned in silence and ran towards the Lamia encampment, pleased that all had gone according to plan. She looked to be devastated. Maél Muire would ask for his assistance soon.

chapter six

Caletum

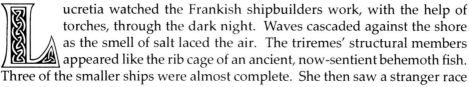ucretia watched the Frankish shipbuilders work, with the help of torches, through the dark night. Waves cascaded against the shore as the smell of salt laced the air. The triremes' structural members appeared like the rib cage of an ancient, now-sentient behemoth fish. Three of the smaller ships were almost complete. She then saw a stranger race through the line of sentries holding a parchment. He turned to face the Lamia.

"Are you Lucretia?" the messenger inquired as he licked his lips as though hungry.

Lucretia nodded her head. "Give me the message, and then you may rest for the evening."

The messenger smiled for a moment before glancing around. "I bring you orders from Mandubratius," he explained. "He is in Éire, in the old kingdom of Connacht near the capital of Ráth Cruachan."

"I thought he was in Britannia," Lucretia countered, confused.

The messenger shook his head. "He went to Britannia, but left for Connacht soon after staying at the stronghold in Bath. He wishes you and the others to join him in Éire."

"I see." Lucretia smiled, exultant at the idea of seeing her sponsor again and presenting him with a surprise in Connacht. "After you return to him, tell him that we are in the process of shipbuilding. We will continue building ships until the fall equinox, I believe. We will join him in all due haste. Give him a status report, and then after you are complete, I wish you to tell him that I have a gift for him. Then I want you to say this name, 'Marcus Galerius Primus Helvetticus'. Tell him I need instructions on what to do with this present." She looked around, hearing the telltale signs of a mortal daring to interrupt her. She could see nothing and so returned her ready gaze back to the messenger.

Mandubratius' servant nodded his head. "As you wish, my lady, I will leave first thing tomorrow evening."

Leandros backed away from the trees that protected him from the Lucretia's line of sight, before turning to run in the other direction. He could have sworn that her glowing eyes could see him behind the veil of leaves. Leandros raced towards the cart, hoping for safety. Instead, he nearly knocked Sitara off her feet. The bowls she carried broke on the rocky ground, shattering into clay pieces.

"What is wrong with you, Leandros?" she asked. "I thought you went to get wine to go with our meal."

Leandros noticed Marcus and Berti look up from a large, bronze horn that made the most annoying noises whenever either one of them attempted to play it. After glancing at his periphery, Leandros waved Marcus closer and then whispered in his ear, "There is danger. I overheard…" He stopped before hissing a breath. "A courier just arrived to speak with Lucretia." Leandros inhaled again, fearful of discovery. "The dispatch is from someone named Mandubratius. She told the messenger to return to his master and ask what to do about you."

"Where did this traveler come from?" Marcus queried, after handing the horn to Berti. His entire face became dark, and Leandros grew frightened at the sight.

"I could not hear the entire conversation," Leandros answered. "However, this message bearer intends to leave tomorrow evening after sunset."

Berti grabbed Sitara, huddled with them, and murmured, "Then we must make plans quickly. That means there is a ship that is seaworthy and ready to sail."

Marcus pushed the thin slave away gently as the stranger trembled in a mixture of fear and need. Slaves always seemed to have a fear of death, yet many humans found the lingering taste of mortality to be addictive. It numbed the pain of a day of backbreaking labor and made one forget all but the sweet promise of rest.

The slave's eyes radiated delight, finally, as if the spell had broken. He blinked his brown eyes and turned away.

Marcus grumbled before looking over the remainder of slaves wandering through the camp, their movements listless, their eyes hollowed, and their wearied steps heavy. After a few minutes, he could smell the Legate nearby.

"You should watch for your enemy, Marcus," Patroclus murmured with a chuckle.

"And who might that be?" Marcus asked after regarding the legate.

"Oh, as if you do not already know that it is 'she'." Patroclus inclined his head in a direction to the south where they could see Lucretia pace the perimeter. "Granted, she is enemy to most of us here, however. Your enemy asked several of us to keep an eye on you." The legate's smile soon faded. "As a professional courtesy, from one former mortal soldier to another, I am telling you to watch your back."

Marcus nodded his head and said, "Thank you for that. I will be on guard."

Patroclus nodded back before stepping away and accosting a thin yet lovely female slave as he strode toward the center of the encampment.

"Let's give this a try," Berti whispered as he picked up one end of the sails that Marcus had rolled around himself before dawn. He heard a snore and a sputter. Soon a light rain began to pelt their cloaks and the sails.

"Hush," he addressed the sail-wrapped Deargh Du as Sitara, whose cowl concealed her features, picked up the other end. They soon drew closer to the pair of mortal guards near the bay.

"Our first shipment of sails," Sitara announced with a deep voice in an attempt to sound masculine.

"Are you two blind? This ship already has–" the other guard argued before Leandros killed the guard from behind.

"It took you three long enough," Leandros muttered as he pulled the dead guard towards the woods.

"We came as quickly as possible," Berti replied. After reaching the ship, he and Sitara lowered the rolled sails into the interior of the boat, eliciting a quiet 'oof' from within the sails. Another outburst followed as Berti dropped his half within the lower level of the boat.

"Sorry," he muttered before joining Sitara and Leandros on the upper deck. They then pushed off. Berti, who knew something about sailing a vessel from his various travels, took command and helped Leandros and Sitara get the ship under sail.

As they journeyed northward for several hours, Berti began looking in the distance for the white cliffs, yet the fog and rain kept the coasts of Britannia from his sight.

Lucretia gave a soft purr as she rose from her bed. She soon began sniffing the air, ready for her first meal. She then walked out of the cart, only to notice Lamia milling about with concerned faces. Even the messenger from last night appeared confused.

"Patroclus," she addressed the legate, who gave her a strange smile. He had always been disrespectful to her. "What is going on?"

"Ask our mortal guard," he replied with a chuckle. He then walked away, and his staff trotted after him.

"Well?" she demanded after facing the mortal. Her anger fumed like a protective cloak against the chilled night. She cursed the cold weather, which caused them all to shudder.

The head sentry stared at her before his gaze moved to her feet. "The messenger's boat is gone, as is Marcus. We cannot find him or his mortal slaves."

Before the guard could say another word, Lucretia grabbed him by the throat and twisted his head to the side. The sound of breaking bones did little to sate her anger.

"None of you even saw fit to tell me this!" she growled, while staring at the remaining Lamia and mortals. Mandubratius would be furious that she had allowed his prize to escape, but what could she do? At least the messenger would not tell of this most grievous error. However, she needed assistance.

"Assim!" she yelled. Damn that child for not being around when she needed him.

Assim ran towards her. "What is it?" he asked. A growing fear in his eyes pleased her.

"I need you to return to Rome," she stated. "You must find Amata." She pointed to the south and then pulled him away from the others. "Return with her," Lucretia whispered. "Tell her that it is most desperate. Marcus has disappeared. He probably wishes to return to his precious Hibernia." She then removed a silver ring from her finger and handed it to him. "Present this to her and inform Amata that we need her assistance. Tell her to return with her forces, and let it be known that our ships will be seaworthy soon, but that we could not give chase to the messenger's ship they stole."

Assim nodded his head. "I want a kiss," he whispered, "and to share your blood." He now resembled a pouting child standing under the stars.

Lucretia backhanded him. "We have precious little time for mortal displays of affection. Now leave! Make haste!" She turned away, pleased to hear his soft cries of sadness. She could remember her own tears the first time her sponsor struck her with a fist for disobeying his orders. The sooner this stubborn ass learned to follow her lead, the better. Lucretia strode towards the ships with an impatient gait, leaving Assim to find his own way home to Rome. She soon heard him start to run towards the south.

Béal Átha an Fheadha

Maél Muire took unsteady steps toward Bearach's home and started banging on the door. The armsman appeared in the doorway as his wife Aine peered at Maél Muire. They both gaped at her, but Maél Muire ignored the stares.

"I believe the Uí Briúin attacked and killed Seanán in the dun. They left this behind," she explained as she held up the blade.

Aine started to hand clothing to her husband.

"Chieftain, perhaps this is a diversion," Bearach suggested as she shoved her dirty, bloodied blade back into her belt.

"I know," she answered. "That is why we are going to ask them if they were here. The Briúin and the Máine are not friends, yet I will assume that they will be honorable and honest. After all, while Seanán's clan and theirs fought until recently, they did not fight with ours." She hissed a sigh, trying to hold her rage. "You will join me, and we will ask them what occurred."

"You assume too much honor of Aidan and his clan," Bearach advised as he grabbed his sword and then followed her outside towards the dun. "You and Cennedi had no quarrel with them, but I would not trust them. I suggest we bring our strongest men. I know better than to suggest that you stay here, but Aidan is always looking for a new wife, especially one who has livestock and land. Keep your guard."

Maél Muire nodded her head. "Gather the warriors, Bearach. We leave in an hour's time."

The armed scouts strode closer as the red dawn gave way to the rising sun. Maél Muire and the fifty warriors of the Uí Máine tribe advanced toward the dun of the Uí Briúin, whose chieftain waited behind a vanguard of his clansmen. Maél Muire ordered her warriors to halt and waited for Uí Briúin to act.

Instead of charging, he sent forth five mounted warriors. One of his men, a straw-haired scout, leaned forward on his pony and sniffed at the Uí Máine warriors. He then waved his compatriots forth.

"So, you are the chieftain to the south," he said with a smirk. "I can see why many call you piglet. I heard it told that your father satisfied his needs with animals."

"She and her men smell of the wallows," stated another Uí Briúin.

"Better a sow than what your father laid down with," answered Maél Muire. "Is your chieftain afraid of a mere woman? Is that why he hides behind his noble warriors?" She then cupped her hands and yelled, "Aidan! I need to speak to you. May I approach?"

She could see and hear the red-haired chieftain laugh. "Maél Muire, do you need all your warriors to come over and talk to me?" His clansmen joined him in hooting and whistling.

"Yes, I need all the protection I can muster," she bellowed. "Any woman who comes within a hundred feet of you tends to fall victim to you and your clan's dubious charms." She heard him laugh again.

"You are a most amusing woman!" he shouted back. "Dismount your horse and I shall meet you. Tell your men to back off. However, you may have one escort to protect your virtue, dubious as that is." His clansmen roared in laughter once again.

Maél Muire slid off Biast and handed her reins to one of her clansmen.

She and Bearach, with the armsman a few steps behind, then walked several paces towards Aidan, who glowered at her.

"Well, well, well. Little Maél Muire is growing old. I will wager that you are still growing. You are far too tall for my liking." Aidan smirked at her. "I am quite relieved that your father turned down my proposition to court you."

"As am I," she stated. "Did you think you could get away with killing him?"

"Who?" Aidan asked as he continued to grin at her. "You must specify who you speak of, chieftain."

She stared back at him, feeling fury rise through her entire body. "Seanán Mac Declan, my betrothed. You always envied his clan's holdings. That is why you and his clan fought each other for years." She then pulled out the dagger and held it up for him to see. "Do you recognize this? It bears your mark."

As Aidan walked closer to examine it, she witnessed a glimmer of recognition in his eyes. He attempted to grab the dagger from her hand, but Maél Muire grappled with him for a moment before positioning the blade at his throat. She then heard the noise of his clansmen drawing their blades. "Keep your weapons sheathed!" She ordered. "My issue is with your chieftain!"

Aidan gasped in shock before meeting her eyes. She then watched a tight smile form and pull at his lips. "Atta–"

She sliced the blade through his throat and felt his blood gush onto her hands and arms. Maél Muire dropped the body as time ceased to move. She heard one of his warriors draw close, so Maél Muire turned and threw the Uí Briúin dagger into his chest. Time returned to normal speed as she found her sword and drew it. The dried blood of Seanán's killer still clung to the blade.

Maél Muire watched the survivors of Aidan's clan wander amongst their dead in disbelief. Women and babies cried, and she felt a profound guilt pound at her temples. The desolate dun seemed to wither into the landscape. Instead of the pleasure of vengeance, all she could feel was pity for the survivors.

Bearach placed a hand on her shoulder, and she turned to face her uncle… her armsman.

"What shall we do?" he asked.

Maél Muire looked around and then said, "These lands are mine, now."

"Yes, chieftain," Bearach agreed with a nod. "These lands, animals, and people are your responsibility now."

"Leave the clan here with half of their livestock. We will take the other half with us. One quarter will go to Seanán's clan as compensation for his death. Split the remaining amongst our clan along with the gold."

She stopped and watched as two women and five children strode towards her with purpose and long faces.

"I am Cailin and this is Dechtire," stated the elder blonde. She stared at Maél Muire with exhausted resignation as the younger brunette spat at Maél Muire, but missed. The spittle landed in front of Maél Muire's brogued feet.

Cailin sighed. "I am Aidan's first wife, Dechtire is his second. I am here to ask for mercy for my clan. Ignore Dechtire, she is a fool."

"My only quarrel was with the chieftain, not his clan," answered Maél Muire. "He killed my betrothed, and instead of discussing it with me, he bade his men attack us. My clan will protect these lands now. I am leaving our clan here. However, you two and the chieftain's children will come with us to Béal Átha an Fheadha."

"Will you kill us there in a sacrifice, you godless heathen?" Dechtire hissed.

Maél Muire uttered a harsh little laugh. "No. You two will be sacrificed in another way. You will marry two of my male warriors. Your sons will be fostered by my armsman, and our clans will become one."

Cailin smirked for a moment. "Will we have time to make a decision on a husband?"

Maél Muire shrugged. "You will have two weeks."

"Do we have a choice in who we marry?" Dechtire asked.

"Did you not have a choice before?"

Cailin shook her head. "Neither of us had options," she deadpanned before clapping her hands. "Come children, let us pack for our journey."

Dechtire followed the other wife and stared at Maél Muire for a moment with a confused expression.

"We will leave ten warriors here tonight, and we will take ten of their unmarried warriors with us," she stated. Another realization came to mind. "I need to see Brigid," she murmured.

"We will return to Béal Átha an Fheadha. Go to Brigid with her clan's share of the livestock," Bearach suggested as he patted her hand. "You did all you could." He then gestured for ten of their clansmen to step forth and help her herd the animals toward the southwest.

Cill Ala

Maél Muire walked into the dun in silence, ignoring the servants and the other clansmen. She could take no notice of her surroundings.

"Whose cattle, sheep, and horses are those?" Brigid asked as she walked into the great hall before staring at Maél Muire. "You look... what has happened?" The older woman grabbed her hands and squeezed them.

"Seanán's dead," Maél Muire whispered.

"What?" Brigid asked. "How?"

"I went to my aunt and uncle's to get herbs for him, and when I returned, someone had... killed him. I found an Uí Briúin dagger in his chest."

Brigid dropped Maél Muire's hands and looked at the smoking hearth. Her face grew stoic. "Did he die well?"

"I am certain that he displayed no cowardice," Maél Muire answered.

"And... was vengeance taken?"

"Justice was served," stated Maél Muire. "My clan and I took care of that. I have brought you the eric, the compensation for your son."

Brigid nodded her head again. "He thought very highly of you." She turned back to Maél Muire while keeping her gaze steady. "He served his clan well, and Seanán loved you very much. Even in his younger years, he wanted you at his side."

Maél Muire lowered her head as a single tear moved down her cheek. She wiped it away with a bloody hand. "I will never forget him."

She raised her eyes to Brigid and nodded her head. She then turned away and left the dun, unable to find any more words of comfort for the mother of the dead man she loved.

Béal Átha an Fheadha

Maél Muire dismounted Biast and walked through the door of her aunt and uncle's home without bothering to knock.

They stared at her for a moment and then looked away as if discomforted with their knowledge.

"There is no shame in crying here with us," her aunt whispered.

Maél Muire covered her face with her hands. She could not hold onto her tears anymore. She felt two pairs of hands pat her shoulders and hair. "I feel the same way I did when father died," she sobbed. She then tucked her face against her aunt's shoulder. "Why do I continue living, only to witness those whom I love, die?"

"You live on because you must." Her uncle's warm hands, which smelled of clean dirt and herbs, stroked her plaits.

"You have a duty to your clan, your family, yourself, and the gods and goddesses to experience and learn all you can in this life before you go to the Otherworld and begin again," her aunt added.

"I know," Maél Muire murmured.

"We are born, we live, and we die in a never-ending cycle of three," Fergus added. "It is expected that people die. The living must persevere."

Maél Muire backed away. "Of course. I know. Will I ever find someone to love and marry again, or am I bad luck?"

"You will find someone, or perhaps he will find you," her aunt replied.

"Am I still a druid after all this?" Maél Muire queried. "Druids do not ride into battle. They do not return with blood-stained hands that sought vengeance."

"You did what you had to do," uncle Fergus pointed out as he gave her a hard stare. "If you did nothing, it would have been shameful for us all."

"Your first responsibility, since that fool Cennedi left, is to take care of your clan," Sive added. "The druids did that in the past. When your duties change, you can step away from your chieftainship. You will continue your training, though you do not have much left."

"Can I stay here tonight?" Maél Muire asked.

"Of course," Fergus answered.

She noticed them exchanging looks as if agreeing to a plan.

Maél Muire woke up with a start as a fierce caw echoed in her ear. She sat up and found Taliesin resting against her, his green eyes closed in the peaceful sleep that only cats seemed to enjoy. After sliding her legs off the bed, she stood up. The cat yawned and stretched before meowing and following her. She soon realized, however, that no one other than she stood within the silent, little house.

Taliesin nudged her with his head, so she leaned down to rub his ears. She soon left the house to go to the dun.

Several horses and a cart waited outside her home as she walked to the front gate. Bearach came out and gave her an unsteady smile. "Seanán's immediate family and yours are here preparing the body for his trip home. I took the liberty of letting them in and treating them as honored guests.

"Thank you," she murmured, before following him through the gate and into the dun. "I feel like a very naughty host for not being here to stay with our Uí Briúin guests."

"I am certain they managed fine," he replied. "Do not forget, they are your clan now."

She nodded before moving into the great hall. The smell of oil and wine covered the stench of death that now faded with the passage of time. However, sorrow still infiltrated the dun.

Seanán's younger sisters and brothers looked her way with gray faces. His youngest sister held a bundle of linen. Brigid and her uncle assisted as her aunt leaned over to sew up Maél Muire's oldest friend, Seanán, who looked at peace.

She felt startled as a hand rested on her shoulder, but when Maél Muire turned, she recognized Father Padraic, one of the few local priests who did not outright condemn her family, since the elder cleric relied on their skills to combat his arthritic hands.

"You should have remained at your aunt and uncle's," he said as he patted her hand.

"I am chieftain, and I am needed here," she murmured.

The priest nodded his head in silence.

Aunt Sive stood up from kneeling in front of the table to walk over to them.

"God has given you great talents, Sive," stated Father Padraic as the priest watched Seanán's family begin to wrap him in the linen. "I cannot even see the stitches."

Sive took Maél Muire's hand. "God is not the only giver of gifts. Éire has had a history of divine gifts long before we knew of God."

Father Padraic chuckled, before looking again at Seanán's family and then back to Maél Muire. "Is there anything that you wish to bury with him?"

"His favorite sword and battle armor," answered his brother, Seamus.

"And his father's torc?" Maél Muire asked. The new chieftain would have their own. Seanán wore his, last she remembered. He did not take it off for anything or anyone.

She watched Seanán's family begin their search.

"Perhaps the killer removed it," commented Seanán's eldest sister, Sorchae, who looked at Maél Muire. "Did Aidan possess it?"

"I did not know to look for it," stated Maél Muire as she scratched the top of her head in thought. "I will go ask Aidan's widows if they have seen it."

She then walked out of the great hall and into a small room to the side. Bedding lay strewn over the floor as Aidan's children and his wives stared up at her, their games and lessons interrupted.

"Cailin, did your husband have a torc that had a bear's head at both ends?" Cailin seemed to be less likely to lie.

Dechtire sighed. "He did not possess such a torc."

"She is correct," Cailin replied. "The only torc he possessed is now worn by his eldest," she said as she nodded to her son.

The boy's eyes met hers and betrayed fear. "It is mine now," he said as he placed his hand over the large torc.

Maél Muire nodded her head. "I would not take your father's torc from you." As she walked away, the children began to play their quiet games again.

She soon took the passage to the room that she and Seanán had shared many times. Maél Muire took an unsteady breath before walking inside. The smell of oil grew stronger after opening the door. Crushed herbs and salt lay scattered throughout the room. A wet spot covered the middle of the floor where she had discovered Seanán and the blood-soaked bedding. The empty room seemed to echo her breathing. All that remained were the stone and wooden walls and the dirt floor.

After standing in the room for a few minutes, Maél Muire returned to her family. "They know nothing of his torc," she stated, "and I believe that they are being honest." She then bit her lower lip as she stared at the linen-wrapped form on the long table.

"Chieftain, the bards and the cart are here," Bearach announced before walking over to her side. "Biast is saddled and waiting. I thought you would prefer to ride to Cill Ala at the head of the procession with the warriors and myself.

She nodded her head.

Seanán's brothers picked up his body and then carried him into the sunshine. The others followed her to join in the march to her beloved's home.

Cill Ala

The musicians strummed their harps with a rigorous fervor and deepening passion. Hands clapped, and the celebrants raised their drinking vessels. One woman stood watching them with unshed tears in her moss-colored eyes. Maél Muire sipped her drink with little enthusiasm.

Connor watched her stare at the green grass beneath her feet as though she could not stand to look anyone in the eyes. He felt a sudden compulsion to embrace her, but an insistent tap on his shoulder interrupted his endeavors.

He glanced around and saw no one, until a pair of strong, pale arms pulled him into the surrounding apple grove.

His mother smiled at him... that strange smile that proclaimed such foul knowledge. The trees seemed to wither with her proximity, though her pale face and dark, staring eyes entranced him.

"We see you focused on the next objective," she purred in the soft tones of a satisfied cat. "Does it not please you that your competition has died at your own hand? Yes, the draining of life force is seductive, especially when they are surprised and frightened. We have tasted another's death." The druid smirked before crossing her arms over her chest.

"As usual, your words are mad yet meaningful," he whispered, hoping no one could hear them. He then looked back at the solemn figure, with long, red curls which cascaded down her back, standing outside of the circle of dancers.

"What must I do to woo her?" Connor pleaded.

His mother laughed for a moment while covering her mouth with a dirty hand. "Wooing will not bring her to your bed, my son. You have damaged young Maél Muire beyond repair. She will never love again." Connor frowned as his mother touched his hand. "However, she will seek you out if you offer her stability and security."

He stared back at her in silence, confused with her suggestion.

His mother sighed as though exasperated. "You must attack that which brings her stability and security. She is already weak," Seosaimhín whispered before placing a pouch in his hand. "Take this and put it in her mead. She will grow groggy and feel sleepy within a quarter of an hour. Then you must take her. She smells of fertility and the full moon. Enjoy her, our child."

As the dancers continued circling the grounds outside of the dun, Maél Muire took another sip of her mead and continued to ignore the entreaties of Seanán's family, friends, and her own clansmen to join in the celebration. The mead tasted as though mulled with the spices of the harvest.

The dancers encircled the outdoor fire again, and soon their faces grew wild with the rhythm of the dance. Around and around they danced, presenting a dizzying spectacle. Despite the twirling, however, she felt eyes staring at her, as though to draw her out and away from the crowd. Maél Muire gazed at the dancers and witnessed Mandubratius watching her with a small smile as he held the hands of two of Seanán's sisters. When Maél Muire tried to focus on him, he had turned around and disappeared behind the figures of the other dancers.

In disbelief, Maél Muire stared into her drink and noticed that she had only consumed this one goblet of mead and that he must be just a figment of her mind. After all, why would he show his face here when he still searched for his treasure?

When she glanced up to look at the dancers, she saw Mandubratius once again, this time in a crowd of people, and his green eyes revealed merriment.

Maél Muire backed up and studied her mead a second time. Did a growing insanity build within her mind? When she looked up, however, the smiling figure had disappeared again behind the leaping flames.

"Too much to drink and too little sleep," she murmured as though diagnosing her own illness. "Yes, far too little…"

His face beamed at her again.

No, this is no fantasy. It must be reality.

Maél Muire stepped toward the circle to confront him, but once again, she lost him amidst the circles of spinning men and women.

At that moment, the back of her hair lifted, and she felt a gentle fingertip slide across the back of her neck. Maél Muire inhaled at the soft caress and felt a cold chill pass over her body. Then one of Seanán's clansmen seemed to notice her shudder and then grabbed her arm.

"Seanán is here!" he yelled. "He came to wish us and his love well!"

The crowd cheered, but Maél Muire felt so tired that she closed her eyes for a moment and felt a great weakness overwhelm her. She then stumbled toward the dun. Soon the loud exultations seemed to be mere background noise. She lurched into one of the back rooms and found a soft bed of furs and blankets. Maél Muire barely had a chance to remove her belt and sword before she fell, face-first, onto the bed.

Maél Muire's body ached as she struggled to sit up. As her mind began to clear, she soon felt fluid dripping down her inner thighs. Knowing it was too early for her monthly bleeding to start, she slid her left hand under herself and wiped some of the sticky liquid onto her fingers. She then held up her hand to the light entering the room through the spaces in wooden walls. A pearly white fluid covered her hand.

"No," she whispered in horror upon realizing the nature of the substance. She then stood up on shaky legs and ran for the back of the dun. The noises of the wake echoed through the night as she rushed towards the flowing stream behind the dun.

Maél Muire threw off her léine and jumped into the stream, ignoring the chill, before washing herself in the cold water, splashing it about her lower regions furiously. Then, after a few desperate moments, she wiped her face as she realized that if anything, she had increased her chances of bearing a child.

Maél Muire whimpered as she grabbed her léine. She then dried herself and ran back into the dun. Before her lay several sleeping forms wrapped in blankets near the hearth. Maél Muire stepped around several sleeping forms to find her aunt, who she recognized from her graying, red hair. "Aunt? Aunt Sive?" she whispered as she shook her aunt's shoulder.

Her aunt opened her fox-like eyes and stared up at her. "You are dripping water," she stated.

"I need your help," Maél Muire whispered.

"You are fertile."

"Hmmm? Yes," Maél Muire murmured as she continued staring at the sprigs of drying herbs from the small bed in the Brigid's herb room. The smell of lavender, mint, and fennel clung to the air and made her cough. As the tang of honey moved up her throat, she felt as though she may vomit at any minute. Still, she managed to refrain from doing so and instead focused on her aunt's ministrations.

Sive closed her eyes and placed her warm hands on Maél Muire's abdomen. "One can just tell these things," she whispered while pulling down Maél Muire's léine. "You smell of fertility and sleeping powder. Someone tricked you, Maél Muire, and perhaps several other women. That someone has knowledge of herbs and magic." Aunt Sive then poured the brew she had been making into a goblet and handed it to Maél Muire.

"This will cleanse your system and bring on your monthly bleeding. It will last for five days and nights, and it will not be pleasant. Drink it slowly."

"It smells horrible," Maél Muire whispered before taking a sip, but instant revulsion coursed through her body.

"Yes, well, the choice is to do this or raise a child without a husband," Sive explained and then sighed. "Raped women have done it before, and I have watched them hate that child and themselves. This is the right thing to do in this situation," she advised. "Do you remember anything about what happened? Did anyone loiter near your drink?"

Maél Muire pinched her nose shut and started to gulp down the rest. After a few swallows, she shook her head. "I thought I saw Mandubratius dancing in the circle. It must have been an effect of the powder, or perhaps it was not an idle fantasy and this is his way of getting even for lying after the vision quest," she suggested to her aunt.

"I know little of the ways of blood-drinkers," Sive mused aloud while sitting on the floor next to Maél Muire. "Yet, I imagine if he came to wreak vengeance on you, he would simply kill you."

Maél Muire finished off the potion and gagged. "Yes, that makes sense. Perhaps it could have been a friend of Aidan's." A sudden gurgling sensation brought her stomach immediate discomfort, and so she grabbed her abdomen and rolled onto her side. "I think it is working already," she whispered.

Her aunt nodded her head. "Try to rest. I will tell Brigid and her family that sadness overwhelmed you. We will go home tomorrow morning."

Mhuine Chonalláin

Connor urged his horse forward as they trotted towards Béal Átha an Fheadha. The sun had set, and a thin sliver of the moon arched in the night sky like a scythe.

He could not help but smile at the thought of Maél Muire in his bed. She had to be one hundred times better awake than in her unconscious state last week. His mind soon drifted to their child.

When will she realize that she is pregnant? Perhaps she will learn in a month or less…

Without warning, Lugh snorted and whinnied in fear before rearing to his full height and striking out with his hooves. Connor could feel himself start to slide when a cloaked figure grabbed the reins of his mount. Lugh then calmed and became still, as though caught in a spell.

Mandubratius smiled up at him. "Chieftain Connor, how are you?"

Connor inhaled as he watched the creature run his tongue across elongated canines, much like a wolf staring down a lamb.

"I am well," Connor heard himself reply as he attempted to swallow his fear and meet the blood-drinker in the eyes.

"You are heading to the west," Mandubratius surmised with an all-knowing smile. "You are going to visit 'her'."

"Yes, I am." There appeared to be little point to lying.

Mandubratius pat his horse and then drop the reins, but Lugh remained motionless. "Do you plan on going without a present? Women have always loved gifts," he asked as he handed a box to Connor. "Give this to her."

"What is it?" Connor asked before sniffing the box. It smelled strange.

"Frankincense," Mandubratius replied.

Connor opened the box and looked inside. "Beeswax?" he asked. He had plenty of that, and it did not smell so intrusive. "Thank you," he replied, hoping not to sound rude.

Mandubratius laughed. "It is not beeswax. It is resin from the frankincense tree, to be precise. It is sacred and used in religious rites to purify and protect. It is of great monetary value and comes from Arabia and Africa. She is a druid, so she will know its true value."

"Then I thank you for this gift," Connor answered. "I am certain Maél Muire will appreciate it."

"Of course she will," Mandubratius acknowledged with a smirk. "Maél Muire will love every gift we give her."

Connor stared down at the box. "What is your interest in her?" he asked in a near whisper.

"Nothing you need be concerned about, Connor," the Lamia argued. Mandubratius then leaned in and added, "I am certain you will get your heir. I trust you enjoyed taking advantage of an unconscious woman. I will send you the presents, and you will give them to her. After all, Maél Muire deserves some small amount of joy, does she not?" The blood-drinker smirked at him.

Connor bit his lower lip, unsure how best to respond.

"Your secret is safe with me," Mandubratius purred, sounding like a cat that enjoyed spending time batting around field mice. "Just remember, she is not going to be yours forever, only her property and belongings. I need her assistance. Good night." Mandubratius backed away and then turned to leave.

For what purpose does he need her?

Béal Átha an Fheadha

"Chieftain," Oisín whispered in Maél Muire's ear as he leaned over her shoulder, "another guest has arrived."

His words interrupted her thoughts as Dechtire and Cailin discussed their marriage preparations. Their future husbands smiled at her as the two women chatted about dresses and food.

"Excuse me," Maél Muire bade while taking Oisín's arm, "what guest, Oisín?" She could not help but be desperate for the idea of someone who would not speak of wedding matters after her own dreams had ended in spilled blood.

"Chieftain Connor Mac Turrlough Uí Niall," Oisín replied. "He waits outside. He would not come in until he sees you first."

"Have Basala set more places at the table, and prepare an extra bed for our guest." She then walked outside to join Mac Turrlough and tried to smile. Connor turned to face her, and a familiar smell laced the air. He held an ornate, wooden box and smiled.

"Chieftain," she greeted as she nodded to him. Connor's hair glimmered under the pale light of the stars, dressed to impress someone. When he stepped in closer to her, he smelled of clean herbs.

"Maél Muire, I have come with a present, to…" he said before pausing with a smile, "to express my fondness for you." He then handed her the box.

Maél Muire smiled as she accepted the gift. "Let's go inside," she suggested before taking his arm and leading him into the dun. She felt better inside anyway, as the air outside had chilled. "You did not need to bring a gift," she stated as they approached the main doors. "You have given so much already."

Oisín opened the doors, and they walked inside the dun.

"Open it," Mac Turrlough requested with a smile.

Maél Muire caught a glimpse of her other guests as they vied for vantage point to watch her open the mysterious box. The box itself seemed old, but it bore several carvings and seemed to be inlaid with gold. However, when she flipped up its golden clasp and opened the lid, a surprise greeted her... many amber-colored nuggets. She placed the box under her nose and wafted the strange substance.

"This smells wonderful, and yet somehow familiar," she stated, before holding up the box so her guests could catch whiffs of the wafting aroma. "Thank you, Connor. I do appreciate this lovely gift." Of course, she did not say that she had no idea what the little pieces of resin could be, as that would be the height of rudeness.

"I am so honored that this small gift has brought a smile to your face,"

Connor murmured before kissing her forehead. "I shall return," he promised before walking out of the dun.

Maél Muire stared down at the box before looking over at Dechtire, Cailin, and their betrotheds. "What is this?" she whispered to them.

"Chieftain, this is a most expensive gift," stated Cailin.

"This is worth more than a flock of sheep or cattle," Dechtire added as she leaned in to get another whiff. "The priests burn this during the high holidays of Easter and Christmas. It is called 'frankincense'."

Cailin chuckled. "Perhaps Mac Turrlough may be your next love. You may find yourself married to him before our wedding days."

Maél Muire felt her smile fade away. Unable to take further delight in the frankincense, she closed the box, although she regretted the effort with which she closed the lid, as it made a sharp rapport through the dun.

"I am sorry," Cailin whispered as she patted Maél Muire's hand. "What I said was callous. However, he needs an heir to his lands and livestock. You could do worse. He must be very powerful and rich to give something such as this."

Maél Muire shrugged as she put the box down at the table, more gently than when she had closed its lid. "I will try to remember that."

At that moment, Mac Turrlough returned to the dun.

"You will join us and stay tonight," she stated. "You know very well that I will not take 'no' for an answer."

The elder chieftain returned her smile. "I would be a fool not to accept."

Maél Muire handed the spoons and wooden bowls to Basala, who inclined her head towards Mac Turrlough.

"You need to speak to him," she murmured. "I can handle this."

"Alright," Maél Muire whispered before walking over to Connor, who had leaned up against her chair.

"Did you like my gift?" he asked.

"You gave me resin," she answered with a straight face. "I am not upset, but I am curious. Why was I given resin? What is it that they do?" She concentrated on not smiling.

Mac Turrlough stared at her as if stunned. He then lowered his face and laughed, apparently realizing her game. "You know very well what this is, Maél Muire. You just like to play coy." He then sat up and scooted his chair closer.

"So you have a window into my thoughts now, Connor?" she asked.

"No, I cannot see your thoughts, but I know what you are thinking right now. Any druid worth their weight in salt would know this is frankincense, and you are worth far more than your weight in salt."

Maél Muire felt her face grow warm. "I see a flatterer has entered my dwelling. You are correct. I am very grateful and appreciative for this gift." An utter lie, but she hoped that he could not tell.

"And I appreciate your company and the meal," he replied.

"Well good–" she began to say, but Connor held up his hand to interrupt her. He then leaned in closer and began to whisper in her ear.

"Know that I am here for you if you need me," he murmured.

"In time, perhaps," she stated in reply. She sensed no ill intentions from him, other than the fact that he appeared to want her, but he shifted a bit as though uncomfortable. She decided to lean in and gave him a quick kiss, which he returned.

"Goodnight," he whispered.

"Goodnight." She turned away as exhaustion overwhelmed her. Perhaps a remainder of the potion stayed within her body.

"Frankincense!" Uncle Fergus exclaimed as she walked in the door with the box. He took it from her, opened the box, and inhaled deeply.

Maél Muire chuckled. "So, someone else recognizes it."

Sive smiled and said, "I am glad to hear you laughing again. Fergus, stop being greedy. Let me see it." She smirked as she pulled the box away. "Who did you get this from?"

"Connor," she answered.

"Mac Turrlough?" her uncle asked with a smirk. "No, I do not think so."

"He is doing very well then," her aunt surmised with a smile. "Perhaps, his mother's influence wanes." She then shrugged.

"This is worth more than what he could afford," Uncle Fergus stated. "May I hold a piece?" he requested while looking at Maél Muire. "I have never touched it."

"Take as much as you need," Maél Muire answered. "I would not know what to do with this. But, I should keep some in case he asks about it."

She watched her uncle smile before placing three pieces in a pouch.

"Odd," she muttered as she closed the box.

"What?" her aunt asked.

"I have smelled this recently," Maél Muire answered. "Yet, I cannot imagine who... Marcus... Marcus is that merchant who stayed with you, he smelled of this, as do his correspondences."

Fergus chuckled. "You are right. See, that is who I would suspect to have

Heather Poinsett Dunbar & Christopher Dunbar

a treasure such as this. A rich merchant can afford this luxury, not a chieftain."

Maél Muire grinned. "Perhaps Mac Turrlough has more than we believed."

"Perhaps," answered Sive, though she still continued to look dubious. "Still, after all he has lost, one should hope for him to experience some bounty."

Maél Muire plucked the box from Fergus' vicinity and smelled its remaining contents. "Perhaps Father Padraic would appreciate one or two of these," she stated. "However, I want to keep one for myself. The scent grows on me."

chapter seven

Môr Hafren (Estuary of the River Severn)

"Look at those stars," Berti whispered as though in reverence. "There is nothing like a starlit night on the high seas." He then glanced at Marcus, who stared with contentment at the sails, which furrowed with the gathering cool winds, bringing them closer to Britannia.

The former Roman general seemed to adjust his gaze and take in the stars. "Yes, it is lovely, Berti," he murmured. "However, it is not home until the rain drenches us."

"Do not say that, Marcus," Sitara scolded while frowning at him. "It is already too cold. Rain would chill me to the very bone."

Berti watched his friend unfasten the broach at his throat and pull off his cloak. Marcus then tossed his gray cloak to Sitara. "I prefer the cold, and I have no need for warmth, unlike mortals," he stated.

Sitara looked at Marcus with questioning eyes.

Berti watched as Sitara adjusted her tight clothing before wrapping the cloak around her shoulders. She then stared down at the bowl in her lap and gobbled down the fish Leandros had prepared earlier, as if her appetite had suddenly appeared.

"Marcus," he whispered again, hoping Sitara's ears could not hear this question. "Is Sitara looking rather large to you?"

Marcus choked on his blood wine, which he had found earlier in the messenger's well-stocked ship. The blood-drinker covered his mouth as he guffawed with gusto. The return to home, or close to it, had improved the Deargh Du's spirits. "Oh really, Berti? You have just noticed her transformation?"

"Well… no, of course I noticed it much earlier," Berti explained. "She is bigger now than she was when we first met her."

"Well, Sitara's appetite has increased of late," Marcus added as he lowered the jug. "However, I think there is another reason for her size."

Berti watched his friend smirk. In response, Berti sighed and rolled his eyes. "I hate it when I am left out of these secrets. Tell me what is so amusing, Marcus, or I shall find a way to destroy your stash of blood."

"As if you would do such a thing," Marcus countered before taking another sip.

"Is she ill?" Berti rubbed his hands together as Marcus took over guiding the ship for a bit. "Why has she grown so?"

"I think she is with child," Marcus deadpanned.

Berti gulped as he felt a sudden nausea swell over his body. "How could such a thing happen? What child? Whose child?" He watched his traveling companion roll his eyes.

"Honestly, Bertius... the child is yours!"

"How did this happen?" Berti whispered while sitting down, though his stomach continued to turn.

"I think you know how this happened," Marcus teased. "I cannot believe I must say this, but I will try... when a mortal man and a mortal woman love each other very much–"

"Marcus, I meant..." he argued, interrupting the smirking Deargh Du, but then all he could do was sigh. "I just meant, how do we know that she is big because she is pregnant?"

"There is a test I learned from the Chiang Shi. It is almost foolproof. Wake Leandros and get him to handle this, and we can find out for sure."

Berti strode his way to where Leandros slept, awoke him, and nodded toward the rear of the ship. He then followed Marcus to Sitara's side.

Sitara gave a small belch and stared at them for a moment. "What is going on with you two?" she asked as she eyed them suspiciously.

Marcus smiled. "Sitara," he murmured as he sat down next to her. "Berti and I are a little worried about you. Your appetite seems to grow, as do you."

"I am fine," Sitara stated. "You just think I am fat," she grumbled at Berti.

"True, Berti thinks you are fat. However, I think you may be growing something else," Marcus suggested as he leaned in closer to Sitara. Before Berti could say a word, the Deargh Du rested his ear against her belly.

"I hear another heartbeat. That means I am correct, Berti," Marcus announced with a smirk.

Sitara stared at Marcus and then turned her gaze on Berti. "A baby? I am going to have a baby?" Her voice seemed incredulous.

"It is a common side effect of coitus," Marcus explained while looking rather pleased. He then gently patted Sitara's belly before pulling away. "You will be a fine mother."

Sitara seemed to ignore Marcus' words and continued to stare at Berti as he tried to fathom the idea of having a child with Sitara.

"You are not going to stone me, are you?" she asked with tears in her blue eyes. She soon started to wail while covering her face with her hands.

Berti knelt beside her and pulled her into his arms. She tried to push away, but he maintained his grip.

"Sitara, I love you," he told her, not caring who heard at this point. "I want to be your husband. We will raise the child, and he or she will be honored. I would have married you anyway, even if you were not pregnant." As he rubbed her back, he could feel her tears wet his léine. "We will marry in Éire."

Sitara started mumbling something in her native tongue. She finally sat up and wiped her eyes. "In my culture, we do not marry for love. Marriages are arranged at a young age," she announced.

"Well, we do marry for love in mine, sometimes," answered Berti. "And your family is not here to reject our marriage."

"But my father cannot approve of you or this marriage," Sitara argued before wiping her tears with Marcus' cloak.

Marcus walked over and sat down next to Sitara on her other side. "I accept you into my clan, Sitara, which makes me the closest thing you have to a parent. You have my permission to marry Berti."

The news overwhelmed Berti.

"You do? I can!" Sitara beamed at them both. She then leaned into Marcus' shoulder for a quick embrace.

"Of course, granted my clan is very small, and I have no proper dowry of sheep and cattle for you," Marcus drawled before chuckling.

Berti heard some other comments from Marcus, but Berti found himself kissing his betrothed, and he forgot Marcus' words. Soon, however, he heard a throat clear.

"What was that, Leandros?" Berti asked, breaking his embrace with Sitara.

"If you three are finished with your marriage contracts, I see a port ahead of us. Is it Abona?" he asked Marcus.

Marcus faced the crest of the land and the village named Abona. "Yes, that is it. From here, we can travel to Bath," he cheered, grinning. "I am almost home, outside of Éire home, anyway."

Abona

"You three must be silent," Marcus whispered as he nudged them away from the numerous docks lining the industrious and noisy port into a dank inn, which reeked of disgusting matters. Mice squeaked and other vermin scurried across the floor.

Leandros gagged, and Marcus feared he would retch.

"This is the most disgusting place I have ever seen. It is worse than the slums of Rome," Berti murmured. "You cannot–"

"Berti," Sitara whispered before clamping a hand over the mouth of the father of her child.

After Marcus tapped the innkeeper's shoulder, the odiferous man turned toward his guests. "I am looking for Quintus," Marcus informed.

"The rain is a lovely sight," replied the innkeeper.

"Not as beautiful as the night," Marcus answered.

The innkeeper nodded and then waved to a curtain behind him. "Open the cellar door and go through the passage," he whispered. "The code-word is 'Cernunnos'."

Marcus walked around the innkeeper and gestured for the others to follow him. He then walked into the storeroom.

"Where are we going?" Leandros whispered.

"A safe place," replied Marcus.

"We are going to a safe-house?" Berti whispered. "This is so exciting." Marcus saw Berti tug Sitara's hand. "I have never seen one. Even Sáerlaith did not invite me to the stronghold in Ard Mhacha."

Marcus chuckled as he grabbed a torch. "Follow me, if you will." He then started to walk down the dark passageway when a thought occurred to him. "Do not touch the walls," he advised Sitara.

"There are traps set?" she asked.

Marcus shook his head. "No... it's a mess." He chuckled. "That's an Ekimmu Cruitne trait." He soon grew silent as they ambled towards a ladder. He then climbed up and knocked on the door.

A latch clicked and then the trapdoor opened. Immediately, a sword slid out and pointed at his nose.

"Password," Mac Alpin's servant challenged while staring down at Marcus.

"'Cernunnos'," replied Marcus. "I suppose Claudius had a hand in this password, since it is one of the honored titles of the Lord of the Wild Hunt."

Edward stared at him in silence as he withdrew his sword, but then Claudius pushed him aside.

"Marcus?" Claudius called. "I thought I heard you complaining about my choices of passwords. Edward, go fetch your master."

Marcus finished climbing the ladder and started to assist Sitara into the room.

"I remember this associate," Claudius stated while glancing down at Berti. "But I do not remember this one." Claudius beamed at Sitara.

At that moment, the door to the room with the trapdoor banged open, and Mac Alpin walked in wielding a massive claymore.

"Marcus?" Mac Alpin boomed as he waved his sword. "What brings your Roman carcass to my doorstep? I already play host to one of your countrymen," he guffawed with great merriment.

Marcus watched Berti, Leandros, and Sitara back away with a large amount of trepidation in their eyes.

"Why, you have brought us dinner!" Mac Alpin roared. "Eithnè," Mac Alpin bellowed for his servant, "bring me my gold... no...," Mac Alpin's brown eyes turned to Marcus, apparently realizing his error, "bring me the silver chalices!"

Marcus shook his head. "Sorry to disappoint you both, but these are my friends and traveling companions. You already know Berti. This is his wife-to-be, Sitara, and this is Leandros, who aided our escape from the Lamia. Thank you for bringing us into your home, Mac Alpin."

"Well, no one can say that I am a poor host," Mac Alpin boasted. "Please, join us, and perhaps Edina can find some sustenance for your mortal friends. Edward, put away all the gold before our guest finds himself ill."

Marcus and the two other blood-drinkers stared into the hearth while sipping on bloodmead, as the mortals slept in one of the other rooms. These hidden apartments stood in stark contrast to the filthy inn. Even a light, wafting scent of honey floated through the rooms. Mac Alpin's home abounded in luxury. A polished, wooden floor appeared to extend through all the rooms, and a few rugs, which could have been from Shiraz, graced the floor with their elegance. Although, despite the elegance, an ornate table revealed stains and cuts.

Marcus turned to regard the right side of the underground home and found himself staring at a blue-painted head on the wall. "Mac Alpin, I know there must be a good explanation, but why is there a human head on your wall?"

Arwin shrugged and turned to where Marcus stared. "Oh, that is to remind me of the days when I was a mortal."

Marcus sighed before turning to his hosts. "I need a favor from both of you." He watched as Claudius met his stare, before taking another sip, and Mac Alpin lowered his drink. "I need to go to Bath and take over the Lamia's stronghold there."

Claudius made a small hiccupping sound before looking over at Mac Alpin as if expecting an outburst.

"Indeed, young Marcus," Mac Alpin enunciated with a strained chuckle. "That is quite a request to make."

"I hear that the Ouphe are nearly defeated," Marcus added.

"You are correct," Claudius replied. "Help us defeat the last pit of them, and we will assist you with ridding Bath of the Lamia. After all, I grow weary of them treading over my new home"

Marcus glanced over at his former lieutenant and the Scots blood-drinker and then nodded.

"Yes, I will look forward to defeating those Roman…" Mac Alpin spat before catching himself. He then smirked at them. "They have outworn their welcome."

"And you two have an army to assist us with this raid?" Marcus asked, finishing off the bloodmead before closing his eyes.

"You don't need an army, lad. You've got me!" Mac Alpin rallied.

"Mac Alpin, I have seen these soldiers of Rome tear through mortals in a blink of an eye. They are not that easy to kill." Marcus wondered whether overconfidence permeated his associates' hearts.

"The Lamia have a weakness of course," replied Claudius. "They do not tend to change their plan of attack or defense." He then passed over the jug to Marcus. "There is always an antidote to our old methods."

"However, we should concentrate on handling this situation with the Ouphe first. They are on the run and are vulnerable. ++They cannot create more of themselves when they have no place to take them for their transformation," Mac Alpin interjected.

"We have narrowed down their location," added Claudius. "We were going to take care of them tomorrow night, and I know you would not turn down a fight with them, after that bloodbath you experienced the last time you were with us."

Marcus refilled his drink and then stared into the concoction.

"Besides, Deargh Du seem to be able to survive the Ouphe's scratches and cuts that plague our kind." Mac Alpin grinned before adding, "That, and Edwina says he has a secret weapon. Let us hope he will not set us afire."

"You will join us, won't you, General?" Claudius asked, grinning.

"As if I would turn down a fight with those lycanthrope monsters," Marcus answered. "Consider me in."

"Me too!" Berti chimed in as he leaned out the door from the other room. "It sounds too fun to miss."

The darkness welled and pooled as Marcus crept closer to the Ouphe sentry. Marcus then willed the dark stillness to expand, and the Ouphe did not seem to realize his predicament until blindness overwhelmed him. One of Marcus' gladii made quick work of him as both head and body fell to earth.

"That is a very useful trick," Claudius whispered in Latin. "Someday, you must teach me how you do that."

Marcus watched as the joined forces of Ekimmu Cruitne and Sugnwr Gwaed surrounded the cave that held the remaining Ouphe. Soon he noticed

Mac Alpin trotting over to them. "Are you certain this is a wise idea?" Marcus asked in Briton as he turned to face the Ekimmu Cruitne.

Mac Alpin chuckled softly as the three of them turned to watch Edward toss a mysterious package into the cave and then back away.

"We've practiced this many times," Claudius assured him.

"Aye, it is a most simple plan," Mac Alpin confirmed before motioning them toward the front of the cave. The gathered forces then drew their swords. "Edward's contraption sets them on fire, they run out, and then we remove their heads." The blood-drinker then looked up for a moment and added in an ominous tone, "Let's just hope that he does not set us on fire."

The gathered forces stared at him, until the sound of a huge, booming noise, falling rocks, and inhuman howls drew their attention. Soon after the explosion, the first set of Ouphe, smelling of reeking, burnt hair, ran out of the cave towards the gathered warriors. Seemingly blinded with pain, the Ouphe trundled, oblivious, into the midst of the small party.

The animalistic screams grated on Marcus' ears as he and his companions slaughtered the Ouphe as they exited the cave, frenzied with the fire that had enveloped them within the caverns. Roaring, flame-covered, beings with human eyes tried to make it toward the water, only to fall to their enemy's waiting swords. After several minutes of fighting, howls of pain and rage still echoed from the cave.

"Endina, it's time for another one of those, I think." Mac Alpin suggested as he motioned to his mortal servant.

In response, Edward lit a piece of string with fire before tossing a bag of what looked to be powder into the caves, and then another explosion shook the countryside. Nothing else exited the cave. Only the stench of death and burnt hair remained.

"Again," stated Mac Alpin.

Edward nodded as he gathered the materials again. This time, he mixed the powders with a strong-smelling liquid. The explosion made the land shake, and then the entrance to the cave closed as rocks and boulders cascaded over the opening.

Marcus faced Edward as the fires from the explosions started to move towards the expanse of grass and grains. "Mac Alpin!" Marcus shouted as he grabbed the shoulder of the Ekimmu Cruitne, who was enjoying a premature, celebratory drink with the warriors.

"Yes, fine, Marcus, here's your drink," Mac Alpin answered, but then his eyes grew wide as he stared at the fire. "Edward!!!!" he bellowed, apparently remembering his associate's real name, for once.

"Yes?" Edward turned and then seemed to study the fire in the distance.

"You started another fire, you blundering fool!" Mac Alpin growled. His voice grew animalistic. "I should never trust these plans of yours!"

Edward regarded the fire in the distance. "Now sir, that fire is totally under my control. The land is brushy and overgrown. It needed a fire to thin and clean it anyway."

Claudius smirked. "Then I hope the farmers will forgive us for destroying their crops, Edward," he said before finishing his drink.

"Nonsense, Claudius," Edward replied. "The fire will stop at that river..." he said before pausing. They then watched as the winds changed direction, and then the fire began to drift towards the nearby village.

Edward started to run towards the fields of grain, and the blood-drinkers followed him, hoping to control the fire that threatened to rage through the tranquil farms.

Hrothgar stared at the smoking cave as the other blood-drinkers returned from putting out the fire. The figures from over a mile away were tiny, but his eyesight assisted with the watch. He then turned to face the two other survivors of the assault by the Sugnwr Gwaed and Ekimmu Cruitne and shook his head, aggravated with the night's events.

"We need to go into hiding," he stated in a half-snarl. "Let them believe us dead."

Eryk and Aluen nodded their heads.

"How long will we hide?" Aluen asked.

"After the Saxons cement control of this wretched isle, we will return," Hrothgar replied, before closing his eyes, allowing the transformation to take place. He then called to his brothers, and together they loped into the distance. Soon, Hrothgar let the disappointment slip away. One night, they would rule this land.

Later that night at Mac Alpin's home, Claudius watched as Arwin sat down in front of the hearth. "Are you comfortable?" the Ekimmu Cruitne purred to Sitara. In response this obvious flirtatiousness, Claudius could see Marcus smirking and Berti rolling his eyes a bit before returning to his mead. The mortal did not display jealousy, just amusement at their host, who seemed to find Sitara's exotic looks to be enchanting. Mac Alpin seemed to present her with extraordinary gifts and comforts, to the exclusion of his other guests.

"I'm fine." Sitara smiled as she looked over the new bracelet the blood-drinker had given her. Mac Alpin must have hoarded a great many treasures in his life, of course Claudius also kept his own treasure troves, hidden away.

"If watching him were not so amusing, I would be jealous," Berti murmured softly to Marcus.

Claudius cleared his throat twice in hopes of getting Mac Alpin's attention. "Now, what is this business you request of us, Marcus?" he asked.

Marcus set down his mead and then looked on as Mac Alpin left Sitara's side to join them. He then began to explain the mission. "I need to steal something."

"So… you want us to become petty thieves?" Claudius inquired with a smirk, suspecting this was not the case. "Whatever happened to our honor?"

Mac Alpin started to laugh. "Why, any child in the street could do that. Why are we needed?"

"No child could handle this duty," Marcus replied. "I need to steal an important artifact from the stronghold of the Lamia in Bath. It's part of a statue of Mars that was stolen from the temple in Rome."

Berti continued. "If they reunite it, they believe it will help bring a new age of dominance for their kind. So you see, Claudius, it is an honorable cause."

Mac Alpin leaned forward. "And what does this artifact look like?"

Marcus chuckled. "It is about the size… of a rather large cucumber."

Claudius raised a brow. "Are you joking? What part of a statue?" he guffawed after a brief pause. "Oh wait, I have heard the Lamia fables about the Phallus Maximus. I believed them to be nothing more than that."

"You Romans and your strange obsession with cucumber," Mac Alpin jested, before glancing over at Sitara, as if to make sure she was not offended.

Sitara stared back at the men. "I do know all about the Phallus Maximus. I am not a woman who needs protection from such things."

"Is that an insult, Arwin?" Claudius asked as he rose up to refill his drink.

"Not at all… well, yes, but I mean it in the nicest way," added Mac Alpin.

Claudius passed by Marcus to rejoin them at the hearth. "I bet he hasn't used his cucumber in a few centuries," he whispered, before asking in a conversational tone, "So, you want us to break into the Lamia stronghold and get past how many Lamia to get this most sacred, treasured cucumber?"

"I believe about two hundred, including their leader, Mandubratius."

"What?" Mac Alpin roared, and then the entire company jumped.

At that moment, the door opened and Edward peeked into the room. "Yes sir?"

"I did not call for you, Edena!"

The mortal smile, betraying a great deal of patience on his features. "Sir, whenever you utter such an exclamation, I assume that I am being summoned," Edward stated.

Mac Alpin rubbed his forehead, revealing his frustration. "Eithnè, I will call you when I need you. Now, go back to your room and play with your alchemy equipment, but do not blow up my home."

Edward withdrew from the room and then closed the door behind him.

"What is he working on?" Sitara asked.

Mac Alpin took a gulp of mead. "Who, chroí?"

"Edward, of course," she replied.

Mac Alpin's brow furrowed as he contemplated her question. "'Edward'? Who is that?"

"Your mortal servant," Marcus clarified.

"Oh Edwina! He's working on some other vile concoction from lands far to the east of Persia. If he can get it to work, it might be useful in this endeavor." Arwin then clasped his hands together and asked, "So, when do we leave?"

Outside Divio

Assim stopped behind the pack of Lamia as they continued their midnight journey through the lands at top speed, or rather at the top speed of the mortal slaves who lingered behind them, tripping over rocks as tried to catch their collective breath. He removed a pouch from his pocket and began to drink... a night's rations.

At least until dawn creeps near with her red cloak, and then we shall feed!

Assim soon felt a tickle as a soft, white hand rested on his. He raised his head and stared into Amata's blue eyes. "You are a most quiet Lamia," she purred. Her eyes revealed a gentle patience he had not seen in years.

Assim shrugged. "I am thinking about our enemy, the Deargh Du," he answered, before facing away from her gaze. He still found himself fearful of them, of what power they must wield in order to keep those in line under their sway. He then looked at Amata again. Even though she traveled the harsh trail with them, she still emanated a regal, chilly beauty that haunted him.

"You display a cautious fear," she stated. "Such fear can be both dangerous and wise. Tell me what worries you, young one."

Assim gestured with his free hand for her to walk with him away from prying ears, and she followed. Free of eavesdroppers, Assim answered.

"My lady, what I have to say is... truly frightening to me. As a mortal, I have seen many blood-drinkers." He paused, as the wind rattled the trees. "However, Marcus is not someone who we should trifle with, especially if the other Deargh Du are the same as he. I witnessed him force Lucretia to do much against her will, including drinking animal blood," he whispered. "He attacked her, and she could do nothing. I am worried for our kind, Domina." He then handed her his pouch, which she took and began drinking from it.

"If all Deargh Du are as gifted as he is," Assim added, "we cannot win."

Amata laughed. Her guffaws sounded quite different from her voice, which never seemed to rise in anger. She seemed like a delicate desert flower, a world apart from Lucretia. "But Assim," she continued once she stopped laughing, "Marcus is better than four Deargh Du put together."

"What do you mean?" he asked. A quick glance revealed that the army waited for Amata.

What makes this one Deargh Du different? Are the others still to be feared?

"There is something special about Marcus," she began to explain, "but it is something that I cannot identify, Assim. However, I mean to discover what he hides." She then handed the pouch back to Assim. "You will soon see that we are as strong as most Deargh Du."

Assim took the pouch. He felt a trace of reassurance from her words. "I still have my concerns," he said, "yet I must admit to a great deal of ignorance on my part. Lucretia did not wish to impart much knowledge to me. She preferred to keep me in the dark." He smiled.

Amata revealed a twist of a smile. "It surprises me that Lucretia did not teach you more. Ask me questions, young one, whenever you feel a compulsion to ask." She then met his eyes. "The dawn nears, Assim. Tell me about your life before."

"I was a shah, the leader of my people in Shiraz," he answered.

"Most impressive," Amata commented.

Her words, however, were soon interrupted by a Lamia servant. "Domina, the scouts advised that there is something you must see to the east!"

"Let us see what this is," Amata suggested before taking Assim's hand. Before he could answer, they started to run, passing the servant. They sprinted through fields and stands of trees as they headed for the mountains, but then they stopped upon reaching the stench of death. Amata joined a scout and stared at the bones and rotting bodies, seemingly immune to the smell.

"This is where the Goths and Franks attacked us," Assim explained, while trying not to gag, although he managed to join Amata and the scout.

"Tell me of this skirmish," Amata inquired as she turned to face him. At that moment, several Lamia soldiers arrived and began to take in the spectacle.

"There were almost 2,000 of them," Assim began, "versus two hundred of us." Assim continued to share the rest of his recollections of the battle as the sky grew brighter.

"When you described this fray, I had no idea how large it was. We have not engaged a force this size in some time. I have forgotten how efficient our army is." Amata grinned, revealing her fangs. "I owe my noble soldiers an apology. I feared that they had grown decadent." She then looked up at the soldiers. "We will camp away from this squalor. However, make sure the men know that my confidence in them grows and doubles each night."

Outside Ráth Cruachan

After avoiding the fae mound and the sacred caves, due to his last experience at Brú na Bóinne, Mandubratius neared the outskirts of Ráth Cruachan. Soon the sounds of sleeping mortals grew, while his senses reveled as he prepared to feed. All external distractions of the forest and its creatures ceased as he concentrated on his need to find food. He moistened his lips in eager anticipation as he crept closer to a farm house with sleeping mortals within. Nothing could compare with the pleasure of feeding, save feeding and coitus.

Before Mandubratius could enter the dwelling, he jumped in silent surprise when a hand wrapped around his forearm and pulled him around. Before him stood the ancient druidess from Brú na Bóinne who stared at him with a satisfied smirk as he attempted to cover his shock.

"We understand you have designs on our daughter to be," the crone intoned as she stared at him.

Mandubratius glanced around the forested realms, waiting to see the druid's companion.

"'We' have heard?" he queried, feeling a smile tug at his lips. The old woman, for her powerful insight, seemed a bit crazed, though the forest appeared to wither at her proximity. "Wherever did you get such an absurd idea, crone?"

"We hear it from the trees, from the bees, and from the flowers. We hear it from the stones, for she always speaks to us."

"Well, that is simply not true," Mandubratius argued.

The druid growled as she grabbed his other arm. "It is true!"

Mandubratius took a step back after the old woman released him, regaining his composure. "Such accusations are uncalled for, old crone. If it were true, then what are your designs on Maél Muire?"

"We seek one to follow us and learn our ways, one who is strong in the ways of nature corrupted," she answered.

"That does not sound like the Maél Muire I know," he commented.

She sighed as though exasperated with him. "We want the child of Maél Muire!"

"Child?" Mandubratius inquired after inhaling in shock.

"Yes, child of Maél Muire, child of our bloodline, child of my useless son."

"Maél Muire is with child?" Mandubratius asked again.

"Thunder cracks, yet the stag does not heed. Yes! That is what we said!"

"I had no idea that she carried a child," Mandubratius stated.

"The trees are green, yet he only sees black," the druid sighed, revealing her impatience.

"If I take her before the child is born, I do not know what will happen to the child. It may die, it may be born mortal, or it may be born into darkness. If it is born into darkness, will it ever grow?" he asked, revealing his concerns.

What if the child were to display the strengths of a blood-drinker and the mortal ability to walk under the sun? Perhaps–

"That is not acceptable to us," the old woman countered, interrupting his musing.

"Fine," Mandubratius answered. "I will wait until after the child is born, but it will need nourishment."

The crone laughed, revealing her teeth. "The child shall feed off the she-wolf."

Mandubratius nodded. "Then it is agreed."

"The white crow caws its pleasure," the druidess murmured as she nodded her head.

The sound of falling branches made Mandubratius turn away from the ancient mortal. Seeing nothing out of the ordinary, he turned back and saw that nothing remained of the old woman except for a lingering presence, which faded into the mists. He ignored the inner warnings in his head about making deals with people such as her, for the insane could not be trusted. However, the idea of ignoring the ancient taboo of sponsoring an expecting woman grew on him. A child like that could cement the Lamia hold on the world of night.

Mandubratius grinned before turning his thoughts back to his hunger. It denied him the chance to worry anymore about that strange druidess, yet the idea of rearing a child grew more and more enticing. After all, as a mortal, he had left behind a son and a pregnant wife to go to Rome. This could be his chance for another son or daughter who could wield the power of a Lamia and the hidden blessings of a mortal. He could not deny himself that temptation.

Béal Átha an Fheadha

Basala opened the interior door of the dun and sighed in utter disappointment as Mac Turrlough's dark-eyed messenger presented a box in his hands. "Oh, it is you again," she stated, trying to keep her voice respectful. However, she could hear the disdain.

"I have a gift for you, beautiful lady," purred the brown-eyed flirt with a mischievous grin, before handing her the box. "At least I wish I could give it to you, but it is from my chieftain, and he wishes for you to present it to yours."

"That's what you said about the gifts from yesterday," Basala answered the departing messenger before placing the box near the others stacked in the corner. Before she could close the door, Maél Muire walked past her holding a scroll.

"I heard you at the door. Who was it, Basala?"asked the chieftain.

Basala said nothing, deciding instead to point at the new box.

The chieftain frowned. "I should do something about those."

"When a man gives me unwanted attention with gifts, I return them," Basala stated.

Maél Muire chuckled. "But Basala, I do not wish to be rude. He has given me so much."

Basala shrugged her shoulders. "Well, you could bury or sell them, except for," she added, glancing at a pair of combs in one of the few opened boxes.

Maél Muire stared at the pile of boxes. "No, this is ridiculous, Basala. I will go speak to him and stop this extravagance." She sighed before picking up the wooden box of combs and handing it to Basala. "Every woman needs something pretty of her own."

Basala reddened for a moment, turning away. "I have no need–"

Maél Muire pushed the box toward her. Basala looked at the other woman's determined eyes and decided to accept the gift.

"Thank you." She took the box and felt a genuine smile pull at her mouth. The chieftain then gave her that slow, half-grin in return.

Basala watched Maél Muire study the skies for a moment.

"I think it will rain soon. The skies smell of rain," announced the chieftain.

"I think the sun will shine, Chieftain," Basala said before pausing, for the druids usually were right on these matters. "I will find your cloak."

Maél Muire slowed Biast to a trot as she noticed Connor ahead of her, assisting with the repairs of a clansman's roof. She halted the horse, before patting her chestnut neck, and whistled to Connor.

He glanced over, smiled at her, and then headed for the ladder.

She gestured for him to follow her into the stand of oaks so their words would not be overheard, and then she walked Biast over there. The horse nickered as Connor walked over to the side and looked up at Maél Muire.

"Maél Muire, to what do I owe this pleasure?" He smiled at her. "You are not wearing the combs I gave you, nor the silk léine. Is it too short?"

"This is the reason I am here," Maél Muire began to explain as she stared down at him, trying to smile. "I appreciate your generosity, but I fear that it is misdirected. I would rather you give such lavish gifts to your clansmen. I think they would benefit more from your generosity. I feel uncomfortable receiving these gifts amongst my kin for fear that I am not providing as well for them as I could. I look selfish."

She watched Mac Turrlough turn red as if embarrassed. "Have you given away or sold anything?" he asked in a near whisper.

"I gave the combs to Basala. She deserves a reward or two for her fidelity. I shared the frankincense with my uncle and a priest, who has shown my family kindness and much understanding. However, I have not given away anything else," she answered. "I seek your permission to do so. I feel it would only be honorable."

"I am sorry for placing you in this awkward position," Connor stated. "By all means, please do what you will to help your friends and clan. What would you like instead?"

Maél Muire grinned before shaking her head at his insistence. "I do not need material things that you have to offer," she answered.

She heard a chuckle from him, and in response, she stared down at him. His blue eyes met hers as if daring her to say more. "You are a challenging woman to woo."

Maél Muire raised her brows, affecting surprise. "Oh, so you are trying to marry me? Why would any man want such a thing, since I have proven to be such bad luck?"

He patted her leg and stared up at her with a wary smile. "I feel we are destined to be together. My heart is yours to do with as you please." The last sentence became a soft purr, accentuated by the sound of the birds chirping.

Maél Muire stared at the lush green oaks for a moment, trying to think of a proper reply. Finally, she said, "I must say that I am intrigued by your intentions, but I have my doubts that we would have a fulfilling union."

His right hand slid over hers. "What must I do to convince you that we were meant to be together?" Connor's fingertips stroked over hers.

"I will say this," Maél Muire countered. "Lately, you have been missing the mark. Perhaps you should redirect your aim."

"Then I shall endeavor to please you," he murmured, before kissing the palm of her hand and then releasing it.

"I must be going. Have a good day," she stated, before nudging Biast with her heels. This had not gone according to plan. Now, she almost wished Mac Turrlough had been upset with her dismissal of his gifts. A general confusion on all matters dealing with her neighbor to the east weighed on her head.

She could almost hear a spoken, muttered reply on the wind as Biast's strides lengthened into a canter.

chapteR eight

Bath

itara nibbled on one of the apples that the men had found for her, relishing in its sweetness. Still, the sugary taste grew more with the addition of honey. She dipped her right index finger into the golden sweetness, stuck the digit into her mouth, and savored its subtler flavors.

Something about sticky, rich substance made her feel relaxed, and so Sitara reclined in an outdoor lounge and gazed at the splendorous sky above as the sun drew ever so closer to dusk, its beauty bringing tears to her eyes. The departing sun basked the gardens within the old Roman villa in brilliant, long light, revealing the bright colors offered by blooms and fruit of every conceivable hue.

"It is a pity that they cannot see this," she commented to Edward, who managed to remain awake while Berti and Leandros still slept, exhausted from their journey. She could not help but wonder how they managed to stay awake for so long and make do with little rest.

"Yes, this villa is very beautiful. No wonder Claudius loves talking about his home," Edward said before yawning. "Excuse me, for I am still weary from travel. I am sure that the night skies to them are magical."

Tired of her sticky fingers and mouth, Sitara lifted herself out of the lounge and walked over to a wash basin. "May I ask you something?" Sitara inquired as she began washing her hands with the clean, warm water of Bath. After their arrival, Claudius and Marcus had insisted on bathing in the balneum in the villa, which seemed to be a Roman custom, and a very long process. She had wandered, in the early morning hours when no men were about, into the bathhouse to experience this Roman custom, but she could not stand the heat from the first room and instead had visited the middle room. The servants' explanation of the proper bathing process only confused her.

"Go ahead, before they awake," suggested Edward. "Otherwise, I may have to be running errands for Arwin. It's not another bath question is it?" Edward laughed as he ground a black substance into a fine powder.

"I am afraid I will never understand that," Sitara replied, "yet my query is about you. Why do you stay with Mac Alpin?" she asked, wanting to coax his story from him. "Do you owe him money, your life, or is it something else?"

Edward chuckled as he started filling small, porcelain containers with powder. "I have enough money to pay off Mac Alpin, but I do not want to leave. My family has always taken care of its friends. He saved my grandfather's life when my family had arrived from Saxon Germania. We swore to stand with Arwin if we were ever needed. Sitara, I would be most miserable if I were stuck working on a farm or trying to impress a mortal master with my skills. Even though Mac Alpin would never openly praise my abilities, he knows my value." He then motioned her away as he started to close the powder capsules.

Respectful of the ominous warning, Sitara took a weary step backwards while holding onto her abdomen.

"Besides that," Edward continued as he met her eyes, "I have been able to learn and study during our travels, no matter how arduous. I would not be able to do that if I were to live here in Britannia on my own. I hope Mac Alpin would not insist that I move on if my familial debt were repaid."

"I can understand why you chose to stay with Arwin," Sitara stated. Soon, the sounds of footsteps down the walkway drew her gaze, and she spied Marcus yawn before joining them, staring as the remaining trace of sunset vanished.

"How are you feeling?" he asked while looking at her expanded stomach.

"Very well," Sitara answered while patting her belly. "Edward has kept us fed." During Sitara's pregnancy, her stomach ceased giving her problems from certain foods, though now it just demanded more and more food.

Marcus grinned for a moment. "I am glad to hear that. Edward, you must be a resourceful and stalwart individual. Sitara needs a strong force of arms to keep her safe. It would be a personal favor to me if you would protect my clanswoman from harm. She needs to rest in this safe-house."

"I do not need to rest–" Sitara argued, but she stopped when she heard the footsteps of the other warriors as they gathered by the hearth.

Berti had appeared from nowhere, his face set in a strange half-smile and a pout. "Sitara, you do not really want to go join the battle at the Lamia stronghold, do you?" he inquired while wrapping an arm around her. Berti began to pull her along through the house, but not before she glanced back over her shoulder to watch Edward nod his head and salute Marcus, or at least she assumed it was some sort of salute, and then she saw Marcus copy Edward's actions. Soon, however, she found herself outside of the house.

"I love this part of the day at the cusp of nighttime," Berti shared as he released her arm, before sliding his fingertips over her hand to entwine hers with his. "To see the sun give over reign to the moon and to watch the stars glimmer is beyond description." Then he turned to her. "Sweet poetry aside, you must stay here."

His hand splayed over her belly. At his touch, she felt movement within and jumped a bit.

"He recognizes you," she murmured.

His lips parted into that strange, mysterious smile. "Yes, he does." He then leaned closer and brushed his lips over hers. "Please stay here with Edward."

"I will," she agreed as she leaned into his embrace.

She could soon hear the secret doors open and close as other blood-drinkers wandered past them into the house. Men and women in battle armor stared at them and then smiled while whispering to themselves. "What did they say?" she asked. Sometimes hearing the different languages confused her.

"They consider it fortuitous to see an expectant mother before battle," Berti said, before rubbing her stomach again. "Now, we should discover their plans." He then led her back towards the house.

"Some of us have tracked them in and around Bath," Claudius stated, before rolling out a scroll detailing the Lamia quarters. The others scooted or stood closer to get a better look.

"We have counted nearly two hundred troops that come in and out of this back entrance here," another Sugnwr Gwaed stated, "yet their movements have decreased of late."

"Many of us keep watch on the safe-house. The old villa above looks to be deserted," added one of Mac Alpin's warriors, "and yet we know the basements underneath are not. They are large and complex. Many of our mortal spies have returned to us confused, although several mortals, and even our own kind, have forfeited their lives for these floor plans."

"This underground compound must be huge to house so many," Mac Alpin acknowledged as he stared down at the scrolls. "And the sentries?"

"Fortunately, most of the sentries are mortal servants to the Lamia," another Sugnwr Gwaed explained. "The Lamia defenses have slipped."

"They have grown lazy while the Ouphe have been keeping all of us busy," Mac Alpin added with a chuckle.

"Since their defenses at night increase, the best time to attack would be during the changing of the sentries." Marcus smirked for a moment. "Before daybreak, I hope all of us are prepared to spend the day within the stronghold. I am certain that there are plenty of hiding places. Remember, this is a mere scouting mission to find the treasure. I suggest we split into two groups. The first will deal with the sentries. Mac Alpin, Claudius, and I will find the entrance to the underground compound."

"When will we put this plan into effect, Gen… I mean Marcus?" Mac Alpin asked, his face flushed with embarrassment for a moment.

"In approximately five hours."

Marcus sat and started, before discarding the blankets covering him. He then stood up in the small room he shared with many of the others waiting for battle. The attempt to sleep during the night did not go well. After a few seconds, he walked out to join other sleepless blood-drinkers, only to find Mac Alpin sharpening his blade.

"You cannot sleep either?" the Ekimmu Cruitne asked while drawing his whetstone down the edge of his blade. "I never could before a battle or even a mere exercise to search for a treasure. Even as a mortal, I had my own little habits that I had to follow for luck, you see." He chuckled weakly.

Marcus nodded his head, allowing silence to grow between them.

Mac Alpin paused in his sharpening to hand him a pouch. "Most Deargh Du would sooner spit on my kind than share a drink."

"I have never even met one of my kind," Marcus admitted with a smirk. "I imagine they would sooner spit on me as well."

Mac Alpin barked a laugh. "Perhaps, perhaps. They are very strange and very solitary, almost standoffish." He shook his head a bit. "No, Marcus. They are standoffish. There are a few who are not, but they are the exception to the rule." Mac Alpin eyed his sword as he added, "At least they do not try to conquer this land."

Marcus gulped down the fiery liquid. "Excellent," he murmured, before handing it back to Mac Alpin.

"Edward has many talents," Mac Alpin conferred while taking back the pouch. "If he did not make this so well, I would consider discharging him, as he has repaid his familial debt to me. By the way, do you wish to meet this Mandubratius and kill him yourself? Claudius says you and this Lamia have a bit of unfinished business."

Marcus shook his head. "If you see him, kill him before he can say a word. Many say he can manipulate with words better than most of the Sugnwr Gwaed."

Within the first few moments of battle, the first wave of warriors overwhelmed the mortal sentries, dispatching them in silence from the sky. Then Berti and a few blood-drinkers took their places in the sentry defense.

Marcus joined the others at the small entrance door.

"I hear four heartbeats," Claudius whispered.

"And I hear dice," Mac Alpin bragged with a smirk.

Marcus closed his eyes, allowing the darkness to surround them. Claudius opened one of the doors as Marcus grasped the other. The sound of swords leaving their sheaths grew louder until the three of them surrounded the

Heather Poinsett Dunbar & Christopher Dunbar

guards and cleaved their heads with swift strokes.

Marcus released the darkness, which melted into the atmosphere. Claudius and Mac Alpin then followed him through two other rooms, before reaching a room containing more mortal guards. They dispatched the sleeping guards and found the main staircase. Unlit torches lined the stairway.

Within moments, they reached the second level of basements and stared in amazement at the barracks for four to five hundred men. Marcus then motioned for Mac Alpin to guard the staircase before glancing back at Claudius, who waved Marcus to join him at the end of the hall. After Marcus linked up with Claudius, he saw that the last set of barracks revealed kits and weapons, indicating that someone was using these as living quarters.

They leaned up against the last door and, after hearing nothing, opened it. A dank smell of old blood greeted them. In the corner stood several barrels of wine and ale, waiting to be mixed with blood. They then walked back to the main hallway and noticed Mac Alpin hold up his left fist, motioning for them to halt.

Marcus leaned toward the noise and could hear the sound of two soldiers speaking in Latin. At that moment, voices stopped, and he heard a call for help and then footsteps, as one of the Lamia ran down to the lowest level.

The one remaining soldier raced, with sword drawn, towards Mac Alpin, who grunted as he swung his sword to meet the high cut of the spatha, but Mac Alpin's blade shattered to pieces.

Claudius stepped in and blocked the soldier's cut and then removed the Lamia's head from his shoulders.

"Go for the reinforcements," Marcus called to Mac Alpin, who then flew up the staircase and outdoors.

Marcus turned to Claudius before taking a step down the stairs.

"Should we wait for the others?" Claudius asked.

"Since when have I waited for reinforcements?" Marcus answered, before starting down the long staircase, hearing Claudius follow. Once they reached the bottom step, Marcus looked around. He could hear the sound of a spring bath. Soon he beheld huge columns holding up the roof and torches lighting the entire passage, revealing remaining Lamia who waited for them in a combat formation.

Claudius caught up to him and asked, "So, it is the two of us versus fifty?"

Marcus glanced over his shoulder for a moment and answered, "You take the twenty five on the right." He then drew down darkness, leapt into the area above the Lamia, and attacked the three soldiers in the back row, cleaving heads from bodies as he and Claudius flew over the Lamia forces, leaping, twisting, and flipping. The Lamia turned to face them, ignoring the reinforcements that soon arrived, Berti among them.

Marcus held the darkness in place as he heard the clanging of metal bashing against metal and the grunts of effort from both the slayers and the slain. After a few moments, the blackness dissipated into a filmy mist. Marcus watched as the reinforcements hacked at the remnants of the fifty Lamia defenders.

He then noticed the gleaming resplendence of the Lamia general, who Mac Alpin would soon run though. "Arwin, hold!" Marcus ordered as he flew over to the leader and held one of his gladii at the general's throat. "This is their general," Marcus addressed Mac Alpin in Briton. "Mandubratius is not here. Disarm him."

Mac Alpin kicked aside the discarded swords and knives of the general.

Marcus then kicked the general. "To the floor, on your stomach," he ordered in Latin. "Double check him," he said to Mac Alpin in Briton.

Marcus then realized that the ensuing fight had finished.

"Extra knife," Mac Alpin grunted as he tossed aside the weapon.

Marcus then reached down and pulled the general to his feet. "Tell me where the Phallus Maximus is," he yelled in Latin, but the Lamia stared back at him in sullen silence. "Again," Marcus hissed, feeling a strange sensation overwhelm him. At that moment, a blissful numbness, which reminded him of feeding, slipped around him. "Now, where is the Phallus Maximus?"

"Intelligence says Éire," the general deadpanned, as his eyes grew lugubrious.

"Where in Éire?" Marcus asked, feeling his strength surge.

"Mandubratius says Connacht, the western coast. His last missive revealed he searched for it there."

Marcus then beheaded the general. "Thank you for the information."

"What was that?" Mac Alpin asked. "Claudius, did you see what your general just did? He made the Lamia talk. Berti, you must have witnessed this."

"Deargh Du do not have that talent," Claudius stated, while meeting Marcus' eyes.

"He has done it before," Berti murmured. "He must have picked it up from some other group of blood-drinkers."

"We must speak on this," Mac Alpin suggested, "some other time in the near future." The Ekimmu Cruitne's attention soon drew to his broken sword. "This was my father's sword. I will have vengeance against every single Lamia," the Scots blood-drinker huffed. "I am exhausted. Must we do all this cleaning?"

"I will call forth the men of Bath," stated Berti, "and tell them that the victims of a rare illness are here. I may need some help with convincing them of that. However, I am certain Claudius and his friends will help."

"What does the house above us look like, Arwin?" Marcus asked.

"I have not seen the inside," Mac Alpin answered.

"Let us take a quick look," Marcus posed to Claudius. "I am certain there must be a secret entrance to the house from here."

The victorious blood-drinkers avoided the sun as it pooled through the magnificent windows. Marcus also had to duck away from the gold leaf in the columns and statues. Still, what he and the others beheld seemed marvelous.

Cobwebs clung to marble arms. Tiles and marble decorated the floor, and on their immediate right, a large, painted mural sprawled across the wall. Gods played with beautiful nymphs, Venus smiled at them from a large couch where she reclined, and Cupid sat at her feet, pulling an arrow from his quiver. A statue of Venus and Mars stood in the foreground. Dust covered the marble of the statue, giving it the appearance of a dull finish.

Claudius coughed as he pushed a door open.

They then sauntered past several empty pools, fountains, and what could have been a garden, if it were not so overgrown. Each new room revealed more beauty than the last, yet all remained in a sad state of disrepair.

"Very sad," Marcus muttered under his breath. "This place must have been beautiful."

"I think this may have been the viceroy's home," Claudius replied. "I believe I have visited here, yet memories fade after hundreds of years."

"I wonder what it would look like if they replaced the gold with silver," Marcus added. He then closed his eyes for a moment, imagining what it may have looked like in its heyday.

Marcus finished up his fifth cup of mead. The ensuing celebration for the dead kept everyone awake as beautiful mortal servants kept goblets filled.

"What do you think will happen to the Lamia fortress?" he asked Mac Alpin and Claudius, who both appeared intoxicated.

"I suppose it will be set upon by squatters," Claudius answered. "I got my home in London that way. The Lamia owners mysteriously disappeared."

Mac Alpin laughed and then belched. "You want it. I could tell, or rather Claudius could and told me. You realize that if you plant your backside in the chair and rest your swords on your arms, no one will ask you for the title."

"Hmmm, unfortunately, I cannot take it over right away," Marcus stated. "However, Leandros could, though with some assistance. I am certain you two know of a few associates who might be interested in a safe-house in exchange for some light guard duty."

"Sure. I am certain something can be arranged," Mac Alpin answered while crossing his arms over his chest. "Well, we have assisted you with this task of taking over the Lamia compound, but now we are needed here in Bath and back home." The Ekimmu then began to mumble as he faced away from Marcus. "Besides, Leandros will need assistance, I am sure. Who knows, the Ouphe may also return. Yes, that is it. We must prepare for another battle. Yes, we must..."

Marcus heard the Ekimmu Cruitne continue muttering about this and that, but soon he heard Arwin mention something about crossing the waters of the Irish Sea, and then, "Nonsense!"

"What about your fury at the Lamia for breaking your sword?" Claudius smirked a bit. "I thought you did not put aside your grievances so easily."

"This has nothing to do with another battle." Marcus met the old Scots warriors' eyes. "This is about fear, Claudius. Well, I suppose that means the oaths of the elder Ekimmu Cruitne means little."

Mac Alpin gave Marcus a dark stare back at him.

"Imagine that," Marcus added. "So the rumors are true. There lives on an island a powerful race of blood-drinkers who are afraid of the water."

Mac Alpin's face grew flushed. "I am not afraid of anything, Roman. Do not test what you cannot understand. We are not afraid of the water, are we?" He looked at his contingent of warriors.

Before anyone could make a reply, Edward walked by with a bucket of soapy water. He then tripped and ended up splashing water on Mac Alpin.

"Edwina," Mac Alpin growled, "that was not entertaining." Mac Alpin shook himself out. "As you can see, we are not afraid of water," he stated with a sneer.

"No, we just do not like flowing water of any kind," one other of the Ekimmu Cruitne finally admitted in a quiet voice. They then all lowered their heads a bit as though embarrassed.

Marcus met Mac Alpin's eyes again. "I was not accusing any of your kind of being afraid of the water. I have yet to see any cowardice from the Sugnwr Gwaed or the Ekimmu Cruitne." He chuckled a moment. "If you do not want to go to Éire, you cannot carry out your sworn vengeance against the Lamia. Oh well. I will make sure they receive your regards."

Before Marcus could stand, Mac Alpin grasped his arm and then looked over at his warriors. "Fine," he hissed, "we will go." The warrior's bluster disappeared and the crowd grew silent in a pregnant pause.

"I did not hear that," Berti said.

"Bertius, we all know you are not deaf!" Mac Alpin groused. "We will go!"

The others soon began to dispense through the villa, for sunrise neared.

"What is it about the water that puts you ill at ease?" Claudius asked.

Marcus watched Mac Alpin glance around as if making sure the others were gone. "There is the legend of the geis," Mac Alpin replied.

"Geis?" Claudius asked.

"That which is forbidden," explained Berti.

"We are all familiar with that concept," Marcus added. "Who placed the geis on you?"

Mac Alpin uttered a choked laugh. "You have not heard the tale, young Marcus? I suppose it is because you do not have contact with others of your kind. Our blood is part Deargh Du and part Ekimmu. When the two transformed the first of our kind, the Morrigan placed a curse on us. She found the very thought of our creation so monstrous that She wanted to keep us here."

"Fascinating," Berti murmured. "So you cannot leave the isle?"

"No, we can leave," Mac Alpin replied. "Yet, flight becomes impossible with the first smell of that salt air. Illness overcomes us."

"And if you traveled on a boat?" Claudius queried. "Is it easier to cross then?"

Marcus heard Mac Alpin laugh. "No. Then it is worse! We suffer nights of illness, compounded by the way the boat rocks up and down and up and down." His face turned green. "The best way is to do it as quickly as possible."

"I suppose that means we will have to help you across to Éire," Marcus reasoned aloud with a smirk. "Unless, you would prefer to travel on the boat Berti, Sitara, and Edward hired."

"Oh very amusing," Mac Alpin grumbled.

The skies grew dark as the new moon hid her face.

"Take good care of our new home, Leandros," Marcus said as he placed the bags of silver in his hand. "Before you do anything else, take out that gold leaf and repair the baths. Hire whoever you feel can help."

"Thank you." Leandros backed away and bowed. "I will make sure it is ready for your return."

Marcus turned to Mac Alpin. "Are you ready to try this?" he asked.

"I do not appear to have much choice in the matter," Mac Alpin growled. "All I can say is that you had better not drop me in the water."

"If the smell of the sea is such a problem, perhaps some strong oil will help," Sitara suggested, before holding a vial of perfumed oil.

Mac Alpin took the vial and opened it. He then made a face and shuddered. "It smells," he said as he glanced at Sitara while trying to smile. "Sorry, chroí."

Sitara laughed before grabbing the vial. "Fine, then. Go across and be ill."

"Desert flower, this oil of yours smells like cat piss!" Mac Alpin objected. "I cannot abide smelling of stink!"

"I think a bag over his head may work," Berti added, "in the way one would lead a frightened horse through fire."

"I take much umbrage at your comparing me to a horse, Berti." Mac Alpin sniffed the oil again.

"I have no more patience for this." Marcus grabbed the vial out of Sitara's hands and flicked oil onto Mac Alpin. "Stop whining. I promise to drop you into a river, and then you can take a bath."

He watched Mac Alpin wheeze a bit and close his eyes. "We should leave before I change my mind," he told Marcus.

"Have we reached the water yet?" Mac Alpin asked as he squirmed about.

"No," Marcus lied. He could see Éire in the distance. "Stop moving or I will drop you." He already held Arwin by the scruff of his neck.

"We are near the sea. I can feel salt breezes," Mac Alpin said. "You had better not drop me, because I never learned to swim."

As Marcus flew, he could soon see the waving torches of the Sugnwr Gwaed at the shores. He then landed and set Mac Alpin down near the other Ekimmu Cruitne.

"I lied," he admitted to Mac Alpin. "We are in Éire."

"We shall rest here tonight in the caves," Claudius stated. "Our scouts have found some a mile and a half to the west. They are clean and dry."

"I am sure most of our coterie will be glad to hear that." Marcus smirked. "How fare the other Ekimmu Cruitne?"

"Seasick, but alive," Claudius answered with a weary chuckle. "And unless there is some other duty that must be done, I am going to go drag a few to the caves. I know you would rather do what you normally do. Sleep well, General."

"Thank you, Lieutenant."

Once the others had left, Marcus kneeled underneath a large oak and began to dig a hole, smiling as the black clods of rich dirt began to cake his hands and nails. A peace settled over him as the island sung a welcome hymn and then smells of night flowers drifted through the air. Even the fresh scent of mistletoe grew steadily in his mind.

He sighed as he slid into his earthen bed, before pulling Éire's clean blanket over himself.

Caletum

"Lucretia, I had assumed that the ship construction would be almost complete by now." Amata watched Lucretia jump at what seemed to be unexpected words. Through the corner of her eye, Amata could see Assim glower at his sponsor. She did enjoy surprising the young ones.

"Yes, we have had some issues with inclement weather." Lucretia pulled aside the thick strands of hair hiding her eyes and seemed to try to regain her composure. "Where are the reinforcements?"

"They wait for my word," Amata answered. She then noticed Patroclus awaiting her with his usual patience. To Lucretia she said, "You appear to be busy. I will discuss things with Patroclus." She could see Lucretia's dark eyes widen, and then a false serenity came over the other Lamia.

"I have work that I must attend to," Lucretia quipped before scurrying off. Relief seemed evident on her face at the terminus of their conversation.

Amata glanced at Assim before gazing at the Lamia and mortals building their ships. "Go find refreshment," she told Assim before patting his arm. The former shah could be needy at times, but his devotion to her was now unquestionable. Amata suppressed a smile as she watched the shah bow to her and turn away. How short-sighted Lucretia must be not to see the value in such devotion.

To her right, Amata could see Patroclus stand with placid patience. With a slight nod of her head, she indicated for him to walk with her. Together, they strode toward the opposite end of the encampment, away from Lucretia.

She knew of the Legate Patroclus' proclivity for the enduring state of Rome. He had swore himself to that duty centuries ago during the era of the Emperor Trajan, when the Lamia believed in Roman honor and ideals. Amata longed sometimes to describe Patroclus as simple-minded, but the legate seemed to be more single-minded. She found him fiercely loyal, as long as she and Mandubratius presented themselves to be the preserving and serving the ancient honors of Rome. It seemed a bit strange that such matters were all-important to Patroclus, who possessed fair skin, fair hair, and looked Gallic.

"So, what is the truth of the matter, Patroclus?" she asked, knowing he would be honest about the progression of their agenda.

Patroclus smirked. "We are actually on schedule, Domina. Lucretia knows nothing about the building of ships, so her words are but foolish guesses."

"And how did our friend, Marcus, leave?" she queried, wanting to make sure that Lucretia's and Assim's messages were true.

"He and his mortal companions stole the messenger's boat. We had completed a new ship for him many weeks ago, and he now sails to Connacht to deliver the message to Mandubratius."

"Tell me about the construction. Will there be space for our other soldiers?" Amata queried.

"We started on new triremes when the messenger left to find you."

Amata nodded her head. "I am glad to hear this."

"Domina, I predict the voyage will be a slow one," Patroclus added. "Lucretia has not realized that the weight of the weapons will decrease our speed."

Amata chuckled. "Yes, I realized that, Patroclus. Have no fear, for you and I will have her out of our plans soon. Mandubratius will dispatch her himself. I am certain of it." She then took his hand and stroked her thumb against his knuckles as a gentle promise of future escapades and honors. After all, one had to get the attention of men in one way or another. Plans for her dominance required it. If those plans remained viable, who knew what would happen in the next few months and years?

Patroclus gave her a noncommittal smile as he brought her hand to his lips. "Of course," he answered. He released her hand before walking back to rejoin the builders.

Ráth Cruachan

Mandubratius paced within the great hall of the dun, remembering his own dun and his past glories, until his present intruded, interrupting his contemplation.

So many plans, so many…

He turned to Wicus and cleared his throat. "Is there any word of our treasure from the men on the excavations in the area?"

"No sir. There is no news yet of the Phallus Maximus."

"And the merchants?" he queried.

"We have discovered nothing," Wicus answered. "The merchants we have found have been manipulated into searching for it, but so far, nothing."

Mandubratius nodded before facing away. The smells of the sea distracted him, and he could have sworn he heard strange voices from further down the coastline. He began to run, and Wicus followed him. Together they sprinted to the perimeter of the village. He could hear the sentries speak to each other, and then the outline of a messenger came into view as he dashed towards the village.

"Call forth everyone to the dun," Mandubratius ordered while rubbing his hands a bit. "This may be news that we all need to hear." While Wicus retreated, Mandubratius hiked to wait for the message in the dun.

A few minutes later, all of the Lamia and mortals not on guard duty gathered, and then he took a seat in the chieftain's chair.

The messenger stepped toward him and saluted. "I bring word from Lucretia," the messenger stated before looking around at the gathering. "The cohort is leaving from the continent to join you soon. Amata is arriving with the second cohort within the month."

"Excellent news," Mandubratius replied. "The sooner we take over this desolate place, the sooner we can return home with our treasure and our rightful place of honor."

His plans regarding the continent would fall into place, then. In due time, they would leave the temple and move to the Vatican hills and the Lateran Palace. The pope could be convinced he needed protection.

The messenger nodded before opening the vellum scroll to reveal more news. "Lucretia told me to tell you that she has encountered an old friend of yours who is looking for you."

"Oh, and what is this old friend's name?"

"Marcus Galerius Primus Helvetticus," answered the messenger. "He stole my ship and–"

Mandubratius stood before he could think to reply and grabbed the messenger, ripped out the blood-drinker's throat, and then tore off his head. He heard the gathered forces grow silent as he licked the blood off his fingers. Without a word, he picked up the scroll the dead Lamia had held and started to read it.

"Good report," he said to the headless corpse. "I think you deserve a promotion." He then faced the others and felt satisfaction as he watched them cower a bit. A show of force always kept these people in line.

With his display at an end, Mandubratius walked towards his staff and began issuing orders. "We need more scouts along the coastline," he stated, pleased that they finally met his eyes. "These scouts will signal our fleet and escort them to the encampment. That way, the mortals will stay away from Ráth Cruachan. They may become suspicious of our actions soon enough."

Ard Mhacha

Caoimhín walked to Sáerlaith's door, pushing the mortals aside who insisted she slept now and could not be disturbed. "I must speak to her now," he demanded. "The sun has yet to rise, and she must know what I have learned about the Lamia."

Sáerlaith opened the door and peered at him. Her dark hair hid her almond shaped eyes. 'Young woman' did not describe her, but her face showed no wrinkles, and only a few gray hairs silvered her hair. Adhamdh had chosen her for her wits and skills in magic, not for her beauty, and yet her intelligence only enhanced the magnificence reflecting in her eyes.

Sáerlaith slid her fingers around his arm and then pulled him into her room. "What have you learned?" she asked with soft and gentle words before closing the door behind him.

"I found them in a village south of Ráth Cruachan. Reinforcements will arrive in a few days, or perhaps they are there now, but who knows... they may be five hundred strong by now," Caoimhín explained. "Also, the Roman Deargh Du, Marcus, was with the Lamia on the continent. He must have been spying on the Lamia. Apparently, he and Bertius stole a messenger's boat." Caoimhín grinned before adding, "I also heard it whispered in the village that this Marcus and Mandubratius knew each other as mortals."

"Indeed?" Sáerlaith acknowledged with a raised brow.

"I also heard murmurs about what had happened to the messenger," he added. "Mandubratius ripped out his throat and tore his head off."

"And the soldiers?" Sáerlaith asked, seeming to hold her breath.

Caoimhín stared at her. "They looked as they had known one another in the past, during the height of the empire, Sáerlaith."

He watched her head lower for a moment, displaying a fearful defeat, yet her eyes displayed a fierce, green fire.

"I will call the council, and you will be there with me to confirm this truth. I will not have my kind hide and melt away into the green grass. I will not allow the Lamia to take over our home. Our kind hides behind a cloak of magic, but we must step out from behind our cloak and make our presence known, again, within these dark nights."

He watched Sáerlaith open the door to dispatch her mortal servants.

Sáerlaith then turned back and clasped his hand. Her eyes reverted to their natural brown again. "I cannot sleep now. Will you help me part the mists? I need to commune with the ancients. It will give me strength."

"Of course," he replied. "I am honored."

Sáerlaith watched the council join her in the small grove. Caoimhín stood at her side as the gentle breezes played with his pale hair. The others stood with them in the midst of the oaks.

"We must decide now what we are to do about the Lamia in the West. They desecrate the home of our beloved Mother with their presence near her cave. They manipulate the very things the Phantom Queen charged us to protect and venerate. They disturb the balance. We must remove them, or we will be doomed to wander the earth as a vagrant race," she announced.

"And what is wrong with that?" Emer asked. "We can go to Britannia and Alba. You always complain that we do not see more of the world. I am not a warrior, Sáerlaith. I was not even an ovate. I am a bard. You were no warrior either."

"I was a warrior," Finn said. "There is no need for us to leave when we can negotiate with this Mandubratius. He is a Briton, and he will see sense when we offer to assist in finding this treasure of theirs."

"You do not understand," argued Caoimhín. "They do not mean to negotiate with us. Even if they promise to do such a thing, we cannot trust them. This Mandubratius rules with an iron fist. He may smile and place honoraries on us, but a Briton rules the Romans because he is feared. They have turned many mortals into Lamia, most against their will. How can we let them do this?" Caoimhín shook his head. "The one we have alienated does more against them than we. How shameful is that?"

Sáerlaith watched Etain and Nuadin for their responses.

"They are hunting mortals, not Deargh Du," Nuadin clarified. "I say we hide as the Tuaths did. The Lamia's influence will wane, and we will regain dominance when they cannot find their treasure. The balance will favor us again soon."

Etain met Sáerlaith's eyes. "I feel that this is a matter we all must discuss. Perhaps the others in our home will have their own opinions."

Sáerlaith stared back at them. Her disappointment tasted of bile. "This is not our finest hour," she countered. "Very well, we can meet in two night's time. Call forth all the brood of Morrigan who can participate."

Soon she could sense a mortal's footsteps and watched as a young woman with an unsteady and fearful heartbeat approach, bowed, and then held out a scroll. Sáerlaith took it and shooed her away. She took a quick cursory glance at the scroll and then returned her gaze to the council.

"I have much to think over, so forgive my distraction," she said. "I bid you all goodnight." She then motioned to Caoimhín before murmuring, "Send a message to Bertius for me. I need his council."

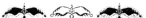

Upon sensing a strange ripening smell gracing the wind, Marcus inhaled and closed his eyes. Intuition informed him that a Deargh Du neared. Perhaps it was passing from one part of Ulster to another. He knew this scent from before, but it had never come to him so strong and demanding.

Besides, where was Berti? This Deargh Du should just be a reply from the council. Would it be yet another rebuff? An official 'thank you, now please leave our island because you are nothing more than bastardization to our perfection'? Almost in answer, Berti's scent soon entwined with the Deargh Du's. Even so, Marcus still had to protect himself, just in case, so he drew his gladii and cloaked himself in darkness. After all, this could be a trap.

The footfalls paused as they stopped behind the safe-house.

"Something from the shadows draws near," Marcus murmured in reverence before allowing his voice to grow aggressive. "Berti, who is that

Deargh Du with you?"

"Marcus?" The doors opened, and he could sense Berti staring into the shadows trying to find his way. "Where are you? I hate it when you do this!"

Marcus peered through the edge of the darkness so he could see the Deargh Du. Her graceful movements and luminescent radiance caught his eye as she moved her gaze to stare directly at him. The winds played with her hair as she pulled it back with an impatient hand. The female Deargh Du continued to look into the void, revealing no fear, but a hint of a smile played at her lips.

"Marcus Galerius Primus Helvetticus," she called out, saying his full name. "I am Sáerlaith Ní Adhamdh, chief of the council of the Deargh Du. I have not come to harm you. Rather, I have come to congratulate you."

Marcus watched her for a moment before releasing the darkness.

Berti smirked as he said, "Thank you. I will take my leave now. I am sure Sitara is hungry again."

Sáerlaith nodded before turning her gentle smile to Berti. "Thank you," she said while bowing her head toward the mortal. After Berti left, her luminous, brown eyes regarded Marcus. A few of her silver hairs sparkled in the firelight.

"I apologize for my deception," Marcus stated. "You are the first Deargh Du I have encountered, and I wished to know your intentions before I revealed myself." He would have said more, but he heard owls hooting outside, which caused a bit of a fright, as he still halfway expected some sort of trap.

"It seems as though you have mastered one of Morrigan's many gifts to Her chosen children," Sáerlaith replied. "I can call on mists, but I did that as a mortal druid. I feel my skills lie within the creation of illumination, not darkness, which taxes me."

Marcus chuckled. "Obviously, I do not draw it down well enough to hide from you."

"In time, you will have the mastery of many skills we share. May we sit and talk? I am weary from flying."

Marcus motioned towards one of the wooden chairs near the hearth. "I will tell you now that I do not feel as though I am Deargh Du, Sáerlaith. I feel a connection with Morrigan, but not with the others of our kind."

Her eyes stayed on him. Her gaze made him feel like glancing away as the connection became too much and too painful. "I have spent many years in Ulster, yet I have never met another Deargh Du. To what do I owe this pleasure?" He delivered the last sentence in a sarcastic hiss. Despite feeling an anger exude from his entire being, he bowed.

"I can tell by your tone that you are not pleased to see me." Her words were accented with a soft lilt and wane.

"I might have been pleased three hundred years ago to meet another of our kind, but tonight, I feel no satisfaction in meeting a fellow Deargh Du," he answered, lacing his words with venom. "Why have I been alienated and isolated?"

Sáerlaith's stare moved to the hearth. "We Deargh Du are a proud group, and we are alienating, as well as alienated, from the other lines. All Deargh Du are from Éire except for you." Her eyes returned to his and challenged him for a moment.

He soon pulled his anger away like the dark cloak. "You do not feel that way," Marcus ascertained.

"You are correct."

"And you have not tried to meet me face to face?" he replied.

"I do not rule the council of the Deargh Du with an iron fist, Marcus. I rule to sway the plurality. They have deemed you an outcast, and the punishment for talking to you was too great to risk until now," she answered.

"What is the punishment?"

Sáerlaith revealed her fangs in a harsh smile. "Banishment to daylight, then I would be staked and chained with gold to the ground."

His anger drained away and met her eyes. "Then you risk a great deal to see me tonight."

Her smile grew soft again, like a gentle breeze. "Normally, yes. However, in recent nights we have gathered more intelligence, which leads me to believe that the Lamia will soon be invading in force. I am here because I need your help. All Deargh Du need your help."

"My help?" He could hear the disbelief in his words.

"Yes." Sáerlaith's eyes grew black. "Unfortunately, most Deargh Du cannot see the truth, the truth of the invasion, the truth of how strong you are. Berti has told me of your exploits in following Mandubratius and searching for the Phallus Maximus. You, your companions, and I know that the Lamia are a strong presence here and that they have an invasion force arriving." Her words grew fevered. "We do not have much time, Marcus."

He closed his eyes, remembering Morrigan's face and Her charge to him. "I respect you for this and for asking my assistance. I look forward to proving my worth. What do you wish for me to do?"

chapter nine

Ard Mhacha

Marcus followed Claudius and Mac Alpin into the large meeting hall. He could smell nothing but the frankincense and myrrh they wore to mask their scents. They crept toward the center of the hall and then stood motionless, keeping their cloaks in place and their heads covered. Marcus attempted to peek at his surroundings, but the hood did not allow for him to examine much of the Deargh Du stronghold.

Marcus could hear the gathered Deargh Du murmur and mill about, and through the small gap in his cowl, he could see them sipping at silver chalices, their graceful steps and height distinguishing them from the mortals. Soon he could hear Sáerlaith chattering with someone as she walked to the front of the room. Her linen léine swished against the floor as she walked.

When Sáerlaith reached the council table, she hit a stone gavel against it, causing the fifty Deargh Du present to flinch in surprise. "I call this meeting of the Deargh Du to order. I will forgo with our veneration of Morrigan because of the dire news that sweeps our home." This statement drew murmurs of displeasure from the crowd. "The Lamia are in Connacht. I will now turn over the meeting to Caoimhín, who has returned from their headquarters."

The Deargh Du cleared his throat before speaking. "There are five hundred Lamia present in our homelands. They march like the Roman soldiers in their heyday. They are well armed and well trained, and they know our weaknesses. Some of their armor and weapons gleam of gold."

"This is ludicrous!" another Deargh Du shouted from across the room. "Why would the Lamia invade us? We have nothing they need."

"On the contrary," Caoimhín replied. "There is a fabled treasure of their gods called the 'Phallus Maximus'. The Lamia believe it is here and that they can use it to usher in an age of dominion over all other blood-drinkers."

"You believe this fool's tale?" a female Deargh Du scoffed.

Sáerlaith answered before Caoimhín could say another word. "Whether we believe that they could have power or not, all that matters is that they believe it has power and that they have searched for it for over six hundred years. They have scoured the known world, and now their forces are here. They know it is here."

The din of voices soon grew, until Sáerlaith roared, "Silence! This night, we must decide how to respond!"

"Let us send a peace envoy. If we find this object and give it to them, they will go away," suggested a voice.

"The Lamia are conquerors. They will only leave by brute force," Caoimhín challenged.

"We can give up Connacht and placate them," rejoined another.

"If we do that, we will be pushed out of Éire by our own cowardice," Sáerlaith answered. "I love my home. I do not want to become lost overseas!"

"Is there anything else we can do?" a voice queried.

"Yes, there is something we can do," Marcus shouted in answer from the concealment of his cowl. "We can defeat them!"

"Who are you to suggest such rash action? We have no army," another shouted back.

Marcus pulled back his hood and dropped his cloak, revealing his modified uniform and weaponry. Mac Alpin and Claudius followed his actions. "I am Marcus Galerius Primus Helvetticus, the only Roman brood of Morrigan, and I wish to raise an army of Deargh Du and our allies to defeat them."

Many Deargh Du backed away, hissing and hurling insults.

"Weapons are not allowed here! This is our sacred home, and it is not to be tarnished by bloodied swords!" a red-bearded Deargh Du shouted.

"Be gone, bastard of Morrigan!" another rallied.

Marcus heard Sáerlaith growl, demanding order. Caoimhín hit the bench repeatedly with the rock as chips of the wooden table flew.

Marcus decided to recapture everyone's attention, so he closed his eyes for a moment and flooded the entire room in darkness. Silence ensued. After a few seconds, Marcus released the billowing cloak, and then light returned. He soon noticed Sáerlaith staring at him for a moment with surprised, yet thankful, eyes.

"I have invited Marcus and our new friends from across the sea. This is Claudius Metrius of the Sugnwr Gwaed and Arwin Mac Alpin of the Ekimmu Cruitne. These three have been fighting the Lamia for centuries, and they will teach us how to win back our home."

The red-bearded Deargh Du glared at Sáerlaith and then turned his green eyes on Marcus. "We need no lessons from this low-born whelp and these cursed ones."

Marcus felt a fury grow within him, and so he brought down the darkness again before leaping over the gathered Deargh Du, somersaulting in mid-air and landing behind the intended target. He tapped on the arrogant Deargh Du's shoulder and released the darkness, just as the other Deargh Du spun around. Marcus greeted the arrogant Deargh Du by laying one of his gladii at the blood-drinker's throat. The Deargh Du stared at him with fearful, round eyes.

"There are practical aspects to our skills, which I hear are just used as mere entertainment now," Marcus stated softly while looking over the gathered Deargh Du. "You have strengths you have never used because the majority of you have not been in combat since you were mortals. Oh, you may have fought a few mortals that got in your way, but you have never fought a well-trained, well-armed army of blood-drinkers. My companions and I are willing to teach you how to utilize these strengths and how to exploit your enemies' weaknesses."

Marcus returned his gaze to the Deargh Du in front of them and then retracted his gladii before sheathing it. He then walked back towards the wildly grinning Mac Alpin and the serious Claudius. The gathered Deargh Du allowed him to pass without jeers.

"Snobs, all of them, excepting Sáerlaith and her assistant," muttered Mac Alpin. "They still believe themselves too good to dirty their hands with an honest night's battle."

Claudius guffawed. "Arwin, did you ever notice how good a Deargh Du's hearing is? It may be unwise to insult them when we are trying to enlist their participation. We should save the insults for later... during training."

After sharing an inconspicuous smile with his friends, Marcus turned back to face the gathered Deargh Du, only to noticed that one of them, a dark-haired woman, had walked up to him and met his gaze with contempt.

"I am Emer," said the dark-haired Deargh Du. "Prove your skills in battle. You call forth the darkness with great expertise. However, the Lamia will find a way around that trick. The council of five, four," she continued, while looking over her shoulder at three others, "wishes to witness your skill."

A male Deargh Du bellowed a challenge before shrugging out of his cape. Soon the room erupted in chanting... 'Niall! Niall! Niall!'

"This must be their champion," Mac Alpin said with a ready grin.

"Yes, but he looks like he is trying to do more than prove a point," Claudius stated in a loud whisper.

"His aggression may be to his disadvantage," Marcus reasoned aloud as he watched the Deargh Du raise his arms as if seeking more praise. After a few seconds, someone brought the champion a large claymore. The crowd then drew away from the challengers, allowing more space for the men to fight.

Niall began to swing around his mighty sword a bit, before assuming some sort of warrior's stance. He then taunted Marcus to fight.

Not wanting to waste any time, Marcus drew one of his gladii and rushed forward to meet the supposed champion. Marcus ducked around the clumsy, wild swing of the claymore and removed Niall's right arm at the elbow with a precise cut. Immediately, he heard the applauding and shouting Deargh Du stop mid-cheer, and the room plunged into silence.

Marcus could see Niall staring at the bloody stump where his arm used to be and then at his severed arm on the floor, which still clasped his sword.

"You need to learn to fight with both hands," Marcus stated before glancing at the speechless Deargh Du around him. "The Lamia have no concept of the honor of a champion." He then uncorked a pouch of vitae before handing it to the speechless champion, who quickly finished off the pouch.

Marcus looked on as Emer and a few other Deargh Du walked over to Niall and helped him out of the council chamber, but Emer soon returned to the room, joining Sáerlaith, the other councilors, Marcus, and his friends.

"It appears this barbaric display has proven Marcus' worth," Sáerlaith commented.

One of the Deargh Du Marcus presumed to be a councilor met his gaze and began to speak. "I am Finn of the council. Why will you teach us this? You have every reason to hate us for abandoning you."

"Because I have deserved most of your hatred," Marcus answered. "I came here as a general of Rome, along with a very mortal Mandubratius. We were in the midst of invading Britannia when we landed here by mistake. Ten of my men and I left to find provisions, and when we returned, the rest of my comrades were dead." He inhaled a sharp breath. "I lashed out in fury. My remaining men and I slew an entire village of innocent mortals who only wanted to protect themselves. We soon came across a grove and killed many of the druids there, but then a Deargh Du annihilated my men and transformed me. Perhaps Morrigan saw my transformation as a fitting punishment."

Marcus closed his eyes again, regaining his earlier calm. "You have forgotten so easily that you are the sons and daughters of the Lady of Battle and Blood. She weaves a beautiful magic, but she also destroys with one hand and creates with the other. That is why I must help to keep that balance."

Finn turned to regard Sáerlaith and nodded his head. He then looked at Marcus and said, "On behalf of the council, we accept your offer to raise and train an army to fight the Lamia." Addressing the crowd, he added, "We ask all who are not in the council to retire while we deliberate what we shall do."

Most of the Deargh Du walked with their soft grace past him, their faces devoid of their past arrogance, though a strange, palpable fear lingered.

"This place makes me uncomfortable," Mac Alpin murmured. "I need to go outside and see the stars."

"I as well," Claudius whispered. "Something lingers here that reminds me of the great contest with Cernunnos, and I don't quite feel prepared for that."

Marcus watched them follow the Deargh Du through the doors towards the exit, before taking one last look over the room in the Deargh Du sanctuary. He then noticed Sáerlaith walking over to join him.

"Thank you so very much," Sáerlaith praised, beaming at them. "This ended better than I thought it would."

"This was the easy part, Sáerlaith," Marcus stated. "The hard part will be overcoming the Celtic tendency to fight for oneself rather than for the unit."

"And that is how the Romans were able to deal death to the Gauls and Britons?" she queried.

"Yes," he replied. "We put the needs of Rome before ourselves, and that is what made us victorious every time."

"That will be the most formidable reason that you can teach us. We must all fight for Morrigan and our home."

Marcus nodded his head. "We shall fight for the balance. The balance will be maintained." He then watched as Sáerlaith raised a questioning brow at his words, causing him to wonder whether he had said too much.

"We must set up a training camp in Connacht. Do you know where we might be able to do this?" she asked, seeming to ignore his last sentence. "It will help me solidify our plans with the council.

Marcus smiled. "I know a chieftain named Maél Muire. She is also a novice ovate."

"Maél Muire Ní Conghal?" the Deargh Du known as Caoimhín chimed in as he joined them. "Excuse my interruption."

"One and the same," answered Marcus. "She is young, but wise. She would consider such a task her duty and an honor."

Sáerlaith turned to Caoimhín and asked, "And your thoughts on her?"

"She is faithful to the old path," Caoimhín stated. "We would not frighten her. I have met her twice. She is not a fool, and she knows Lamia and the dangers they present."

"She sounds to be the perfect choice to ask for help, then. I will approach the council with this news." Sáerlaith then turned away to rejoin the other four council members at the great stone table.

Béal Átha an Fheadha

Maél Muire woke up to the pealing of the alarm bells. She rushed out of her bedding in her léine and grabbed her cape and sword. She could not help but fear the worst. "Bearach, what is going on?" she asked as she followed the other servants and clansman to the center of the village to grab torches.

"The sentries have seen fifteen burly men on horseback. They clank," he added. "The sentries think these men may be attacking us under the cover of darkness, Chieftain."

Once the gates of the village opened, Maél Muire peered out into the night. She saw the riders, who seemed to be waiting, but they remained still and silent. Soon, they all dismounted, while holding his or her reins, save one.

Heather Poinsett Dunbar & Christopher Dunbar

She stared into the starlit darkness. "I cannot tell who they are, yet they appear to be waiting for us. Perhaps they are just looking for lodgings or supplies." She handed her torch to Druce and then turned to Bearach to say, "Let us go see what they need," while gesturing for her armsman to join her.

As she walked with Bearach towards the party through the thick grasses, the bleating of sheep grew louder. Maél Muire spied a few horses and cows staring in the direction of the strangers, but they soon returned to their nighttime grazing. She then stopped as the strangers regarded her. One of the gazes, which caught the moonlight, seemed familiar... diamond blue eyes.

Marcus?

She smiled and grew transfixed for a moment before shaking her stupefaction away, blaming her stare on her lack of sleep. "You have entered the domain of the Uí Máine. I am Maél Muire Ní Conghal, and I bid you welcome."

The strangers nodded, as though exhausted with their travels.

She walked over to Marcus and raised a brow. "Marcus, it has been so long." The same serene beauty that rested on the Deargh Du swarmed over him like a cloak. "It is good to see you again." She then rushed into his open arms and gave him a fleeting kiss on his right cheek. "And it is an honor to have one of Morrigan's representatives in my lands again."

She heard a soft chuckle from Marcus. "I see I can hide nothing from you," the Deargh Du teased as he smiled at her. "It is good to see you as well. I am traveling with friends tonight." He then gestured towards the party. "These are my associates, Claudius Metrius, Arwin Mac Alpin, I believe you have already met Caoimhín, and this is Berti, Sitara, and Edward."

Maél Muire bowed her head toward them in respect. "Berti?" she queried, before coming forward to embrace the trader. "Your amusing tales and horrible prices are missed here."

Berti grinned. "I had no idea that you were the Maél Muire Marcus spoke of, Banbh."

Maél Muire felt her face grow red. "Berti, I will hurt you if you ever call me 'Banbh' again." Through her peripheral vision, she could see Marcus smile.

"Before anything else is said, unless I am wrong, Sitara should be resting. Bearach, please show them to my quarters. Honestly, you men should be ashamed of yourselves, making her travel in her condition." She watched Berti and Sitara leave towards the dun, exhaustion apparent in their movements.

Sitara looked back at her for a moment and smiled.

Maél Muire nodded to the other woman. She prepared to ask about the status of the search for the treasure, when Marcus' hand slid around her arm.

"I apologize for cutting short these pleasantries, but we have urgent business to discuss with you," he said.

She turned back to Marcus. "Indeed? My home is yours. What do you need?" She then felt a moment of nervous indecision come over her, as the smiles and welcome had disappeared. Anxiety seemed apparent on Caoimhín's and the others' features as they regarded her.

"Marcus and our associates from Alba and Britannia have been charged by the council to prepare the Deargh Du for the incoming Lamia invasion," Caoimhín stated, before pulling the cowl of his cloak away from his face.

"We are here to ask a tremendous favor of you," one of the strangers stated.

"I…"she muttered, before looking at Marcus. "Congratulations. Do you need supplies, gold, silver, or something else?"

"We need a place in Connacht to train," Marcus stated. "The Deargh Du are not equipped to handle this kind of combat."

"I last spied on the Lamia near Ráth Cruachan," Caoimhín added. "They have since left the village to keep their whereabouts secret. They are expecting us to immediately fold and leave for the continent or Britannia."

Maél Muire paused before saying anything. An uncomfortable silence descended. "I know of the Deargh Du's fondness for life, and because of that, I know my people will not be in danger due to blood-thirst. However, I am concerned about causing panic, since there will be so many Deargh Du that must be fed. I can ask for donations of blood, but it may be traumatic for the Christians here. They will have nightmarish fears of demons killing them."

"You do not need to worry about that, Chieftain," Marcus answered. "Most Deargh Du have preferred hosts. There will be enough mortals living with the Deargh Du to keep us fed. You have my promise that there will be no panic."

Maél Muire sighed. "What about the Lamia, Marcus? I have met at least one, and they have no honor that would keep them from striking my clan."

"A group of sentries will protect them, and we will set up protection wards and spells. You, your aunt, and your uncle could help us with this," he replied.

She looked skyward for a moment and then noticed Bearach rejoining her. "This is my armsman, Bearach." She looked at Marcus again. "It is an honor to assist the Deargh Du and their friends. You all look exhausted. Please follow me to the dun. Bearach, would you go fetch my aunt and uncle?" The then led them towards the dun. The weariness in their steps seemed almost palpable. Once everyone was inside, she closed the door behind her guests. Servants and some clansmen and women soon gathered blankets, food, and bedding for her guests.

Now how do I get them to volunteer what my guests really need?

Maél Muire cleared her throat to get her everyone's attention. "Our guests are very special," she explained. "They are Deargh Du and friends of the Deargh Du." Silence exploded around her as everyone stared at her. "They need our help, and we in turn need theirs. They are here to protect us from another group of blood-drinkers who wish to take over Éire." The servants still looked at her as though she had grown another head. "The fact is, they need sustenance. It is not painful to volunteer blood if you wish to do so." She then turned to Marcus and lowered herself to her knees. "Do you need to feed from me?" she asked, before rolling up the left sleeve of her léine.

Marcus took her left hand and met her eyes with his now glowing, green eyes. "I thank you for this honor," he whispered as he pulled her closer to him and rotated her wrist. She then watched as his fangs entered her flesh.

Just before penetration, she lost all sense of herself. She felt a moment of pain, but then she experienced a flush of pleasure. Maél Muire could sense a smile tug at her lips as she lost track of everything except for the sensation that exuded from her arm. She soon felt him gently lower her hand before pulling her towards him in an embrace.

"Do I need healing?" she asked, inhaling that familiar smell of frankincense.

She heard a throaty laugh. "No, you appear to be in fine health," Marcus answered. "Thank you." He released her, and then she watched her servants feed the eleven others.

"It is my honor and duty to take care of those who come to me," she answered. "You know very well that I will offer hospitality to those who come to my home. Now, please introduce me to your blood-drinking friends once again," she requested. "I was so surprised to see you that… well, I must confess… I forgot who was who."

Maél Muire sipped on her cider as she watched her guests and servants happily drinking. Mac Alpin's servant, Edward, snored near the hearth, much to Mac Alpin's apparent chagrin.

"Then we left Ulster, charged with this task," Berti concluded as he finished his mead. Maél Muire poured him some more.

"That is a most exciting tale," she said, feeling her face turn up in a smile. Maél Muire waved in her aunt, uncle, and Bearach as they joined the celebration.

"Balancer of…" her aunt murmured as she began to kneel before Marcus.

Maél Muire watched him smile before motioning for them to sit.

"Our hostess saw to my needs and the needs of all," he said.

Maél Muire stood up and began to refill drinking vessels. She then sat down next to Claudius and Mac Alpin and refilled their drinks. She could not help but be interested in their kind. "I am… curious," she stated.

"About?" Claudius asked while raising a brow. A half smile made him look almost mortal. While he and Mac Alpin were not as pretty as the Deargh

Du, she could feel the thrumming power that they exuded.

"Hmmmm, I sense you want to know how a mortal becomes Ekimmu Cruitne and Sugnwr Gwaed," Mac Alpin reasoned aloud.

"How did you…" she started to ask.

"Every line of blood-drinkers has its gifts," Claudius told her. She felt as though each of his words glimmered in a soft, warm honey.

"Stop playing the Gan-Ceann, Claudius," Mac Alpin said with a smirk.

"It was just a demonstration of my talents. I do not let my words tempt women to desolate pastures," Claudius replied with a touch of pique in his voice. "My kind is created to join in the wild hunt at the behest of Cernunnos, the Lord of Hosts. Cernunnos selects mortals He finds interesting. We participate in a contest with other mortals to see who is most worthy of His honors." She then watched Claudius glance over at Mac Alpin. "Most Deargh Du refer to Ekimmu Cruitne as 'the cursed ones'."

Mac Alpin guffawed. "Claudius is being polite, Maél Muire. We are Morrigan's bastards! Our creation came about when two lines fed a nearly dead mortal both their blood. Morrigan found us to be an abomination, so She turned Her back on us."

Maél Muire felt her face redden a bit.

"Do not look embarrassed, Chieftain. I rather like being who and what I am. I would be miserable as a Deargh Du, for they are too perfect for my liking." Mac Alpin smirked as he tipped his drink against hers. "Let's all drink to being who and what we were meant to be."

She raised her glass and began to drink down her cider as the two others finished their mead.

Marcus ducked into a small room on the other side of the hearth and sat down to clean and oil his weapons and his leather. Soon, however, the scent of another mortal drifted in from the east. He heard the servants start to mill at the arrival, and so he leaned forward to see Basala shake Maél Muire out of sleep.

The chieftain grumbled and then came to her feet before splashing water onto her face from the bowl the servant held. Maél Muire then shook out her unruly hair as curls slid from her plaits, before dusting off her léine and standing at attention.

Marcus returned his attention back to his armor, hoping the interruption would not be too loud, since the gathered blood-drinkers still slept amidst the covered windows.

"Maél Muire," a man's voice echoed in the dun over the snores. Marcus looked back as a mortal walked carefully through the sleeping bodies.

"Connor?" Maél Muire's voice revealed surprise and still sounded of sleep and mead. Everyone had consumed too much last night... even his thoughts still swam in that dark ale.

The stranger's face belied hurt feelings. "You had a celebration last night, and I was not invited? Who are these people? Most are not even your clansmen."

Marcus could hear the jealousy in Connor's words.

"These are friends of mine," Maél Muire replied. "This was not a planned event. Had I been prepared, believe me, you would have been invited."

Marcus soon noticed a naked, disheveled Mac Alpin walking on the ceiling of the dun toward the mortals.

"Edwina!" Mac Alpin shouted as he came up to the stranger. "Why are you upside down? I am out of mead," he drawled with a wide grin on his face, before presenting his cup to Maél Muire's guest. Mac Alpin then closed his eyes and fell to the floor in front of the two mortals.

Marcus saw that Maél Muire's face broke into a smile, and then her eyes met Connor's.

"Deargh Du?" he whispered.

"I am sorry, but he did that last night too," Maél Muire murmured in reply as she patted his arm.

"W-what?" Connor stammered.

"Last night, he seemed to believe I was his mortal sister, Lia," Maél Muire stated.

"But he was standing on the ceiling and fell... how did he?"

Marcus could see the mortal wipe at his sweaty face.

"Well, he passed out and lost his concentration," stated Maél Muire.

"I mean, what and who is he?"

Maél Muire studied the snoring Mac Alpin for a moment. "You know of the Deargh Du?" she asked.

"Yes, I know of them. Is he one of them?"

Marcus could hear impatience in Connor's voice.

"No," she replied. "He is like them, a relation to them almost."

"Like the Lamia?"

Marcus stood up after hearing the question.

Maél Muire's voice grew quiet. "How do you know of the Lamia?" she queried.

"My mother taught me of the other blood-drinkers," Connor answered. "I still do not understand why he is here."

The visitor grew less jealous, but managed still to look worried. Marcus joined them, hoping to smooth things over.

"If you know of the Deargh Du, you would know that they like to visit mortals, and they always love a party," Maél Muire replied. Upon seeing Marcus, she smiled, although her blood-shot eyes now revealed that she still needed sleep.

"Good afternoon," Marcus greeted Maél Muire. "Chieftain, might I introduce myself to your guest?"

Maél Muire rubbed her temples. "Ah, I am a horrible host. Please do so, Marcus."

He then regarded the guest and said, "I am Marcus Galerius Primus Helvetticus. My full name is a mouthful, so I go by Marcus."

"I am Connor Mac Turrlough, Chieftain of Mhuine Chonalláin, the village to the west. You are Roman?" Connor queried, as he seemed to study Marcus.

"My family is Roman, but I have lived in Éire most of my life," Marcus replied. "I met Maél Muire a few years ago."

"I am so sorry. Would you two care for a drink or food or...?" Maél Muire inquired while eying at Marcus. Her eyes glimmered for a moment.

"I would like to speak to you regarding a private matter," Mac Turrlough said to Maél Muire, and with glance to Marcus, he added, "It was nice to meet you, Marcus."

Marcus smirked, understanding that he had been dismissed.

"The dun is full of sleeping people. We can go outside, if you do not mind," Maél Muire suggested. She then took the other chieftain's arm and lead him to the door. As they walked, she looked over at Marcus with an apologetic smile.

Marcus gave her a slight wave as the door opened and the mortals left the building. He could eavesdrop, but decided to return to his weaponry. Maél Muire could take care of herself. However, he would keep an eye on the chieftain until the Deargh Du arrived. Something about Mac Turrlough seemed suspect. Perhaps it was his knowledge of the Lamia. Maél Muire appeared to be suspicious about that as well.

Maél Muire wandered out into the afternoon sun, shading her eyes. She considered that the purpose of Connor's visit was to ascertain whether his gifts had yielded their desired effect, but more important thoughts dominated here mine. She therefore decided to try playing coy with him. "I can smell the lavender growing," she said, desiring to appear a little absent-minded. "I love the smell of lavender, because it always calms me. I prattle sometimes, my apologies, Mac Turrlough. What did you want to speak about?"

His blue eyes met hers and held them for a moment. "What would you find to be good traits in a husband?" he asked.

"A good heart, a sense of humor, a will to protect those who need it," she said before shrugging, not really knowing what characteristics would make her heart beat faster. She tried to think of Seanán, but she could not find words.

"So, what kind of traits do you see in me that may be what you would search for in a husband?" he asked.

Maél Muire chuckled a little, feeling nervous at his direct question. She then noticed him lower his eyes like a pitiful young man. It made her feel wretched. "My apologies," she said as she patted his shoulder. "I was not aware of the seriousness of your question. I find that you have several pleasing qualities. You care for others, you have a good eye for selecting livestock, and you are gentle." She tried not to blush at her response.

Livestock? Gentle? I must look like an awful fool.

"Well then, why have you not responded to my messages?" Connor inquired. "I was worried and concerned. I thought we had drifted apart and that our relationship needed mending." He then slid his hand around hers.

"Our relationship has not changed," she answered. "I just have been busy with my duties, and my guests are a handful, as you can see."

"I noticed that." She saw a small smile light up his features. "I would like to be invited to your clan's festivities. I have been told that I appear to be happy whenever you are near. You seem to find some pleasure when I am close to you as well."

She gave him an uneasy smile and said, "I am flattered," since she could not afford to make her neighbors angry.

"Do you feel anything when I am near?" he asked.

"Of course," she lied. She then looked up, pretending to hear something. "I think I am needed inside. Do you want something to drink?"

"Yes I do," he replied, before following her back inside.

Marcus noticed Maél Muire trying to keep several people between herself and her jealous suitor. While speaking to Caoimhín, she glanced over at Marcus. As she strolled closer, Marcus observed that her hair appeared to be free of its messy plaits and gleamed like dark fire. She also now wore a pale-blue léine.

"I heard the others will arrive before dawn's break," she said to him, after motioning for Marcus to follow her outside.

"You are avoiding someone. I do not need the Ekimmu Cruitne's mind reading capabilities to notice that," he stated.

"Yes, but he practically proposed to me," Maél Muire muttered. "I am not sure whether I should accept. I do not have any feelings for him."

He stretched for a moment before saying, "It would be strategic to your situation. You would have your neighbor in your bed. Think about it."

"Yes, but he…" she muttered under her breath. "I do not want to have to marry him," she answered. "Stop thinking like a Roman, Marcus. Everything is not black and white." As she spoke, it seemed as if something about his expression made her cease her argument. "Oh, I am sorry," she apologized before chuckling a bit. Maél Muire then extended her arms to him. "Have you fed yet?"

He looked into her eyes, seeing the wish for a moment of forget and release. "No, I have not." He then rolled up her sleeve and turned over her arm. He felt her body go slack for a moment after the initial pierce. Soon a small smile soon played at her lips. After he finished feeding, Marcus kissed the wound and pulled away. "Thank you, Maél Muire."

Her eyes met his, gleaming with pleasure. "I should go back to my hosting duties, now."

"I think I will go check on the arriving troops," he said with a laugh. "Troops? What am I thinking?"

As he headed away from the dun, Marcus heard the door to the dun open, and then he saw Mac Turrlough walk toward the barn, jump onto his horse, and gallop away. The promise of finding a connection to the Lamia proved to be too enticing, and so Marcus flew behind the horse as it galloped to the west.

Mhuine Chonalláin

Marcus edged around the back of the thatched house Mac Turrlough approached, attempting to ignore the stink coming from a bubbling cauldron within. As he crept around the outside of the house, it seemed to sink inward. The sight of frightening vegetation twisted around dead trees and the stench of rot from the surrounding grove almost made him ill. Despite his trespassing, the grove, along with the birds that watched him with foreboding warnings in their vacant eyes, remained silent. He then noticed a large spider crawl into view.

Soon he heard the chieftain's horse trotted toward the back of the house and stop. Marcus could then discern the chieftain dismounting.

"Maél Muire is coming around," the chieftain said to someone… a person Marcus had not sensed due to the stench. "She may even start loving me."

"What, no kiss for us?" an old-sounding woman's voice answered, pique in her words.

"Sorry, mother." There was a pause, and Marcus assumed the ever-dutiful son gave his mother the respect she had requested. "Did you hear, mother? She is interested in me, and I think soon she will love me."

"Of course," he heard the old woman reply, though her words revealed sarcasm. "That is excellent news, my son, for it is as we foretold. We assume you had assistance in wooing her?"

Laughter echoed forth from the house, which seemed to startle the chieftain's horse, as it walked over to Marcus and gave him a nudge. Marcus sighed before scratching its right ear.

"You do not have any confidence in me to woo a woman all by myself?" Mac Turrlough asked, incredulity evident in his tone.

Marcus heard the dry laughter of the woman. The horse's eyes rolled back, revealing fear, and then the horse trotted away to the edge of the grove, where green grasses peeked through dead vegetation.

"Alright, alright, I had help, Seosaimhín. Help from the one you call the 'being of power'."

"Ah, the dark one, the Lamia. How goes his search for the treasure?"

"The treasure?" Mac Turrlough asked, sounding confused. "I think they know where it is, but they are waiting for something. Perhaps they wait for more help."

"Where do they think it is, our son?"

"Somewhere in Connacht," Mac Turrlough replied.

"Ah, of course! The soulless ones infest this part of Éire. I can see why they need help here," the woman answered.

"Especially at Béal Átha an Fheadha," commented the chieftain.

"Indeed? You have seen the soulless ones?"

"Yes, there were several there. One is Deargh Du, but he was from Rome. And there were others, Britons and the Albanach."

A pause grew, and then the elder asked her son, "Did you see their eyes?"

"Blue, like the color of lightning," the chieftain replied.

Marcus heard a quick intake of breath.

"The soulless ones have allies. Did you notice anything else about this one with the lightning-blue eyes?"

"Nothing, but he did walk on the ceiling as if he strolled on solid ground," answered Mac Turrlough.

"Could it be that the bastard offspring of the soulless ones have come to Éire?" There was more raspy laughter. "We must meet these soulless… bastards."

"What do you want me to do, mother?"

"Find out more about this army the Lamia send, and tell the 'being of power' that we wish to see him again."

Being of power?

"I will seek knowledge of the Lamia, and I will ask Mandubratius to meet with you," Mac Turrlough answered.

"Be off then, and walk with Nagirrom," the crone answered.

Marcus heard the chieftain walk away in search of his mount. A moment later, he sensed the mortal depart on horseback. Marcus then closed his eyes, preparing to leave for Béal Átha an Fheadha, when a voice from inside the house interrupted his thoughts.

"You may come in. I know you are out there, soulless one. Come visit us. We are just simple Seosaimhín," Marcus heard the woman say, but then he felt an insistent tap on his shoulder. He whirled about to find himself staring down at the old woman. He attempted to keep from looking surprised.

A white crow clutched at her shoulder and cawed at Marcus, as if finding him to be an irritation.

Marcus then returned his gaze to Seosaimhín. "Who are you?" he asked, while trying to escape the crone's stare, which threatened to swallow him whole.

"We are the mist that covers the fog in the predawn of the morn," the woman answered with an expansive smile.

"What are your intentions, Seosaimhín?" he asked.

"Oh, soulless one, the mist always seeks to obscure and permeate whatever crosses its path."

A great unease continued to settle within him, and an unnamed trepidation gripped him. Marcus could find nothing else to say, while the druid continued to assess him with her eyes.

The white crow soon took flight before landing on the roof.

"So, this soulless one who stands before us is Roman. All the others are of Éire, yet not you." Seosaimhín grew silent and almost awestruck for a moment. "You, who are a most beautiful moonlit dream, the bastards of the soulless ones, and those who run with the beasts are the only ones not of Éire. However, you are not a bastard of the soulless ones, and you are not one who runs with the beasts."

At first, Marcus wondered what she meant by 'soulless one', 'bastards of the soulless ones', and 'those who run with the beasts', but soon he realized she referred to the Deargh Du, the Ekimmu Cruitne, and the Sugnwr Gwaed. In truth, her entire manner and speech seemed quite mad.

Seosaimhín guffawed while shaking her head. "Very curious indeed, Soulless One of Rome. Are you in league with the dark one that you call 'Mandubratius'?"

Anger overwhelmed his earlier discomfort. "I mean to destroy the one called 'Mandubratius'."

"As he wishes to destroy you," the crone said, and then a strange smile spread over her face. "Now our eyes can see you clearer. You are not a full Roman. You are a Gaul, are you not? The mist seeps into your eyes and finds

Heather Poinsett Dunbar & Christopher Dunbar

your true heritage."

"Yes," he replied, "my mother was a Gaul." He wondered why he bothered talking to this woman.

Seosaimhín laughed again. "By blood, you should have been one of the dark ones and Mandubratius should have been one of the soulless bastards, perhaps even just a soulless one. Often, we see him alone, staring inwardly out of desire to be something he is not."

"Seosaimhín, why do you tell me these mist-filled half-truths?"

"The mists seep everywhere and see all. Until now, the mists have not seen the soulless one of Rome. Bide our words, Deargh Du. One night, Mandubratius and you shall meet again, and the mist will be there."

Marcus watched the druid began to fade away into the heart of the darkness that permeated the dead grove.

"One more thing," the mad crone added before becoming completely enshroud. "The unborn druidess grows more within your hostess."

Maél Muire is pregnant?

Soon, Marcus could see no trace of her... only darkness remained. He then backed away and extended his senses, trying to find her, but the scent of decay had faded, and so he took to the air, never wanting to inhale such filth again.

chapter ten

Béal Átha an Fheadha

Upon returning to the dun, Marcus heard the angelic sounds of a harp, interrupted by the deep grumbles of a bronze horn. He looked around and saw Maél Muire sitting in her chair, while the gathered mortals played games and ate. Marcus walked over to her, placed his right hand on her shoulder, and whispered in her ear, "We must speak."

Maél Muire did not immediately look up at Marcus, as she seemed entranced with the performance. "Berti should be a bard," Maél Muire informed him in a far-away voice. "He is full of good stories." She then turned her head to regard Marcus and seemed to notice the frown he wore. "What is it?" she asked in a more focused tone.

He leaned closer to her and whispered in her ear, "Your friend, Mac Turrlough, conspires with the Lamia, Maél Muire. I followed him to his mother's home, and he spoke of them. He even mentioned Mandubratius."

Marcus heard Maél Muire inhale audibly, prompting him to pull away. As he drew back, he noticed her moss-green eyes grow wide. "I tried to follow him," he explained, "but his mother found me. She is... strange."

"I know. She was normal as any druid, once," Maél Muire replied. "She taught my aunt a great deal. However, her husband was the victim of a Dearg Du in transformation, and Seosaimhín never recovered."

"Yes, the first night," Marcus murmured, remembering his own experience. "I could not find Mac Turrlough after we spoke. I had hoped I could follow him to Mandubratius. However, Mac Turrlough disappeared into the mists. Strange... He seems to care for you, though. I would continue your relationship with him for now. Make no promises, but do not turn him away." Marcus contemplated how to explain the next bit of intelligence, but sometimes it was best to just spit it out. "Also, Seosaimhín believes you to be pregnant. Are you?"

Her skin turned pale, almost bloodless. "Could you get me a drink?"

"Of course," he answered, before getting up for some mead.

"I hope these warriors will understand the concept of 'fas est et ab hoste doceri'," Marcus heard Claudius murmur as they neared the mist-covered fields, which grew obscured with mist.

Mac Alpin grumbled. "More Latin-talk. You two do remember that I do not know Latin very well."

"'It is right to learn, even from the enemy'," Marcus translated, feeling the quote from Publius Ovidius Naso fit his training situation. Of course the question remained... could the warriors of Éire learn from a former enemy?

"I fear that sentiment will be hard for these warriors to accept," Arwin suggested. "On the other hand, it will be amusing to watch this."

Soon the mist parted, revealing Maél Muire holding an oak branch.

"Chieftain Maél Muire," Marcus greeted her.

"This is not as easy as it looks," she explained after closing the distance with the blood-drinkers. "Then again, your job seems much more complicated." Maél Muire seemed to accentuate her comment by nodding toward the gathering of Deargh Du that milled about in the field.

"Two hundred and fifty Deargh Du, plus we Britannic and Alban blood-drinkers," Claudius observed aloud as he rubbed his chin. "Mandubratius has nearly twice that."

"'In war, numbers alone confer no advantage'," Marcus added, hoping he exuded confidence. "Some eastern philosopher-warrior said that." After a few moments, he could see a figure he recognized in the distance. "It's Sáerlaith." Although she did not stand alone.

He then started walking towards the her and the other Deargh Du. He heard Maél Muire wish them luck as Marcus, Claudius, and Mac Alpin, with the other Britons in tow, walked towards the waiting Deargh Du warriors. These looked different from the Deargh Du of Ard Mhacha, appearing less like druids and more like the battle-hardened warriors he remembered seeing as a mortal first landing on Éire.

"Perhaps, you should do that dark clouded mist thing, you do," Claudius suggested.

"Aye, we can listen to them then," Mac Alpin stated.

As Marcus closed his eyes and called down the darkness, Claudius and Mac Alpin walked behind Marcus, and each blood-drinker placed a hand on one of Marcus' shoulders. The three seasoned warriors then crept in closer to the gathered forces. As they approached, Marcus could hear the banter amongst Sáerlaith and the other Deargh Du.

"Sáerlaith, where are these great warriors you promised?" one yelled.

"They will be here soon, Idwal," Sáerlaith replied. "I suggest you all sober up and think over what you must do to take care of the Lamia."

"I know what should be done," the one known as Idwal hissed. "Bring in someone who is truly interested in solving the problem. I can handle the training. I fought with Cu Chulainn and The Red Branch."

The gathered Deargh Du issued forth a derisive hiss.

"Idwal, you wish you were with the Red Branch!" a woman shouted in reply. "That was a bit before your time. Sáerlaith, where is this Roman Deargh Du we hear murmured about on Mananan Mac Lir's breeze? Where are these blood-drinkers from Britannia and Alba?"

"They will arrive soon," Marcus heard Sáerlaith reply. As he watched through the edge of the blackness surrounding him and his friends, he could see her staring at the gathering. "I know you all are suspicious," she continued. "Just remember, Morrigan whispers Her wishes to the council." However, her words appeared to be wasted.

"You doubt my skills, Ula?" Idwal shouted before giving Ula a push.

Ula laughed, before whirling about and twisting Idwal's arm around his back. "I doubt nothing about your lack of skills." The two Deargh Du separated and then began circling one another, growling.

Marcus heard Sáerlaith sigh as she backed away from the center of the clearing, while the others surrounded the challengers, waiting for the bragging to stop and the true fight to begin. Soon, a blinding display of fist fighting ignited between the combatants.

Now is the time.

Marcus extended the darkness to surround the other Deargh Du. He then, along with Claudius and Mac Alpin in tow, flew over the blinded Deargh Du and hit Idwal in the face, sending him sprawling backwards to the ground. Marcus then cleared the black mist, revealing himself and his two companions. He could see the other Deargh Du stand in shock, while he noticed Sáerlaith smile and shake her head.

"I am Marcus Galerius Primus Helvetticus!" Marcus yelled while crossing his arms over his chest and staring at the sputtering crowd of Deargh Du. "These are my associates, Claudius Metrius Sertorius of the Sugnwr Gwaed and Arwin Mac Alpin of the Ekimmu Cruitne."

The gathering erupted in general grumbles and few mutters of 'cursed ones', which he chose to ignore for the moment.

"Sáerlaith requested that I teach you all that you need to know in order to defeat the Lamia. I have some experience in the realm of Roman tactics. I arrived in Éire during the first invasion of Britannia, leading the seventh legion under Julius Caesar. I recently have been spying on the Lamia, pretending to be one of their own."

A Deargh Du near him scoffed, "If you were on your way to Britannia, how did you end up in Éire?"

Marcus strode over to the proud warrior who asked the question and stared down at him. "Our general had requested that I take the mortal whelp known as Mandubratius to his friends on the western coast of Britannia. That whelp now holds the leadership of the Lamia."

"You wish our trust to belong to someone such as this bastard of Morrigan?" another Deargh Du queried while staring at Sáerlaith. "Our battle methods are not questionable. They work." To Marcus, the Deargh Du added, "I will not fight in an army with this mistake."

"Alright then," Marcus replied. He could not help but smirk at the gathered warriors. "If you wish, you can go back to your homes and villages... that is if one of you can defeat me in single, unarmed combat." He observed several Deargh Du staring at him with murder in their eyes. Wishing to provoke them further, Marcus took a few steps closer to some of the more battle-hardened warriors... to one in particular who seemed ready to accept Marcus' challenge.

"Then toss aside your sword and this armor of yours," the warrior replied. While the warrior spoke, his eyes burned a bright green.

Marcus smiled at the warrior and then turned back to regard his friends. He began removing his weapons and handed them to Mac Alpin. He then walked to the edge of the circle, removed his armor, and placed it on the ground. After setting down his armor, Marcus turned around and met the Deargh Du's stare.

The Deargh Du warrior yelled a battle cry and then raced towards him.

Marcus stepped aside at the last moment, grabbed the blood-drinker's right arm, and elbowed him in the throat. He heard a soft inhalation from the impact. He then pulled up the Deargh Du, getting a good look at the pale, pretty features, and punched him with his right fist. Marcus watched the unconscious warrior land ten feet away. The stranger left behind five teeth, including a fang.

Three other Deargh Du warriors raced toward Marcus, snarling, and so he fell flat on his back with the sudden impact. He then kicked at the middle one, who collapsed into a ball, moaning. Next, Marcus shot out his arms in a rapid motion, and then the other two tripped and staggered back towards him as he leapt back to his feet.

Marcus stepped in front of the smaller one and pulled him off balance by kneeing him in the on the inner-side of the warrior's left knee and yanking down on his left shoulder, dislocating it. He then felt a fist from the other warrior connect with his chin.

Marcus looked up into the eyes of two others warriors, who joined the one remaining warrior, wielding knives that reflected the moonlight. He soon felt a strange pull within, and then without the concentration he usually needed, the darkness cascaded down around him and the warriors who surrounded him. He then flew up and over one of the knife-wielding combatants and managed to plunge the warrior's knife into her own stomach.

Marcus lost himself in the momentum of the battle as other Deargh Du warriors joined in the fray, enraged that a Roman had defeated their friends with trickery, Marcus reasoned. He attacked from the air, from chest-level, and from the ground, and never from the same place. He struck with fists, elbows, arms, and the warrior's own weapons, careful not to kill his opponents.

When he could sense no other challengers stood to face him, he sent the darkness away. The moonlight skies returned, revealing a dozen moaning warriors on the ground who clutched at their wounds. He then noticed Sáerlaith smirk. Marcus dusted off his hands and looked back into the sea of beautiful faces, those who did not challenge him. "So, does anyone else want to go home now?" he queried.

The Deargh Du stared back at him as if uncomfortable. No one came to the aid of the fallen warriors to offer them blood or healing.

"So, now you wish to stay," Marcus continued. "When I first started in the Roman legions, I was taught that a disorderly mob is no more an army than a heap of building materials is a house." Marcus walked away from the pile of moaning bodies towards his armor. As he donned his armor, Mac Alpin, Claudius, and the other Ekimmu Cruitne and Sugnwr Gwaed, who had waited at the fringe of the crowd of Deargh Du, pushed through the Deargh Du to gathered in front of him.

Marcus collected his weapons from Mac Alpin and then turned to regard the Deargh Du. "You do not need to like me. I am not here to be a friend to anyone. However, I am here to mold you into an effective fighting machine that can go against an army bred for conquest. I need ten volunteers. Those who wish to volunteer can walk to the front."

He looked around the field, hoping to see a hand raised, but instead the only movement he witnessed was Sive holding what appeared to be a branch of rowan. No Deargh Du moved forward. "So no one wishes to volunteer?" Marcus queried, feeling a hint of a smile curl his lips. "Well, what method of persuasion should I use to elicit ten volunteers? I suppose I could offer a dozen heads of cattle to each of you who walks forward."

Beautiful eyes stared away from his, studying the ground, the trees, the Ekimmu Cruitne, the Sugnwr Gwaed... anything to avoid meeting his gaze.

"Well?" Marcus chuckled. "Then perhaps twenty pieces of silver? Mead?"

The still and silent Deargh Du yielded no answers.

"I see a pattern," Marcus said, before pacing amongst the gathered Deargh Du. "Well then, if such material matters do not motivate you, I will select volunteers." He then started to his right, following the path of the sun. Any Deargh Du who managed to meet his stare, he selected, until he reached the eighth.

A low, feminine voice drawled, "I wish to volunteer."

He turned to stared into the fierce, blue eyes of a plaited, blonde warrioress. Marcus raised a brow. "You have an open invitation. What is keeping you?" He watched her motion to another, and together they raced to the smaller gathering. Marcus followed them. When he reached his friends, he announced, "Mac Alpin, you will handle the training of these ten, who are now in positions of leadership."

The Ekimmu Cruitne rubbed his hands in delight as they all left. "Do not worry, for your fates are already sealed," Mac Alpin stated. "You ten are bound to me now. I will make it as painful as possible." He then turned on his heel and yelled at the ten lucky Deargh Du to follow him.

Marcus faced the other Deargh Du and stated, "The rest of you will start by getting your bodies and minds prepared to fight." He then called for Claudius over his shoulder.

His former lieutenant in the tenth legion ran over to him and said, "Yes gener… Marcus." Marcus saw Claudius catch himself in the motions of a salute, before lowering his right arm.

Marcus closed the distance with Claudius, and then in a hushed voice, he said, "Besides your usual duty in my personal guard, I have another task, one that I know is beneath you, but I need to ask it of you regardless. We are in need of someone to assist me in getting these warriors to learn how to stand in straight lines."

"The honor is to serve," Claudius replied.

Marcus felt the cool, early morning breeze blow through the night sky, as the horizon began to brighten to the east. The calls of birds echoed through the whispering trees as he, the rest of the warriors, and the others who accompanied them walked back towards the dun.

A few minutes before, Marcus had dismissed the Deargh Du soldiers, instructing them to dig holes in the ground to serve as their shelter from the sun. Now, their grumbled complaints rivaled the sounds of the waking day.

He followed Claudius, Mac Alpin, and the druids on the path leading towards the dun. Marcus then noticed Maél Muire stray from the group, walking at a slower pace, with her head down as if lost in thought. Just as the others disappeared into the shadows that still remained, Marcus edged back towards her, matched her pace, and gazed into her now upturned eyes. It seemed her eyes reflected a growing astonishment. Perhaps the large gathering of Deargh Du and druids had been too much for her to take.

He broke eye contact with Maél Muire and then stared ahead of them, thinking about how to prepare for the next evening's work, when she interrupted his thoughts.

"I have never seen this side of you," she said in a soft whisper. "Marcus, how could you be so brutal? Your actions were vicious, even for a Gael, and I have seen many bloodthirsty Gaels."

"As a general under the command of Julius Caesar, I had not the patience or tolerance for insubordination, or the outright defiance that these Deargh Du display, and–"

"You were a general?" He could barely hear her queried interruption.

He stopped walking and noticed that she had stopped next to him. "I have never lost a battle using these tactics, Maél Muire. My men were part of a unit, and we fought for the cause of Rome. We were all unified in our struggle." He paused for a moment. "I am just doing what I feel needs to be done to save Éire. I do not wish to offend you, but the methods I use yield winning results." Marcus chuckled softly. "Besides, their limbs will grow back."

As he started walking again, she paced in step with him, her shorter legs having to take two steps to make one of his.

"How are Berti, Sitara, and Edward?" he asked.

"They are all doing well," Maél Muire answered, though her tone seemed dismissive, as if she desired to speak on a more pressing topic. "We are going to see my aunt and uncle tomorrow so they can check on Sitara's progress. My knowledge in such things is limited."

A pregnant pause grew between them, but soon she asked, "So, how did you become Deargh Du? Why did Morrigan choose a Roman general? Before you, She only blessed the people of Éire with Her gifts."

Marcus sighed while trying to think of an appropriate half-truth. "Maél Muire, I do not know why the Goddess allowed it," he began to explain. "They left me to my own devices, abandoning me to the mortal world."

"So, did the Deargh Du encounter you within Rome, or were you in Éire? When did your transformation take place?"

"I was in Éire," he answered, hoping she would end the interrogation soon.

"When?" she asked. "Where in Éire?" Maél Muire's questions grew more demanding.

"Near Loch Garman," Marcus answered, "nearly six hundred years ago."

He heard Maél Muire stop in her tracks. He then turned around to regard her and saw pain etched across her face.

She drew her sword from its sheath and stared at him while moving into a defensive posture. "You were the Roman general who led the invasion there? You ordered the slaughter of the villagers and the druids in that grove?" Tears welled up in her green eyes.

Marcus said nothing, and yet he knew is posture exuded the guilt he felt.

"And you participated? There are still stories told of your cruelty." He heard her voice grow wrought with emotion. "They spoke of a Roman soldier in red and gold whose swords raged like lightning strikes, a man possessed by the elements and driven with bloodlust."

Marcus opened his mouth to speak, but she continued. "They invented words in our ancient tongue to describe you." She finally grew silent, awaiting his answer. Her eyes now swam with angry and fearful tears as her palpable emotions intensified.

"Yes, that was me," he confirmed, "when I was mortal. I had my reasons for being that way, Maél Muire."

She uttered a soft cry. "I will not hear another word from you. I–"

"Please hear my story before you judge me," Marcus pleaded. "Caesar made a deal with Mandubratius. We pledged our assistance in helping him regain his lands in Britannia. We invaded Britannia, yet there was a stalemate, and Mandubratius led one of our ships to what we all believed to be the western coast of Britannia. Instead, we found ourselves in Éire, and while ten of us went scouting for Mandubratius' comrades, the local chieftains and their warriors killed my men. The soldiers were scattered over the beach, their bodies desecrated."

Marcus stopped speaking to let her brain digest the information. He then continued, "The Britons were nowhere to be found. The one survivor of my men told me, before he died from his wounds, that Mandubratius' friends had spurned us and joined with the Gaels. We then turned our fury on Mandubratius." He decided to leave out the details of the punishment. "Then, we went to find the killers, burning the forest as we marched, killing whatever dared cross our paths. It was about justice, Maél Muire, justice for my dead men. Don't you desire justice?"

"But you still have not told me how you became Deargh Du!" Maél Muire raged. "The bards say Morrigan Herself came down to slay the invaders! Why did She choose you? How could a murderer such as you be accepted by Her? I cannot believe this!" Maél Muire then pointed her sword at him. "If you did not have the blessing of the Council, I would insist you leave immediately. However, because you do, I will only insist that you not present yourself in my dun. Bearach will bring your things to your dark hole," she hissed.

Marcus watched Maél Muire storm off with her jaw and fists clenched in utter fury.

Ráth Cruachan

Connor presented himself to the Lamia forces outside the dun. His nighttime race to the center of Connacht had not allowed for much time to think through his current predicament.

The guards took him to the pacing Mandubratius. Teá followed Mandubratius, venerating him with her luminous eyes.

Connor waited to speak, fearful of angering the vicious blood-drinker.

"Mac Turrlough, what is it now?"

When the Lamia fixed a stare on him, Connor heaved a heavy breath, trying to avoid Mandubratius' green eyes. He tried to think of a way to say that the Deargh Du were in Béal Átha an Fheadha.

"Your silence grows wearisome," Mandubratius spat in an impatient manner laced with threatening overtones.

"Other blood-drinkers have come to Béal Átha an Fheadha!" Mac Turrlough stated. "Maél Muire entertained several last night."

"Indeed?" Mandubratius inquired with a smirk.

"Yes," Connor answered. "Most were from Éire, but several were from Alba and Britannia. One was even from Rome."

Mandubratius said nothing, but he stopped pacing. He then stared at the chieftain's chair.

"I see," Mandubratius murmured, apparently lost in thought for a mere flicker of a second. "I would have thought the Sugnwr Gwaed and the Ekimmu Cruitne too busy with the Ouphe to bother coming to Éire." Mandubratius then whirled about and sat in the chieftain's chair. "Very well. We shall send a team of Lamia scouts out at dusk tomorrow. In the meantime, you will return to Béal Átha an Fheadha with two of our mortal scouts in the morning, Mac Turrlough." After a brief pause, a beaming smile lit his face and his features grew soft. "Is my investment working?" he asked.

It took Connor a few moments to realize to what Mandubratius referred. "Yes, she is pleased with the gifts," Connor said, not wanting to tell the truth. He hoped the Lamia would not bend his mind, as he had done to Seanán.

"Excellent," Mandubratius stated, though his appearance grew hard and cold like a dagger again. "I will have other gifts for her when you leave tomorrow."

Connor nodded his head. "She will like that," he answered, deciding it was better that Mandubratius did not know the truth.

Béal Átha an Fheadha

Sitara watched their host slap the reins of the cart against the horse's rump with a determined frown as she, Maél Muire, and Berti rode to Maél Muire's aunt and uncle so they could check on Sitara's progress. The chieftain's bad mood seemed to continue unabated. Perhaps the nights and days of sleeplessness had caught up with her.

Berti, on the other hand, beamed with a contented smile at the pastures of land that offered the first harvest. A celebration called 'Lughnasa' would come soon, he had said earlier, and Sitara welcomed experiencing the event with her new husband. She felt happier than she had ever felt before. Of course Maél Muire didn't seem so happy. She tapped Berti on the arm and gestured to their host.

Berti nodded and then turned his smile on their traveling companion and asked, "What are you so upset about, Maél Muire?"

"I am not upset," Maél Muire grumbled. "What do you know of Marcus' earlier days before he was Deargh Du?"

"You know, it is funny... I know he was a general under Julius Caesar, yet beyond that, we have not talked about it." His smile faded for a moment. "It seems like he was a hard man, but he has mellowed like a fine mead," Berti added.

"He never told you about how he was made Deargh Du? Nothing about who had transformed him? Not even about why?" Maél Muire's frown made her appear older.

"No," Berti replied before holding Sitara's hands. "He did not tell me."

"Are you protecting him?" Maél Muire hissed in accusation.

"I do not think Marcus needs my protection," Berti chuckled at her question, either oblivious to her undertones or above them.

"Berti, I am being serious. How do you know he has not committed atrocities as a Roman general? You do realize he may have killed your ancestors? After all, he fought against the Britons."

Berti patted Sitara's hand. "If the Goddess has forgiven him and granted him the gift of being Deargh Du, then perhaps he has earned our pardon."

Maél Muire grew silent, as if studying his words.

"Besides," Berti continued, "in all the miles I have spent traveling with him, I would not have wanted anyone else at my back."

Sitara noticed the chieftain's green eyes study hers. She decided to voice her thoughts. "He is the most generous man I have ever met, next to my child's father," Sitara stated. "If he was cruel in his past life, something changed him that pleased Morrigan. He is no longer that man."

"I still do not know how to feel," Maél Muire admitted. "My emotions are conflicting with my thoughts. After all, I have experienced his kindness." She sighed before continuing. "He pulled me out of my burning home a few years ago."

"Is this when your father passed?" Berti asked.

"Yes, that is when he was murdered." The chieftain's small smile passed into a frown again.

"Murdered by whom?" Sitara asked.

"We do not know to this day who did it," Maél Muire answered.

Sitara leaned against Berti's shoulder. "Are we almost there?" she asked softly. "I am not feeling very well."

"We will be there in a few minutes. There is the grove," Maél Muire stated as she motioned to a stand of trees within their view.

"Dismissed," Marcus called to the gathered warriors. He then judged the moon's placement in the sky and determined that he had about an hour to return to the grove to sleep under the sheltering arms of the oaks.

"Where are you going?" Mac Alpin asked, while meeting his stare.

"To the grove. Death by burning is not something I really want to experience," Marcus answered.

"Arwin, stop being rude," Claudius added, before grinning at Marcus. "We all know Marcus is not allowed in the dun. Gods, you did not grope Maél Muire, did you? If you did grope her and managed to escape her rage, then you should consider yourself lucky. She is in a most foul of moods."

"Indeed. Whenever you are brought up, she mutters and leaves," Mac Alpin added. "What did you do?"

"I did… something long ago," Marcus replied. "It cannot be undone."

"She will forgive you eventually," commented Mac Alpin. "They are bringing forth the new batch of ale for Lughnasa before sunrise. I suppose we can bring some out to the grove, if you are still awake."

"I will be waiting," Marcus replied, hoping they would not forget.

Sáerlaith closed her eyes as the sponnc filtered through the misting rain. The very same soft and meager drops had been whispering to the Deargh Du warriors for the past week. Sáerlaith inhaled and exhaled, rocking back and forth, waiting for the smoke to take effect.

"Show me," she whispered. "Tell me where to find him. For seven nights I have pleaded for insight. Show me."

A dark tunnel shrouded by the mist opened in front of her. She took careful steps towards it, knowing that a misstep could lead to an unexpected turn of events. The denizens of the Otherworld enjoyed visitors, but sometimes their presence grew addictive, like the taste of sweet mead sparkling on one's tongue.

Sáerlaith witnessed a figure watching her. A shadow obscured the being. It motioned her with an elegant finger.

She wondered whether it would ask for more than she could offer. It pointed to a window, and Sáerlaith leaned into it, waiting. She exhaled again, before inhaling, still feeling a tingle from the sponnc.

Trees blew in the gentle breezes, and beings as bright and as radiant as pearls formed shapes, melding and then distancing themselves. She almost forgot her purpose in entreating their aid.

"Ruarí?" she whispered. Had he joined in the eternal games and joyful battles here?

The trees branches dipped, entwining and growing together.

A vision formed amidst the wood and leaves.

She studied the pictures forming in the swinging arms of the oaks, willing herself to remember the landscape and the caves.

"Western jewel, home of your mother," voices chanted. Beings entreated her to join them, as the skies of the Otherworld grew dark. She backed away, and then a face formed in the trees with a veiled eyelid.

"One-eyed seer," Sáerlaith whispered.

The seer said nothing, but She did open Her eye. Sáerlaith gripped the sides of the window as the force of the vision bore down on her.

Ruarí ran away from a lightning-filled grove. A group of bloodstained Roman soldiers stared in surprise and fear at the gathering storm. They disappeared in a breath's time, and then only one remained. The full moon grew black with the influx of ravens.

Morrigan stepped out of the furious, swirling mass as the black forms of the ravens grew into a cloak. Time seemed to speed up, and before Sáerlaith could blink, she watched Morrigan's vengeance on Marcus, his own rage replaced by anguished pain.

The Phantom Queen paused in Her attack and smiled, before ripping at Her wrist with Her teeth and placing Her wrist at the mouth of the nearly-comatose warrior.

Time moved along as she watched Marcus tending the grove amidst his isolation, feeding on an exclusive diet of animals, protecting a young druid, and being released from the bonds of his punishment. Then Berti and Sitara joined him in a journey across the lands of the known world of men.

As the seer's eyelid began to lower, the last scene revealed Marcus and Maél Muire returning from training. She then raised a blade in a defensive gesture, as large tears gleamed in her moss-green eyes.

Sáerlaith turned to study Marcus as he stared back at the chieftain. A steady pain grew in his eyes. Marcus seemed physically to experience pain as Maél Muire told him never to set foot in the dun again.

The seer closed Her eye, and Sáerlaith felt the mists to the mortal realm part once again.

Sáerlaith crawled toward the small house, hoping that someone would have mercy and open the door. She heard her name called as two sets of arms lifted her, carrying her into the druids' home. Soft, mortal whispers pulled her to reality with gentle obstinacy. Sáerlaith felt caked dirt and blood on her arms.

"What happened?" one voice queried.

"How can we help you?" the other chorused.

Sáerlaith opened her mouth, feeling nothing more than an exhale of air from her lungs. "Her other son," she whispered, feebly. "I saw her other son."

"Who's other son? What do you mean?" the female druid asked.

As the memories grew clearer, she could recognize Sive and Fergus.

"Thank you for taking me in," Sáerlaith said. "I do not wish to trouble you for long, but I must see your niece as soon as possible."

"Rest," Fergus said. "I will go find her."

Maél Muire strode into the house with some amount of trepidation, knowing that soon she would come face to face with Sáerlaith, the head of the council of Deargh Du. She could not decide whether she should be frightened, honored, or a little of both. She then slid aside the curtain, which covered the dark room that served as a place to dry plants. The soft, sweet smells of flowers drifted to her nose.

"You came," Sáerlaith murmured as a smile spread over her face. As she sat up in the small bed, her eyes bespoke of exhaustion, and her hair revealed tangles from sleep.

Maél Muire bowed her head and then met the Deargh Du's eyes. "I am honored to be called upon. What can I do for you? Do you need sustenance?"

Sáerlaith shook her head. "Your aunt took care of my needs. I wish to tell you about Marcus."

Maél Muire felt her guard rise. She could not help but frown, feeling a dark mood settle over her. "Did he ask you to speak with me?"

"No, Maél Muire, our Goddess did. I searched for Ruarí, our arch druid this night past. The Seer revealed much to me. I will need your assistance searching for Ruarí tonight. Returning to my friend, the mists melted, and the oaks imparted on the origins of the Deargh Du known as 'Marcus Galerius Primus Helvetticus'." Sáerlaith paused. "Only one thing surpassed the pain of the severe, torturous experience of his creation, and that was the many years of this life trapped in a grove."

Sáerlaith wrapped her arms around her knees and met Maél Muire's eyes. "The Goddess meant for him to kill himself in the rising rays of the sun, yet he never gave up. He learned the ways and wisdom of the druids from memories long forgotten in shrouded lives in the past, and he tended the grove. He also saved a mortal druid, who had found him, from death at the hands of a pack of Lamia. The oaks displayed still more memories... they revealed his actions in following the Lamia. I even saw him pull you out of your father's home as it burned."

Maél Muire sat down next to the Deargh Du, forgetting her earlier resolve to stand in respect. Sáerlaith reached over and placed her cool hand over Maél Muire's.

"He has gone through much," Sáerlaith told her. "No one should have to endure such punishment and alienation. His actions were not premeditated."

"He saw it as justice," Maél Muire said, recalling his confession earlier. "Who transformed him? Who is his mother or father-in-darkness?"

"The mists are not clear on that," Sáerlaith answered. "They do not wish to reveal that being's identity."

Maél Muire blinked back her tears and inhaled the scents of drying herbs. "Is he yours?"

"I did not create him as he is," Sáerlaith answered. "Though, I am trying to mother him as a Deargh Du. I would appreciate it if you could find it in your heart to forgive Marcus, as Morrigan has."

Maél Muire rose to her knees before kissing Sáerlaith's hand. "I will forgive him, Lady of Balance. Thank you for telling me this."

Sáerlaith arose in a seamless motion, displaying the beauty of the Fae. "I must discuss the business of Ruarí with Marcus and the rest of the officers at dusk. Please inform them of this."

With gentle hands, she pulled Maél Muire to her unsteady feet. Sáerlaith's eyes glittered like the bark of a gnarled oak. "There is one more thing."

"Yes?"

"Please be mindful of your choices, my child. They may lead you down paths you do not wish to tread upon," Sáerlaith murmured.

Outside Ráth Cruachan

Cennedi watched a group of confused Lamia scouts from the horizon as they neared the new headquarters, situated a few miles away from their old location in the village. The scouts stopped in the center of the tents with questions in their eyes. The other Lamia soldiers and the mortal slaves continued with their duties of establishing and settling the new headquarters, which greatly resembled the old series of tents and portable storage buildings.

Mandubratius pushed past him as Cennedi tried to ignore the adoration pooling in Teá's eyes as her sponsor marched to his soldiers.

"Sir!" the lead scout exalted as he saluted Mandubratius. "We were on our way towards the village of Béal Átha an Fheadha, yet we ended up here. A great mist surrounded us."

"You are utter cretins!" Cennedi heard Mandubratius yell at them. "You have not heard of that ancient trick of the druids?" Cennedi watched Mandubratius motion to his lieutenants, knowing something awful awaited these poor soldiers who stood awaiting orders.

Why don't they run away?

"Give them the usual punishment," Mandubratius murmured in Latin, "and we will go talk to the arch druid. He will know of a way to dissipate these mists."

The leader of the Lamia walked past Cennedi, taking his wife's arm. Before following Teá and Mandubratius, he heard the screams of the scouts.

Without conscious thought, Cennedi turned and witnessed the soldiers chaining the armless scouts to the ancient trees. He closed his eyes.

"Cennedi! Hurry!" Teá's shouted as if barking orders to him.

He needed to find a way out of this encampment, or perhaps it would be easier just to die in the sun.

Mhuine Chonalláin

Connor knocked at his mother's door. She had left a message in the dun the night before, nearly frightening poor Etaoine out of her wits. He heard no welcome and decided to walk in anyway. He could see Seosaimhín stirring the cauldron. "Mother?" He heard an angry sigh as she looked up from her brew.

"Sometimes child," she murmured, "we find it hard to believe that you came from our womb... of course the mists know the truth."

Connor blinked in shock. "What do you m–"

His mother shook a finger at him. "You led him here, you fool!"

"Who?" Connor had to wonder whom she spoke of again.

"The soulless one of Rome!" Seosaimhín roared. "He was here and spoke to us because he followed you! I had to keep him busy, leading the rabbit with a carrot tied to a stick, so he would not follow you to the dark one. I cast misdirection on that one. Be thankful for us, Connor."

"So, what did he hear?" Connor asked his mother.

"He is wise to your movements, yet not our reasoning. You should be suspicious of your Maél Muire, because the Soulless one will tell her what he has learned."

"What should I do?" Connor asked as he sat down in the other chair.

"Propose to her," stated his mother, while stirring the cauldron again.

"Why? I thought you said to be suspicious of her," Connor replied, growing more confused by Seosaimhín's ideas.

"Our goal is for you to wed her. That goal has not changed, Connor. She carries your child, now."

"Maél Muire will not come, and if she does, she will not agree to marry me," he argued.

"Here again, I see evidence that makes me suspicious that the Fae left me a changeling child. Can you not see the ingredients I prepare in this concoction?

Can you not smell the unique odors of this potion?" Seosaimhín groaned as she slapped her forehead with her right hand. "It is a wonder I bothered to teach you anything. Always with your swords, you played, so ignorant of the greater lessons."

Connor bowed his head in a moment of shame. "I am sorry that I did not become who you wanted me to be."

"I considered once removing your genitals when you were young to see if that would make you listen. However, it would have meant that I could not have any grandchildren."

"Mother, I cannot believe–"

"Be silent," Seosaimhín hissed, stirring faster now. "I am making the potion that will make her say 'yes' when you propose to her. She will think Aonghas Og offers Himself to her. If you did any study of Druidism, you would have known that." Her words dripped with disdain. "You could have been so much greater."

Connor clucked his tongue. "I will host a feast and ask her then."

"The potion takes a week to prepare, Connor. When she answers 'yes', be certain to make sure the ceremony is within a month."

"Why a month?" he queried.

"That is how long the potion lasts. If you have not married, she will reject you and never look back," Seosaimhín replied, before returning to her attention to her cauldron.

Béal Átha an Fheadha

Sáerlaith waited with anticipation, while standing in the shadows of the dun's great hall, as Chieftain Maél Muire and many of her guests gathered to listen to Sáerlaith's plea. Ruarí needed her help... well, Marcus' help.

The chieftain cleared her throat as she sat in her chair. "Thank you all for coming to the dun on such short notice." She then met the gaze of the others. Marcus, Mac Alpin, and Claudius stood, watching her. Bearach stood at her side, Berti and Sitara held hands from the door of her room, and Caoimhín watched her from the right side of the hearth. "A crisis looms on the horizon that Sáerlaith will explain."

"Thank you, chieftain," Sáerlaith added before strolling to the center of the dun. "I took a vision quest last night, and I have learned the location of Ruarí, our arch druid. I wish for Marcus to lead a rescue party. The trees and the Seer told me the details of the guards and their marching routes." Sáerlaith grew quiet as she stared at the ground for a moment, before steeling her resolve. She then looked up and continued. "I do not need to inform you how important Ruarí is. He will be a vital personage in our war with the Lamia. We must rescue him."

"I grow weary of these orders," Maon complained as he finished another cup of mead.

"Well, I grow weary of these foreigners telling us how to fight," Fianait hissed as she finished her drink. "That Marcus had the gall to tell me that I could not walk in a straight line!" she grumbled with a hiccup.

"He would probably tell us how to do everything with efficiency, if he could," Declan added. "Am I right?"

The dozen gathered warriors raised their mugs of bloodmead.

"And allowing those cursed ones to join us," Aidan whispered. "The Goddess doubtless grows furious for casting our lots with such as those."

Soft grumbles echoed in the field.

"Let us prove ourselves worthy of the council's laud," Breacán stated with a slight slur. "We shall take the head of Mandubratius."

"Yes," Declan cried, raising his full mug, "we can subdue that worthless, cursed guard and steal weapons from the armory."

They then arose from the ground, ready to put their plan into motion.

"The group looks rather sparse today," Mac Alpin muttered, before heading towards the front of the lines and ordering, "One step at a time!" Arwin wished he had managed to talk Claudius into a game of dice to see who would be stuck with this duty. He then noticed the door of the armory swinging open, back and forth.

"Halt," he barked before racing towards the door. One of the Sugnwr Gwaed lay bloodied on the grass. Empty slots for swords and other equipment caught his eye. "Crieche! Edwina!" he called out as he raced to find his servant.

"Yes sir?" the mortal answered as he came out of the dun, dusting off his hands.

"You will take over training the Deargh Du," Mac Alpin ordered as he smiled at Edward. He then grabbed the mortal's arm and dragged him towards the waiting trainees.

chapter eleven

Outside Ráth Cruachan

he Lamia scouts gestured to a group of drunken warriors, who were waving swords and spears about. The smell of blood abounded from these men and women, and their loud voices seemed to harken from a lack of discipline.

"This Mandubratius should not be that hard to find," one of drunken warriors commented in a boisterous voice.

"Go to the encampment and tell Wicus," the lead scout ordered in a whisper, before continuing to follow the warriors.

Mandubratius could hear a loud commotion of clanking armor echoing from outside of the tent. He pulled away from Teá's embrace to walk outside. One of his lieutenants stood nearby. "What is going on here, Wicus?"

"Sir, there is a group of what we believe to be a dozen Deargh Du coming toward the encampment," Wicus answered, before glancing towards Teá. "I was about to inform you, but I did not wish to interrupt you."

"I see. Take forty of our soldiers and try to subdue as many as you can. The arch druid is of little use to us these nights. We can torture them, and they can help us find a way past these nocturnal, magical mists."

Marcus hovered near the Lamia encampment, cloaked in shadow, and listened to the Lamia below.

"That damnable mist," hissed one of the guards. "If that fool of a druid spoke on how to part the mist, we could get out of this and back to our regular duties, or even drink with the others."

Marcus levitated in closer to the back of the thatched sod house. A growing stench multiplied as he landed near the two Lamia soldiers guarding the back of the windowless dwelling.

"I consider ourselves quite lucky that we did not die," the other guard commented. "Mars is on our side that we are needed, since the mortal guards are now scouts during the day."

Marcus slid from the cloak of darkness and without a sound, beheaded one guard and then the other. He then motioned the five others forth. Claudius, Caoimhín, and three Ekimmu Cruitne landed outside the dwelling. Mac Alpin had remained at Béal Átha an Fheadha to train the troops.

Marcus held up two fingers and pointed to the front of the house. Torches flickered on that side. He pulled on his old helmet and straightened his uniform before marching to the front. His armor clanged with each confident stride toward the remaining guards.

"Halt!" the guard on the left called out in Latin.

Marcus removed his helm and stared at them. "I have come to take the prisoner," he answered.

"No one takes the prisoner without authorization," replied the other.

"You have my authorization to release the arch druid to me." Marcus sensed the others hovering above the guards, awaiting his signal.

"And just who are you?" the guard on the left queried.

Marcus pulled back on his helmet, signaling the others to drop on the guards. "I am he who brings your doom." He then watched the soldiers' heads roll before their bodies, spurting blood in diminishing pulses, collapsed in a pile. Afterwards, Claudius and one of Mac Alpin's men landed.

The brush nearby rustled as four more Lamia, with their weapons drawn, came from their hiding places. Within an instant, the other Ekimmu Cruitne warriors took care of the new Lamia threat.

"I found two others at the eastern edge," Caoimhín said as he joined them, before sheathing his bloody blade. "No alarm has been raised."

Marcus nodded before addressing the three Ekimmu Cruitne. "Please guard the door." He then gestured for Caoimhín to open the passage first.

"What a stench," Claudius murmured as they followed the silver-haired Deargh Du.

Marcus felt like responding, but the sight of the arch druid held his tongue.

"By... the Goddess'... sacred..." Caoimhín stammered with a soft cry. "What did they do to him?"

Marcus stared at the abused Deargh Du, his features unrecognizable.

"It is called crucifixion," Claudius answered in a toneless voice.

Twisted iron spikes, sparkled with gold, impaled the arch druid's arms and feet. Golden chains wrapped around his body bound him to the wood beam behind him. The glare from these golden chains made Marcus wince, forcing him to stare at the ground for a moment in discomfort. He managed to look up and see that Caoimhín appeared similarly affected. Marcus felt his stomach clench, and so he went outside to join the others. Caoimhín joined him.

"Oh," Marcus could hear Claudius state from inside the room, "the gold. I will remove it." Claudius said nothing more before entering the passage.

Marcus expected to hear screams or some sort of noise, other than the sound of chains and metal, and yet only a disturbing silence grew. Soon, a few scuffling noises departed from the small dwelling, leaving him to wonder whether the arch druid, exhausted from his previous trials, could be unconscious.

The shuffling of feet drew his attention, and he looked on as Caoimhín rejoined Claudius and the arch druid. Soon, Caoimhín said, "Are you well enough to travel, Ruarí?"

The arch druid's raspy voice replied, "Are you a prisoner, Caoimhín?"

A brief pause ensued, and then Caoimhín answered, "No Ruarí, these are our new friends."

"Who would have thought that the other brood of Morrigan and The Hunters of Britannia would have joined us?" Marcus heard a soft intake of breath. "Such happenings mean great things will come to pass, Caoimhín. Please tell me your names."

"I am Claudius Metrius Sertorius of the Sugnwr Gwaed," he heard Claudius reply. "I am honored to be at your service. There are others, Arch Druid. More introductions can come later, for sunrise is almost upon us. We must return to our sanctuary."

"Very well, let us leave here and never look back. I may need assistance in traveling, Caoimhín."

Marcus heard their steps and turned. Caoimhín guided the arch druid out of the hut. He then looked into Ruarí's eyes and felt his own eyes widen in disbelief. The druid who had called down Morrigan stood before him.

"You," Ruarí mouthed in silence, his eyes revealing a mixture of fear and anger.

No one else appeared to see their reaction to one another.

Marcus finally found his voice. "We must all go, now." The all then took to the sky.

Fianait raised her right hand and called, "Hold! I smell something,"before sniffing the air. A few Deargh Du stopped next to her and inhaled the breezes. Breacán continued past them with three other warriors.

"Lamia," Maon whispered.

A rustle of brush answered his guess, as a group of Lamia appeared, marching through the vegetation. Their shields hid all but their feet as their armor clanged with a remorseless beat. The three warriors rushed the shield wall, but the Lamia fought with precision and discipline, cutting at the opponents to either side, not the one in front. Breacán and two others fell.

Maon yelled a battle cry as he drew his blade. He then rushed towards the front line, hearing the others join with him. He swore that his blade screamed in near desire at the thought of the ensuing bloodbath.

MacAlpin watched the fevered battle with awe for a few moments. Perhaps the Deargh Du could hold their own, but then a second formation of Lamia troops came from behind, and soon only handful of Deargh Du remained. He grumbled to himself before taking off in an attempt to save these misguided warriors.

He ran behind the second line of troops and then threw himself sideways at the densely packed group. He felt an intense rush of pain and excitement as he knocked over nearly half of the Lamia. The broken line could allow for a victory. Mac Alpin rose to his feet and began to stab the bodies beneath him. The surviving Deargh Du joined him, and he watched them finish off more of the Lamia.

The sound of a horn shifted the battle plan of the Lamia. Mac Alpin roared in glory as the defeated Lamia ran away from the one-on-one fights. With the battle over, Arwin decided to take stock of the dead. He then noticed that one of the dead Lamia wore gold armor and bore gold weapons, whereas the others possessed normal steal armor and weapons.

The sounds of bodies being dragged drew his attention back to the weary bloodied Deargh Du, who started to pick up their fallen comrades.

"Look," Mac Alpin said as he picked up the Lamia leader's golden sword. As he held aloft the gold sword, the Deargh Du stared at him with veiled fear. "Do you realize that if everyone you encountered had wielded swords like this, you would all be dead?" he queried.

"Is it Mandubratius?" the female warrior asked.

"No, he is a Briton, with green eyes, or so I've been told." Mac Alpin shrugged. "This is a Roman." He then kicked the beheaded soldier's boot. "Now, the one thing you should have learned about fighting Romans today is that you must break their formation with an attack from behind or above."

They stared at him for a moment in their beautiful way and then nodded.

"You demonstrated the value of that lesson today," the tallest one commented with lowered eyes.

Mac Alpin shook off his desire to give them all a verbal thrashing and suggested, "Let us go back to the dun with our fallen friends. I am sure there are Lamia reinforcements on the way." He then picked up the Lamia leader's weighted body, weapons, and armor and started at a jog. Mac Alpin wanted to show the rest of the Deargh Du what kind of warriors and armaments they would come against.

Though ill-advised, this tragic foray of these now deferential Deargh Du might help quash the arrogance in the others, or so Mac Alpin hoped.

Béal Átha an Fheadha

Marcus could smell the smoldering of brush as he approached the training grounds near the village. As he landed, he saw mud-covered Deargh Du and several distraught mortals, all of whom appeared to be quite confused.

Maél Muire, Berti, Sive, and Fergus stood around Edward, who shivered from being wet.

Sive shook her right index finger while yelling at Edward. Her speaking grew in volume with each word. "Rain! We had to call down rain! If Sáerlaith had not helped us, the fields would have gone up in flames!"

"What in the name of Mars happened here?" Marcus bellowed in Latin, forgetting that they would not understand him. He then repeated himself in Irish.

"Arwin had to run after a few drunken Deargh Du, who had taken it upon themselves to relieve Mandubratius of his head," Sáerlaith replied.

"They would not stay in formation," Edward explained with a shrug. "They did not want to train with a mortal, so I thought I would show them what I could do, and my concoction had a far greater effect than I had thought possible, but we took care of it."

"Edwina!" Arwin roared upon landing, carrying a gold-clad body. "What happened? Gracious Goddess of the earth, what was I thinking?" He then dropped the body that he carried.

Several weary Deargh Du set down behind Mac Alpin, bearing their fallen comrades.

Desiring an explanation, Marcus faced Mac Alpin, but before Marcus could say anything, Mac Alpin muttered, "They wanted to take care of Mandubratius."

"So I heard. How did they fare?" he asked.

"As well as any crazed group of barbarians who did not know how to kill Romans properly," Mac Alpin growled with a smirk.

"So, I suppose you showed them how to do it correctly," Marcus ascertained aloud while coughing back his laughter.

"It was that or watch them be slaughtered. You do wish to punish these six, correct?" Mac Alpin looked back at the Deargh Du as the mortals helped them take their slain brothers to the meat storage room until the next night.

"If this was the Roman army, they would be flogged for not obeying orders to remain here," Marcus answered. "However, we must remember that these are Deargh Du. Perhaps the best punishment is promotion."

"What? Are you daft?" Mac Alpin asked mid-bellow.

Marcus noticed Edward look up at his master's usual exclamation.

"Those six survived the Lamia, granted it was with your assistance. Almost none have done that in the last one to two hundred years. They survived and learned a valuable lesson that will make them victorious. We need them to motivate the others."

Mac Alpin barked a laugh. "I suppose that may help in the long run. You are the general, after all. Did you find the arch druid?"

"Yes. He is in the dun with Caoimhín, who is tending to him."

"I need to tend to my own needs. Sunup draws near," Arwin looked up at the sky, "and my bed calls."

"Oh yes, how lovely for you." Marcus chuckled. "I will think of your fluffy, warm bed while I slumber comfortably in my hole."

For the first time in several nights, Ruarí could feel his body relax, though his mind still bore scars from the emotional turmoil he suffered at the hands of the Lamia, and at seeing that face... that monstrous face staring back at him after so many years. Oh, how that face had haunted him each day since the grove... since the monster butchered the villagers and all of his students at Loch Garman.

Movement drew his attention away from his waking nightmare, and he noticed Basala handing Caoimhín a set of clothing.

"This should fit," she said. "Do we need more hot water?"

Ruarí saw Caoimhín look at the brass tub in the back room before answering, "No, I think we have everything we need. Thank you, Basala."

Caoimhín glanced over at Ruarí before walking toward him carrying clothes and a wide piece of linen. "Basala found clothing for you," he said before picking up a comb and mirror and handing them to the arch druid.

Ruarí stared at him in silence, ignoring the comb and mirror for the moment. He could not find words to explain to Caoimhín his experiences, how Mandubratius had tortured him, and the memories dredged up by seeing Marcus once again. At that moment, a soft knock interrupted his thoughts. He wrapped the linen around himself before standing.

"It is Sáerlaith, may I come in?"

Ruarí nodded to Caoimhín and then allowed the clean léine to cover him.

Sáerlaith walked in and lowered her head in respect... an odd movement for the chief of the council.

"How do you feel?" she asked, before sitting on the stool near the tub.

Ruarí inhaled and then murmured, "I have seen a monster today."

"Yes, Mandubratius," Sáerlaith intoned as she took his left hand. "I am sorry... I did not mean to take your chair." She then arose.

"No, no," Ruarí answered. "You sit. I mean that Roman, the one who led my rescue." He heard his words end with a soft hiss. "He is the monster!"

"Calm yourself, old friend," Sáerlaith murmured as she took his hand and met his eyes. Her calming, brown eyes entranced him for a moment, and he felt weak. "You have nothing to fear from Marcus. He is with us."

Ruarí shook his head vehemently from one side to another.

"Ruarí, she is right," Caoimhín added. "He is Deargh Du."

Ruarí continued to shake his head in a violent manner, denying their words. Marcus could not be one of them... could not... must not be.

"Shhhh," Sáerlaith cooed as she took his right hand.

"Find your peace within," Caoimhín whispered while patting his back.

"Let me tell you what that monster has done," Ruarí stated in a hoarse whisper. "He came to Éire as a conqueror and set his troops loose on Loch Garman. He and his men even murdered the druids. I did what had to be done!" His words grew in volume. "Morrigan Herself came down from above. I called Her and saw Her arrival. I thought Morrigan had taken him, but now I see he's been walking Éire. You tell me how this can be possible! Does our Phantom Queen punish us?"

"Ruarí," Sáerlaith explained, "Marcus could not be Deargh Du if She had not forgiven him."

"Perhaps he is a plague She set upon us for forgetting our duties," Ruarí grumbled, though he could not fathom how the Deargh Du could have earned Her vehemence. Before he could dwell upon the idea of Morrigan punishing the Deargh Du, Ruarí felt the sun begin to pierce the night sky. Soon, other blood-drinkers came into the dun.... Deargh Du, Ekimmu Cruitne, and Sugnwr Gwaed.

"Give him time, Ruarí," Caoimhín urged.

"Fine, I will reserve judgment on him. Until I see what he is, I will accept that She forgave him. There is some redemption, but as a man who witnessed his deeds, I cannot fully accept his full deliverance. I will still see him as a monster until he proves me wrong." He then wiped tears of exhaustion and anger from his eyes. "I must sleep now. I feel as though I may fall asleep at this very moment."

Outside Ráth Cruachan

After completing his feeding expedition, Cennedi walked towards the encampment, feeling a strange pride that he had managed to feed from several victims without killing anyone. He then he heard Mandubratius' voice, and so Cennedi decided stop by the trees outside of the encampment and listen.

"There you are," Teá teased Cennedi as she placed a hand on his left shoulder and smiled at him. "You left without me to guide you. Do not tell me that already my assistance is not needed. You must be careful because the Deargh Du are afoot."

He hushed her and then demanded, "Tell me first what is going on."

Teá sighed before pulling him out of the forest. "You shall see." They then walked to the edge of the encampment to watch the excitement.

As soon as Mandubratius came into full view, her sponsor's face appeared dark with silent fury, and yet when he spoke, his voice remained calm.

"Forty left our outpost and only ten returned," Mandubratius stated as he looked over the defeated soldiers. He then gestured for his lieutenants to join him.

Cennedi witnessed a few shudder. "Why do I have a feeling that everyone will be punished for this?"

"Not everyone, you will see," she hissed.

The lieutenants gathered all of the troops to stand in front of their leader.

Cennedi soon heard the sounds of chains clanking, and then he saw an officer pouring colored stones into a helmet. The officer then walked up to each soldier, who drew a stone from the helmet. Seventeen out of the one hundred and seventy soldiers drew black stones. Each soldier bearing a black stone stepped to the front of the formation.

"Failure is not an option, here or in Rome!" Mandubratius shouted, before facing one of the seventeen. He then drew out a branch he had been hiding behind his back, whirled it around, and then staked the soldier through the heart with it.

Other assembled soldiers joined in, staking their comrades who had drawn the black stones. After wounding the seventeen, the rest the Lamia staked their bodies to the ground and chained them in place.

"They say that the mortal Roman legions did this," Teá whispered in Cennedi's ear as he winced in pain. "They called it 'decimation', I think."

Cennedi closed his eyes as mortals and Lamia set up chairs in a perimeter surrounding where the seventeen soldiers lay staked and chained.

"Make sure they stay still," Mandubratius stated. "Kill them if they move."

Cennedi opened his eyes, but then he felt his jaw drop as the soldiers and mortals began to urinate on the unlucky seventeen.

"And they dare call us the barbarians?" he gasped before covering his eyes once again at the abject show of humiliation. "Why do they not revolt against this?" He then heard a sigh of exasperation from Teá.

"Because this is the only means of controlling an army," Teá answered. "You are such a fool to think anything else could work." She then started to drag him towards the tents.

"Other things can work," Cennedi stated upon opening his eyes.

"The sun rises soon," she replied, apparently ignoring his statement. "Go back to your tent with the others." She then left his company to join her sponsor and link arms with him.

Cennedi obediently walked to his designated tent, but then from the entrance, he glanced back at the seventeen staked bodies, and him.

Mandubratius gazed back at Cennedi with a strange, all-knowing smile.

What can I do to get her to see the malice and manipulative talents of her sponsor? How could she stay with such a being as this?

Cennedi thought for a moment of joining the others in the sun, but he noticed Mandubratius turn away from Teá towards the staked victims. The orange and red sun moved slowly from the east. Cennedi looked on as the Lamia leader watched the burning figures until he could not bear the light of day anymore. As they both turned away from the sun and sought cover, Cennedi could still hear their screams, but only briefly.

Béal Átha an Fheadha

Marcus heard leaves crunch as someone kneeled down next to his hole. The smell of dusk and early harvest permeated the air, as well as the scent of the chieftain. Marcus heard the sound of Maél Muire patting the ground. She then started hitting two small rocks together. He then opened up the hole, pushing aside the cover of twigs, dirt, and leaves.

She looked down at Marcus before backing off to give him room to ascend. "How do you like the accommodations?" she asked with a devious smile.

"It is cramped, but infinitely better than sunshine," Marcus answered as he looked up at her. Her eyes danced with bemusement, growing greener as his eyesight improved. Even a glow graced her cheeks tonight.

"You are cheerful. Why is that?" he asked.

"Will you come out to talk to me, or do you wish to remain in your hole?" She then offered him her right hand, but he could see that she regretted the decision as his filthy hand latched around hers.

He climbed out and then started dusting himself off. "Do me a favor and hand me the bag behind that rock. It has my clean clothes, my kit, and armor in it."

Maél Muire chuckled and backed away. "You have to bathe before I come any closer. You smell horrible." She held her nose and made a face at him.

He laughed, finding strange amusement at her bearing. "Then walk with me to the river," he suggested as he picked up his bag.

"As long as you get clean," she answered.

"Well, this is a pleasant change from the last week. You are being civil, if not congenial," he said, while starting for the river. Of course the previous conversation remained clear in his mind, not to mention the guilt her accusations had drudged up, but perhaps she now saw past his previous transgressions, but how? What did she now know?

"I talked to Sáerlaith about you," she began to explain while shaking the dirt, mud, and dead insects off her hand.

"And what did she tell you about me?" Marcus asked, curious.

Maél Muire cleared her throat and said, "She told me that by your own deeds, you were redeemed in the eyes of Morrigan, and that She allowed you to become one of Her brood." Maél Muire paused for a moment before meeting his eyes again and smiled. "It is funny. I can almost see a young boy under all those layers of dirt."

Marcus chuckled while shaking his head. "That boy disappeared over six hundred years ago."

Maél Muire looked away. "You have done much good around me and for me. I believe you are not the same man you were as a mortal. I wish to forgive you and hope that you can forgive me for doubting you." Her eyes then focused on his, and a mixture of emotions played out on her face. She reddened with shame, or what he assumed to be shame.

"No," he said, feeling a small pout wrinkle his features. "I will only forgive you if I get to stay in the dun again."

"Oh, alright," she replied, before stopping at the river's edge. "Well then, we are friends again?" Her earlier embarrassment seemed to have faded away.

"Of course." He then dropped his bag and strolled closer to the river.

"Excellent! Then take your bath," she said before pushing him into the river.

He smiled as she noticed that grime and dirt caked her hands and arms. "That serves you right," he chuckled while pulling off his wet clothes and then throwing them onto the low-hanging limbs of an oak.

Maél Muire made a face before pulling off her clothes and jumping into the chilly water with him. She started splashing herself in an apparent effort to become used to the cold, before following Marcus towards the middle of the river, where the water ran over her waist. The night breezes lifted her hair for a moment, and after it passed, her curls lowered. She then shook out her tresses for a moment before pushing them back with impatient hands.

Marcus ducked under the water and returned clean, or so he hoped. He then broke away from the trance of watching a mortal in the mundane process of washing to ask, "How is the arch druid?"

She floated closer and then cupped her hands to gather water in order to rinse the remaining dirt from his left shoulder. "He is doing well," Maél Muire replied. "He is speaking again and starting to become sociable. They made horrible torture on him. He speaks of mirrors reflecting sunlight onto him and being nailed…" She grew silent and closed her eyes, leaving the rest unsaid.

She then ducked into the cool, running water. Upon surfacing, she exhaled and began pushing her wet hair out of her face. "He did not talk," Maél Muire added. "He held onto the belief that Morrigan would save him, and She did, through you."

Marcus treaded closer and began feeling a growing serenity. "You have some dirt on your left ear," he observed before rinsing it off, gently rubbing at her left lobe. He then asked, "Has he spoken of me?"

"He has not said anything, although the others say you keep your distance whenever he goes outside," Maél Muire answered.

"Arch Druid Ruarí and I met once before when I was a mortal. He was witness to some of the atrocities my men and I carried out. Ruarí survived our slaughter of the village and the druids." He then lowered his eyes and turned away as the guilt resurfaced. He wished he could be rid of it.

Without any warning, Maél Muire pulled Marcus into an embrace. Her warm fingers traced across his back, moving up to his hair. After sliding his arms around her, his hands wound up in her soft curls. He then rested his chin against the top of her head.

"You are not who you were then. The Goddess allowed you to become what you are. She knew these nights would be upon us."

"I know," he murmured into her hair. He then kissed her forehead, but he felt a little uncomfortable, so he pulled back from her.

"Are you alright now?" she asked.

He felt relieved she had not realized the intimacy of the embrace. "I believe I am clean enough to return to the real world." He then trampled back to the shore. As he dressed and combed his hair, he noticed that she continued to watch him, but after a few moments, Marcus watched her squeezed water from her hair and rejoin him on land.

She pulled on her léine before looking at him and saying, "You look pale."

"Maél Muire, I have not had a chance to feed tonight," he answered.

She then pulled her hair away from her throat. "Here," she offered as she drew closer to him. "It is an honor as always."

"You know it is more of an honor for me," he murmured as he pulled her toward him and bit into her throat and began stroking her hair. After a moment of feeding, he felt his strength begun to return. Soft warmth pulsed within her blood, allowing him to realize a thought he did not dare voice. She felt something for him. A raw surge of emotion laced her vitae, adding delicious flavors. Once sated, withdrew and kissed the wound.

"Thank you," he whispered in her ear, deciding it would be best to wait to speak about her feelings after the issue of the Lamia could be finalized. He then took her arm, as she stared back at him with a dazed expression, and started to lead her back to the dun. Neither of them uttered a word.

Caletum

As Amata surveyed the ongoing ship construction, a messenger arrived and handed a scroll to Amata. She read it and then turned to Lucretia and Patroclus, who stood next to her overlooking the docks. "Mandubratius writes that they have discovered Deargh Du in Connacht. They have encountered activities that lead him to believe that the Phallus Maximus is in the area. We are to move with all due haste to join him. Also, he desires that we send a small group to Britannia to find Marcus and his friends in case the Ouphe do not take care of them."

"We can leave in two weeks time, Domina," Patroclus replied. "However, our journey may be delayed by the weight of the boats."

"The golden armor and weapons will be necessary," Amata stated. "We will go to Connacht as quickly as possible."

Béal Átha an Fheadha

Through the mist of her dreams, Maél Muire heard a voice call her name. Then she felt a soft, feminine hand shake her shoulder. Maél Muire awoke and began to rub the sleep from her eyes. "Yes, Basala?" Maél Muire asked, while meeting the steady gaze of her servant.

"A messenger from Connor Mac Turrlough is waiting for you outside. He says the message is of great importance and that I should wake you immediately. I am sorry for interrupting your sleep."

"It's alright," Maél Muire said before standing up. "What time is it?"

"Almost two in the afternoon," Basala answered.

"I see." Maél Muire rubbed her forehead. "Could you wake Marcus and ask him to meet me in the great hall?"

As Basala left, Maél Muire went to her water bowl and splashed her face, before moving to her hands and feet.

"What is this about a message?" Marcus asked as he joined Maél Muire in the great hall. Although her servants had taken great pains to prevent the sun's entry into the dun, he still felt drained, even grumpy, when woken up during the day.

"It is Connor Mac Turrlough's personal messenger, and I thought you would want to hear this message and assist me in responding to it."

Marcus nodded his head. "Excellent suggestion," he replied before taking her arm and leading her to the chieftain's chair. He then stood at her right side and motioned for Druce to open the door. Marcus covered his eyes as a blade of brilliance stabbed into the dun.

The messenger walked into the corridor of the great hall and bowed his head. "Connor Mac Turrlough humbly requests your presence at a celebration he holds in your honor tomorrow night."

Maél Muire looked over at Marcus for a moment.

"And to what do I owe this immense pleasure?" she asked the servant. "I have not done anything to earn such honor and praise from your chieftain."

"His motivations are unknown to me, my lady. I just know that he desires your presence and that of any guests who you wish to accompany you," the messenger replied.

Marcus nodded his head in an almost imperceptible, terse movement, but Maél Muire seemed to noticed.

"Thank you," she said. "Please communicate my acceptance to your master."

"Thank you, Chieftain." The then messenger bowed his head and left.

Maél Muire stood up. "You believe that this is a way to learn more about our enemy," she surmised aloud.

Marcus smiled, happy that she understood his motives. "You are wise, chroí. Those were my thoughts."

"Do you think we will see our friends, the Lamia?" she asked.

"Perhaps," he answered as he crouched closer to her. He then inhaled.

"Does that mean I need another bath?" she asked with a chuckle.

"Not today," he acknowledged with a grin. "It means you smell of wildflowers." He then plucked a small flower from her hair.

Maél Muire's face seemed to heat up for a moment. "I hope you will join me at this celebration, then. I have a feeling that I may need your protection," she said as she stared up at him.

"I will, as well as a few of my trainees who I wish to reward and challenge."

Maél Muire chuckled. "Please make sure they dress appropriately."

"I will make them aware tonight so they can make the necessary preparations. Now, if I may, I need to get back to sleep."

Maél Muire turned his face back to hers and kissed his cheek. "Sleep well, and have pleasant dreams."

Mhuine Chonalláin

Connor felt his entire body lose feeling as the faceless creature continued drinking his blood. Soon he awoke, drenched in sweat, and sat up. He then uttered a fearful noise, upon noticing a figure in his chair.

"How nice of you to join the awake," Mandubratius drawled.

Connor opened his mouth to speak, but Mandubratius lifted a finger.

"The next words you utter should be, 'hello, my friend, what can I do for you?'. Otherwise, I may become uncharacteristically rude."

Connor exhaled. "Hello, my friend, what can I do for you?"

"It has come to my attention that you are throwing a celebration tomorrow night, a celebration where you plan to propose marriage to a certain chieftain."

Connor felt all feeling drain from his face and found it difficult to breathe.

"You look stunned, Mac Turrlough. Surely, you realize that I would have associates here who watch over you and yours. However," Mandubratius said before pausing for a moment, "I find that hard to believe, since I thought you would tell me such a thing. After all, is it not tradition to invite one's closest friends to a gathering wherein one proposes marriage? Is this not a tradition?"

"Yes, but…" Connor began to explain, but words failed him.

"Are we not close friends?" Mandubratius smiled again.

"Yes, but–"

"But you did not invite me." The blood-drinker sighed. "I am hurt that you did not consider me a close enough friend to invite to your proposal party. I cannot tell you how this wounds me so."

"Mandubratius, I would very much wish for you to attend our celebration," Connor said, while trying to keep his breath steady.

"Thank you. That is a most gracious invitation, my friend. However, I must regretfully decline."

This it ridiculous! All of that effort just to turn down an invitation?

"I am sorry to hear that," Connor answered.

Mandubratius arose. "Thank you for the invitation. By the way, did Maél Muire accept your invitation?"

"She did," he replied.

"Excellent. Do you believe some of her blood-drinking friends will join her?" Mandubratius queried.

"I believe so," Connor stated. "I invited her to bring her guests."

"Then I have a request to make." Mandubratius' mouth twisted into a smile.

"Of course, anything you wish."

Mandubratius paced the room for a moment. "Some of my mortal cohorts grow weary of guarding us during the daytime. Do you have any vacancies in your personal guard that could be filled for the party?"

Connor nodded his head. "I would be happy to add them to my staff."

"Very well then, thank you. I shall take my leave. Until we meet again, Chieftain."

Connor watched the Lamia leap through the window and disappear before Connor could say another word.

Maél Muire dismounted Biast outside of the gates. She then dusted off her cloak and looked over her guests as the sounds of harps and flutes echoed over the walls and toward the small huts outside of the dun.

"Do we pass inspection?" Sive asked with a chuckle.

"Of course," Maél Muire answered. "Although, I have this idea in the back of my head that we are under-dressed." Just in case, Maél Muire looked over the three Deargh Du and her aunt and uncle, who all wore clean clothing.

Why display finery at an event that we know so little about?

"It's too late to go back and change," Fergus added through a yawn, before sniffing the air.

Maél Muire stepped forward and then knocked on the door and waited.

The gates opened, and they walked into the courtyard of the dun. Fires roasted the finest meats as three bards holding oaken branches of silver bells sang to the gathered village. Everyone looked to be decked in his or her finest. As people turned to face them, she could hear whispered comments about their clothing amidst the sounds of sizzling meat and song.

"Are they always this rude?" Maon muttered. She watched Maon and Marcus grin as if pretending not to hear the insults.

"Only within the last few months," Sive replied.

She watched Aidan raise a brow after hearing a comment. He opened his mouth to reply to the short and intoxicated clansman, but Marcus pulled him off to the side before Aidan could say anything.

"Do not allow yourself to be singled out, Aidan. Our assignment now is to protect the chieftain and find out what we can about our enemy." She heard him pause for moment before continuing to whisper. "The best way to do this is to disappear into the crowd, and I do not mean by drawing down the darkness."

She heard a terse 'yes sir' before Aidan left them.

He traversed the courtyard before drifting towards the ale barrel. Maon then gave her a bit of a shrug before joining the milling crowds that danced.

Maél Muire walked over to Marcus and leaned toward his ear. "I have a bad feeling about all this," she whispered.

"Why do you say that?" Marcus asked. "Other than the fact that we are the poor bastards, here. It looks like he spared no expense."

"That is the problem. Look at this expense and waste," she huffed. "Mac Turrlough knows the dark time comes soon, and I hope for his sake that they have enough supplies in store. He has been trying to woo me, and this is his bid for me to become his betrothed?"

Marcus chuckled, "It would seem so, Maél Muire."

"'It would seem so, Maél Muire'?" she mimicked, imitating his tone. "I have no idea what to say to him. My heart says run away, but my mind knows that my friend Marcus has a plan." She grinned.

"Yes, I believe he has a plan in mind," Marcus teased as he wrapped his arm around her.

"And this cunning plan of yours?" she queried.

"Basically, a continuation of my old plan, with a twist," Marcus answered. "Agree to the proposal and then spy on him for the Deargh Du. We need to know how many troops they have now, where they are located, and when they plan to attack."

She heard her voice grow stern. "You expect me to agree to marry someone I do not love who is working for the enemy? How can you expect me to do this?"

"You do not have to marry him." He rubbed her arm for a moment. "You merely have to make him believe that you will and make him trust you enough to lower his guard. You cannot disagree with the feelings of your heart. However, we need your assistance. Please do this. Help us maintain the balance."

She stared into his eyes for a moment, watching them momentarily gleam silver. He stood in silence, awaiting her answer.

"You are right," she grumbled.

She watched his eyes dart over to where Maon stood near the musicians and make eye contact with him. She then noticed him look over the rest of the celebration and saw Aidan drinking ale, paying attention to little but the goblet he held.

Marcus squeezed her arm briefly with a gentle hand and then marched over to join Aidan.

She began to walk through the crowd on her way to get dinner.

Marcus turned back around to find Maél Muire, arm in arm with Mac Turrlough. She smiled, revealing her teeth, yet on closer examination, she looked nervous and somewhat confused.

He could not hear their conversation over the general roar of the gathered clansman, and so he tried to find Aidan again, but the crowd blocked his line of sight.

"I have an announcement to make. Everyone please quiet down!" Mac Turrlough called, as everyone turned to face him... even Marcus, for the briefest of moments. "I did not just throw this celebration for our enjoyment." A soft release of laughter died, and then all grew silent.

"As many of you know, there is someone special to me who has traveled to be here with us tonight. I find her to be the most beautiful thing in the world."

Marcus could see the chieftain step back to allow the crowd to look at Maél Muire. Marcus then ducked around more mortals, trying to find Aidan. He was not by the ale, the mead, or the musicians. Concerned, Marcus motioned to Maon to look for Aidan as well. The other Deargh Du started walking through the gathered mortals.

Then, amongst the quiet gathering, Marcus heard the host chieftain utter, "Maél Muire, will you marry me?"

He could hear a soft exhale in the silence. Marcus glanced up and saw Maél Muire meet Mac Turrlough's eyes for a moment before closing hers. "I will," she replied.

The drunken crowd roared with applause.

"Then we will have our wedding in three weeks at our church in your new home… here."

He noticed Mac Turrlough hand her what appeared to be a goblet of mead. Marcus covered himself in shadow and rushed behind her, stealthily taking the mead from her hand and replacing it with his. Once out of the way, he sniffed her mead for a moment, smelling a variety of different things, the very least of it being honey. "I cannot find Aidan," Marcus whispered upon sensing Maon behind him. "Keep an eye on Maél Muire, Fergus, and Sive. I will search the dun."

A side door beckoned to him. As he slid into the dun, a strange scent almost sent him reeling. Marcus then grabbed a servant as he attempted to evade his hand, pulling him back.

"You have an odd fragrance," he advised. "Have you made some new friends lately?"

The servant attempted to bolt from Marcus' grasp.

Marcus in turn threw him against the wall and held him up by his arms.

The servant's spindly legs bucked and kicked as he tried to reach the ground.

"Where is the Deargh Du known as 'Aidan'?" Marcus asked. He felt a flood of strength overwhelm him, which became gentle waves of growing power.

"Where is Aidan?" he asked again.

"You will never find him. I will not say where they took him," the servant hissed.

"And who are they?" Marcus demanded.

"Our masters," the servant whispered.

Another thrum of energy invigorated Marcus. "Where did they take him?" he asked.

"They did not tell me. Mandubratius wished to question him."

"And what information does Mandubratius seek?"

"I was not told." The servant tried to escape looking into his eyes.

"What was your reward?" Marcus stared into the servant's hazel eyes.

"They offered us immortality as Lamia," the servant answered.

He tried to ignore his growing fury, but could not. Marcus pushed his enemy against the wall and fed until the body grew cold and still.

Seosaimhín felt the crow land on her right shoulder as a perch. Soon her hair tangled with the crow's claws. As she watched her old student join in the dances, she shook her head.

Torches lit the dun as if they celebrated one of the ancient feasts of old. Revelers indulged in drink, food, and the dance.

The crow tipped her head in study of the celebration.

"So much more that one could have done if she had stayed with us, instead of leaving for Britannia. She should have concentrated more on her lessons before she got married." Seosaimhín then rolled her eyes. "No, it is not our fault. Sive left for other reasons. No, we cannot take her back. She is gone from us. She is the mist that pours from our fingers."

The crow exhaled a strange half-caw.

"Oh, we are not worried. There is always salvation in the night's kiss." She pointed to Maél Muire, who received her son's embrace with subtle tells of confusion evident on her face. "There is the daughter we will have and the child I shall teach. There is much that can be learned while in the womb of her mother. The body is new, yet the soul is everlasting. She is there."

The crow looked at Seosaimhín again.

"Our son seeks to wed her, but he is so misguided. He cannot woo such a strong-willed person. Of course, we made a love potion so she would fall for him."

The crow interrupted her.

"Ah, the Lamia's servants come about. Thank you for telling us, minion of Nagirrom. They seek the gateway through the mist. We know of this gateway. Perhaps we will share this knowledge with them, yet we will consult Him first. You have our word on that." As she watched, the crow took to flight, its snowy wings illuminated like a fierce light against the night sky.

Maél Muire laughed at Connor's joke, hoping that she was not too obvious as she looked out for Marcus. She then felt a hand on her shoulder and turned to see Maon. He leaned in to whisper in her ear.

"Chieftain, may we speak for a moment without company?"

She nodded her head. "Connor, please excuse me," she said to her betrothed. She then followed Maon to the side door of the dun.

"Please wait here," he said, as his blue eyes met hers, allowing glamoury to illuminate him and reveal his beauty.

"I will wait," she agreed. Maon then turned and drifted away like the mists. She exhaled before turning her back to the dun and surveyed the celebration. She soon heard the door creak and turned to open the door.

"Maél Muire, it is Marcus. Do not turn around. They are watching, and I cannot be seen now. Maon is helping me remove the body of a servant of the Lamia who worked here."

Maél Muire lowered her arm and stopped her movements, trying to relax.

"I fear your life is in danger," Marcus explained. "We are all in danger here. I had no idea to what lengths they would go. The servants we see here are bound to the Lamia. They captured Aidan and spirited him away before Maon and I could give chase."

Maél Muire stared at the dirt gathered near the door. "How did they incapacitate him?" she asked. "It would not be easy for mortals to subdue a Deargh Du."

"I did not see it happen," he answered. "I just know he is gone, and Maon and I cannot find him, although we did find his goblet." He paused for a moment. "Perhaps there is something he drank that incapacitated him, but first we need to get you and your family out without causing too much suspicion."

"Are all the servants here in league with the Lamia?" she asked.

"I would act as if that were the case," he answered.

"I will handle it. Be ready with the horses on the road to home," she stated. Afterwards, she heard nothing more. Maél Muire cautiously opened the door and found nothing else in the silent dun. She then backed away from the door, before noticing Maon watching her from across the field of dancers.

He nodded to her and then disappeared.

She took a few steps through the dancers, thinking how unreal it seemed. While her clan stowed away food and spent all day baking bread to use the grains, Connor's people danced and dined as if the world would end tomorrow.

Maél Muire attempted to smile, but she felt arms grab her and pull her into the circle of dancers. She looked up briefly at Connor, who had pulled her in.

"I am glad you found me," she murmured as she tripped over her léine, before righting herself from her stumble. "A messenger came for me, and I must return home."

Connor pulled her back out of the circle before smiling and tracing a finger down her left cheek. "I would beg you to stay if I did not know what your duties entailed. Have a safe journey home. I will come by soon, and we can make plans." He then pulled Maél Muire in close, and she allowed him to kiss her for longer than she had planned. After all, it was what he wanted. Even though the kiss felt as though she were suckling on poison, she needed Connor's trust to get information about the Lamia's plans.

Maél Muire pulled back, not wanting to meet his eyes. She could feel Maon's eyes, so she started for the gate with him following behind her, allowing for some distance between them. Once she had walked outside of the gate, she rubbed her mouth against her right sleeve, trying to get the taste of Connor out, before climbing onto Biast. She did not want to say a word to anyone after that.

Béal Átha an Fheadha

"Here is Aidan's goblet," Maon said before handing it to Fergus.

Maél Muire rubbed Taliesin's belly as the cat purred with a soothing murmur. The cat then rolled onto his back and kneaded the air.

She did not say much after leaving the feast. She wished to calm herself and find some tranquility before joining the Deargh Du and her family.

"How do you know it's his?" Fergus asked while accepting the goblet.

"Aidan usually marked or scratched the 'beth luis nion' symbol for the white fir tree whenever he was given something. He always tended to lose his things otherwise," Maon replied.

"That sun cross?" Marcus asked while leaning in to get a better look at the Ogham scratched into the goblet.

"Yes," Sive said.

"He always hated the idea of others taking his portions," Maon stated while scratching his beard. "I thought it was amusing."

"And this?" Sive asked, before reaching for the goblet Marcus had in hand.

"Mac Turrlough gave it to your niece. It smells of things other than mead," stated Marcus. He then passed over the empty goblet. "I am sorry I did not manage to save the mead."

Taliesin pulled away from Maél Muire and began nuzzling the goblet.

"Catnip must be one of the ingredients," Sive chuckled. She then pulled the goblet away from the curious cat. "I think we will be able to discover what was in it." She inhaled the scents from the goblet as Fergus took a piece of clean linen and ran it around the other cup. A glittering dust clung to the material.

"Gold dust," he stated. "It appears Aidan was poisoned, I suppose, although I have no idea what sort of things happen to a Deargh Du who has ingested gold."

Marcus raised a brow at Maon. "I just know what I feel whenever I come close to it. Have you ever ingested it?"

Maon looked at the linen and shuddered. "Yes. Even a small amount can render a Deargh Du unconscious."

"So, this was their method of kidnapping Aidan in hopes of finding a way to break through the mists," Marcus reasoned aloud as he sat down.

Sive shrugged. "Now, let's discover what was in this brew." She turned around and added some clean water to the other goblet before pouring it into a cauldron. Steam released the fragrances into the house.

"I smell Roses and catnip, of course," Sive said before sniffing again. "Then, there is aster, barley, and sponnc. I know what this is." Her face grew dark for a moment. "This is a mixture that Seosaimhín taught me."

Maél Muire leaned closer to the pot. "Is it a love potion?"

"No, now it is just steam and essences," her uncle stated.

"However, with the correct intentions, can it become that?" Marcus asked, noting the look of surprise shared on everyone's faces. "I have not done much work with potions, as I tend to avoid such practices."

"Deargh Du have very little need for such things," Sive replied.

"For mortals, intentions mean everything in our works," Maél Muire said. "Even in simple prayers. The intention is what would give this brew power."

"Without intention, these herbs, flowers, and fruit are just a stew," Fergus added.

"So, this chieftain knows Druidism?" Maon asked, in an apparent attempt to catch up on the conversation.

"No, but his mother Seosaimhín does," Sive answered.

"This merely confirms all the suspicions we've had," Marcus assented.

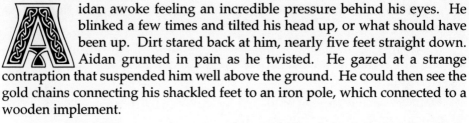

chapter twelve

Outside Ráth Cruachan

idan awoke feeling an incredible pressure behind his eyes. He blinked a few times and tilted his head up, or what should have been up. Dirt stared back at him, nearly five feet straight down. Aidan grunted in pain as he twisted. He gazed at a strange contraption that suspended him well above the ground. He could then see the gold chains connecting his shackled feet to an iron pole, which connected to a wooden implement.

Aidan closed his eyes, knowing this could be the apparatus that these monsters had used on Ruarí. Aidan then opened his eyes again as he began to rotate in the opposite direction. Soon, a wooden door came into view, and through it he could see row upon row of orderly tents, distant trees, and a half-finished wooden palisade. Soon the pressure behind his eyes lessened, but then another ache infiltrated his ankles and wrists. He looked up at his feet and noticed sparkling, black shackles.

He tried to levitate, but he felt too week. Aidan then started to swing back and forth, hoping the momentum would allow him to swing up and pull the shackles free from the iron bar. However, with each movement, an irritating itch teased him before burning into a fierce pain that he could no longer ignore.

He then glanced at his arms after feeling a painful tingling sensation when he noticed that his wrists were encrusted with dark blackness, and he realized that his captors had slit his wrists. Still, the ground seemed bereft of his blood, so they must have collected his vitae.

At that moment, a noise alerted him, so he twisted his head in order to discern its source. Then he saw that a series of figures strolled closer to him, and he felt an odd moment of fear as they neared. Their faces showed nothing... no contempt, no loathing... nothing. The one in front even smiled. Just like the rows of tents, these warriors all stood in well-ordered lines.

He heard a quick series of instructions in what he assumed to be Latin.

Aidan stared past the Lamia as the green-eyed leader asked something in a voice so devoid of emotion or humanity that he tried not to shudder. Suddenly, Aidan let out a cry as a series of welts stung his back. The sound of snapping leather awoke him to a newfound pain, along with the aching tickle of gold. He looked at who he assumed to be Mandubratius again. The face of his captor reminded him of an ancient druid who specialized in battle surgery. That druid never seemed surprised at the facets of death and dismemberment, almost enjoying the secondary pain he wielded. Aidan closed his eyes until he heard Mandubratius speak in Gaelic.

"You know something that I wish to know as well." The even-tempered words revealed little. Mandubratius continued, "I will do anything, short of killing you, to get that information." Mandubratius then started to pace. "If you tell me what I need to know, Aidan, I will give you peaceful passing to be with your Goddess," the Lamia added before stopping inches away from Aidan, staring into his eyes.

Aidan squeezed his eyes shut, willing himself not to hear the voice again, yet his determination proved weak.

"If you do not tell me what I wish to know, I have means of directing and focusing sunlight onto your body. I will be safe from harm. However, I can burn off parts of your body. They will grow back over time, but I assure you that when I remove your limbs, you will feel it." Mandubratius smiled at Aidan. "Now, do you have anything that you wish to say before I begin?"

Aidan exhaled, remembering his first night as Deargh Du and Her whispered words. She promised times of trial and also times of pure ecstasy. Morrigan foretold a balance between joy and adversity.

"I have nothing to say to you," he answered.

Mandubratius smiled. "I must admit, I admire such bravery. Please reconsider." He then pulled up the cowl of his cloak before motioning for mortals and his underlings to pull a covered object into the room. As they removed the cover, Aidan witnessed his reflection in a mirror.

"Are you certain this is necessary?" Mandubratius asked in confirmation. Once again, his host's face grew still and silent.

"I have nothing to say to you," Aidan repeated.

"Very well." Mandubratius then turned to his underlings and ordered, "Remove a few of his fingers."

Mortals grabbed his right arm and centered a beam of light onto his thumb and index finger. Aidan tried to pull away, but he could not move. He screamed as the searing light carved away his fingers, leaving singed blackness.

"I know there is a way to get through the mist," Mandubratius stated. "Just tell me how to get through it."

"No," Aidan whispered, adding a silent plea to Morrigan to bind the pain away.

"The left foot then," his captor drawled.

The itch in his left ankle became full-force fire. He watched in tears as his foot blackened to dust. With his left foot gone, his crispy ankle slipped out of the shackle, causing Aidan to fall and tip to his right side, before swinging back and forth by his one remaining foot.

"Are you sure that you do not wish to tell me how to walk through the druid's mist?" Mandubratius inquired as he paced about again.

Aidan inhaled and then let loose a scream. "Never will you know!"

"Take his left arm," Mandubratius intoned while walking away from Aidan, while showing a terrible smile.

The burning smell of his flesh made Aidan start to heave, and then a surge of blackness overwhelmed him. "Gracious Goddess," he whispered before passing into the silent darkness of unconsciousness.

Béal Átha an Fheadha

Maél Muire leaned over Marcus, preparing to wake him. He smiled for a moment in his sleep before opening his eyes.

"I am sorry for waking you," she whispered. "I just need your advice on this message that Connor has sent to me. He arrives in a few hours to discuss wedding plans."

Marcus murmured something she could not quite understand. He then sat up, reaching for the customary bowl of water she held. "What advice do you need?" he asked after washing up. He arose and then stretched his arms and neck.

She felt herself grow red after watching him.

"How do you feel about this wedding?" she asked before opening the door and walking to a small alcove off the kitchen. He followed her.

"In wartime, it is necessary to use deception to gain information from the enemy," he explained. "I would accept the circumstances, understand that I do not have feelings for him, and realize that this is needed to thwart the Lamia's plans."

She sighed before rubbing her forehead. Her thoughts seemed confused... a jumble of reasons and feelings. "So, you have no problems with my going through with this?"

He seemed to hesitate for a moment before turning away from her. She wondered whether he wished to avoid meeting her eyes. "I would rather you not have to go through with the ceremony." His voice seemed to grow older with each word. "Yet, circumstances dictate that you must, for the balance." The last sentence he uttered grew as dry as sand.

"But why do you..." she began to ask, but then footsteps interrupted her words.

Oisín cleared his throat, neared them, and said, "Chieftain, I am sorry for the interruption, but your betrothed is waiting outside."

"We will continue this later, Marcus." Maél Muire then pushed away her frustration and walked out of the interior of the dun with a smile frozen in place. "Connor," she greeted, while leaning in for an embrace and a quick kiss. Maél Muire hoped that he would accept it as a play at being coy. She then gestured for him to sit in the soft grass. "How are you?" Maél Muire asked as she joined him and then stretched out her feet and toes.

"I grow anxious for this wedding to arrive," he said, after sliding a finger over her hand.

She pulled back, hoping that he would not try it again. She then arched a brow as he caught her eyes. "Let us wait for fun. It will make the time go faster," she suggested.

"Or even slower," he purred, before taking her hand. "So, let us discuss this happy event."

"I want it small," she requested. "It is late in the season. Samhain nears, and with it comes the darkness. We should not make our families suffer for our pleasure."

"Nonsense," Connor bade before kissing her hand. "I know your clan has not had a good season, but we will help. There is no need for you to pretend with me."

"How do you manage to do so well?" she asked while tracing a finger over his knuckles.

"I have made treaties," he began to explain, "treaties which have brought us wealth and prosperity."

"Oh indeed," she drawled, continuing playing the fool. "That is very fortunate for all of your clan and mine."

"We are prepared for the cold winter," her betrothed replied. "We have anticipated this celebration for some time."

"How long have you been planning this?" she asked.

"Well, the planning was originally for Brian's wedding to you," he stated. As soon as he spoke, his eyes grew sad for a moment.

"I miss him," Maél Muire said, lying, as she squeezed his hand, "yet I am glad that you are here."

Connor's sadness soon passed. "I miss him too, but we should not mourn for him. I suggest that we have the ceremony at the church near my dun. Who would you like to marry us?"

Berti patted a horse before looking over at three cows.

"Do you really think this is a wise idea?" Sitara asked as she looked over the livestock. "I know nothing about farming. Do you?"

"It is just some livestock for us to keep here, Sitara," Berti answered, while rubbing her belly. "After he or she decides to join us, we can decide what to do. We can open a shop here, go back to Ard Mhacha and open a shop there, or travel again, though I would prefer to wait on that."

She pouted a bit. He and all the other men, mortal or otherwise, could be utterly brainless at times.

"I know this is not much to start with," he began.

"No, I am not thinking about that. Rather, I am pouting because Maél Muire marries a man she does not love in a few weeks. We love each other, and we have a child on the way, and yet we are not planning a wedding. Why are you not planning?" she demanded before hitting him on the shoulder and frowning. She felt a lapse of guilt as he seemed to realize her anger and became sheepish.

"With all the travels and activities, it did not seem to be the right time." Berti met her eyes. "I believe it is the right time now."

She grinned, forgetting her annoyance. "What kind of wedding should we have? We come from two different places with different customs."

Berti began to stroke a strand of her hair. "Talk to me about your customs, and I will tell you of mine. Then we can decide what to do."

Maél Muire headed back to the dun when Berti called to her and began to approach her, with Sitara in tow. Both seemed breathless. Their bright smiles seemed like a pleasant contract to her own frown for the departing figure of Mac Turrlough. The two lovers seemed to sense her mood, so she gave them a small grin. "Sorry... I am not much fun to be around, am I?" She then focused on them. "Is it about the house? You can still stay with me if the roof is leaking."

"It is not that," Sitara replied with a smile.

"We wish to get married as soon as possible," Berti added.

"Wonderful!" Maél Muire pulled them both toward her for a hug. "Congratulations. What help do you desire from me?"

"We desire to be wed by a druid," Sitara answered.

"All the other details are just that, details…" Berti suggested.

"Is there anyone in particular you had in mind?" Maél Muire started to count on her fingers who she knew could perform the rituals.

Ruarí walked into the great hall and beamed, looking like his old self. "Excuse me, but I could not help but overhear that you two wish to be married and need the assistance of a druid. Might I offer my services? I have married many happy couples, and it would be an honor to help those who love each other honestly." His raised a brow and genuine grin suited his features better than misery and fear, though his eyes still seemed haunted.

Berti's jaw dropped in pleasant astonishment.

"We would love that," Sitara stated, sharing in her beloved's unspoken awe.

Ruarí chuckled. "Lovely. When should we commence the ceremony?"

"As soon as possible," Berti replied, still in an apparent bit of shock.

"Tomorrow night in the grove, then," Ruarí suggested. "I will prepare for it tonight after I assist in raising the mists."

"Let us find you some suitable wedding clothing," Maél Muire recommended as she took Sitara's arm. "My cousin Caile is a seamstress. I am sure she will have something."

"Do you think she will have a red dress?" Sitara asked.

"We can find out," Maél Muire answered. "If not, I have something."

Mhuine Chonalláin

Caile clucked her tongue as she started hemming up the red dress on Sitara. "Two hours is not much time," she groused while looking at Maél Muire.

"I am sorry, Caile. It was a rushed journey to get here. Thank you." Maél Muire chuckled, as marriage seemed to suit her cousin, well, most of the time. Although, Caile's early pregnancy made her a bit snappish.

"My thanks as well. This is beautiful," Sitara stated, while looking down at Caile.

Maél Muire watched Caile grin. "I am making a similar dress for our chieftain. It's green." Caile shook her head. "That is a bad luck color for a bride," she explained after turning to Sitara. "We believe that green attracts the fae. Many tell stories of fae suitors who run away with new brides dressed in green."

Sitara giggled. "Perhaps she wants that."

"Sitara, stop gossiping about me, or at least wait until my back is turned." Maél Muire found her new and then stroked a finger along the green linen. "Green is my lucky color," she replied, trying to keep her secret thoughts from being known to all. The feelings increased night by night. She felt her face heat as she twisted a curl in her finger. She soon noticed Sitara smile at her, and she tried nervously to smile back.

"All done. This color suits you nicely," Caile said after finishing the hem.

Béal Átha an Fheadha

Maél Muire arrived at the wedding oak with Sitara in tow, much later than she had anticipated, although the grove smelled of sweet herbs, a low fire burned, and the night skies gleamed with gold and silver lights. The arch druid, her aunt, and her uncle conversed quietly amongst themselves.

Maél Muire left Berti and Sitara on their own before noticing Marcus watching them from the shadows of the grove. He seemed afraid to interrupt

---

their preparations, watching them like a silent specter. The arch druid then began the ceremony by calling the druids of the past, present, and future to join them, before parting the mists between this world and the land beneath the surface with a soothing ease of a being accustomed to the magic of the earth and Otherworldly realms.

"Marcus," she whispered, feeling what was probably a most foolish smile slide over her face. Why did he have to exude such grace? She felt herself transfixed between him and Ruarí. She then watched as Marcus left the oaken leaves, moving towards her with lips curled in a smile.

"You hide so well," she said, noticing him tense as the arch druid turned his eyes on them. His stern disapproval silenced them for a moment. Marcus seemed almost fearful, yet she gestured for him to walk closer to the gentle canopy of the great oak in the grove.

"Did you find a set of rings for them?" Marcus asked her in a hushed tone.

"Of course. Such things are my duty," she replied in a whisper, realizing that the set of rings were another thing she would need to think of for her wedding. "I spent most of my day with them going through the details." She grew silent as the arch druid, Aunt Sive, and Uncle Fergus faced them. Sáerlaith and Caoimhín joined them as well.

"Gods and Goddesses of our world, we humbly ask for your blessing on this our ceremony," the arch druid intoned before closing his eyes.

Sive motioned them forward and then led Berti and Sitara closer together.

The arch druid nodded before glancing back down at the silver sickle and dagger in his hands.

Maél Muire bit her lip, feeling some quick wave of jealousy. Wreaths of trailing ivy and holly leaves covered their heads. She wondered for a moment whether she and Seanán would have looked as blissful. Just then she felt Marcus' hand slide about hers, so she glanced over at him. His eyes reflected green at her, before melding into silver again. She swallowed her confusion, but she felt rising tears as he squeezed her hand in a comforting movement. His skin seemed warm, for he must have fed before nightfall. For some reason, she wondered whether he could sense her thoughts. She then turned back to the couple. The scent of apples, honey, and lavender wafted around the circle.

The arch druid continued the invoking ritual. "We stand upon the blessed and unveiled lands to witness the Sacred Rite of Marriage between Bertius and Sitara. Just as we come together as part of a great family here at one of the sacred homes of the Tuatha dé Danann, so we ask the Great Ones to be present here within our Circle. May this Sacred Union be filled with Their Holy Presence. We invoke the God of Love, whose name is Aongus mac Og, to be present in this Sacred Place. In His name, love is declared."

Maél Muire watched the arch druid's eyes rest on Sáerlaith for the briefest of moments. She looked on as Sáerlaith gave a slight nod before approaching the couple.

"We invoke the Goddess of the Bright Flame, whose name is Brigid, to be present in this Sacred Place. In Her name, peace is declared," Sáerlaith rejoined.

"All things in Nature are circular," Sive called out. "Night becomes day, and day becomes night again. We can see the moon wax and wane. We are surrounded by those who act in accord with nature as a balance to life and death. There is spring, summer, autumn, winter, and then the spring returns with her blooming bounty. These things are part of the Great Mysteries. Do you bring your symbols of these Great Mysteries of Life? This symbol of circular balance?"

"We do," the couple replied in unison.

Ruarí nodded his head. "Then before all present, repeat these words, Sitara."

Maél Muire watched as Sitara pulled a ring off her thumb.

"'Accept in freedom this ring as a token of my vows. With it, I pledge my love, my strength, and my friendship. I will bring you joy, now and forever. I vow upon the unyielding force that brings balance by taking your name. I will honor you above all other men'." The arch druid looked at Sitara with a patient smile.

Sitara began repeating his words as she placed the ring on Berti's left hand, while attempting to avoid biting her lip. Her voice grew louder as her vows grew in strength.

Maél Muire studied Berti for a moment and saw a flash of emotion light his eyes and face.

When Sitara finished, the arch druid nodded and then addressed Berti. "Now, repeat these words, Berti. 'Accept in freedom this ring as a token of my vows. With it, I pledge my love, my strength, and my friendship. I will bring you joy, now and forever. I vow upon the unyielding force that brings balance by taking your name. I will honor you above all other women'."

Berti repeated the vow.

When Berti finished delivering his vows, Fergus pulled forth a sword from the small altar in front of the wedding oak. "Do you swear upon the Sword of Justice to keep sacred your vows?" he asked the couple.

"We swear," the couple answered in unison.

"Then seal your promise with a kiss," Sive enthused as her mouth curled in a smile.

While the couple kissed, Maél Muire smiled as she stroked the fingers of the hand that encircled hers, but the arch druid's words interrupted her silent thoughts.

"Beneficent Spirits and Souls of our Ancestors, brothers, sisters, and children, accept this union. Help them, guide them, protect them, and bless their home and the children born of their union. May their life together reflect the harmony of all life in its perfect union. May they work together in times of ease and times of hardship, knowing that they are truly blessed. From this time forth, you will walk together along Life's Path. May your way be blessed. This Sacred Rite of Marriage ends in peace, as in peace it began. Our most honored guests are welcome to stay if they wish, with our thanks."

The soft whisper of the mist fell, parting the Otherworld from the mortal one.

Muir Mhanann (Irish Sea)

Assim felt waves rock and pitch the trireme gently in the night. As he leaned against the railing, he heard chatter between sailors as a merchant ship neared. After a complex series of signals between the two ships, a boat passed, and he watched a Lamia soldier step towards Amata and the Legate, speaking to them in quiet Latin. He followed them towards a middle cabin in the lower decks out of his own curiosity, and of course concerns for his safety.

"Who is this?" he murmured.

Amata's steady, blue-eyed gaze fell upon him, and he felt a thin trace of fear move down his spine. Amata seemed to grow more distant and impatient as each night passed, but she only displayed it in her eyes. He noticed Patroclus watching them, and then averted his eyes. Assim then heard the door open and close behind him. A note of Lucretia's cloying perfume drifted into the cabin. He watched Lucretia study the soldier.

"This is Alannus. He was telling us about recent activity in Bath," Amata answered.

Assim inhaled.

"Well, go on. I am here now," Lucretia stated, prodding the soldier.

"As I said, the Ekimmu Cruitne and Sugnwr Gwaed overwhelmed our forces," Alannus repeated. "I am the only one who escaped the massacre. "I was on my way to Éire onboard a merchant vessel when I saw the ships and the familiar banner."

"I believe this calls for a splitting of forces," Amata suggested. She then began to pace the cabin.

"I agree," Lucretia chimed in.

Patroclus muttered under his breath. "Despite what some think is the right course of action, Mandubratius expects us to arrive on time with our full force. If we short him in meeting these objectives, he will come after us in a fury."

Amata stopped pacing. With her back turned towards them, she nodded her head.

"Besides," the Legate added. "It would be easier to return to Bath once this business in Éire is completed."

Assim began to speak, unable to curb his tongue. "You are turning your back on a strategic fortification? From what I have learned in my short time as a Lamia, the British Isles hold vital trade routes. Without our Bath headquarters, we cannot receive the revenue that we need to wage war. All is invested in these golden armaments, and we know little of the effects of this gold on our enemies. What if the effect is so mild that it makes no difference?" He then took a breath.

"Patroclus is right, Assim. We will take back Bath soon enough. There is no more discussion on this." Amata's eyes bore through him.

Assim watched Lucretia pout for a moment... how he hated her pouting.

Amata still stared at him, as if daring him to say another word.

A small fire of rage began to build within him. He might be young, but he understood battle and what impeded war. "Very well," he muttered. This was not the time to challenge her. Whatever small alliance they may have had, it now seemed to slip through his fingers.

Mhuine Chonalláin

Maél Muire yawned as Caile pinned up the hem on her dress.

Her cousin then clamped several bone needles between her teeth. "Mmmmph…" Caile mumbled as she pointed to the left, so Maél Muire turned.

A noise soon drew Maél Muire's attention to the door, and she saw Connor smile at her as he walked into Caile's home. "How is my bride-to-be?" she heard him ask before rushing over to kiss her brow.

"Fine," she answered, with what felt like a tired smile. "I just have not slept well. My guests are sometimes a little restless at night."

Connor chuckled. "Your own fault for being such a good hostess," he commented. "Well done, Caile." He leaned in and traced his right index finger along the left arm of her dress. He then slid that finger over her collarbone.

"Thank you," Caile muttered through a mouthful of pins. She then stood up and removed the pins. "I have to find my special thread. I shall return," she chuckled before walking off.

Maél Muire remained standing in the middle of room by the open window.

Connor grinned before taking Caile's stool. "I have been making plans for our future," he said.

"Oh indeed? What plans are these?" she queried with a forced smile.

He took her right hand gently. "I speak of the unification of my family and yours."

"If that is my clan's wish," she advised. "You realize, of course, that it is ultimately their decision, as it is your clan's decision to extend an invitation."

"I am certain that will be no problem. Power lies in numbers. Many of our neighbors to our south are taking advantage of our friends, and perhaps soon we will be their targets. We must be prepared for more raids." Connor's thumb stroked over her fingers.

Maél Muire nodded her head. "I understand your concern, but my father negotiated with them, and they have yet to do more than the odd raid or two of cattle and sheep that wander–"

"Yes, but he was forced to negotiate with them," Connor interjected. "That will change when you and I are wed." He then kissed her fingers.

"Even with our increased numbers, we are still but a quarter, or even a third, of theirs," she argued.

Connor chuckled. "We will have new friends in this endeavor. By the by, my mother would like to have you join us tomorrow night for dinner." He then arose before leaning in for a wary kiss, trying to avoid the pins.

"Yes, of course," Maél Muire replied with a ready smile. Caile rejoined them before snatching back her stool from the chieftain with a chuckle.

Béal Átha an Fheadha

The sunset turned the sky red and orange as Maél Muire neared the dun. She heard voices echo within the dun as she slid off Biast and handed the mare over to Druce. She then marched in before slinking into her chair. It seemed to be hers now and no longer a place held in waiting for Uncle Cennedi. Here, guests waited for darkness to fall. As she rubbed her forehead, she felt her aunt's hands on her shoulders. "I am to go to dinner tomorrow night with Connor and his mother," Maél Muire muttered.

"And she believes you are pregnant." Marcus' voice came over her left shoulder. She looked up and watched him smile a bit.

Maél Muire stood and turned around to face them, wedging a knee on the chair.

"That is easy enough to take care of," Sive said. "We will just place a water-proofed pouch on her stomach."

"I do not think she will be that easy to fool," Marcus replied. "Seosaimhín is very astute with all five of her senses."

"She is still a mortal," Maél Muire stated.

Marcus leaned in closer, as if worried that someone might hear him. "She found me, without my sensing her, remember?"

Sive hummed in thought. "Perhaps we can catch a mouse and drug it. We

Heather Poinsett Dunbar & Christopher Dunbar

can stash it within the pouch. A little berry juice and ruam on her cheeks and she will glow, I think."

"Yes, but–" Maél Muire countered, only to have Marcus interrupt her.

"Pregnant women have a certain scent, though," he stated. "Go visit Sitara and ask for her clothing, or better yet…" he said before pausing for a moment, watching them, "collect her sweat within oil."

"That is a strange request to make," Maél Muire replied.

"Alright then. It is decided. Maél Muire, I will tell Fergus to find that pouch he is fond of, and we will place compartments in it. You talk to Sitara." Sive then turned to Marcus. "Deargh Du are very good with animals. See if you can catch a mouse, or ask Claudius for assistance."

"Alright, but first, tell me more of this Seosaimhín," Marcus requested, grabbing Maél Muire's arm as she walked by. "Best you hear about this as well."

"I am not sure where to start," Sive answered. "I will try to make this as short as possible. Even though those with druidic knowledge are hard to find at times, many of us still belong to specific groups or orders. Seosaimhín was quite gifted, and many of the young wanted to learn at her side, even though she was perhaps a decade older than her students. This was after her husband had died at the hands of a young Deargh Du caught in the transformation. She was asked to train many of us. However, she also had a strong interest in death. She…" Sive trailed off as she looked around the room, appearing to be nervous. "She wanted to learn more about death and would torture animals to discover the secrets of mortality. Some of my friends assisted her in a search for the hidden life essence of animals. They would channel it into their other works. I have heard stories of a substance called the 'Philosopher's Stone', which can grant eternal life. Perhaps that is the closest thing in name to the substance she wished to find."

"Many have tried to understand such secrets and became crazed in the process," Marcus commented.

"Some of us were horrified by these practices," Sive continued. "We went to the druid council. Our implications led to our council taking her students and her honor. No one would speak of her anymore." Sive then grew silent for a moment. "Yet, it was not so easy to forget," she added.

Maél Muire shuddered before wrapping her arms around herself. "Please tell me no more." Fear made her cold. "I will go find Sitara." She then walked away, wanting to forget what she had heard.

"There. You look… two months along now," Sive teased as she patted Maél Muire's fake stomach.

Uncle Fergus held the essence out to her. "Two months? Why two…? Oh, sorry, chroí."

Maél Muire dabbed it on carefully. She then closed it up and motioned for Marcus to come closer. "Does it smell right?"

She watched him close his eyes and inhale.

"It is not perfect, but it is close enough," Marcus answered.

Bearach watched the performance. "I want to go. I do not trust that old crone. I saw her once when I was just a lad, and the memory of her eyes still frightens me."

"Bearach, the last time we went to Connor's home dun in Mhuine Chonalláin, the Lamia kidnapped a Deargh Du. If this is a trap, I would feel more confident with another one whom I trust. I am afraid that means Marcus will have to assign his duties to others tonight." She then looked at Marcus and gave him what she assumed to be a nervous grin.

Mhuine Chonalláin

Marcus watched Maél Muire slide off Biast onto unsteady feet. A young boy took the reins of their horses and led them away towards the lean-to barn.

"Are you sure you want to do this?" he asked after taking her arm.

"Want? No," Maél Muire murmured softly as she pulled her arm back. "I can stand, thank you." She then smiled a bit. "It is too late now," she whispered, as another servant approached them.

"I am Maél Muire Ní Conghal," she announced.

"Of course. We are expecting you." The young man looked over Marcus for a moment. "Would you like your servant to wait in the kitchen?"

Marcus tried not to be stung by the comment.

"No. My friend will dine with my betrothed, his mother, and I, if it is alright with the chieftain." Marcus watched Maél Muire smile at the servant, knowing that denying anyone from dinner was an insult of the highest caliber.

"I am certain it will be an honor. The chieftain awaits you in the great hall. Please follow me." The servant then turned and then walked into the dun.

Marcus heard whispers as they came closer to the table.

"Do not say anything stupid," he could hear Seosaimhín hiss at her son. When in view, they both smiled at their guests.

"Maél Muire," Connor called as he stood before pulling her in for an embrace and a kiss. "We were growing concerned." He then looked over at Marcus and smirked. "Welcome again. Come join us."

"Please excuse us for not standing," Connor's mother added as she continued to smile at them. Marcus had to wonder whether she would acknowledge their first meeting. "Child of our loins, why have you not told us of this most handsome guest of yours? He is not known to us. We wish to know his full name."

"Of course, mother this is–" Connor began to say, before Seosaimhín interrupted him.

"Let the one who stands give wind and thunder to his name."

In spite of her lack of sanity and her age, she always seemed ready to challenge anyone. "I am Marcus. My full name is too long to–"

Seosaimhín shook her head. "Give us your full name."

"Marcus Galerius Primus Helvetticus," he answered.

"Oh?" Seosaimhín queried, raising her brows. "A child of Rome stands beside us, yet your eyes, of course, bespeak your true heritage… Gaul, if your beautiful eyes do not lie."

He nodded, finding himself bemused at her discernment and memory again. A moment of silence soon settled between them.

"Mother," Connor interjected, interrupting the strained tranquility of the moment, "this is Maél Muire, our–"

The elder druid's eyes moved towards Maél Muire as she stood, studying the younger woman, and then she smiled. "The white crow has told us of your strong bond with the earth and all that lives." The woman then paused in contemplation a moment before saying, "Come here, closer, child."

Maél Muire walked around Marcus and stood in front of her.

The crone looked her up and down. "It is good to hear your heart beating among the walls of this home. You bring life and vitality with you wherever you step," Seosaimhín murmured before closing her eyes. "Please sit at our humble table."

They sat, and Connor motioned to a woman at the hearth to begin bringing forth food and drinks.

Marcus looked away from the plate placed in front of him.

"I apologize," Connor began, before stopping one of the servants. "Remove Marcus' plate. I forget you are Deargh Du and do not partake in food."

Marcus watched the serving woman's eyes widen as she reached for his plate.

"It is quite alright, Chieftain. I like to try to pass as a mortal," he replied as he handed over his plate to the young woman.

"I offer my life essence if you need sustenance," she offered while bowing her head.

Marcus felt a bit overwhelmed with the offer. He considered rejecting it, but he realized it would be considered an insult. "Thank you." He then took her right hand and bit through her wrist, taking a few swallows. Once he finished, Marcus pulled back and healed the wounds, since she was not as healthy as Maél Muire, who never needed healing after feeding. As he felt the servant's blood revitalize him, giving him sustenance, he could smell the others eating their fish, mutton, bread, and carrots.

"Oh, you are one of those who traipse in the shadows and suckles off the life force of the living," Seosaimhín ascertained aloud. "One of those who consider Morrigan their matriarch."

Marcus felt Maél Muire's hand pat his for a moment. "Yes," he said while smiling at Seosaimhín. "She is our progenitor and more."

"Yes, yes," the elder sighed. "A race of blood-drinkers descended from a Goddess. How in tune you must be with Her. How glorious it must be to serve such a noble and powerful One."

Marcus smiled at Seosaimhín. "It is a gift," he said, deciding to leave it at that.

The elder druid seemed to change topics. "So the wedding is in two weeks. We have seen the bonds of matrimony solidified many times. We remember well the splendor when Connor married his first wife, Líadan. What a grand occasion it was. The air was full of mirth and joy. Such a disappointment it was when she died bearing our grandson."

Marcus closed his eyes for a moment, trying not to choke on his drink. He could feel a strange knowledge on the air that Seosaimhín may have had a hand in Líadan's death. He then turned back to meet her eyes.

"Oh well," Seosaimhín deadpanned, as her eyes bore deep into his. "We never liked her much anyway."

"Mother!" exclaimed Connor, as his voice displayed unease and bewilderment at her admission. Food dribbled from his mouth.

"She was but a seedling of a daughter, compared to the great oak you are about to wed, son. Maél Muire has strength and a wise mind. Líadan had no desire to learn." Seosaimhín chuckled. Marcus could now feel heat escape Maél Muire. "She could not discover the difference between a poultice and a potion. By contrast, the mountains echo loudly with praise of Maél Muire's mastery of the natural arts."

Maél Muire gave a nervous chuckle. "I am hardly a master."

"She insults us?" Seosaimhín asked as her voice grew harsh.

Everyone stopped eating. Marcus glanced at the elder druid and then Maél Muire.

"Excuse me?" Maél Muire asked as she stared back at Seosaimhín.

"The one who guides you in your journey learned her ways from us. She was a master on all accounts. Therefore, you should be as well."

"I apologize." Maél Muire smiled again. "I was trying to be humble. I received very good lessons, and I appreciate the skills you taught her."

Seosaimhín smiled. "The clouds have dissipated, and the sky is clear. Sunshine is restored to the earth. Will the pitter-patter of little feet grace our humble home?"

"Of course," Connor answered. "We are looking forward to many children."

Marcus smirked as he felt Maél Muire kick him.

"Perhaps many feet," Maél Muire added.

"Will the brood of our brood learn the ways of the land, seas, earth, air, and life?" Seosaimhín asked.

"If it is their calling," Maél Muire replied.

Seosaimhín frowned.

"I am certain you realize that these teachings cannot be forced on the unwilling or inept," Maél Muire stated before starting on her fish again. She then swallowed and added, "It is dangerous for either to pursue being a druid."

"The evening wind carries a scent of wisdom on its breeze. If these old bones have not yet turned to dust, we would be honored to guide your bairn down the enlightened path," Seosaimhín offered.

As Maél Muire smiled, her eyes moved to the table, before darting to Seosaimhín. "I would be honored." With her meal finished, Maél Muire pushed back her empty plate. "That was delicious."

"We cooked it," Seosaimhín stated. "Unfortunate, you could not enjoy it, soulless one."

"Excuse me? I do not think I heard what you said," Marcus asked as he smiled at Seosaimhín.

"The white crow has whispered to us the burdens of those who serve the Phantom Queen in the life after. We are honored by the presence of our daughter-to-be and her companion. We wish the hills and valleys accept our endorsement of this bond." The elder druid then arose. "May your fields grow plenty of grain, and may your children develop fit and quick of mind."

"Thank you." Connor helped Maél Muire to her feet and gave her another quick kiss. "Good night, chroí. Be careful on the way to our... I mean, your home."

As Marcus stood, he glanced at Seosaimhín's plate. While her food looked disturbed, her plate still appeared full, though he recalled seeing her go through the motions of eating, did he not? Maél Muire's voice soon drew Marcus out of his reverie.

"You have nothing to worry about," Maél Muire replied. "Goodnight."

The echoes of 'goodnight' drifted on the winds as they left the dun. As they walked, Marcus could not remember what had taken his attention before.

"Thank the Gods that our meal is over," Maél Muire whispered to Marcus before climbing onto her horse.

Connor heard the sound of a fist slam against the table. Bowls wobbled and cups toppled over.

"Why was he here?" his mother roared. He felt truly frightened of her at this moment. She then stood and began to pace the room.

"I do not–" he began to say before being interrupted.

"We did not anticipate or desire these walls to reverberate any utterances from you in respect to our question!"

"Then why–"

"Silence!" His mother's eyes seemed to gleam with utter fury. "Do you realize, young whelp, that the soulless one brings bad tidings? He is a sign, like how the dark clouds reveal the coming of the storm. We must deal with him before he interferes further with our plans."

"But that Mandubratius has tried to rid Éire of the Deargh Du," Connor said, managing to get out a sentence before being crushed by the voice of his mother once again.

"That is enough from you!" His mother sighed before growing silent for a few seconds. "We grow more doubtful of the powers of the dark ones as each cycle of the night passes. Perhaps the dark ones cannot defeat the soulless ones. Sit, child."

He sat down as she continued to pace. "The only reason we have not taken care of Marcus ourselves is that it would give Maél Muire pause to rethink her marriage plans. She worships that soulless one of Rome. Perhaps that is the closest she can come to love, now." Seosaimhín shook her head. "Talk to your dark friends and tell them not to do anything until after the wedding. On second thought, I will tell them," she said, before patting his head. "You be good and watch over the dun while we are away."

He heard her walk away.

"Mother?"

The door slammed behind her, leaving him speaking to the air.

chapter thirteen

ilence graced the ride back towards home for the first ten minutes. Marcus watched Maél Muire lean forward to pat her horse's neck.

"Your future mother-in-law could silence a banshee," he said with a smirk.

She turned to him with a raised brow. "Would you stop carrying on as if I were going through with this?" she teased while smiling at him. "I want you to stop talking about her for the rest of the night."

He smiled back at her, feeling a strange compulsion to stop the horses. He watched, fascinated when she lowered her eyes. Then the winds pushed her hair aside in a seductive movement, but soon a familiar and unwelcome scent made him forget about staring at Maél Muire. He held up his hand before pulling his horse to a stop. She stopped and glanced at him.

"Ambush," he whispered to her, before jumping off his horse. Maél Muire dismounted as well. Marcus indicated the woods opposite of where the Lamia waited and began to lead his horse there. Maél Muire followed.

After covering their tracks up to the road, Marcus grabbed her, shrouded them in darkness, and then levitated into the woods. They quietly floated around and behind the Lamia, downwind of their location. Once they touched down, Marcus whispered into her ear that she should unsheathe her blade with as little noise as possible. Marcus followed suite, drawing one of his gladii.

At that moment, a small patrol of three Lamia walked by, following their tracks in the dirt road. The Lamia wore woolen cloaks, not uniforms, looking very much like the local farmers.

"When will we find this food?" one of them asked.

"Soon enough," another said as he leaned down to study the tracks in the dirt.

Marcus whispered to Maél Muire that he would fly over them and attack from the other direction. He then explained that he wanted her to attack from behind.

In response, Maél Muire whispered, "Understood," into Marcus' ear.

Marcus then leaped into the air, still covered in darkness, and landed silently behind them. He smiled as he beheaded the first Lamia to his left. The other two Lamia turned around with shock on their faces. Marcus then released the darkness and then attacked the one on the right before either could draw their swords. He could hear the last one unsheathe his sword as Maél Muire's footsteps approached. Marcus paused, watching her creep behind the other Lamia.

"You tire as a mortal does," the Lamia jeered at him with a grin.

"And you will die like one," he replied, upon seeing Maél Muire's blade thrust through the Lamia's heart. He then beheaded this one before the Lamia to heal. Marcus then wiped his bloody blade against the lifeless corpse. "And what took you so long, chieftain?" he asked Maél Muire.

"I do not move as quickly as you do," she replied. "What do you think they were doing here, Marcus?"

He dropped to his knees and started rummaging through their purses. "Here are their orders," he said before reading the scroll he found. "This is an advance patrol, dressed as locals, that is trying to find their way through the mist. However, in the typical Lamia tradition, they have been robbing and feeding on their victims."

Marcus looked up at Maél Muire, who still held her bloody blade, and believed she almost resembled Morrigan, yet the Goddess had never appeared to be so worried.

"I wonder how far their influence has spread," she pondered aloud.

"The powers of the Lamia allow them to control the minds of the weak," he told her. "They could have many mortal allies." He sniffed the air again.

"Are their friends coming?" Maél Muire asked.

"No," Marcus replied, "not now, but we should leave before our actions attract the attention of other patrols."

Béal Átha an Fheadha

As they moved back past the mist, Maél Muire felt a small release of fear and disgust, yet the first thing she needed to do before going inside her home was to take a cold bath.

"I have to get clean," she stated as they neared the edge of the river. She dismounted Biast and then continued, "and I need to release this mouse, which was so much help fooling Connor's mother." She then looked over at Marcus, feeling her body burn with a newborn desire. She smiled at him, feeling shy for a moment. He stared back at her with a crooked smile and glowing, green eyes. "Last one in the river has to get married in two weeks," she dared him, after freeing the mouse, and then took off at a run.

She giggled, feeling a rush of wind move past her. In the distance, she could hear Marcus laughing, and she looked on as he tossed off his clothes. She started running faster, flinging off her cloak and brogues.

"You are so far behind!" she heard Marcus yell out to her.

"Not for long!" she yelled back before tossing off her belt and léine. She was almost there, though he just stood on the bank, appearing to be supremely confident.

Then her foot hit a rock, causing her to tumble. Maél Muire felt herself fall toward Marcus, and then they both fell over into the water. She sputtered and coughed a bit, still chuckling. She tried to stop as they both regained their footing.

He waded closer to her and started to push back more of her hair so he could see her face. "So, who won?" he purred softly while tracing his right index finger down to her chin.

"Does it really matter?" she replied. Her arms moved around him before kissing him, tasting the sweetness of mead from their bitter meal. His lips remained warm from the servant's small donation.

Maél Muire felt his arms encircle her and pull her closer. One of his hands slid into her hair, while the other she felt move down her back. She then opened her eyes and looked up at him. After pulling back for a moment, she asked "Do Deargh Du…" but embarrassment left her breathless, as she tried to find the best way to speak of intimacies.

His fingers ran over her hair as she felt a soft kiss on her forehead. "Yes," he murmured, before kissing her again. This time, the kiss grew more demanding. His hands moved down her hips and then over her backside. He suckled at her lips and then bit down, drawing two little trails of blood into his mouth with a hungry, engulfing kiss. The insignificant pain gave way to pleasure, as she felt him begin to suck on the wounds. Their tongues dueled, his stroking her mouth to ecstasy.

When she felt a hardness rub at her stomach, she slid her left leg around him. She could taste her blood on his lips and in his mouth while receiving another bittersweet kiss.

He soon slid his hands underneath her, caressing her limbs and raising her to meet him at the same time. She wrapped her other leg around his waist, moving her fingernails down the planes of his back as their movements became more frenzied. Breathless, urgent gasps caught in her throat as her skin slid against his. She felt him lower his head to tease the apex of her shoulder and throat and then move down lower.

Maél Muire heard herself moan as he filled her in one swift motion. His arms wrapped around her waist, stroking her back as she arched against him, grinding herself into him, losing herself in the delirious rhythm as they writhed together. She moved with him, loving each pumping caress as he plunged deep within her, over and over again. She then bucked against his body, clenching at him with each frantic movement, as her breathing grew quick and shallow. Soon, her hands moved back into his hair.

Maél Muire then heard Marcus cry out with each harsh rush of her breath as they joined again and again. She heard sweet reassurances in Latin as he abandoned himself to pleasure. Her own passion crested as he throbbed within her. She felt a moment of delicious delay when the world seemed to stop for just one moment, combining pain with pleasure, as an orgasm ripped through her body. She clenched deep within as she convulsed around him. The intense bonding exhausted her. Maél Muire then leaned her head against Marcus' shoulder as he continued to hold her.

Outside Ráth Cruachan

Seosaimhín walked towards the entrance of the Lamia encampment, thankful that her foolish son had told her the location earlier. For some reason she had yet to fathom, Mandubratius trusted Connor with that information. As she stepped up to the two guards at the meager front gate, she observed that these Lamia needed to do more if they wished to keep Deargh Du out of their encampment.

"Halt and identify yourself," challenged the guard to her left in Latin.

"We are Seosaimhín. We are here to see your dark master, Mandubratius," she announced.

"We are under orders," replied the other guard. "We cannot allow you through."

She smiled at them. "You shall part like the mists when a cool day warms the land." She then strode closer towards them and looked into their eyes. They said nothing more as they opened the gates. As she passed through into the encampment, she heard their words.

"Why did we let her pass?" one asked.

"Because if we had blocked her way, I believe we would be dead now," replied the other. "You obviously had the same feeling I did. That was not someone I wanted dealings with. Did you see her eyes?" the soldier hissed.

Seosaimhín noticed others back away from her as she walked through the encampment. Conversations even halted as she made her way to what she assumed to be Mandubratius' quarters. She then stopped outside and stared at his guard as he stared back in a rather contemptuous fashion.

"What business do you have here?" he asked.

"We desire to see your master, Mandubratius," she answered.

"Old crone, he is not available," he said.

"My child, we have not spanned the hills and valleys through the mists to hear the mountains echo that he is not available!"

The guard looked startled at her words. "Who is we?" he asked.

"We, who will pluck your eyes and suckle on their salty jelly if you do not step aside," she growled.

The guard moved aside, pulling back the flap of the tent.

Seosaimhín walked into the tent toward another set of flaps. She then closed her eyes and whispered a chant to make herself disappear. She pushed the flap aside and noticed Mandubratius with two women. His lips pursed for a moment before a grin settled across his face. His arms wrapped around a blonde woman with eyes the color of blue ice. This one was the aunt of her daughter-to-be. His hands rested on her hips as she faced away from him. A lovely brunette lay beneath the blonde.

Seosaimhín licked her lips, dropped her cloak, and began to loosen her belt. Soon she removed her léine and made herself be seen.

She watched Mandubratius open his eyes as she made eye contact with him, and then she strolled closer. "It has been a long time," she drawled.

The two women stopped and stared at her, stunned and silent in their fear or surprise.

Mandubratius stopped his movements to stare up at her. He then leaned back on his knees. "Teá, Xenia, leave us," Mandubratius ordered.

The two women continued staring at her, not moving at all.

"Be gone!" Mandubratius shouted as he slapped Teá's backside hard. Seosaimhín watched as the women grabbed their clothes and raced out of the tent.

Mandubratius moved off his knees to recline against several pillows. "Your clothes do much to conceal how fit you appear to be, druidess."

"Seosaimhín," she said, before sauntering closer. "The life of a druid is full of toil and hard labor at times, but it does sculpt the body."

"And what brings you here?" Mandubratius queried.

Seosaimhín kneeled down in front on him before sitting down. "We came to give you a message," she cooed as she traced a finger over a muscle in his chest, "but we have something else on our minds right now," she purred, before leaning in to nibble at his throat.

His movements were quick, and she found herself on her back, staring up at him. Seosaimhín willed him not to bite her.

"And what is this message you want to tell me?" he asked.

"Later," she purred.

Mandubratius watched Seosaimhín gather her clothing, still disappointed that she had not let him feed from her. "Now, what is this message?" he asked again.

Seosaimhín tossed her clothing over her shoulder. "There will be a wedding in two weeks between our son and Maél Muire. Do not attack the soulless ones until after the ceremony is complete and Maél Muire becomes my daughter."

"I may not be able to–"

"No more talk from you, Awvarwy," Seosaimhín warned, smiling. "We will not take 'no' for an answer."

How did she know my name?

He watched her pull up the first flap, stepping past his table, desk, and chairs. Then she walked out into the night. The camp grew silent as Mandubratius watched her, fascinated with her resolve, yet he remained bewildered by her power, and furious that his guards allowed the woman to have her run of the place. With the druidess out of sight, Mandubratius turned away to dress. He would have words with those guards soon enough. They would be lucky to escape execution.

Mandubratius watched the floggings with mild interest. Soon he heard Wicus address him, so Mandubratius turned to meet his lieutenant's eyes. "What is it?" he asked.

"Sir, there is an advance patrol from the fleet at the gates," Wicus replied.

Mandubratius motioned to the new guards at the gate, and then the doors swung open. He noticed a familiar face within the small group of Lamia. Patroclus, the legate, walked past the flogged soldiers, paying them no heed.

"Ave, Mandubratius," Patroclus called while saluting him.

Patroclus had always been one for the old signs of honor and respect. It could be annoying at times, yet none could claim that Patroclus displayed anything but fidelity to the current Lamia leaders. Amata found him amusing and attractive most of the time. Mandubratius found Patroclus a bit dense and shortsighted.

Mandubratius nodded before saluting back. "Patroclus, what news do you bring from our invading fleet?"

"They shall reach landfall within a week at the designated point, which is at the mouth of the River Moy, or as the locals call it, 'Abhainn na Muaidhe', just north of Béal Átha an Fheadha" Patroclus replied.

Mandubratius smiled. "Excellent, most excellent. How was your journey? I realize how far it is from Rome."

Patroclus met his eyes. "Sir, may we speak in private?"

Mandubratius nodded his head and motioned for the legate to follow him into the tent. Once there, he sat down.

"Please take a seat," he said to Patroclus. "Wine?" He then poured red wine into two goblets without waiting for an answer.

"To our victory!" Patroclus cheered as he took the goblet.

"Indeed, Roma vitrix," Mandubratius replied. "So, what is it that you wish to tell me in private?"

Patroclus took a sip of wine before saying, "Marcus escaped."

Mandubratius could only see red. He stood up, throwing down his goblet, and sensed his chair falling backwards behind him. "What?" he roared.

"Somehow, Marcus found out we were on to his charade. He overcame the guards protecting the messenger's vessel and sailed away. We believe he headed for Bath to find you."

Mandubratius closed his eyes in mute shock. "I had reports some time ago that our headquarters in Bath was attacked," he murmured. "Marcus must have led the attack on our home. Well, I will deal with him personally when we conclude our business here and the Phallus Maximus is in our hands." Mandubratius soon found himself pacing the tent.

"With it in our grasp, I can turn over the residents of this fetid island to our will. I resolve that our forces will invade Britannia on our way to conquering the rest of the known world. I plan on personally removing that bastard's head after I disembowel him and perform other acts of retribution to his body." Mandubratius then turned back to stare at Patroclus. "Who do you believe told Marcus of our plans?" He watched the legate think that over for a moment.

"Sir, I believe that it was Lucretia. Your sister Amata believes this as well."

"That deceitful little bitch," Mandubratius hissed. "You are certain of this?" he asked as he stared at the legate.

"Yes, I am quite certain," Patroclus replied.

"I plan to deal with Lucretia later. Until then, tell no one else of her treachery," Mandubratius warned.

"Yes sir," Patroclus answered before finishing his wine.

"Is there anything else I need to know?"

"There is nothing more, sir," Patroclus answered while rising from the table.

"Please tell the quartermaster to give you quarters," Mandubratius stated. "Thank you for your honesty with this news."

The legate saluted him and then left the tent.

Béal Átha an Fheadha

Maél Muire grinned while entwining her fingers with Marcus as they led the horses back towards the barn. They had both stayed silent during their walk.

"Why does Berti call you piglet?" Marcus asked with a smirk, breaking the silence.

Maél Muire giggled, despite her desire to keep her voice muted. "Because

I will sometimes snort when I laugh," she admitted, feeling her face aflame. "I cannot believe I told you that. Just promise not to reveal that to anyone else."

He passed over the horses to Druce, who waited patiently for them in the stables. Marcus then smirked at her again as contemplated how to use this embarrassing nickname to his advantage. As he held open the door to the dun, she stepped in, taking his offered hand again. "And what will you give me if I promise to keep this important secret?" he whispered. He then stumbled, nearly stepping on someone, as the floors appeared covered with many sleeping people.

She caught him and grinned back at him, but then she jumped a bit.

Marcus looked down and noticed that Mac Alpin had seized her leg.

"Refill this, chroí," Mac Alpin mumbled.

Maél Muire turned around and kicked his hand off her leg and then jabbed him in the stomach.

"I am awake!" Arwin yelled while dropping the goblet. The clatter seemed to wake the rest of the house. Mac Alpin rubbed his eyes for a moment as they turned to the color of lightning and back again to a hazel-brown.

"Oh," Maél Muire moaned in apparent embarrassed as if realizing he had been half-asleep. "I suppose you thought you were grabbing someone else?"

"No... I mean yes, I was thinking of the time I..." A slow grin grew over his face.

"Some other time, Mac Alpin," she whispered. "We all need some sleep. Tell me this history lesson another time."

Marcus noticed Mac Alpin staring at her hand as it remained in contact with his hand. Mac Alpin then raised a brow and smirked, before nudging Claudius with his left foot.

Marcus caught sight of Maél Muire's lips curve up a bit in a foolish grin before walking past them and tugging on Marcus to follow her.

As they left, he could hear Mac Alpin say to Claudius, "Wake up, Claudius. I won our wager."

Marcus glanced back and saw Maél Muire's face redden again as she opened the door to her room, pulled Marcus in, and then closed the door with her left hip.

She crossed her arms over her chest and moved in closer towards him.

He slid his hands over her hair, and his thumbs traced over her cheekbones as he pulled her in for another kiss.

Mhuine Chonalláin

Once Seosaimhín had marched into her home and closed her eyes, a soft caw echoed in her ears. She smiled. "Forgive us, white crow. Sometimes, the all too human needs must be answered." The crow grew silent.

"Yes, yes, we know that the dark one is not to be trusted. His motives are never clear, and he enjoys the game of manipulation far too much." Seosaimhín chuckled, before gathering her largest cauldron and hanging it over her fire. She then began to start work on a potion.

"He thinks nothing will stop him from this grand invasion, white crow. Yet, we know a secret of the weather. His troops will have more than they ever bargained for. Yes, yes," Seosaimhín whispered. She then closed her eyes, seeing the storm intensify off the southern coast.

Muir Mhanann (Irish Sea)

Assim climbed up the stairs as the trireme rocked and lurched in the furious sea. He came to the upper deck in the middle of an argument between Lucretia and Amata. Assim found it difficult to stand as the two women raged against each other.

"I recommend we go north to make landfall," the navigator yelled over the storm.

At that moment, the ship dipped, and more water came aboard. Assim watched as another trireme capsize.

"We must make a decision, now!" the navigator shouted as he stared at Amata for an answer.

"This is not acceptable," Lucretia replied. "You will continue guiding us to the west."

The captain joined them. "Do not be a fool! Our ships and equipment will be destroyed, and the mortals will be lost."

Lucretia argued, "We do not need–"

Amata cut her off with a curt wave of her hand. "Yes we do, Lucretia. Captain, order the fleet to sail north and make landfall. We will wait out the storm and then disembark from the coast to continue sailing west and then north to Connacht."

Assim watched as Lucretia pouted in a very childish manner. He then felt the ship turn and begin to lurch towards the north. As he grasped the railing, he heard two soldiers comment on how green he appeared to be.

"If that one was mortal, he would be making an offering to Neptune now." The two soldiers then started laughing.

"They are right," Lucretia teased as she moved to his side to stare at the raging seas, swiping rain off her brow, "You do look rather green."

"In my defense, this is my first time on a ship, as well as my first time in a storm. I was the shah! I had command over thousands of men. If my warriors had insulted me that way, they would have been executed," he hissed. "Now look at me! I am shah no more. Because of my present circumstances, I cannot properly punish these men for their lack of manners."

Lucretia chuckled as she said, "I see the viper has lost his fangs."

Before Assim could think, he slapped her. The two guards turned back away from them as Lucretia rubbed her face. Assim palmed a knife that somehow came into his hand from his belt and then covered the first one's mouth with his left hand, slicing the blade deeply across the soldier's throat and then the back of his neck with the knife in his right hand, severing the warrior's head, drenching the deck in blood. Assim then turned and shoved him and his startled comrade overboard.

Assim turned back to regard Lucretia, before shoving his dagger back into its sheath.

Her eyes radiated disgust as she turned and walked away.

Southeastern Coast of Éire near Loch Dá Chaoch

As the triremes ran aground, Amata closed her eyes, whispering the promise of proper offerings to Neptune, Mars, and Venus for surviving the storm. Some of the ships had capsized on the way to beach. She followed the others onto the rocky shore, watching the sailors, mortals, and soldiers grabbing the lines leading to the ships and pulling them from the water. However, the rain continued to pummel them.

Finally, the fifteen surviving ships rested on the beach, and everyone wearily trudged towards a cave the scouts had found. She then turned to face Patroclus' replacement, Laegeus. "Have the mortal sailors watch the boats in shifts, and have them keep an eye out for Lamia whose ships sank. We will stay here until the storm settles and then disembark. We will deal with the issues of lost supplies tomorrow night."

She wanted nothing more now than to sleep.

Amata woke up shivering as other Lamia blew on sputtering flames in the cave.

She could hear and feel the rain and wind rush through the cave opening, still managing to hit them. She could even hear the roar of the ocean. As mortals carried in the rain-soaked supplies, she moved in between two soldiers, hoping for some warmth.

"We are Lamia, why must we be affected by this cold?" Assim asked while meeting her eyes.

Amata shrugged. "I wish I knew," she murmured.

"They say the Deargh Du thrive in this kind of climate," muttered one of the soldiers.

Amata chuckled. "Utter nonsense," she replied, wanting to lift spirits. "How many hours until nightfall?"

"Four," Lucretia replied, though she appeared to shiver under the wet blanket around her shoulders.

Amata leaned closer to the small licks of flame. "And our ships, they can be salvaged?" she asked.

The gathered Lamia seemed to shrink away at her question.

Amata swallowed her rage. "I suppose that this silence means that the triremes are not seaworthy."

"Yes," Lucretia answered. "The mortals are unloading our armor and remaining supplies, but it is a slow process."

Amata stared into Lucretia's brown eyes and saw only exhaustion. "Tonight, we will see if perhaps we can salvage our ships. In the meantime, we will send out a party to see if we can buy or take blankets or something else to assist us with the cold and rain."

Amata stared at the wreckage and shook her head, knowing the worst. A light misting rain still pelted her soldiers. She then tottered back into the cave.

"Domina, we cannot find all the armor," Laegeus said, softly.

Amata turned to him. "Yes, I thought as much. Laegeus, I know our mortal associates and our brothers and sisters grow cold. We must find something for them. However, we must make up for lost time and our lack of speed. I will take Lucretia, Assim, and four mortals to that nearby village to find supplies." She pulled out a map. "I want you to take the rest of our troops on a hard march to this point north of us. Strange… we are a little over twenty miles west and a little south of where we found Mandubratius all those years ago, Loch Garman." She paused as she refocused on the matter at hand. "Anyway, we will meet you there as soon as possible." She also handed him a scroll. "Send your fleetest messenger to Mandubratius in Ráth Cruachan with this message."

Laegeus saluted her and then left.

Amata glanced around the cave and spied Lucretia and Assim warming their hands over the fire.

It was now time for them to earn their keep, she thought with a smile as Felician came to mind. Sometimes she missed his sage advice.

She walked up to them and said, "We are leaving to find cloaks for our army." She could almost feel her eyes gleam an angry red as she stared at them. Lucretia almost immediately lowered her head.

As Amata and the others trudged towards the village, she heard Assim begin to complain.

"I have never been so cold in my life," Assim muttered, "and I am soaked. I have been soaked for two days."

"Silence your tongue!" Amata growled. "We all share the same miserable circumstances as you. Do you hear Lucretia, those mortals, and I complaining about our misfortunes? No? So be quiet, or I shall cut out your tongue and feed it to those noisy ravens." Assim grew more insolent with every step he took. No wonder Lucretia had lost all patience with him.

Assim glared back at her. "No woman will tell me when I can and cannot speak," he challenged.

Amata whirled around and grabbed him by his genitals. "You will keep silent," she demanded while meeting his eyes, "or shall I remove these!" As she squeezed, she saw a brief moment of pain flicker on the fledgling's face. She smiled and released him. Amata then caught up to Lucretia, wondering why she had yet to complain.

"Do you think we will meet our objective on time?" Lucretia asked.

"We may be a few nights late, but if we keep up a good pace, perhaps we will make it in time," she replied.

"Our army could go faster without the mortals," Lucretia suggested.

Amata grimaced, hating to have to explain things to this simpleton. "Yes I know. However, we need them and they need us. They protect us during the day and we feed from them at night. We give them power. We must protect them, as one would a child. Without us, the Deargh Du would kill them all." She then watched Lucretia nod her head.

"Yes, you are correct," Lucretia stated. "I am merely frustrated that we cannot join with Mandubratius sooner."

Amata continued smiling at the other woman. Lucretia had always nursed a soft spot for her sponsor. "It has been a long time since either of us has seen him, Lucretia. Sometimes, I almost forget what he looks like. I am sure he will be happy to see you too. He may even reward you for this dedication." She tried not to laugh. Mandubratius found Lucretia to be a bit demanding, to say the least.

"I cannot wait," Lucretia answered.

Amata said nothing more in an attempt to keep her thoughts to herself.

Outside Ráth Cruachan

Mandubratius raised his goblet as Patroclus held up his, and they both began to drink. Soon after, a messenger ran into the tent and held up a scroll for him. Mandubratius took the scroll, opened it, and read, scanning over the message, before tossing the cup to the ground, giving it another dent.

Patroclus looked at the goblet and then at him. "How many more dents will your cup suffer?" he asked.

Mandubratius closed his eyes for a moment, fuming at Patroclus' joke before he started to laugh. Mandubratius then opened his eyes and shook a finger at the legate. "If you were another man, I would have killed you, but that was quite amusing," he congratulated with a sigh. "This is from Amata. There was a storm, and they managed to make landfall, yet their ships were destroyed. The remainder of our force travels by foot to our present location from the southeast coast."

"Sir, is there a reply?" the messenger asked while looking up at him.

"Yes. Go back and tell Amata to come and join me here."

The messenger nodded before leaving the tent.

Mandubratius walked over to his scrolls and pulled out a map, along with the invasion plans. "From the message, our forces made landfall near Loch Dá Chaoch in the southeast." He grabbed a quill and ink and drew a dashed line. "With mortals in tow, it will take nine or ten nights to get here at a hard march. Hmmm," he purred. "What a coincidence that this is after that wedding Seosaimhín insisted that we wait on."

"What do you mean?" Patroclus asked.

Mandubratius closed his eyes for a moment. "Oh, that story is too long to divulge in one night." He looked back at the legate and decided to tell some of the tale. "There are machinations at work here in Éire that may help or hinder our mission. There are rumors of Deargh Du gathering in force, yet when we send out scouts to find them, the scouts end up traveling in circles, surrounded by mists, and come back to us confused."

"By… mists?" Patroclus asked, looking back at him.

"Yes. They would move in a straight line into the mists and come out someplace else, believing they were on the other side. No one has been able to penetrate this barrier."

"I see," stated Patroclus. "Where is it that you feel the Deargh Du are massing?"

"A village called Béal Átha an Fheadha. It lies to the northwest of us. It is ruled by a chieftain named Maél Muire Ní Conghal. For weeks, I have tried to discover more about the Deargh Du by posing as one. The druids have great respect for them. It is as if they believe they are truly the emissaries of Morrigan," Mandubratius replied.

"And who is this Seosaimhín, and what about this wedding?"

"There is another clan to the east of Béal Átha an Fheadha," Mandubratius answered. "We have allied ourselves with them in order to gain a foothold in this forsaken land. We have manipulated the chieftain of that clan, Connor Mac Turrlough, to marry Maél Muire as an incentive to his assisting us. Seosaimhín is Connor's mother. I have to say I have never met a woman such as her. I know she is a druid and she is also quite mad, but I know little else about her. She has her own part to play, and I have not yet ascertained what it is. She also seems oddly formidable for a mortal."

"I see." Patroclus took another sip of wine. "Tell me of the strengths of the Deargh Du. Marcus hid those well."

"We have encountered a few of them in battle," Mandubratius began to explain. "We even managed to capture two. As individual warriors, they are formidable, yet they seem to be without skill or discipline. Against groups, they are easily defeated. However, I have heard rumors that someone is training them to fight in units. If that is true, then they may be fearsome on the battlefield."

"How strong is the effect of gold on them?" Patroclus asked.

"It is toxic to them. It burns their tissue when exposed directly. It has the overall effect of making them weaker than a mortal." Mandubratius watched the legate drink more of his wine before considering the matter. Patroclus tended to mull over all the angles of every decision in minute detail. It could be aggravating at times, but despite his simplemindedness, or perhaps because of it, Patroclus managed to always make the wisest of choices.

"Let me consider these things, Mandubratius," the legate requested as he stood and saluted Mandubratius.

Béal Átha an Fheadha

While the late afternoon sun continued to warm the soft, green summer grass, Marcus could tell Maél Muire still slept in her room. He had woken earlier and decided to wake the others in order to get a game going. Despite grumbling from his friends about getting up while sunlight still reigned outside, Marcus managed to start a dice game with his friends.

As he held up a gaming cup, shaking the dice within it, he felt distracted by what he swore sounded like a raven cawing.

"Well?" Claudius asked as he looked across the board at him.

The other blood-drinkers and a few mortals watched with innate curiosity.

Marcus shook the cup again. "Sorry... just thinking over what to consider for training tonight." He dumped out the three dice on the board. "Six," he hissed. He then handed the cup to Sáerlaith, who gathered the dice.

"From what I have seen of the training, our army develops nicely," Sáerlaith complimented while shaking the dice. "How soon do you think they will be ready for combat?" She then emptied the Cup of dice on the small table. "Seven!" she shouted with a smile, celebrating her fifth lucky roll.

"A week, I believe," Marcus answered as he watched Claudius glance at Mac Alpin, as if considering whether the Ekimmu Cruitne might have assisted Sáerlaith.

"Why again must I sit this out?" Mac Alpin grumbled.

Claudius sighed. "Because you like to manipulate the results of games of chance, Arwin, like almost every other Ekimmu Cruitne I have met. I will only bet with you on things you cannot directly manipulate."

Mac Alpin barked out a laugh and said nothing more.

Berti took the cup and scooped up the dice.

"They still have several hard lessons before they are ready," Marcus replied. "In fact, I intend to send out a large squad to find the main Lamia force and test their strength. We have scouting reports on where the encampment is. I believe we need to take the marginal soldiers and scare them a bit."

Berti rolled out his dice and chuckled. "Seven," he said with a smirk. He then passed over the cup and dice to Caoimhín.

Marcus felt a hand latch onto his shoulder. He looked over at the hand and glanced up at the arch druid.

"The sun sets. Walk with me," Ruarí said before turning away.

Marcus met Sáerlaith's eyes as he rose from the bench. The others continued gaming as he left.

He watched the arch druid's strides lengthen as the Deargh Du headed in the direction of the grove. Marcus rushed to catch up with Ruarí and considered asking what the elder planned to speak about, but he remained silent.

The arch druid stopped and turned around to face Marcus. Marcus watched the other blood-drinker looked him up and down, wondering whether he needed to consider drawing his gladii.

"Why are you here?" Ruarí asked. "For centuries, I dreamt of your horrible, grotesque death at the hands of our Goddess. The attack you led caused great death and destruction." The arch druid's hands met each other and folded. "That village never fully recovered. The survivors fled to surrounding villages. Only five of my thirteen students survived." The arch druid paused as if to catch his thoughts. "Despite this destruction and massacre, I was surprised to find that when I had visited the old grove, it looked pristine. It was almost as if a druid or Deargh Du returned to maintain it. I knew of none in that region who took over its upkeep." Ruarí gazed upon the grove. "There is a lot of love and tenderness that goes into maintaining a grove such as that. My teachers always said that a grove was like a person. If it is fed properly and given proper lessons, it grows with joy. However, if it is hurt or sick, it will eventually die. Yet, you reversed the damage done and made it more vibrant than it was in my fondest memories." Ruarí's words became low as he started to walk in a small circle, studying the trees. "You later saved the life of that young novice, Muirgel. Then you helped Maél Muire out of her burning home."

Marcus could sense the arch druid wrestling with his thoughts.

"Then you assisted in saving me from that... Lamia," Ruarí hissed. "I am having a difficult time understanding you and why you are what you are. I know that your transformation to Deargh Du was not by choice. In fact, it was supposed to lead to your demise, and yet you are stubborn and resilient." He looked back over at Marcus. "You chose to live then, when confronted by your jailer, instead of falling on your sword. You accepted the punishment. Your assistance with our warriors still demonstrates your character. So... why are you here?" The arch druid became silent, awaiting his answer.

Marcus tried to assemble his thoughts. "I wish to prove that I am a Deargh Du, not to mention that this is my home, Ruarí. I cannot have invaders try to make it into something it does not wish to be. Éire is like the grove of which you speak. The Lamia would simply destroy it out of blind stupidity. That, and I grow fearful at the thought of Mandubratius using the Phallus Maximus to subjugate all the blood-drinkers."

"No," Ruarí said. "Why are you here, really? Why did you not die? In the grove when you were first transformed, why did you defy Morrigan?"

Marcus grinned in spite of Ruarí's intense questioning glare. "It is part of my nature to be stubborn. I could say after all those years that it came from soldiering, but the reality is, I merely hate to lose. There was never a battle or campaign that I fought in where we gave in. We fought under some very harsh conditions. Many times, we went into battle starving. I was not about to let a barbarian Goddess win, so I survived simply because I am obstinate."

The arch druid met his eyes. "There is only one other individual who challenged Morrigan without becoming one with the soil: Adhamdh, the progenitor to all Deargh Du. It is interesting to examine the parallels between you and him. You are both invaders, and neither of you gave in to death's sweet, siren call. I believe I understand now. It would seem your immediate future is before you."

Ruarí looked at the ground directly beneath his feet, before closing his eyes. "The others are leaving to start training. I must go now to help raise the mists," he said as he opened his eyes to look at Marcus. Then Ruarí smiled for a moment, before walking past him.

chapter fourteen

Outside Ráth Cruachan

andubratius rubbed his hands together as he sat in one of the chairs in the front room of his tent. Dawn approached soon. He had sent for Patroclus in hopes the legate had a plan to get through the mists. He then sipped his mead, when he noticed Teá sauntering up to him to slide her right arm around his back. He tried not to roll his eyes at her feeble attempts at flirtation.

"I cannot wait until we arrive in Burgundy and reclaim my ancestral lands," Teá purred in the manner of a satisfied kitten.

"Yes, of course," he murmured, wondering what she was talking about now.

"I grow anxious to leave this place. Why did I ever marry Cennedi and settle for this? I yearn for my true home, not this miserable, cold island."

Mandubratius said nothing.

Teá grabbed his arm. "When will we invade Burgundy?" she whined in a persistent fashion.

"I have no plans to invade Burgundy," he replied, a little confused with her queries.

"You promised. What of our agreement?" Teá asked.

"Oh, yes, of course," he answered. "I am sorry, Teá. I will make those plans as soon as our business is done here." It felt almost too easy influencing the simple-minded.

"Good, good, good," Teá mumbled before growing silent for a moment. She then added, "You really embarrassed me when you forced me to run naked through the camp, Mandubratius. I am not a barbarian like the people here."

Soon a guard lifted the tent flap. "Sir, the legate wishes to have words with you," the guard informed.

"Enter, Patroclus," Mandubratius called before turning to Teá. "Leave us."

Teá's forehead wrinkled. "I am not your slave to order about!"

Mandubratius closed his eyes, trying to retain some calm, although her value alive seemed to diminish with every word she uttered. "Please… leave us."

"Very well," Teá huffed. She then pushed her way past Patroclus.

The legate smirked and then sat down.

"I have an important mission for you, Patroclus. I am sure you have thought out our problem with the mist. The Deargh Du we captured told us that the druids cast the mist. I would like you to find out how to eliminate this problem and do so. Also, regarding Chieftain Maél Muire, make sure she is not harmed. She is a tall woman with hair the color of blood and eyes of deep green."

Patroclus stood and saluted him.

Mandubratius saluted back, confident in the legate's abilities.

Béal Átha an Fheadha

Marcus stood in front of the Deargh Du troops, who stared back at him. He shook his head a bit. "Some of you are ready to fight the Lamia. Others of you seem to lack the sense of even the lowest life forms. There is only one way to get those of you not ready prepared. When I call your name, you will march to the front and queue into five columns." He then began to name those who needed a firm hand, and one after another, each warrior fell in line.

"Follow me," he called while gesturing for them to follow him towards the barracks. "Take care of the others," he said to Mac Alpin and Claudius. Mac Alpin shook his head at him.

"You are the laziest set of bastards I have ever seen, with questionable hygiene and the worst nails out of all the warriors in Éire," Marcus yelled, although he never could understand the insult of 'ragged nails'. "We are going on a special mission. We will find the Lamia encampment from our spies' intelligence, we will identify their strengths and weaknesses in their defenses, and then we will return. You will avoid contact with any of the patrols, because if they discover us, the Lamia may send out hundreds of troops. I do not plan on running or flying away," Marcus added with a wide grin.

"I am no coward," he heard a voice say.

He marched over to the offender known as Naohmin and punched him in the face. Naohmin wobbled on his feet for a moment, but he did not fall.

Marcus smirked at his resilience. "When we first met, that blow would have knocked you over, Naohmin. I believe the training has strengthened the will of all of you. None of you are cowards. My concern is that when we are there, we might be faced with six hundred Lamia soldiers. I do not desire a Lamia foothold in Éire, and I am sure none of you do either." He then noticed them stand up straighter. He could almost sense a change of attitude with them. Now that they stood ready, he turned around and led them southeast into the mists.

Patroclus looked over the small party of twelve soldiers that joined him for this mission, and then he studied the mists that shrouded and obscured the land to the west like a blurred veil. "So, how many of you have tried to go through this obstacle?" He turned back to see six held their hands high.

"You there," Patroclus called as he pointed to one to his left. "I am sorry, but I do not know your name. Tell me what happened."

"Quintus, sir," the Lamia answered. "We would start marching in a straight formation northwest or due west, and we would somehow end up back at our original point. We even tried going north and south."

Patroclus rubbed his chin. "Does anyone else have a similar experience?"

"We tried using torches as markers," said another. "It seemed to make the mist worse."

Patroclus walked about them for a moment before coming to a decision. "I need two lengths of rope," he ordered. He then withdrew an arrow from the quiver a soldier carried and tied one end of the rope one of the soldiers had fetched. "Now, start tying the other rope to the end of this one," he said, "then tie the other end to that oak tree."

He took a bow from another soldier after they finished tying the ropes together. Patroclus then nocked the arrow, drew it back, and loosed it. A split second later, he heard the arrow hit a solid object in the distance.

"Alright, we will go in one at a time, keeping our eyes closed as we go. Use the rope as a guide," Patroclus instructed them. He then watched Quintus leave through the mist.

"I am on the other side," Quintus called out. "I can even see stars."

Patroclus motioned for the others to move and then followed them, with his eyes closed, through the mists. Once he had gathered the soldiers on the other side, they followed a trail towards a stand of trees. A small hut outside of the trees spewed a strange-smelling smoke.

"This must be the grove," Patroclus ascertained aloud, thinking a druid must live in this house. They then cautiously began to surround the house. He could hear soft voices conversing in the quaint, local tongue.

Patroclus cautiously looked through the front window. Two figures traversed through the house as a third lay, reclined, next to the fire. The legate raised his hand to signal the others to go inside with their weapons drawn. He then heard several screams before he walked in and removed his helmet. An older man and woman stared at him. Their eyes seemed sharp despite the silver strands in their hair. A young, pregnant woman stared up at him with luminous, blue eyes. She looked… familiar. However, she seemed frightened and mystified by his appearance.

"How do you take down the mists?" he asked in Latin. In response, they said nothing. "I said, how do you remove the mists?"

Again, they spoke not a word. They just looked at each other. Patroclus took another look at the young, foreign woman on the fur and considered that she may know more than she revealed.

Movement interrupted Patroclus' thoughts as he watched the elder druid grab a blade. In horror, he witnessed Quintus attack the old man, stabbing him through the chest. Blood spurted out as the body fell to the floor.

The women screamed again and continued sobbing in grief and in rage.

Patroclus clasped his hands to his ears, but the screaming penetrated into his very core. "Everyone outside, we are returning to the camp," he ordered.

"But why?" one of the other soldiers asked.

"We have accomplished our mission," Patroclus replied.

Another soldier pointed his sword at the women. "What about them?"

Patroclus spared them a glance. "They are women," he stated. "What threat are they to us? Assemble outside, now!" he barked, and then the soldiers ran out of the house and lined up. He watched the door close before turning back to the women who cried over the druid's body.

The crone stare at him with a mixture of shock, horror, and rage.

"This is not what I intended," he told her. "For what it is worth, I am sorry he is dead." Patroclus then turned on his heel and left the warm hut.

Marcus noticed Naohmin and his party land a few feet away from him. As the reports continued about troop movements, they started towards the west.

"The Lamia encampment is southeast by two miles," Naohmin reported. "One Lamia patrol is a half a mile to the north of their encampment."

"How many guards are at their watchtowers and gates?" Marcus queried.

"We counted twenty-three," another warrior replied. "Two at each tower, two at each gate, and several more marching around the gates."

Marcus held up his hand to halt, upon hearing the sounds of rapidly moving feet. Despite being spread out, he heard them stop. Before he could call out for his men to form up in a defensive pattern, a large party of Lamia soldiers attacked them at full speed. Their movements were so quick that he could not even count their numbers.

"To me!" he barked at the retreating Deargh Du. He then turned back to face two of his attackers, dispatching one and then the other.

Have they forgotten their training?

He witnessed a few of his warriors fall before he took on another soldier. He concentrated, allowing the darkness to settle over the Deargh Du and

Heather Poinsett Dunbar & Christopher Dunbar

the remaining Lamia. He could hear the sounds of screams, as well as the thudding of heads and bodies hitting the ground. Soon the surviving Deargh Du moved out of the cloud of black mist, and so he released it. The Deargh Du surrounded him and then gathered into two formations. One group took to the air to fly around the attacking Lamia, while Marcus led the others in a charge against the Lamia forces from the front.

The spilled blood enlivened his senses, while a strange, growing energy expanded within.

Fifteen of the Deargh Du remained, marching slowly behind Marcus. Soon the skies grew purple with a gentle reminder that dawn soon approached. He stopped his men after sensing another gathering of Lamia nearby. As they looked across the expanse of the field, Marcus recognized Patroclus.

"Sir, should we attack?" Tiarnán asked.

Marcus shook his head. "No, we cannot. They realize it too. The sun comes up soon. We may survive an attack, but none of us will survive the sun. I believe their commander will realize the same thing."

Marcus witnessed the legate nod almost imperceptibly in his direction. He responded in kind, keeping his forces from seeing the acknowledgment.

"Let us return home. We are close to the grove, now." He then turned back to the northwest, towards Béal Átha an Fheadha.

Patroclus stared at Marcus across the field. "What is he doing here?" he asked in a whispered voice.

"What was that, sir?" one of his men asked.

"Nothing. We will continue to camp," he stated.

"But sir, we should attack now," another suggested.

"No," Patroclus countered. "That Deargh Du realizes that sunrise is almost upon us. There would be no one left to tell of our victory." He then gestured for his troops to join him as they began to run southeast.

Outside Ráth Cruachan

A few minutes later, the legate stopped at the gates and then pressed through to Mandubratius' tent. The elder Briton Lamia stood in front of the tent watching the skies turn red.

"Were you successful?" Mandubratius asked.

"We killed the lead druid," Patroclus replied, wondering what sort of retribution Marcus would want to have for Patroclus' participation in this plot.

"Was he the one who raised the mist barrier?" Mandubratius asked.

"Yes, though there may be others involved," Patroclus answered, deciding the truth would be best. He watched Mandubratius nod his head.

"We shall see if there is a mist barrier tonight. You are dismissed, Patroclus, with my thanks."

Patroclus walked away, rubbing his chin again. He had heard rumors of a friendship between the chieftain and the Deargh Du leaders, not to mention that their druids also seemed important to them. What kind of retribution would Marcus seek?

Béal Átha an Fheadha

Marcus held up his right hand, stopping the warriors, and faced them. "If you had not joined in and fought as a unit tonight, we would be within Morrigan's ranks now. However, you must learn to maintain a perimeter. As you witnessed, when the enemy invaded the perimeter, they caught us unaware. Get some rest," he ordered before turning away.

As he headed for the dun, he could sense something strange within the home. Marcus drew one of hiss gladii and walked to a side door. He could not smell any of the Deargh Du or other blood-drinkers that normally gathered in the dun. He then opened the door and peeked inside. He entered and silently closed the door behind himself, checking the corner behind the side entrance before walking forward. He could hear two heartbeats. He soon noticed a figure near the hearth, whose back faced him. Her red curls spilled over the floor. Marcus turned and then walked backwards towards Maél Muire, making sure no one else waited in ambush.

"What happened?" he whispered. "Where is everyone?" He then looked down at her. Maél Muire's eyes appeared flooded with tears.

"He is dead," she sobbed. "He was murdered."

Marcus leaned closer to her, rubbing her shoulder. He could still hear the other heartbeat, rising in tempo.

"Who was killed?" he asked her.

"Uncle Fergus," she replied, before wiping her tears with her léine.

Marcus placed his left hand to her back. "Stay here. Someone draws closer," he whispered.

"That is Bearach," she informed him.

The armsman peered around the back of the dun.

Marcus sheathed his gladii and nodded at Bearach.

The armsman nodded and left.

He pulled Maél Muire in and embraced her. She radiated warmth as her arms encircled him. He sat down and pulled her onto his lap. "Tell me what happened," he said as he pulled a curl away from her face.

"The Lamia came to my aunt and uncle's home while Sitara was visiting to make sure the child was alright. Berti had left to gather firewood. Aunt Sive said they wanted to know how to remove the mists. Uncle Fergus then grabbed his sword and went after their leader, but then one of the Lamia retaliated, killing him. Their leader prevented further death and even apologized," she stammered, sounding confused.

"We encountered two patrols," Marcus stated. "One came from the Lamia encampment, while the other came from the direction of the grove."

Maél Muire's tears ceased. "Did you kill them?" Her cold words broke the warmth around them.

Marcus pulled back, surprised at her words. He gently slid her out of his lap, but then he grasped her hand and held it. He stared into her eyes and shook his head, and then he fixed his gaze on the floor. He heard a soft hiss and looked back at her. Her face grew contorted in rage.

"You did not?" Her harsh whisper chilled him even more.

"The sun was almost upon us," he replied. "We would have all died in the midst of the battle."

He watched her eyes gleam with fury. She then pushed him, enraged, causing him to fall over.

She stood up and walked over to the door to her quarters.

He remained in shock.

"My period of mourning is over," she told Marcus. "I will focus my efforts on bringing the Lamia to justice." She then turned and then stormed into her room.

Marcus shifted his gaze towards the hearth and stared into the flames. He could hear the sound of chirping birds in the distance greeting the new day, as he closed his eyes.

"Marcus?" a voice whispered as a hand shook his shoulder. He heard a mortal's heartbeat. Marcus rubbed his forehead, trying to get his bearings. He then blinked and saw Bearach, who held a message.

"This was just delivered for you," the mortal said as he handed over a vellum scroll.

"Who was it?" he asked Bearach.

"He would not say except to mention he worked for an associate of yours." Bearach's eyes revealed a deep concern. He then rolled up his left sleeve. "Here, you seem a bit incoherent."

Marcus smirked. "Thank you Bearach." He took the offered arm and began to feed, taking a few sips, before lowering the armsman's wrist. "I need to leave you some strength, as Maél Muire and I need protection."

Bearach chuckled and shook his head before walking away.

Marcus opened the scroll and read.

Retribution is yours. Outside of the eastern mist, behind the fifth oak.

A Comrade in Arms

Marcus closed the scroll and leaned back against the large, rock-hewn pieces of the hearth, deciding that sleep might help him decide what to do next. He soon closed his eyes again and returned to his slumber.

Marcus carried the cauldron of water for Sive and stuck it over the hearth. She had shown up during the day and surprised him.

"You do not need to cater to my every need, Marcus," she admonished, sounding somewhat irritated. "I am fine, and you should be asleep. It is only mid afternoon." She then dusted off her hands before adding herbs to the potion.

"I am sorry about–" he began to say before she cut him off with a raised hand.

"Let us talk of other things. I am certain there will be a balance. Perhaps I am just denying my anger. I am but a mortal, and I am allowed to be calm now."

"I need you to tell me what happened," he said.

"Fergus grabbed a sword, and a Lamia soldier killed him. In a strange way, I suppose it was not his fault. He merely reacted to a perceived danger." Sive tossed in more herbs and some fragrant, oily mixtures. She then sat down before looking up at him. "It is done, now. Fergus eats from Dagda's ever-filled cauldron until he decides to return."

"I can understand that it may have been a somewhat justified reaction. However, an old mortal is not much of a danger to a Lamia," Marcus said.

"You sound a little like Maél Muire," she commented. "She was very upset. I suppose we all have that right. I will mourn for him later, but now, I need to consider what to do for his burial." She rose and then said, "The sun sets soon," as a slow smirk spread over her features, "but I am certain you already knew that."

As Marcus walked to the outskirts of the mist, he could smell the Lamia. He soon saw a chained figure slumped against an oak. Marcus wondered whether Mandubratius had condemned Patroclus to that spot, so he rushed over to the tree, only to see that the victim was not who he believed it to be. In fact, Marcus did not recognize the bloodied victim at all. Upon examining the blood-spattered face, Marcus noticed that a tight rope bound his mouth open. In addition, a large padlock kept the chains in place, and a key rested within the lock. A clean scroll stuck out of the soldier's blood-soaked tunic. Marcus pulled it out, opened it, and read the message.

I am truly sorry for the accidental death of the mortal druid. When I discovered who he was through our extensive intelligence network, I linked the druid to Maél Muire Ní Conghal and her to you. No one was to die during this mission, especially a harmless mortal. Mandubratius requested that I find a way to stop the mist barriers. One of my men, Quintus, misinterpreted this druid's actions as dangerous and killed him without orders from me. I know that this in no way makes up for the loss. However, your friend Maél Muire and her clan will have some satisfaction in killing her uncle's murderer. I cannot betray my commanders, but I feel that you and I understand one another, and if at some point I can assist you without harming them, I will. May Mars and Venus smile kindly upon you.

Patroclus Statilius Messalinus

Marcus rolled up the scroll into the sleeve of his tunic before twisting the key, unlocking the padlock. He noticed the Lamia open his eyes. They grew wide upon seeing Marcus.

"You picked the wrong mortal to slay," he informed the soldier in Latin. Marcus then hefted the Lamia to his shoulder and started towards the dun.

Marcus heard the grove and the dun begin to come alive with the sound of soft whispers on the wind. He felt no doubts that they could smell the Lamia he carried as he approached. Marcus heard orders resonate with the wind, and then he watched as a strong darkness descended, successfully blinding him for a moment. Marcus sensed several warriors, including a flagon-waving Mac Alpin, surround him.

"False alarm!" Mac Alpin boomed, and then the camp went silent, as the darkness descended to the dirt. The gathering Deargh Du, Ekimmu Cruitne, and Sugnwr Gwaed chuckled as they left.

"You intend to defend the dun with that?" Marcus guffawed at Mac Alpin upon noticing his lack of steel weaponry.

Mac Alpin laughed throatily. "I do not waste drink, Roman," he belched.

"Oh of course... your breath could finish them off," Marcus added.

"This mug was all I had in my hand when I heard the call. Who is this guest?"

"Join us in the dun and I will reveal all–" Marcus forgot his words upon seeing Edward rush in with a smoldering clay pot.

"Edwina, what are you doing?" Mac Alpin roared. He then grabbed the pot from Edward and threw it into the woods. Marcus ducked upon hearing an explosion. The stinging smell of burning grass and wood made him wince.

"Marcus has an oversensitive nose, as does my line," Mac Alpin chided with a sigh. "Let us take care of this fire, Edward, before your mistake burns down the village."

"I thought this would be the perfect time to demonstrate these new capabilities," Edward said with an apparent lack of alarm in his movements. "That forest is full of undergrowth, and a burn would do it good."

Marcus chuckled as Mac Alpin tugged Edward by his ear towards the smoke. He watched other Deargh Du fly for the forests, carrying helmets full of water. Marcus then walked through the front door of the dun and into the great hall.

Maél Muire sat in the chieftain's chair, as Sitara and Sive sat next to her on stools. Sitara rubbed her stomach, Sive dropped powdered resins into a mixing bowl, and Maél Muire spoke softly about some harvest.

Marcus walked over to Maél Muire and dropped the Lamia at her feet. He watched her pale in shock.

"Who is this?" she asked.

Marcus turned to Sive and announced, "This is your husband's murderer." After starting for the side door, he heard Maél Muire call for the guards to find Deargh Du to keep watch on him. He glanced back for one last look and saw that Maél Muire's face betrayed no more shock, but her ire remained. He then faced forward and continued walking, but he sensed her footsteps following him, and so he decided to stop, turn, and face her. Marcus watched her face become soft and gentle at her approach.

"How did you find him?" she asked.

"I have a friend in the Lamia ranks," he replied. "This is his way to apologize."

Her body stiffened. "Was he present at my uncle's execution?"

"Yes, he commanded the mission," Marcus answered.

"Was it his mission to kill my uncle?" Her words grew venomous, and her face grew fearsome.

"No," Marcus replied. "It was his mission to discover how to remove the mists. Your uncle's death is a horrible accident. This friend of mine felt that this action could grant him some redemption."

He watched her grapple with that information, but her face still showed unease and turmoil. "Who ordered this mission?" Maél Muire asked.

"I believe it was Mandubratius," Marcus answered.

"How soon will your army be ready to march on the Lamia?" she queried, as her voice grew forced.

"We are almost ready, yet we need our equipment. Sáerlaith says it will be here within a week."

"Very good." She fell silent for a moment and then met his eyes. "Thank you, Marcus. You do not know what this means to me. We will talk about this soon."

Outside Ráth Cruachan

Amata led the others through the encampment, pleased to see the soldiers bowing their heads in obeisance as she moved by with Assim and Lucretia behind her. Upon reaching the legate, she nodded to him. "Patroclus, please join us," she said.

"As you wish, Domina." The legate turned and then marched in step with her, as Assim and Lucretia walked behind them.

Amata pushed aside an errant tress of dark hair as they stopped in front of Mandubratius' tent. She then held up her hand to the guard, motioning him to stand aside and allow them passage.

The guard lowered his head and held back the tent flap. She heard rustling, as well as the sounds of copulation. Amata tried to keep her laughter under control. She motioned Patroclus, Assim, and Lucretia to join her in the front room of the tent and then watched the guard drop the flap. She could see Mandubratius clasping a blonde woman's back and breasts as he continued to grind himself against the stranger's backside, oblivious of his guests.

Amata decided to pick up a cup and slam it against the table.

"I ordered you not to interrupt–" Mandubratius shouted before looking up at her and grinning.

Amata chuckled, noting the sheer embarrassment on his companion's face. "I see you are up to your usual entertainments, diddling your former food."

"Perhaps you would like to join us," Mandubratius suggested.

Amata raised her brows at him. "I would prefer not to trouble myself with younglings." She glanced back at her party and noticed Assim look surprised and just a bit angry about her assessment.

"Lucretia, it is nice to see you again." Mandubratius rose, pulled on some clothes, and then walked over to Assim. "And who might you be?"

Amata watched Assim begin to answer.

"He is of no importance," Lucretia interrupted.

"Let him speak, Lucretia," Mandubratius warned.

Amata watched his eyes narrow in Lucretia's direction, becoming serpentine.

"I am Assim Ibn Kalil," Assim spoke as he bowed. "We have met once before, several years ago. I am the Shah of Shiraz, Dominus."

She watched Mandubratius bow in return.

"Impressive," Mandubratius said. "And who sponsored you?" he asked.

"I did," Lucretia answered in a meek voice.

Mandubratius walked over to Lucretia, who stared at the ground, apparently afraid to meet his eyes.

"In the days of my predecessors, you or another would have been killed to keep the numbers of the Lamia population even. You should be thankful that we are at war and therefore need all of the soldiers that we can make. However, you are supposed to ask a superior for permission." Mandubratius looked at Assim and then turned his green eyes back towards Lucretia.

Amata could feel him study her.

"Would you and the shah kindly leave so I can remind Lucretia of the chain of command? Teá, you may leave as well. Your services are no longer required."

Amata placed a hand on Assim's shoulder and walked him out of the tent. She wondered whether this reminder would be more about the loss of Marcus than Assim's sponsorship.

Cennedi Looked Up as Teá stalked into the tent they shared and began to pace about the small space. "I am so tired of being treated like this by that... Briton!" she fumed.

Cennedi watched her for a moment before returning to his contemplation of a simple cross he had drawn in the dirt. He started playing again, moving his finger around the cross and turning it into a quartered circle. He then studied his wife again, when a strange, young woman covered with a coarse blanket entered the tent. Her tears appeared to blind her.

She moaned softly as she walked to the center of the tent.

"You have blood running down your legs," Cennedi commented. "Sit," he ordered the stranger. "Tell me what happened. Did a Deargh Du attack you?"

Teá laughed at his question. "It is obvious what happened," Teá snapped, her words impatient. "This is one of Mandubratius' disobedient children,

Lucretia."

"What do you mean?" Cennedi asked Teá. "It is not obvious to me."

"Husband, there are some things not meant to go between a woman's legs," Teá answered.

"He used a scroll tube," Lucretia murmured.

Cennedi looked at her in disbelief. Maél Muire had to be older than this one. Her soft, brown eyes welled with unshed tears.

"I know you will heal, but you still need to stop the bleeding," he said to Lucretia while looking around for something. He then grabbed Teá's softest linen léine and handed it to Lucretia.

"No, she cannot have that!" Teá yelled, "It will be ruined."

He ignored her and moved in closer to Lucretia as the young woman raised her dress. He tried not to be disgusted as he tore the léine and held it in place using gentle pressure. "Here," he told her as he placed his arm in front of Lucretia's mouth. "Feeding will help you heal."

The young woman took a weak bite and started to suckle from the wounds, before collapsing to the ground, unconscious.

"Why are you helping her? She has not exactly pleased Mandubratius recently," Teá stated.

"And you have?" He felt a small smile turn his mouth up. "How many times have I witnessed you running out of his tent without clothes, tail between your legs, scrambling to hide your shame?"

He felt a strong sting across his face as she slapped him.

"How dare you help this… harlot?" Teá's face grew red.

Cennedi started laughing, almost rolling into an amused ball. "What role in this tragedy do you think you are playing, mhuirnín?"

"How dare–"

Cennedi interrupted her. "If anyone has been the harlot, it is you, Teá. You cavort with Mandubratius, the soldiers, and our food. The only one you do not cavort with is your own husband. I do not know if I consider you a wife anymore."

Teá grew silent. Had he rendered her speechless?

"You would divorce me, here and now?" she asked.

"Yes, I would," he replied, his voice calm and even.

He watched Teá smirk for a second before tossing aside her robe.

"I think I just remembered why I married you," Teá purred. Her lovely, graceful movements made him forget his fury with her.

Assim felt a hand grasp his shoulder. He turned and saw Amata stare at him with red eyes.

"I swear to Mars that I will kill you if you ever make me look like an idiot in front of Mandubratius again," Amata hissed before pushing him away.

He stared at her retreating back as she stalked away. He soon heard voices in a tent speak of leaving, and so he snuck closer to eavesdrop.

"I think that your plans for the invasion of Burgundy were nothing but folly for Mandubratius," a male voice said.

"I do not want to hear this," a female Lamia replied. "We are supporting him."

"I see. In your eyes, there is no other choice," the male Lamia snapped in irritation.

Assim watched the male Lamia leave, heading towards the supply tent. Assim stood up and started to follow the native into the tent, but he soon found a sword at his throat. The stranger motioned him inside.

Assim held up his hands and slowly followed.

"Who are you and why are you following me?" the stranger asked. His blue eyes turned red in the dim light from the lamps.

"I am Assim Ibn Kalil," Assim replied. "My sponsor is Lucretia. I understand that you feel this invasion is a folly and you also feel that chasing this myth is a waste of time."

The sword moved closer, its point piercing the skin of his throat. "Who told you that?" the other Lamia whispered harshly.

"I feel the same way. I wish to leave this camp and live beyond next week."

The stranger then lowered his blade. "Why do you wish to leave?"

"I am tired of being treated as a lesser," Assim replied. "You walk with the confidence of a leader. I was a leader once myself. Have you seen the Deargh Du fight? I believe they can fly. I witnessed one attack Lucretia, and she was helpless and at his mercy. The Lamia are no match."

The stranger gave a strange little laugh. "I was a chieftain of lands to our north, friend. My name is Cennedi Mac Lubdan. I think this Phallus Maximus that Mandubratius searches for is not even real. It is nothing more than a legend. This land is full of such legends that never existed. Of course not too long ago, I counted creatures, such as the Deargh Du and us, among those legends. So, what do you propose to do?"

"In the midst of battle, we can sneak away to caves near the river Moy where we can hide for a few nights. We can then travel to Ulster and decide where to go from there."

Cennedi chuckled. "It may be crazy enough to work. Will anyone else join us?"

"I think I know someone who may join us," Assim replied.

Assim walked over to the side of the legate's tent. He had chanced to see what he believed to be annoyance on the legate's face during their short meeting. Anyone with a mind of their own would be impatient with Mandubratius and Amata. Assim pulled up the back wall of the tent, wanting to keep their conversations private, but yet another sword met his shoulder.

A lamp turned the room bright as the legate pulled him within before sheathing his blade. He then backed away, giving Assim space to crawl under the tent and stand.

"You have an odd way of entering tents, Assim. Please join me for a drink." The soldier then turned toward the front half of his tent.

"Thank you. That would be most enjoyable," Assim replied.

"Take a seat," offered Patroclus as he gestured towards a spare chair, before pouring wine for them both. After handing Assim a cup, they raised their drinking vessels.

"Now tell me why I should not turn you over to Mandubratius for invading my tent?" Patroclus asked.

Assim felt anxiety, but he tried to keep that to himself. "Do you normally invite intruders to drink?"

The legate chuckled. "I find it a good way to judge friend from foe."

"Well, since we do not know each other well, I suppose I do not fit in either category," admitted Assim.

"Before you leave this table, I will know which category you belong in. Now please, tell me your reason for being here." Patroclus met his eyes.

"I have heard people mention that you are a champion of the old ideals of Rome," Assim began to explain. He watched the soldier nod his head. "How do you feel this ideal is being served being so far from home, chasing after a mythical artifact with dubious properties?" Assim asked.

"It is the will of the leadership of Rome," Patroclus replied.

"Is the will of the leadership of Rome serving the ideal of Rome?"

"Such talk is treasonous," the legate replied, steel firming his voice.

"I have heard you are a very intelligent man with strong ties to the Rome of old, yet you must see that Rome's ideal is not being served by this exercise in futility. Though the Deargh Du are few, they are superior in strength and fighting ability. You have witnessed the skills of that one who pretended to be in our ranks. Can you deny their abilities?"

He watched Patroclus brush aside those comments. "I serve the ideal of Rome in my own way. I do not need a pretend usurper to tell me what I need to do."

As Assim gazed at the Legate, he realized that the soldier felt the same way, but he would not put aside Amata and Mandubratius at this point.

"I am afraid I have taken too much of your time," Assim said at last. "Thank you for the drinks."

He and Patroclus then rose at the same time.

"Please leave the way you came," Patroclus requested. "I will pretend that this conversation between us never took place."

Assim nodded before heading for the rear of the tent. After sliding out, he noticed that no one waited for him. Assim then made his way back to his tent. He would speak with Cennedi tomorrow night. He felt slightly disappointed, but perhaps one day, Patroclus would change his mind.

chapter fifteen

Béal Átha an Fheadha

aél Muire's wonder at the Deargh Du's senses reeled again, upon seeing Marcus glance over his shoulder at her, so far away, while he continued to speak with Mac Alpin about battle plans, or something. She moved aside to let others past before ducking behind a corner, pretending she could hide herself, when in truth she knew that they could sense her every breath.

Maél Muire closed her eyes, reliving the last night and day. After a quick judgment on her part, she had carried out the execution with Uncle Fergus' blade, severing the Lamia's head from his neck. Now she, only wished for sleep, and for Marcus.

She could barely hear Mac Alpin say, "Lad, do you think you will get back in her favor?" His slurred sentence demonstrated that he did not know that she stood behind them. "After all, she did push you down."

"Would you stop with that?" She heard Marcus laugh. "She caught me off guard. She probably will not invite me back."

"Oh, but I see doubt in your eyes. I bet you one hundred pieces of silver that she will come up to you, friendly as you please, and drag you to her bed."

She watched Marcus consider the bet for a moment.

"That is not a good wager," she stated, while striding from the shadows.

As Marcus turned to face her, she almost grumbled, seeing him allow himself that spark of glamoury that could hold all mortals captive and entranced. Then the glamoury faded, leaving him the soothing gray and blue eyes that made her stomach quiver and feel awed. He smiled, curling his lips and revealing his teeth. Maél Muire could not help but wonder whether the fangs hurt when they descended.

"Oh indeed?" His smile grew.

"Well," she said. "Are you going to stand there looking like a man who just realized that his herd doubled in size, or will you join me?" She extended her hand.

"Lass, you could have come later," Mac Alpin stated. "You spoiled my bet." A strange twinkle gleamed in the elder blood-drinker's eyes.

She chuckled as Marcus wrapped an arm around her shoulders.

"Mind your manhood, lad," she heard Mac Alpin advise.

"And did you have any brothers or sisters?" Maél Muire asked, fully content to rest against Marcus' chest as his hands stroked her hair. She felt exhausted, yet not so tired as to bother him with questions that would lead to a rather important query. She felt content and warm, for the moment.

"None I know of," Marcus replied. "Then again, I was basically a bastard, and I could have been one of many."

She smiled a bit. "So, what is it like?"

"What is what like?" he asked while tucking a strand of her errant hair behind her right ear.

"Becoming a Deargh Du," Maél Muire replied, keeping her voice low.

She watched Marcus close his eyes for a moment.

"It was very painful," he admitted after some length. He seemed to be thinking out his answers. "It is a test of one's endurance, heart, and resolve on a physical and mental level."

"How do you mean?"

Marcus sighed while stroking her hair with his eyes closed. "One's physical appearance and mental character changes during the transformation," he continued. "This is not the way I looked as a mortal. I had a typical Roman's nose, quite a few battle scars, and I was shorter."

"I had no idea it was so drastic," Maél Muire murmured as she ran a fingertip over his left cheekbone.

"Yes, indeed. It can be very painful, and it was for me. There are other changes as well. You lose all your teeth, and you go insane for a night. I remember being hungry and thirsty and not being able to eat. I had to find out for myself that I needed blood. I had no one to teach me."

"How awful," Maél Muire said as she leaned her cheek against his chest. "So what gifts came with this transforming pain?"

"You already know about glamoury, flight, and the darkness. I can also bring forth light as an effect of glamoury. In addition, I have enhanced senses." He looked at her and grinned. "I can influence others' actions... sometimes, anyway. Now be a chicken for me."

She chuckled and looked at him. "Am I supposed to start clucking?"

"I hope so," Marcus admitted while smirking.

"And the feeding?" she asked.

"That depends. It is not as bad as I thought it would be. We do not kill, at least I do not. Therefore, I do not feel any remorse for what I take. Deargh Du can transfer regenerative strength to mortals and heal small wounds. The glamoury makes it seem like a crazy, yet pleasurable dream."

"Yes, but what does it feel like?" she pressed him.

"I feel a rush of power and a bond between myself and the donor. I can learn a few of their secrets, if they are willing to share, and then I feel rejuvenated. I feel their stronger emotions, and sometimes I will become intoxicated if they are as well," he answered.

"You have never drained someone completely?" she asked.

"Yes, a few times in self defense," he replied.

"Do Deargh Du feed from each other?"

"You are Maél Muire of one thousand questions." Marcus laughed huskily while running his right hand down her back. "I have never let anyone feed from me before."

"Mortals need to feed from Deargh Du in order to transform, correct?" she queried.

"Yes, but I have never gifted anyone with the transformation," Marcus answered.

"That must be very sad," Maél Muire admitted. "If you were to find the right person, would you do it?"

"Yes, when I find the right person," Marcus replied.

"So," she began, feeling her face redden a bit. "Would you transform me into a Deargh Du?"

He fell silent as if considering the situation fully. "Yes, I would," he whispered as he caressed her back again. "You realize that if you do this, we would be bonded together forever." He met her eyes. "You could never see the light of day again. Not to mention, you would feed upon the life essence of living beings."

"I believe that is what I wish for," she said before rolling off Marcus and leaning against his shoulder.

"There is a process I must go through to see if you are a good candidate to be Deargh Du," he answered, before leaning in to kiss her forehead.

"I see," she answered, wondering whether he wanted time to think over the situation. Perhaps this was too rash for either of them. "Does that mean you don't think I'd be worthy?" she blurted.

"Worthy? You're most worthy, more so than many I've met." He then began playing with one of her plaits. "However, there are others I must consult."

"Go consult them tomorrow night, please," she told him. "I think this is right for me."

"Alright." He leaned up against his elbow to stare down at her. "Sleep well," Marcus whispered as his hand traced over her shoulder.

Marcus sat next to the fire, hearing the sounds of marching Deargh Du as they drilled. He stirred the flame with a stick, seeing fae speed through the breathing fire. He then sipped on his mead.

Sáerlaith placed a hand on his shoulder before sitting down on the log next to him. "I apologize for the delay in supplies, General," she said, as her mouth curved into an attractive smile, making her appear youthful.

"I am sure our supplies will be here soon enough," he stated.

"You seem to have a lot on your mind," she said. "I am sorry for the chieftain's loss. I know you and she are close."

"Life goes on. She seems satisfied with the justice. Speaking of changes in the cycle of balances within life," Marcus continued before pausing. Marcus looked about to make sure no one else could hear his question. "Tell me, how does one transform a mortal into a Deargh Du?"

Sáerlaith's expression turned to one of utter surprise. "I thought you knew. You became one, Marcus. Do you not remember?"

"I think due to the circumstances involved, that particular knowledge was not passed to me," he answered.

"I see. Well, let me summarize what happens. A Deargh Du feeds from a mortal, and the life essence of the mortal combines with theirs. The Deargh Du then opens a wound, and the transference occurs. The mortal feeds from the wound until a force pushes them away. They pass out and come before Morrigan herself. She judges them and decides whether they will become Deargh Du or die. If one survives Morrigan's judgment, the body and mind begin to transform. It takes longer for the mind to reorient itself, which causes madness for a time. The desire to feed is so strong that the new Deargh Du will feed on anything and anyone, without regard for the life of the victim. The newborn Deargh Du recovers within the next cycle of night and will return to normal."

Sáerlaith joined him in poking at the fire for a moment before continuing. "The father- or mother-in-darkness has to keep the newborn Deargh Du sequestered, if not bound, to keep him or her from killing mortals the first night. Even after the transformation is complete, they are the guide and teacher of the new Deargh Du for the rest of their lives. A strong bond will exist between the two that will never be broken." Sáerlaith then met his eyes. "Is this something Maél Muire wishes to do?"

Marcus tried to seem surprised that she would know, but Sáerlaith's skills could not be doubted.

"She has asked me to do this, but I did not know the entire process. I wanted to ask before I allowed it, just in case it was something I was not permitted to do. I have been an outcast for so long, Sáerlaith, that I did not want to force my fate on others."

"The number of Deargh Du that walk the night is something that is kept within tight controls. After all, we are responsible for maintaining the balance. Therefore, we must balance ourselves. However, with the many deaths that we have experienced, we have not enforced our own rules." Sáerlaith smiled at him, before placing a gentle hand over his.

"Make sure Maél Muire knows that she is ready. Once the transformation begins, there is no turning back. In addition, I must ask one thing. Are you ready to be a teacher to Maél Muire for the rest of your existence?"

"Of course," he answered.

"Then you have my blessing," she replied.

Maél Muire patted Sitara's hand as her aunt busied herself in Berti and Sitara's new home. The sweet scent of frankincense swam through the air.

Sitara stared into the fire as Aunt Sive mixed other herbs together in a brew.

Maél Muire stood up and then tiptoed past a half-asleep Berti, gathered a goblet, and stared into the brew. She smiled at her aunt. "Go relax and let me help." She then grabbed another cup for Sive.

"I am glad you are calm now," Sive said to Sitara. "I was afraid that you had come close to losing the baby."

"I have seen many close to me die," Sitara said. "Until now, I can say that I never witnessed a friend die. Thank you for sharing the frankincense with us. It reminds me of home." Sitara then seemed to study Sive for a moment. "How are you feeling?"

"I am fine, child," Sive replied.

Maél Muire placed a hand on her aunt's shoulder. "You are not well, and you should be resting instead of fretting over Sitara. Allow me to do that."

"I am fine," Sive replied. Her words grew impatient and forced.

Maél Muire stopped Sive as she was about to place ragwort in the brew.

"And you are planning on using ragwort, or was that a mistake? You wanted to use this instead, correct?" Maél Muire asked as she pulled out a bag of dried berries and fennel and began to add them to the brew. "I believe you need some of this too." She then placed a poultice on Sitara's stomach before handing them both tea. Afterwards, Maél Muire sat down and nudged the fire as she watched Berti sink lower into his blankets.

"When did you decide that you wanted to be Deargh Du?" her aunt asked.

"You are going to become Deargh Du?" Sitara queried as her eyes grew and her voice revealed a growing excitement. "I knew it."

"What?" Maél Muire heard her voice grow timid. "Did he tell you?"

"Not every tidbit about your well-being comes from Marcus," said Aunt Sive. "I have other sources too, you realize."

Maél Muire could see Berti smile a bit.

"Bertius!" she accused.

Berti mumbled something and then started to snore.

Maél Muire grabbed a wet cloth and threw it at him, hitting him in the forehead, but Berti still feigned sleep.

"Berti, did you tell my aunt?" she demanded.

The rag slid to Berti's chest. "For your information, I did not tell her, and frankly I am disheartened that Marcus did not tell me himself, since I presume he is the one you wish to transform you."

Maél Muire rocked back in her chair. "I have not yet decided."

"But it is the ultimate form of service to Morrigan," Sive stated.

"I think you would have made an excellent Deargh Du," Maél Muire replied.

"I have no misgivings about my own path. I am here to help the balance and the Deargh Du, and I believe that Fergus is keeping a spot for me in the banquet hall of the Otherworld for when my duty is done."

"What is keeping you from deciding to be Deargh Du?" Sitara asked, while rubbing her stomach.

"I have been around Deargh Du for the last few months," Maél Muire began to explain. "They seem so perfect in many ways. They walk with grace, they look beautiful, and they even speak and smell perfect. They fight with such a beautiful precision. However, I do not feel as though I am good enough to be one of them," she finally admitted.

"Most of these magical graces are a part of the transformation," her aunt replied. "Your mind and body changes, as if under the watchful eye of a trained sculptor that makes beautiful designs from ugly stone."

"Yes, I know," Maél Muire replied. "Marcus told me of the transformation in gruesome detail, but perhaps you are right. I still wish to contemplate this. I must make sure this is what I want."

"Take time, child," Sive advised, before placing her left hand over Maél Muire's. "This type of decision cannot be rushed. Once you are Deargh Du, you cannot return to mere mortality."

"There is one other thing," Maél Muire said. "I do not want any of you three in danger. Stay away from the wedding."

She heard the sound of grumbles and general disagreement. Berti even pushed aside the pretense of being sleepy to pout.

"Berti!" she exclaimed, placing her hand on his shoulder as she looked over at Sitara. "You have a wife and child to look after now. Several Deargh Du will be watching. I am certain that I will be fine. That goes for you as well, Aunt. No one expects you to be there because of Uncle Fergus. Sitara, you are with child, and no one likes to deal with pregnant women. I am sure everyone would prefer not to have to deal with you. No offense."

She heard Sitara laugh. "No offense taken. I revel in being obstinate."

"Fine," Aunt Sive acknowledged, waving a finger at her. "Just be careful."

"Berti?" Maél Muire glanced at him, though he still managed to frown and pout.

"Alright," he grumbled. "You will be sorry that I am gone."

"I am sure we can keep safe, and Marcus will tell you all about it afterwards. It will be a tale for the ages."

Maél Muire patted Berti's back before returning to the cauldron.

Mhuine Chonalláin

Soft whispers drifted in his ear, pulling Connor back to reality.

"Wake up, chroí," a voice whispered. "Let the clouds part and the rays of the sun shine through."

Connor opened his eyes and saw nothing but his mother's eyes.

She stroked his hair and announced, "Our allies will soon arrive in force." She smiled as she pulled away.

"I have wondered why they had not arrived sooner. I thought they were supposed to arrive earlier, perhaps a week ago."

"Shhhh," she purred. "That is why we called Nagirrom. That silly, impatient Briton wanted to battle immediately, but we turned up the wind and blew the ships to shore. They had to take a longer land route with their mortals slowing them down. You see, they will be ready the night of your wedding. Then, the soulless ones will bother us no more. Then, once you are married to Maél Muire, you will have the loyalty of her clan, control of her property, and you will give us many granddaughters to enjoy."

Outside Ráth Cruachan

Mandubratius joined his staff at the gate as the remainder of their forces arrived. He felt Amata's hand entwine with his.

"Time for all of us to study our battle plans," he told her. "In two night's time, we will have our treasure and hold this island."

Béal Átha an Fheadha

Connor took Maél Muire's hand as they sat next to each other in one of the small rooms off the main room of her dun, where so many of the blood-drinkers slept in the late afternoon. He noticed a few healing scars on her arms and tried to keep his fury in check, which was a difficult thing to do when he could picture so many of them feeding off her like leeches. He pressed a kiss to her fingertips, before pushing those thoughts out of his mind.

"I can hardly wait for the next two days to pass," he told her.

She smiled at him. "I feel the same way," she replied.

Perhaps she would allow him a chance to do more, so he leaned in for a kiss and tried to slide a hand over her stomach.

"Not yet," Maél Muire said, as she gave him a sensuous smile. "I feel too... fat."

"Nonsense, you look radiant," he answered.

She grinned again and then opened her mouth to speak, but a soft knock interrupted them.

Basala opened the door. "I am sorry to interrupt," the servant said, "but Sáerlaith wishes to see you, Maél Muire."

"Thank you," Maél Muire said. "I will be right back," she said to him, before standing up and then leaning in for a quick kiss. She left the room and closed the door behind herself.

Connor stood and gently pushed the door open. He looked into the great hall and slipped into the shadows to see what event woke all the Deargh Du and their associates.

A woman walked to the center of the gathered forces and stood on a chair. The dun became silent. Connor witnessed a beautiful smile from the woman. Her dark hair sparkled with strands of silver, yet she exuded a strange beauty that entranced him.

"Thank you all for your efforts in finding the so-called Phallus Maximus. Our success is due in no small part to Marcus, Berti, and Sitara. Their journeys across Persia and the lands to the east have brought this treasure to us. I will take this to Ulster, and we will keep it safe in our stronghold. However, first we have a wedding to celebrate. Our noble hostess, Maél Muire, is to wed her neighbor to the east. May the husband and his bride enjoy the fruits of a long and joyous marriage together!"

The cheers started as the blood-drinkers started milling around each other. Connor crept back through the shadows and returned to the room. Maél Muire rejoined him a few minutes later.

"What called you away, mhuirnín?" he asked her.

"Oh, most excellent news," she exclaimed, beaming at him. "The Deargh Du found the Lamia treasure. They are taking it to Ard Mhacha after our wedding."

"It would be a great honor to be in the guard that takes it to Ulster," he said.

"That honor goes to Sáerlaith," Maél Muire said. "She is the head of the Deargh Du council."

"Will she return after the wedding?" he asked.

"No. I think she will leave directly after our feast," Maél Muire said. "I wish she could stay longer. She is a most kind and wise woman. However, her duty is to take it to her home as soon as she can."

"I should leave," Connor replied. "I must make final preparations for our wedding. It will be a wonderful occasion." He pulled her in for a hug and kiss. He then ran his hands down her back, enjoying the feel of her next to him, before pulling away.

Maél Muire leaned back against the wall and heard the door open. She grinned when she saw it was Marcus.

"Do you think he took the bait?" he asked, before pulling her up. He gently wiped some of the berry juice from her lips.

"I have no doubt," she replied.

He kissed her as her arms slid around his shoulders.

"I will prepare a battle plan," he said. "In three nights' time, no more Lamia will remain in Éire."

Mhuine Chonalláin

"The soft breeze shall rock our child gently as the sweet fae bring blessings to our home."

Connor watched Maél Muire sing softly to their daughter as the baby smiled at her, perfect in her innocence, but then her voice changed, and he could swear heard his mother sang to him and rock him.

Connor opened his eyes and the dream faded, only to see his mother staring down at him.

"We did not mean to drive you from your slumber," Seosaimhín purred as she stroked his hair. "We who have souls need our rest."

He tried to find words.

"You probably do not remember, but in the mists of time when you were but a lad, we brought you full sleep by singing sweet songs of happiness and joy."

"I remember a little," he admitted. "Mother, why are you here?"

"Does a mother need a reason to visit her son?" she asked.

"Thank you. I am not saying I do not appreciate you here. I am just surprised to find you." He smiled for a moment. "Stay if you wish."

"This is not your usual time for rest is it?" she asked. "The sunlight usually finds your eyes wide open, but not this day." His mother chuckled. "Where did your shod hooves take you today?"

"I visited Maél Muire to go over the last details of our wedding," Connor replied.

"Oh, interesting. Enlighten us... how did that go?" Seosaimhín queried.

"We went over food and drinks to serve," he informed his mother, smiling.

"Ah, but that is not why you are excited. There is another reason for your daytime sleep. We are curious what that reason might be."

"We will have additional, unexpected guests during the wedding," he answered as her hand stroked his hair again.

"Yes. Who?" she asked, as her sweet words fell on his ears.

"We will have the company of Deargh Du at the feast. I am not sure who will be there, aside from Sáerlaith, their leader, and Marcus."

"Oh, Sáerlaith. The wind whispers of that soulless one. Why do they come? Is it for Goddess, gold, or glory?"

"It is to prevent glory," he whispered to her. "Sáerlaith will bring the artifact the Lamia have sought for centuries. After the feast, she will take it to Ulster, where it will be safe and sound."

He watched his mother begin to glow with radiance and excitement.

"Many rewards would be bestowed upon he who informs on the location of the Phallus Maximus to the dark one, Mandubratius." His mother smiled at him.

"How do you know of the Phallus Maximus," he asked her.

His mother patted his head gently. "You should know that your mother knows all that goes on. We have our sources."

"I am leaving late this afternoon to give Mandubratius the news," he said.

"And we shall accompany you, but I require more sleep. Let us leave at nightfall, sweet son."

Connor tried to swallow his shock, "As you wish, mother."

His mother took some of his bedding, and then he heard her begin to sing again. Her quiet words burned warmth into the darkest of places.

Outside Ráth Cruachan

As Mandubratius looked over the weaponry within the supply tent, he shook his head, upset over the fact that his responsibility included noting that several shields and swords had sunk to the bottom of the sea.

"Once, there existed a regiment of soldiers able to perform mundane tasks such as these," he said to the mortal servant taking notes. Soon he heard footsteps as a messenger entered the tent.

"What?" he asked. "What is so pressing as to interrupt my mundane affairs? Is what you are about to tell me so important that you are willing to risk your life?"

The messenger's steady gaze did not relent. "Yes sir, I am quite certain that this information is worthy of your time."

"Well then, will you stand there or tell me what your message is?" he asked the messenger.

"Two individuals wish to see you, sir," the messenger announced.

"Two individuals," he stated, before unsheathing his sword and swatting the messenger's shoulder with the flat of the blade. "You mean to tell me that your life is worth this report of two people who wish to see me? I have an entire encampment of people who wish to see me. You have ten seconds to convince me your life is worth saving."

"They claim to know the location of the Phallus Maximus," the messenger stated, with raised brows.

"Well? Go on," Mandubratius enunciated. "Tell me where it is."

"They would not give me details, sir. They only wanted to speak with you."

"Typical," Mandubratius huffed, sighing in anger. "Just typical. I have a crisis, and someone wishes to speak to me. Someone wants to tell me where the Phallus Maximus is. Do you think that is important to me right now?"

The messenger looked up at him. "Well, it is why we are here, sir."

"Well of course it is important! Bring them in!" Mandubratius ordered before sighing.

"Now?" the messenger ascertained.

"Yes, go on," Mandubratius answered, tired of this game.

"But your sword, sir," the messenger bade, meeting his eyes.

"Oh yes. It is one of the new gold ones. Now, get out there and bring them in, now!" he said to the messenger as he sheathed his sword. Mandubratius then stared at the messenger, who had not moved. "Now!"

The messenger scurried out, and then the tent parted, revealing Seosaimhín and her son walking into the tent.

He felt his mood lighten. "What an unexpected pleasure. Please sit down. May I offer either of you a drink?"

"We will be leaving soon," Seosaimhín answered. "We just wanted to give you some good news."

Mandubratius met Seosaimhín's eyes. "Something about the location of the Phallus Maximus," he murmured in reverence. "Do you know where it is now?"

"Sometimes the mists of time are not so revealing," the druid answered. "There are eddies that we can see through to the other side. There is a soulless one named Sáerlaith. She will come with other soulless ones to my son's wedding in two nights. She will be carrying the phallus that is maximus to Ulster."

"You know this to be true?" Mandubratius raised his brows.

The mother looked at her son, who cleared his throat.

"I overheard a Deargh Du council meeting at Maél Muire's dun where they discussed that they had found it and were moving it to the Deargh Du stronghold in Ulster for safe keeping, Connor explained. "She will leave after the wedding with an escort of several Deargh Du."

"Did you hear anything that would lead you to believe that this conversation was a ruse?" Mandubratius asked.

"No one saw me. They were truthful," Connor insisted.

"Hmmm, you are probably right, but just in case..." Mandubratius paused, deep in thought.

"Just in case what?" the chieftain asked.

"Hmmmm? Oh yes, just in case... I will need a contingency plan." He picked up a golden sword and shield and handed them to Mac Turrlough. "This is a gift from the Lamia to you." Mandubratius then glanced at the door of the tent.

"Is there any way my clan can assist in this nearing battle?" the chieftain asked.

"It is best that you are not seen giving aid to us," Mandubratius answered. "Your clan may not like it."

The chieftain nodded his head. "Thank you for the beautiful treasures," he said as he stood up, as if preparing to leave, though his mother remained in her seat.

"One more thing," Mandubratius said. "I would advise you to ensure your men do not participate in the battle, and make sure that you keep Maél Muire out of harm's way." He then walked over to Seosaimhín and extended his right hand.

She took his hand and stood up, without pressing any weight against him. She met his stare.

"Mandubratius, you will honor our bargain," she stated. Her words seemed soft, yet vehement.

"Yes of course," he replied, wondering whether Seosaimhín believed him. Then the druid and her son took their leave.

Mandubratius followed his guests out. "Centurion," he said to the soldier outside the tent. "Assemble my officers. We need to discuss our attack plan."

Béal Átha an Fheadha

"And that is our plan," Marcus concluded as he looked over the gathered officers. "Any questions?"

He noticed Claudius grin. "An excellent plan, General."

"Yes, a fine plan indeed," Mac Alpin concurred.

Marcus watched Edward's finger move around the map while he held a lit candle over it. "You mean to tell me that the forces will be divided into three groups? I thought in battle, one never divided their forces."

At that moment,. a flaming wick fell to the map.

"Do not just stand there," Mac Alpin raged. "Put that out Edwina! How many times have I told you to stay away from fire?"

Maél Muire swooped in to carefully throw water on the part of the map that burned.

"Sorry," Mac Alpin grumbled.

Marcus chuckled a bit. "I will take the singeing as a sign of good fortune. I have a copy of this plan, anyway. Are there any other questions?" He looked around the table. "Then, let us go to sleep. We will make the final preparations tomorrow." He then felt a warm hand slide over his back as the Deargh Du and the other blood-drinkers left the table.

"Can I have a word with you please?" his host asked. He found himself lost in Maél Muire's eyes. He then wordlessly led her to the small room that they shared. She now seemed nervous to meet his eyes.

"Marcus," she said. "I am not sure that I am ready or worthy to be Deargh Du. I think I would be more confident in a decision if this path were meant to be."

He pulled her in close and kissed her brow. "I am disappointed, yet also relieved," he answered as her lips teased at his for a moment. "I would never force such a decision on you." He felt her stroke him as he became stiff at her nearness. His hands then moved over her supple frame before pulling off her léine. They traipsed over to the bed of blankets and furs, where she threw him down and straddled him.

Maél Muire dropped her clothes by the side of the river and waded into the water, adorned with a small bag of herbs and salt around her neck, and continued her habit of washing after raising the mists. She splashed about, rubbing the cleansing salt mixture everywhere. She paused for a moment and then lowered her hands to the areas below the water, gently washing over the sensitive parts of her flesh between her legs.

"Ah, the Gods would smile if my hand was where yours is now," a voice called out in the direction of the riverbank.

A chill ran up and down her spine as she shuddered a little. The water in contrast now felt warm. She then turned slowly towards the voice.

"You are not pregnant," Mandubratius observed, meeting her eyes. "That is a shame."

"How did you get here?" she demanded, trying to sound authoritative and angry.

As he stepped into the water, fully clothed, Maél Muire took a few steps away from him.

"Your druid's mist barrier is not impenetrable, Maél Muire," he said with a slow grin. "We applied some Roman ingenuity to thwart it, the same way we managed to get to your lead druid. I thought, wrongly, that without him, it would be gone. It is a nuisance now, but not an impassible force anymore."

"That was my uncle," she hissed at Mandubratius. She felt venomous ire wash over her fear as she circled around him, maneuvering towards the bank.

He followed her and kept his eyes on her. "I am sorry," he purred. "He was a casualty of war."

"You had him murdered!" she thundered, before backing out of the water towards her sword.

He followed her out as she kept her eyes on him. "It was just a strategic objective. It was not personal. Believe it or not, his death was not my intent, Maél Muire." He smiled again, so easily. "It was an accident."

"That is why I do not kill you where you stand!" she shouted while stepping in closer to her sword. As Mandubratius followed her, Maél Muire tried not to shiver in the wind.

He chuckled. "You would kill me with your bare hands? My, you are strong-willed. Perhaps a little fool-hardy, though."

"I will give you a chance to leave since his death was an accident," she told him, trying to keep her rage from exploding like one of Edward's ill-timed creations.

"So, you will not allow me to have the privilege to talk to you and explain why I am here? I did, after all, take a big risk in coming here. Your Deargh Du friends are efficient in their patrols. I could be spotted at any moment." He moved in closer to her, further than an arm length away, but still too near in her opinion. "My time here is short, and I would like to make the most of it," he said while squeezing the water from his clothing.

"You enjoy hearing yourself speak, do you not?" she ascertained, trying to keep from sneering.

"Yes," he said, meeting her eyes. "Sometimes, even in a crowded room, mine is the most intelligent voice. At times I have to speak to myself in order to carry on a witty conversation."

She stared at him. "Are you so deranged that that is your only recourse?"

He smirked at her. "Clever girl, but as I said earlier, my time is short, so please allow me to get to the point."

"Very well," she said, still not wanting to take her eyes off him to grab her sword. "Why are you here?"

"I wish to offer you a gift," he said, before taking a seat next to her clothes. She watched him continue to wring the water out of his clothing. A small amount of distaste moved over his features.

"Are you making this offer to the wise salmon or to me?" she asked.

He met her eyes again. "My apologies, Maél Muire, but I wish to make this offer to you."

"What gift are you offering?" she asked.

"Ahhh, this is a special gift," he drawled. "It will help you in your marriage and give you power and influence in clan affairs in this region."

The ridiculous image of his leading a herd of cattle to her invaded her mind. "I gather this does not involve livestock," she stated.

"Your words are quite amusing, but no livestock or gold, I am afraid," Mandubratius answered.

"So tell me, what is it?"

He stood up and sauntered closer again, seemingly allowing himself to appear harmless.

Maél Muire kept her eyes on her sword behind him.

"Have you ever experienced a time when you felt powerless to right a wrong? Or perhaps you had to deal with an obstinate person who did not listen to your words of wisdom, and you wished to do something about it? Have you ever been hurt physically, requiring a long time to heal?" he queried.

She remembered seeing Marcus after he pulled her out of the burning house, but she said nothing.

"The gift I wish to give you would relieve you from experiencing these hardships anymore. You could command the utmost authority." He then started to walk around her as she remained still, but she did follow him with her eyes. "If you were ever wounded, you would recover in a short time."

She could see where he intended to go with this conversation.

"You mean to tell me that—"

"Yes, I do," Mandubratius interrupted her. "Think of it. If you had this gift before, you could have saved the lives of your uncle, your father, and even your beloved, Seanán."

She noticed a slight upturn of his lips into a tiny smile. She felt ashamed to feel tears begin to blind her eyes. "Did you have anything to do with his death?" she asked, hating her voice for growing so meek in sorrow.

She watched Mandubratius' smile grow. "I had help," he replied.

"Who?" Maél Muire hissed.

"Mac Turrlough," he stated.

Maél Muire fell to her hands and knees, crying. She felt him bend over her, as if to comfort her. She then reached past him and gripped her sword by its pommel. In one swift and fluid motion, she shoved it through his heart. His blood drenched her arm.

She could see him still smiling through her tears as she impatiently attempted to wipe them away with her bloodied sleeve.

"That is the second time you have stabbed me," he murmured.

She growled in rage and twisted the sword, furious to see him smile, all the more before collapsing on top of her. Maél Muire then shoved Mandubratius aside and pulled out her sword, before pushing and kicking his body into the river.

She carried the bloodied sword toward the dun, forgetting the small matter of her clothing. When she got home, she felt Aunt Sive wrap a blanket around her, and she finally dropped the sword to the floor, feeling blood splatter on her bare legs.

"She needs me," Marcus told Sive.

"Not now, Marcus," Sive said, her voice becoming steel. "Maél Muire does not need you to see her like this, and you are wasting your breath and my time. My duty is to her now, and I will let you know when you can see her." She shook a finger at him. "And you will not see her a moment before!"

"I am only concerned for her well-being," Marcus answered, hearing himself sound impatient and out of sorts.

Sive placed a hand on his shoulder. "As am I," she replied. "I hear all the new equipment has arrived. Busy yourself with that for now."

He nodded before stepping outside of the dun. He could see the others gather their new belongings, including green-trimmed armor, and so he decided to duck back into the dun and dress quickly. After returning to the parade grounds, his friends came up to him.

"Hmmmm, somebody received very nice armor," Mac Alpin commented while walking toward him. "Why is that, I wonder?"

Marcus smirked. "Who is the general of this mighty force, Arwin?"

"If it were up to me, I would pick the lad who cleans up the horse's droppings at the barn."

Marcus chuckled for a moment. "I am very thankful that this decision was not up to you."

Mac Alpin's laughter echoed through the gathering Deargh Du.

"Claudius," Marcus called to his other friend, "assemble the troops for inspection."

He heard barked orders, and then he watched as faces turned toward him.

"You have all worked hard and have overcome many obstacles," Marcus began. "Tomorrow night, your training will pay off. We will face a well-trained, well-equipped army. There is intelligence that the Lamia have gold weapons and armor. This fact shall not frighten you, for one on one, the Deargh Du are faster and have the advantage of flight. The Lamia do not widely know this. We know that they have bought our ruse. However, in case they have not, we have preparation on our side. All of you know what must be done, and you all have the will and the discipline to do it. Tomorrow, we will bring victory to ourselves, and to the people of our Goddess!"

He heard a cheer, and then a strange noise made him turn to stare at the western skies as an unkindness of ravens passed by, cawing. The entire Deargh Du army grew silent in reverence. Eyes misted with the beauty of the black-winged birds. The gathering of ravens soon passed into the dark skies.

"I grant you liberty for the rest of the night," Marcus added. He heard another cheer as Mac Alpin bellowed that they would meet here at sunset, ready for battle.

Marcus noticed Sive smiling at him from the door of the dun. He then strolled over to her.

"She is well enough, now. I believe she is ready to see you," Sive said.

"Did she tell you why?" he asked, before pausing in an attempt to find words. "Why was she walking to the dun naked and covered in blood?"

"No," Sive answered, "but I believe that she will answer your questions."

He watched the elder druid blink back tears before taking her hand.

"You know she loves you," Sive said, smiling.

"I love her too," he whispered.

"I think you and she would make a good match," Sive said. "I think you compliment her even better than Seanán."

He gave her a small grin.

She leaned in closer and gently patted his face and kissed his cheek. Sive then pulled away with a pained smile before motioning him to the door.

Once Marcus opened the doors, he could see Maél Muire lying next to the hearth. She looked healthy as he neared her, but he noticed the poultice and herbal treatments on her body. Her tear-filled eyes regarded him as she reached for him. Marcus felt her arms embrace him, and he settled into her warm shoulder.

"He killed him. He killed him," Maél Muire squeaked.

"Who killed whom?" Marcus asked, pushing aside a few strands of sweaty hair.

"Mandubratius killed Seanán, my betrothed, the one most dear to me. He killed him, and he lied." She rested the right side of her face against his chest. "I chased him," she continued. "I wounded him, but I did not know who he was, and he said he wanted to give me a gift. Mandubratius wanted me to be like him. How could I be like him?" she asked, mid-sob. "He murdered him… them!!!"

"Be calm, take a deep breath," Marcus cooed while rubbing her back as she continued in her rants. "Please tell me what happened. When did you hear this?"

"He told me!" she insisted.

"Take a deep breath and tell me," he ordered her, for her heart pounded in his ears, and he could barely understand her. He felt her grow calm before taking an uneasy breath.

"He told me. I was bathing in the river when he surprised me. He said that he could break through the mist barrier, as the others had, the ones who had killed Uncle Fergus. He wanted me to become Lamia, and as he was trying to convince me, he told me that if I had been one of them, I could have saved them. Mandubratius smiled at me when he mentioned Seanán. He tried to hide it, but I saw it. It dawned on me that he had been there, that he may have performed the act himself. When I accused him of murdering Seanán, his smile grew and his eyes twinkled in… pleasure! My rage grew to think that during this time I believed he was my friend. I did not even suspect Mandubratius. I cannot believe how blind and oblivious I could be," she whispered, before rubbing her eyes against his tunic.

"Seeing the look in his eyes, I knew he did it, and I punished him for it. I grabbed my sword and thrust it into his heart."

Marcus stared down at her, wondering whether she had killed Mandubratius, whether she had removed his head.

"Still he smiled," she continued. "And in rage, I twisted it, until he fell over dead."

Marcus started to shake his head in disbelief.

"Then I withdrew my sword and kicked his dead body into the river, and the currents pulled it away. I could not feel anything. I left my clothes behind." She still sounded bewildered and confused. "Why are you shaking your head?" Maél Muire asked him.

"Because you did not kill him," he replied. "To kill a blood-drinker, you have to remove their head. Anything else and they can recover."

"No," she hissed, before pushing away from him and standing up.

He grabbed her and met her wild eyes.

"I am going to find him and finish him off," she growled.

"No, you are not going to go yet," he commanded as he held her against the wall, watching her face glow in fury.

"I want him now! I will feel his life drain and see the life dim from his eyes. I will make him feel the pain Seanán did!"

"We have a plan, Maél Muire. You will have your opportunity. Mandubratius will take the bait," he said. "You can kill him then." He watched her lower her eyes.

"He also said my current husband-to-be had a hand in Seanán's death. I realize now that he and his evil, scheming mother have contrived these plans for such a long time. The only reason I agreed to this foolish, damned wedding was to find out more of the Lamia's plans." Maél Muire moved her arms and embraced him again. "Mandubratius believed I was pregnant. They have all talked. I would strongly believe that Connor is just a hostage to their plans and that his mother and Mandubratius are the true manipulators behind it. Connor wants me to legitimize his claim to my properties. They might have designs on the child that I am supposed to carry. I wonder," she said before taking an unsteady breath, "will things change now that I am not with child?"

"You will have an opportunity this next night to make things right," he promised.

"You think we should go ahead with this wedding plan, despite what I have learned?"

"Yes I do," he said. "Mandubratius will be suspicious if we change our plans. I do not believe he will tell Mac Turrlough or Seosaimhín that you know of their involvement in Seanán's death. He knows you are strong-willed and that rage burns within you. Now, I also believe within his sick and twisted mind that he will come for the wedding, just to see you deal justice. We know he wants the Phallus Maximus, and he will take this opportunity to acquire it. He is likely confident in the size of his forces and their armaments of gold. I think if we do not go through with the wedding, it will not only seem like an insult, it would also be a prelude for a Lamia invasion of your village. They discovered a way through the mist," he said. "They will see an opportunity to attack us when we are not in a fortified position. It would be easier to attack with fewer losses in Mhuine Chonalláin than here."

"Your words ring true," she said, though she still seemed disappointed. "I have seen those aspects of Mandubratius. I believe he would find a great deal of pleasure in seeing Connor Mac Turrlough and his mother's demise."

"I sent the troops to celebrate. I should be with them tonight," he stated, before pulling her in for a gentle kiss.

"No," she murmured, before taking his arm. "Marcus, I changed my mind... I wish to become Deargh Du," Maél Muire requested, as her eyes gleamed with defiance.

"But why now, Maél Muire?" he asked. "You only wish to become Deargh Du to have the strength to kill Mandubratius."

"I want to sate my thirst for vengeance," she purred, "by draining the blood from his body."

"I do not think it is a good idea to become Deargh Du just for the sake of revenge," he murmured in her ear.

"Marcus," she said, as her eyes grew calm. "You will do this for me. Please."

"But vengeance," he said.

"Marcus, please understand that this is the tiny pebble that tipped the balance to my becoming Deargh Du. It is not the entire pile. There are many reasons for me to become Deargh Du. This is just a small one."

He stared down at her, trying to decide, though her face tugged at his heart. "We can do this, but to you are far too weak to do it now."

She embraced him again, and he could feel her heart race against him. "You will do it then."

"Yes," he said, before playing with a lock of her hair.

"Then tomorrow in the morning," she said

"But the transformation," he warned.

"Yes," she replied, her eyes alight with emotions.

"There will be enough time for your body to change, but your mind needs a full cycle of the day before it will catch up with the changes," Marcus informed her.

"What are you saying?"

"I am saying, Maél Muire, that you will be gripped with madness during your wedding."

Her fingertips moved down his cheekbone. "You said the change tests one's endurance, heart, and resolve. You have known me long enough to understand that I have a very strong will, and I know that will be able to control myself during the ceremony. No one else will be the wiser, and then once I have dealt with my husband-to-be, I can use my madness to take out Mandubratius and the Lamia invaders."

"I do not know if this is right," Marcus whispered, before pulling her in closer, "but for you, I will do this."

She kissed him, and he soon forgot everything, for the moment. "I love you, Marcus."

"I love you too," he said, while pushing back a plait of her hair. "You need to rest," he murmured, before tucking her into her bed and covering her.

"Marcus, please do not tell anyone else what happened yet. I am afraid that knowledge of this will cloud my aunt's judgment."

"I will keep silent," he answered. "I am curious. What do you plan to do to Connor?"

He watched her smile.

"You will see, and you can use it as a signal to commence your attack, if you wish."

He could not help but smile back at her. "I will, and I cannot wait to see what you will do."

chapter sixteen

Mhuine Chonalláin

onnor walked over to his mother's home, mulling over his thoughts on the wedding. As soon as he arrived, he noticed her hunching over the large cauldron in the hearth.

"What is that?" he asked, while leaning in to smell it. "You did not come in for dinner," he added, trying to place the smells that emanated from the cauldron.

"Come closer," she bade him. "Closer." Her words seemed like a satisfied purring of a kitten playing with a mouse. She then pulled out a wooden spoon and ladled some of the gelatinous substance. Before he could move, Seosaimhín flung the substance onto his face. The heat burned before Connor flung it off.

"What in the name of God was that for, mother?" he hissed.

His mother moved to pat his face. "Pain was not intended. We are so sorry, our son."

A strange feeling overwhelmed him. "It is alright," he said. "You can do it again if you wish." He stared at her, horrified by hearing words from his mouth that he did not speak.

"Ah, success smiles upon us!" she exclaimed, before leaning in and kissing his other cheek. "It's ready. Soon, our son, you will have a wife who will bear me a granddaughter and obey us with no question. Now that you are here, what do you wish to do?"

"I wish to do…" he intoned, "whatever you wish for me to do, mother."

"Ah, I wish for you to put one foot in front of the other and walk to the door."

He turned and walked to the door.

"Now, open the door and hold it with your right hand. Next, put your left hand against the door jam and then shut the door," she suggested.

He followed his compulsion, unable to resist her commands, and then yelled in pain as he closed the door on his hand.

"Oh, poor lad, did that feel good?" his mother asked while meeting his eyes.

"I do not know," he answered.

"It felt good, take our word for it. Now, run home and play with your friends. Perhaps we will need the strength of a rabbit, not a lion."

Outside Ráth Cruachan

Mandubratius walked into the encampment, ignoring the guards at the gate, trying to hide his wound. After stumbling into Amata's tent, he sat down at her table and then noticed her playing with her food in bed again. This time, a nearly dead mortal soldier lay next to her.

"A pity," Amata pouted as she looked up at him. She then grabbed the soldier's left wrist and let it drop. "No stamina." Her lips curled into a soft and sweet smile.

"Playing with your food again, Amata?" he asked as he raised a brow.

"Mandubratius, what brings you to my tent?" she purred, before standing up in her flimsy gown that revealed all. "Do I smell blood on you?"

"I desire to speak with you," he said, ignoring her question. Mandubratius attempted to charm and beguile her, despite his pain.

"Oh? Is this an official matter, Caesar?" she murmured.

"You know I despise that title," Mandubratius replied.

"But it is by honor yours. We are the last true vestiges of Rome, and you, Briton, are our leader." Her ice-tinged eyes stared into his. "Whether you like it or not, you are our Caesar, our Dominus."

"I hated Romans when I was chieftain of the Trinovantes, especially that Marcus Galerius Primus Helvetticus. I will not ever forget that bastard's name."

Amata smiled. "I am sure he has not forgotten yours."

"Oh yes," he said, before turning back to her. "That is right. You spent time with him, did you not?"

"Yes, I did, Mandubratius," she answered.

"I thought it was Caesar!" he growled. "I presume the time you spent with him was intimate."

"Yes, you could say that," Amata answered.

Mandubratius grinned, turned, gripped her throat, and then lifted her. "Then why in Hades did you not kill him when you had the chance?" He dropped her before walking away, feeling his healing wound break apart again. Blood started to seep through his tunic.

Amata fell to her knees. "I am ashamed for allowing his escape, but after the confusion of discovering who he was, I thought that you would prefer to kill him personally. He was my gift to you, my Caesar." He noticed her staring at his chest. "You are wounded," she said.

"Do not," he entreated, but she still peeled off his cloak and tunic before touching his wound. He grunted in pain.

"Let me look at that," she insisted as he pulled back.

"It is not–" He winced as she pulled off his makeshift bandage.

"The wound is not closing properly," she said. "There are bits of steel in the wound. I need forceps. Go sit."

He sat and began watching her as she pulled out her supply bag and extracted her emergency kit.

"Did it go all the way through?" she asked.

"Yes, but I am Lamia. It should heal fine, right?" he queried as she started to extract steel slivers and shards from Maél Muire's sword.

"I do not know if that could heal, perhaps so, perhaps not. Would you want to take the chance to find out?"

"No," he replied, smirking a bit. "Patch me up, please."

He grunted in pain a few more times as she removed more metal and pieces of cloth.

"There. You have started to heal." Amata patted his leg.

"I should be fine in a few hours. It was a rather deep cut," he admitted.

"I hope you took care of whoever did this," she replied.

"No," he admitted as he looked away from her eyes. "She still draws breath."

"She?" asked Amata with a raised her brow. "A mortal 'she'?"

"Yes," he admitted, finally meeting her eyes.

"And you talk about my playing with food. It sounds as if you were playing with your food as well."

"It is a long narrative that I do not wish to go into," he said.

"It seems like an epic to me. Perhaps you should at least summarize it for me." She smiled. "I do enjoy epics."

"I believe the Phallus Maximus is hidden by a clan to the northwest that enjoys the protection of Deargh Du. In order to gain it, I have forged alliances with some of the other clans," Mandubratius explained.

"In other words, you have been gaming again," Amata concluded.

"Gaming?" he asked.

"I know you, Mandubratius, all too well. I know how you love to forge these impossible relationships between people, and then you twist and warp situations that turn people against each other for your own pleasure."

He could not help but nod and chuckle. "Yes, that is my hobby. You do know me so well."

"So, does this woman have anything to do with your latest games?" she asked.

"Yes," he admitted. "She is the center of three games that I am playing. First, I convinced her aunt and her uncle, who was the chieftain of the clan, to abandon their traditions and mortality to become Lamia, for as long as I can tolerate their presence."

"Yes," Amata said with a smile, "your plaything, Teá. She would seem to be quite the toy. And the second game, my brother?"

"I have convinced another idiot chieftain and his old crone of a mother that they have a child on the way via this woman. They are spending money for an elaborate wedding feast." He chuckled again.

"And the third?" Amata inquired with a smile.

"Oh, the third is the most delicious game yet," he purred. "This game is the woman herself. She has never been married, at least she has never made it to the altar. Let us say her other husbands-to-be have so far have died, some by my hand, some by my assistance. Perhaps in a few nights, there will be another." He then took Amata's hand. "Despite all this, she still tries to find love. How pathetic." He laughed. "I have been in the process of making her realize that the world around her is dead, and she must embrace a new life with me as her sponsor," he added.

"So," Amata said, laughing, "in appreciation, she shoves a sword through your chest, twists it, and leaves you for dead? That is quite grateful."

"Perhaps I missed something in the translation from Latin to Gaelic!" he told her.

"Well, at least you still have two good games to play, Mandubratius. Both have good chances for success," Amata stated.

"Yes, that is well and good, but I have invested a great deal of time and effort into this Maél Muire game of mine." As he stood up, he could feel a resolute pout on his face.

"Very well, very well," Amata said. "Continue your game with this Maél Muire if you can, just be careful. Women are beguiling like snakes. We can hiss pleasantly," she said with a smile. "I notice there are no snakes here, and that can make the women all the more dangerous." Amata then leaned in and kissed him.

He tasted the sweetness of death on her lips.

Béal Átha an Fheadha

Maél Muire woke up upon hearing Marcus walk into the great hall and gather her cloak. He then leaned down and smiled at her, and she smiled back.

"You are sure about this?" he asked.

She nodded before sitting up. "Will we do this..." she asked before pausing, and then she looked at the cloak. "We are staying here?"

"No. You have access to too many mortals here. The sun will rise in about an hour," he said. "We will go to your aunt and uncle's home, old home. I have some provisions for us there." She watched him realize his slip of the tongue, and he looked a little pained.

She then grabbed a pair of brogues before slipping into her cloak. After heading out of the dun, she looked back before starting for the grove with Marcus. She followed him, while looking at the green grass and the trees, wondering how they would change after her transformation.

When the arrived, he opened the door and began covering windows to bar the sun's arrival.

She glanced around, looking for openings they may have missed. Maél Muire could hear the birds start to chirp as dawn began to break. She peeled back a window covering to see what she would never be able to see again. She then felt his arms slide around her. Maél Muire dropped her hand, releasing the window covering, as she leaned back into his chest. The house became dark.

"Once we begin this, there is no turning back," Marcus said in her right ear. "Are you certain that you wish this?"

She nodded her head and turned to face him. "I wish this. Please do this."

"I accept your request. This morning, you saw your last sunrise, and you will never see another. After you pass through the transformation, I will teach you the ways of our kind and how we must keep the balance and always maintain it. Just know now that I love you."

"I love you," she replied, before giving him a quick kiss.

She felt his cold hands push aside the hair covering her neck as they kneeled next to each other. His cold breath made her skin prickle with a surprising pleasure.

He gathered her into his arms and then paused, before brushing a soft kiss against her throat. "May She grant us success and deem us worthy this morning," Marcus murmured.

Maél Muire drew an unsteady breath as his mouth lowered over her throat. She felt a gentle scrape against the side of her neck. The original levity that she remembered from the other times he had fed from her faded quickly. She slid her arms around his shoulders as she wondered whether the growing pain would drive her senseless. She tried to calm her racing heart as she could feel her pulse pounding. Maél Muire then opened her eyes.

As a sudden racking pain arced through her body, she squinted her eyes shut. Then the pain disappeared, replaced by a dull throbbing sensation that moved through her body as he continued to drink from her.

Her fingers and toes began to tingle with blood loss as he continued. She had to hope this was as painful as it would be. The pain from the incisions soon dissipated, and then a numbing pleasure began to overwhelm her. A burning bliss raced through her body as his icy lips encircled the wounds on her neck, and he continued sucking her lifeblood.

Maél Muire opened her eyes again. She felt a strong desire to press up against him and return the deadly kiss. This was the first time she had ever had that particular sensation, yet she lost herself in the delirious ecstasy as her vision began to blur and turned to shades of gray.

She soon lost her grip on his shoulders and felt herself beginning to fall backwards. Marcus held her in closer as he continued to imbibe from her. Her mind tried to remember bits and fragments of her life, as her heartbeat continued to slow down. Maél Muire could feel herself falling backwards onto the ground. It felt as though time had ceased moving and that all the noises, smells, and sensations had disappeared.

"Maél Muire." A pair of arms pulled her up as hands tangled in her hair. Something pressed her lips to a wet surface.

She felt a tingle in her bones as she licked at the wetness with a cautious tongue. The substance seemed hot and sticky. Blood. Maél Muire remembered the past few minutes and how the thought of blood in her mouth made her gag. She tried to push away, but the fingers laced in her hair tightened, keeping her in place.

Vitae smeared on her face as she licked at the trails of pooling blood on Marcus' neck, afraid of what might happen next. She could not help but be surprised at the change of taste in the blood. She suckled at the sweetness, with mixtures of honey and spices infused into the concoction. The scents of frankincense and myrrh intermixed with the smells from the grove, but the scents of the house seemed but a brief distraction from the blood.

A breathy sigh echoed in her mind as she continued to drink. She could feel herself move from one extreme of heat into another one where the cold settled in her bones.

Oh, delicious. Oh, never let this end. I could spend the rest of my life here, drinking at this intoxicating nectar.

Any other coherent thoughts disappeared on the wind. When she opened her eyes, blackness remained. Soon, though, she began to feel a tiny particle of brightness begin to spread within her body. It started to distract her from the pleasures in the warm blood. She waved away the nagging warning that voiced itself in the back of her mind.

Another annoyance registered in her mind as a pair of strong arms began to push her away from the flavorful drink. She ignored the noises in her ear and the warnings in her head as the particle of luminous strength grew larger, causing her muscles to begin to tense and then release in a sporadic jolt. Maél Muire continued to disregard the admonition her intuition hissed to her.

Before a final cautionary alarm, her muscles contracted. She could sense a force within, propelling her backwards, away from Marcus, in a fusion of power. She then felt her left shoulder smash into the wall next to the hearth. She moaned as she collapsed on her back, feeling her dislocated and shattered shoulder flail about on its own accord.

She soon grew silent, upon hearing her heartbeat pound in her head. The rapid cadence echoed and pulsed through her body. Then the gentle palpitation began to lag. She tried to open her eyes, but she perceived only blackness. Then time stopped, as did the soft fluttering of her heart.

Maél Muire looked up at the sky and saw that gray clouds blocked the sun. She then took a quick look at the grounds surrounding her. A bloodied corpse stared up at her with a jaundiced eye. The strange putrescent stench of rotting death encircled her in the battlefield. Hundreds, no, thousands of red-tinged bodies lay in the battleground. Ravens cawed to each other before landing on the dead warriors, feeding on their ghastly feast.

She turned and willed her stiffened limbs to move about the land. Some of the corpses wore léines similar to hers, while others were dressed in tunics and long robes. She even noticed that a few Roman helms lay scattered about. She took a few steps closer to study the others.

One near her wore an odd set of léine and brócs that appeared to be made of leaves sewn together. A grouping of three striped arrows rested against his arm. The warrior clutched a short piece of metal that seemed neither a sword nor spear.

Next to him lay a man within a blue coat trimmed with red at the cuffs and neck. A large feathered headdress rested on top of his head. He held a long, wooden staff that ended in a club at one end and metal at the other.

A raven cackled at her as it landed on the blue-clad warrior and began feeding from a red hole in the center of his back.

She turned away and almost stepped on another man clothed entirely in black, except for a strange band of red cloth around his arm. In the middle of a white spot in the red cloth, she saw an ominous-looking black cross-like symbol.

Soon a cacophonous noise echoed in her ears, prompting her to whirl around. The unkindness of ravens flew away from their food and disappeared into the blackened skies, but then she saw them join as a dark mass, swooping down from the heavens toward her. She ducked, throwing herself to the hard ground as the ravens flew past her. She raised her head and stared at the group of ravens as they swirled together into an indiscernible shape of feathers, beaks, and wild, black eyes.

She felt her heart drop into her stomach as a figure emerged from within the sphere of ravens. The figure appeared to be that of a woman.

Maél Muire found her unsteady legs and stood again as the woman, adorned with blue paint and covered in armor, strode purposefully forward. A voluminous cape pooled behind her. Then Maél Muire realized that she beheld Morrigan in the guise of the warrior queen, not the one-eyed crone, which she had seen before.

Heather Poinsett Dunbar & Christopher Dunbar

"Do you see those scattered about here?" the Goddess addressed her, as she strode still closer. Her luminous, black eyes radiated power. Maél Muire could not find the strength to turn from them. She just nodded her head, surprised that she could move at all.

The Goddess turned Her face to one side, allowing Maél Muire to escape those black pools of radiance.

"The balance must be maintained, for there are those who seek to upset the natural order of things. When good gets too benign and when evil gets too destructive, we must step in to restore order to the balance."

"These are those who tried to topple the balance," added Morrigan. "They never had a chance to experience the states of being that the Christians call heaven and hell, what the Hindus call Nirvana, or even our Otherworld. I believe it is a fitting punishment." She then waved the spear in Her hand at the scattered corpses. "These warriors lay trapped within their physical bodies while my ravens feed upon them."

Maél Muire could not find any words. She felt her mouth agape in wonder as Morrigan turned Her fearless eyes on her again.

"Come forward, my child, I mean you no harm or ill-will. I have but a question for you, unless you have changed your mind about becoming a Deargh Du. Do you wish to continue in the life beyond to serve this noble purpose? You will have my eternal appreciation."

Maél Muire took a cautious step forward and then another. "Yes," her voice squeaked. "I wish to serve you and maintain the balance."

"Marcus chose wisely," Morrigan replied, before motioning her forward. "Here is my question for you. It is the question that I give all seekers. Everyone will have a different answer. However, most who come here take the wrong path."

"What path?" Maél Muire asked.

Morrigan pointed to Maél Muire's feet. The dead men and women disappeared, and in their place, a stone-hewn road stretched from the east to the west as far as she could see.

"Some go to the east," Morrigan stated as she motioned toward the east. Maél Muire could see the sparkle of gold on a series of buildings. "Others chose the west," Morrigan continued, while pointing at another village covered in silver.

Maél Muire looked from the west to the east before she found her voice.

"I am not here to follow a path of my own making. I am here to follow you."

Morrigan's lips curved into a smile. The gray clouds then parted, and the sun lighted a path to the north.

The Goddess walked to the new trail and beckoned to her. "Come now, young one. I accept you as my newest child. You will no longer use the name, Maél Muire, although I am sure your old friends will still call you by it. You are now Máire, my child of past bitterness and sorrows who finds peace and tranquility. You will serve me by maintaining the balance."

Máire walked toward the Goddess and took the proffered hand. Soon mist engulfed the dazzling phantom queen. Then the gray mist gave way, back to blackness, and then to unspeakable pain.

Marcus watched Maél Muire sprawl against the ground. Blood dripped from the corners of her eyes and lips. Her left shoulder lay dislocated, underneath her body.

As Marcus stumbled toward her, Maél Muire's eyes opened, and he leaned over for a closer examination. Her green orbs turned black as a moonless midnight. Waves of movement rippled through her body. She then screamed in pain as her limbs, fingers, toes, and neck extended. The undulations of moving tissue continued as her arm tucked underneath her body, slid out, and then corrected itself. Soon, the extension of muscle and skin decreased. Maél Muire started to blink her black eyes before rolling onto her hands and knees.

She then began to gag, as Marcus watched in shock, unable to move. Maél Muire spat out blood and then her teeth. After a few moments, the surges of growth in her body began again. She then sat up on her knees and let out a final, piercing scream, before falling back to the ground with her eyes closed.

"Maél Muire," he cried as he kneeled down beside her, stroking her hair. Its strands felt like fine silk in between his fingers. He then studied her new form, noticing that her hair seemed glossy under the moonlight and smelled sweetly of lavender.

Her new alabaster features reflected the luminous moon. Her body had new muscles, and her supple form revealed beauty. He wondered how she would react if he would pull her toward him. Would the transformation keep her from understanding his motives?

For several hours, Marcus stood vigil over her unconscious form. Then, without preamble, Maél Muire opened her eyes. No longer black, they reflected green emeralds to him. Her eyes locked on his.

"Did you see Her when you were there? Were you tested? Did you succeed?" she demanded. Her new voice sounded fluid and melodious. He had expected giggles and nonsensical ravings, but not questions.

He swallowed his surprise and fished out a lie. "My ascension was punishment. I had no choice in my path. No, I did not see Morrigan."

Marcus offered her his right hand. Maél Muire placed her delicate hand within his and stared up at him. He helped her to her feet before looking her up and down. She stood taller than she did before her transformation.

"I hunger. I wish to feed." Her sibilant purr trembled with emotion and frustration.

"I know," he replied. "You may feast from me, Maél Muire." He wrapped an arm around her waist, preparing to bring her in closer, but instead, she gave him a small push.

"I am no longer Maél Muire. I am Máire. Morrigan named me so."

He could feel a smile work its way over his mouth as he thought of 'Máire', the Gaelic word for bitterness. Morrigan had chosen Maél Muire's new name well. "I think your new name suits you well, Máire." He took her arm again.

She promptly pulled away and chuckled. "Marcus, I do not need you to feed me. I am a woman, and I am Deargh Du." Her words then turned harsh. "I can find my own food. I am not a baby bird that needs a regurgitated meal." She gave him a terse smile. "Do not wait up for me."

"The sun has risen, Maél… Máire." He watched her stop, embarrassment evident upon her face. He then held out a jug of blood and mead mixed together.

She flew over the battlefield, hearing naught but the din of beautiful battle and the caws that She sang into the sky. She felt herself land at the feet of a beautiful, blue-eyed warrior. Then She slipped out of Her raven guise and into another form. The landscape grew dark as She watched the warrior's lips move. Before She could comprehend anything, She fed upon the warrior, feeling his blood slake Her unquenchable thirst.

As Máire awoke, she could feel pain radiating around her neck. She then touched the area of soreness gingerly. Her senses reeled as sounds, smells, and other sensations railed at her mind.

Blood. She tasted her own blood in her mouth as her fangs extended.

She finally opened her eyes and could not believe the sights before her. The glowing fire transfixed her.

When Máire heard her name, she moved toward Marcus with a great deal of speed before she had even considered leaving the hearth. She tried to stop, but ended up shoving Marcus into the stone wall. She then pulled back from him and watched him sit down as if dazed. She smelled blood as drops of it dripped down his face.

`"I have never been as ravenous as I am, now," she murmured as she smiled at him. She then curled down and pulled him in close, finding herself licking at his blood as it dripped down his cheek. She stirred closer to Marcus before biting into his throat with her new teeth. She could feel the honeyed mixture warm her chilled body. She soon heard her breathing become harsh and ragged as she drowned in the sweetness.

"Máire, stop," Marcus ordered while pushing her away gently.

She opened her eyes and gave him a slow smile. She backed off and then arose. "I am ready to kill Connor now," she growled.

She felt his arms pin hers down, and then she collapsed to the floor. Marcus succeeded in pinning her, and she half-growled in impatience.

"The sunlight will destroy you," he whispered calmly while staring into her eyes. "Do not go outside until the sun has set."

"I cannot wait," she heard herself whine. "I must confront him. My hatred for him burns, and flames rage within me." She struggled against him.

"You must wait until the time is right," he purred in reply.

She sighed as she stopped her vain attempts at escape. "Very well then, I am restless. How do we pass the time?"

"I do not know," he said before sitting up and stepping away.

She felt her impatience show and heard Marcus chuckle. She then rolled over and crawled her way into the shadows, smiling at him, feeling his eyes caress her every movement.

"Marcus, am I beautiful?" she asked as she twisted a curly lock of hair around a finger.

"Yes, you are." She watched his eyes move from her breasts to other parts of her body.

"Am I more beautiful or less than before?" she purred.

"More beautiful," he answered. His stare made her feel powerful, yet something needled at her.

"You mean I was not beautiful before the transformation?" she prodded as stared at him, feeling her anger rise. She felt a small plate under her knee as she rocked back and forth on her fours and finally sat up. The plate moved behind her back as she awaited his answer.

He grinned. "I did not say that you were not beautiful before."

She roared in fury and threw the plate at his left shoulder, just to get his attention. "You said I was not pretty. I was 'piglet' correct? At least that is what Berti said."

She watched him flick away the shattered pieces of plate on his shoulder. "You were pretty before and the Goddess's gift increased the beauty you had one thousand fold."

Máire sashayed in closer. "Really? Can I see myself? Find me a mirror."

"Are you sure you would not rather wait until the transformation is complete?" he queried, before leaning in to play with a curl of her hair.

"I want to see myself now, Marcus. Find a mirror."

"Fine," he offered before standing up. "However, we will make a compromise. I shall bring you the mirror, but I will hold it. The mirror will not go into your hands. Is that understood?"

"Why not?" she asked. He could be so stubborn and lovely to watch.

"In your current state, you may break it," he told her.

"Oh, alright," Máire grumbled. "Bring it and show me how I look."

Heather Poinsett Dunbar & Christopher Dunbar

She watched him begin to search.

"In that box next to the bed," she suggested with a sigh. After finding it, he carried it to her and held it up.

"Move it to the right," she ordered. "Alright, tilt it downwards." Máire found herself losing her patience. "Honestly, Marcus, how am I to see myself in it when you keep moving the mirror? Let me use it," Máire demanded as she stretched her hands.

He pulled away. "That was not our agreement. I hold the mirror, Máire."

"But you are doing it wrong!" she exclaimed in frustration.

"Alright then, I will grip it, and you will move it as you require."

She stared at herself in mirror and gasped a bit as she saw that her scars had disappeared. She studied her newly prominent cheekbones, fuller lips, and eyes. "Oh my Goddess," she whispered. "I am gorgeous!" The last three words were delivered in a bemused shout. Máire then wrenched the mirror out of Marcus' hands and started to dance, twirling about as she watched herself in the mirror.

After a few minutes of dancing and hearing Marcus laugh, she kicked off her clothing. "My skin is so white and smooth," she purred, while touching her hand to her arms. "And my breasts are bigger." She stood up and looked at the cauldron hanging from a hook across the room. She remembered having to stretch to reach it, and now she grabbed it easily.

"Am I taller?" she drilled Marcus. "I think I am taller!" She then dropped the cauldron and embraced him. "Thank you for this," she whispered in his ear. "I had no idea it would change so much. Tell me more about what I can do."

Outside Ráth Cruachan

"One last time," Mandubratius stated before pulling out the map for his staff. The remains of the encampment burned within a dying fire as the soldiers and mortals marched to the north, hauling their tents and supplies.

"I and several of the others will be inside the church, enjoying the ceremony," Mandubratius began to explain once again. "After the bride and the groom leave, we will overtake Sáerlaith and her escorts. If I lean outside and give this signal," he stated while extending his left arm with his left thumb pointed up, "I have the Phallus Maximus and will therefore need extra protection. If I hold out my arm bent at the elbow, I do not have it, and then attack whatever Deargh Du you find. I highly suspect that this may be a deceptive trap, but reducing the number of Deargh Du would be useful. Once we have collected our treasure and subdued their forces, we will leave for the south and set sail for Britannia on whatever ships we can acquire."

He watched his staff nod their heads in agreement.

"Cohort nine remains with Wicus at the chieftain's dun in Mhuine Chonalláin. Dismissed," Mandubratius hissed, before pulling up the cowl of his cloak.

"Sir," he heard Patroclus address him.

"Yes?"

"I am curious about placing Amata and her underlings within my cohort," Patroclus stated.

"It seems only fitting," Mandubratius replied. "Take Teá and her husband as well. He seems an able fighter, yet I doubt she has ever held a blade in her life."

Patroclus gave a bit of an odd chuckle, saluted him, and left.

Amata met his gait as they started for village. "So, do you plan to finally deal with this third game that stabbed you?" Amata's mouth curled up into an amused smile.

"I will deal with Maél Muire at the appropriate time," he said while grinning back at her. "During the ensuing battle, if I must."

Mhuine Chonalláin

Berti gathered his cloak and sword, pleased that both Sitara and Sive slept in blankets next to the hearth of the guesthouse Connor Mac Turrlough had provided. It seemed as if exhaustion plagued them already from the wedding festivities, which spanned into the night. The still, red sky promised a bloody night.

Upon opening the door, a loud creak rent the silence that had pervaded the room, and now he knew Sive's eyes had caught sight of him.

"Before you say a word, I have to be there," Berti whispered, before turning around to face her. "Maél Muire needs protection. She will attack Mac Turrlough, and his clan will tear her to pieces. Not to mention, Marcus needs me to watch his back. He has grown soft with these Deargh Du."

"You are stubborn and looking for flimsy excuses," Sive whispered back as she arose and walked toward him, wrapped in a blanket. "I cannot deny you the opportunity to protect your friends, yet I must remind you that you have a wife and will soon have a child. You owe duties to them."

Berti stared at Sitara's back. "I have made certain that my family will live in comfort with or without me, Sive. I also must keep my duty to my friends and to the chieftain who protects my property." He smiled for a moment. "Little Bertius will have the best tutors and a good life."

Sive exhaled through her nose, impatient with him. "Very well, off you go. Do not do anything stupid."

He smiled at her. "Everything will happen as it should, Sive," he murmured before closing the door behind himself.

Marcus stood outside Caile's back room, worried about Maél, rather Máire's behavior. The two women remained sequestered in the back. Caile's husband had left earlier for the pre-wedding celebrations that echoed in the village. Mac Alpin had joined him, after he had requested extra assistance for dealing with Máire, who still appeared to be unfocused and lost within her thoughts, or someone else's. As the night grew longer, the spirits and fae of the Otherworld seemed to whisper the strangest of thoughts on the wind.

"Have you ever spent time with a newly transformed Deargh Du?" he asked Mac Alpin.

His associate chuckled. "No. This is my first time. They are amusing, to say the least. I had considered asking her to join my kind, yet you managed to get to her first," he said, grinning. Mac Alpin then walked to the outside and came back in, rubbing his hands. "Time moves quickly, young general. We need to return to Béal Átha an Fheadha."

"I am certain Claudius and the others can handle moving the forces when it is needed," Marcus said while staring at the back room. "It is kind of quiet in that room," he said, deciding to interrupt. He then walked over to the door separating him and Máire and knocked.

He heard an irritated huffing noise.

"Who is it?" Caile asked in a tone that suggested Caile did like him much.

Mac Alpin laughed into his hand.

"It's Marcus," he answered. "I need to see Maél Muire," he added, remembering to call her by her other name.

"You cannot enter yet. It is not… appropriate," her cousin yelled through the door.

"I need to talk to her, Caile," he replied.

"He will keep banging on the door incessantly," he heard Máire whisper. "Marcus is very stubborn."

He could hear the other blood-drinker cackle over his shoulder.

"I am going to get through this door at the count of five," he warned.

"See, he will not stop," Máire said.

"Oh, very well." He heard Caile storm towards the door before flinging it open. "You may enter." She then peeked around the store as if to see whether anyone witnessed the breach of propriety. Mac Alpin waved to her as Marcus went in. He watched Caile frown and slam the door shut.

Máire smirked at him while wearing a green dress that seemed a bit short and tight. She stared down at him from her stool.

"I must have a word in private with Máire," he said.

"Who?" Caile asked, while raising a brow at him, irritation obvious in her words.

"Maél Muire," he replied.

"But… Máire?" She examined her cousin as she asked, "Máire?"

"Just leave us for a moment," Máire purred. "Do not ask," she said with a chuckle. "It is a nickname for me."

"The wedding is in two hours," Caile drawled.

"I will be ready. You are almost done," Máire told her. "The dress is lovely."

Caile threw up her hands and left the room, before slamming the door shut.

Máire then stepped off the stool. "I have been finding it difficult not to drain Caile's blood. She even pricked her finger once, yet some inner strength kept me from plunging my teeth into her supple neck." She then pranced around Marcus, much like a graceful cat.

"Here," he offered, while raising his arm, "take a sip."

"No, no, no," she refused, grinning. "For what I must do, I wish to save all my thirst. I will quench it with my traitorous husband not-to-be's blood. Will you be in the church during the ceremony or with the other Deargh Du preparing for the Lamia?"

"Neither," he answered as he gently tugged at a loose thread that appeared intertwined with her curls and pulled it out. "I will be waiting outside watching you through a window. My men and women will send up a flaming arrow to signal our movement into the village. I will wait until the Lamia show themselves to take the Phallus Maximus from Sáerlaith. We will surprise them."

"That is an excellent plan, my general," Máire purred again. "I will have my vengeance upon Mandubratius then."

As he smiled, he watched her eyes glow. "You and I both have reason to seek vengeance upon Mandubratius."

"Well, the first to find him will have the joy of killing him. The other will have to settle with the lesser pleasure of just seeing him dead." She then paced around him, sliding a hand over his shoulders. He almost felt for a moment that Morrigan herself moved around him. She walked in front of him and drew her thumbs over his lips before kissing him.

He inhaled as she gently bit at his lower lip and sipped at his blood.

"Oh, I needed that," she whispered, before pulling back. She then closed her glowing eyes. "Yes, that took away the immediate need."

He soon heard banging at the door as Caile yelled from outside the room.

"Are you quite done yet, Marcus? I have a dress to finish! I cannot understand it, Maél Muire and I are the same size, until now."

He heard some muttering from Mac Alpin.

"I need to leave," he said to Máire. "I will not see you until after the wedding." He then watched her turn away. "Good fortune on your wedding night," he murmured, before spanking Máire's backside. He chuckled upon hearing her squeal.

"Stop that!" she said while giggling.

"This sounds like too much fun for a woman who is about to be wed," Caile warned.

Marcus opened the door and then beckoned Caile in. "Pardon my intrusion."

"Finally, now get out," Caile muttered, stomping into the room before he could walk across the door's threshold. "Be on your way," she said, while pushing him out with the door. He could still hear her admonishing her kin. "Remove that smile from your face, Maél Muire. We have a dress to finish. I do not see what you find so endearing about him. He feeds off the living like a leech might."

Mac Alpin chuckled and shook his head, before heading for the front door. "We have little time to prepare, and frankly, I am a bit tired of hearing insults flung at our kind."

Marcus glanced at the back room. "Arwin, could you stay here and make sure that nothing happens?"

Mac Alpin smirked. "You should have remembered your first night, young Marcus." His brow then furrowed. "I will make sure Maél Muire does not misbehave."

chapter seventeen

Béal Átha an Fheadha

fter landing outside of the grove, Marcus watched the Deargh Du divide into formations and gather weapons. He soon noticed Sáerlaith to the side, slicing a knife over the palm of her hand as she made an offering of her blood to several raven feathers.

Apparently sensing him, she faced him and smiled. "Marcus, we have anxiously awaited your appearance," she said before licking the remaining blood from her left palm.

"We must talk," he whispered as he motioned her away from the other Deargh Du and other blood-drinkers. "I did it."

"Did what?" she asked, after taking his arm.

"Maél Muire is now Deargh Du," he said, finding himself returning a smile as Sáerlaith grinned at him.

"Morrigan is blessed indeed to have Maél Muire among her brood. How is she?"

"She went through the physical changes well, yet the mental changes are taking a toll on her. She is definitely crazed," he said before staring into the early night sky.

"You are not watching her?" Sáerlaith asked abruptly while staring at him with a raised brow as if accusing him of being a lazy parent.

"Arwin is watching her," he replied. "He managed to distract her on our way to Mhuine Chonalláin, so I felt he was best for the task."

He watched Sáerlaith's face grow relaxed. "I have a surprise for you," she murmured.

"What is it?" he asked.

"Ruarí," Sáerlaith called over her shoulder.

Marcus watched the arch druid emerge from the mists with Sive following him. He then noticed a large satchel slung over Ruarí's shoulder.

Ruarí shrugged off the satchel, opened it, and removed a large piece of marble.

Marcus looked at Sáerlaith for a moment. "You really found it? This is the broken phallus of Mars from the statue at his temple?"

"We did, but this is not it," Sive answered.

"Well, what is this then?" Marcus asked.

"Our decoy," answered Ruarí.

"I knew where it was since Fergus and I buried it," Sive explained, as her face crinkling into a sad smile.

"We thought that this might work with your current plan. Ruarí found a marble seller in Ulster, and then one of our craftsmen made a duplicate."

"And where is the real one?" Marcus asked.

"It is in a good hiding place," Sáerlaith answered.

"There are ears that might hear us," Ruarí admitted. "It is best we do not mention it now. Oh, I heard there is a new Deargh Du. Congratulations! Maél Muire will be an excellent warrior for Morrigan."

He felt warmth surround him as Sive embraced him and smiled.

"We are honored," she said, before kissing his cheek.

He embraced her for a moment. "I think I need to leave for Mhuine Chonalláin to take my position outside the church. Claudius will take our army out to their positions. You two," he said to Ruarí and Sáerlaith, "join Caoimhín and the rest of your party at the church."

"Best of luck," Sive offered as he pulled away and then headed skyward.

Mhuine Chonalláin

Connor looked through the church as his friends and their families sat at the rough-hewn pews, wondering whether Mandubratius would arrive soon. He witnessed several strangers sit down in the middle of the church, including several Deargh Du, with Sáerlaith among them. She met his eyes, and then a glimmer of green in her eyes made him lose track of thought as he stared at her hair. It seemed to be composed of stars. Her then eyes reverted back to brown, before she turned to face the harpists.

Connor closed his eyes for a moment to enjoy the music. The sounds of sputtering candles and the smell of sacred frankincense added to the mystery that seemed to infuse the air tonight. He then opened his eyes and noticed his mother take a seat next to one of the Deargh Du in Sáerlaith's party.

Why would she sit next to them?

As Seosaimhín smiled at him, her eyes appeared soft and serene.

He smiled back at her. He soon noticed the priest nod to one of the men standing in the back, and then the doors opened and in walked his bride. She looked resplendent in her green dress. Maél Muire took small steps towards him while smiling at him. To say she exuded radiance seemed to be too meager a description. She seemed to be taller, which seemed impossible. He then noticed a dark, cloaked figure float into the church before darting into the shadows.

Máire paused mid-step, upon smelling someone all too familiar. A strange sensation arched through the church and made the air seem tight with frantic tension despite the sweet, cloying scent of whatever it was the church burned during its' sacred rites. She looked at the front of the church as she glided down the petal-strewn aisle. Then she saw him... her betrothed.

As his eyes moved down her form, she felt a flurry of anger rise within. Faces began to blur.

Concentrate.

She closed her eyes, willing out the distractions, yet the presence in the back still needled at her. When could she turn around and confront the eyes of whom she believed it would be?

Marcus took a quick peek through the window, after pushing aside the ivies and leaves of the plants that seemed to envelop this small church like a creature tightening its grip on a tiny pebble. Mac Turrlough, looking self-absorbed, stood near the altar with the priest. He also noticed Seosaimhín sitting next to Caoimhín and felt some concern. Marcus backed away before the druidess could notice his presence.

Then Mac Alpin dashed over from the other side of the church.

"It is a shame," Arwin muttered. "This wedding looks so beautiful, but I believe it will not end well."

"On the contrary," Marcus replied. "It will end exactly the way the bride wishes it to." He inhaled, sensing Máire as the doors opened and closed.

Both Marcus and Mac Alpin chuckled, sharing a bout of nervousness.

Mac Alpin then took a look at the players within the confines of the church. "I am surprised he is not dead yet. What will Maél... Máire do?"

"All I know is that she has not fed much," Marcus replied as Mac Alpin ducked away from the window looking astonished and fearful.

"Why, she could explode like one of Edward's experiments!" he uttered.

Marcus tried to stifle his laughter when he noticed that Mac Alpin looked uncomfortable.

"If I were you, I would keep a safe distance from her for some time, if that is the case," Mac Alpin warned without even smiling. "You should have warned me. No wonder her hands felt like ice."

"I am certain you and I are safe," Marcus reasoned aloud, "but I'm not so sure about the mortal she is about to marry."

He heard the door open and then creak closed.

"I smell Lamia," Arwin whispered.

"I thought they would have arrived sooner and swarmed the church," Marcus whispered back as the door closed. Their conversation ceased once Máire neared the altar, after taking slow, deliberate steps.

Clarity. Calm. Do not rush into anything.

Máire tried to make her mind settle on something other than smashing that man into a thousand pieces, though he deserved more than that. She tried to ignore the spore of blood that diffused to her nose and pulsed in her ears.

Connor's smile made it all the worse, rankling and needling at her already unsteady thoughts. How could someone like him stand there and smile at her through his intoxicated state as though he had won?

As she walked, the mortal heartbeats seemed to grow louder. How could the other Deargh Du ignore the constant barrage of noise? She tried to smile as she walked closer, but then she noticed an unkindness of ravens sweep into the church. The others seemed blind and oblivious to the black-feathered messengers that landed on heads, cawing from perches near the ceiling of the church. Some started walking across the stone altar. She then heard a soft caw as one landed on her shoulder. Did Morrigan walk with her now?

A soft whisper tickled at her left ear. "Yes, my beloved brood?"

Máire felt a moment of light-headed joy.

Thank you for giving me the strength and clarity to do what I must do.

After a few more steps, Máire reached the front of the church where Connor waited for her. After stopping at his side and facing him, he offered her his warm arm. She wondered whether she should wrench it out of his socket or wait for something to happen. She then felt a breeze as the raven on her shoulder took to the air, and then she and Connor turned to face their wedding guests.

And there he stood, looking directly into her eyes. She could see Mandubratius' face as he stared at her, stunned at her transformation. She could not help but smile a bit and wonder whether she appeared deranged.

She is a Deargh Du!

Mandubratius felt a strange shock and outrage overwhelm him. He then exhaled a sigh as he looked up and down her form. She appeared... radiant, more than she ever had before. The Deargh Du had such beautiful trickery. He felt stupefied, knowing that her eyes held his. He could not help but lose himself in the thoughts that she might charge him then and there.

What will you be like in battle now?

The movement of her lips interrupted his thoughts, and he could hear her words on the wind.

"I was expecting you," she whispered as her smile grew and her eyes glimmered like exquisite emeralds. Her skin gleamed like a luminous pearl.

Has she grown taller?

The priest cleared his throat and then smiled at them, before gesturing for everyone to turn towards him.

Connor turned to face the priest, finding himself still lost in his bride. Her hands felt frigid, like an icy morning. Her right hand lowered a bit to release his, but he could not let it go. He then leaned closer, smelling her. Her glossy hair seemed to burn with a red fire. She stood straight and tall, resembling a breathing marble statue. Maél Muire almost appeared to be a new person. Of course many said pregnant women changed this way.

The priest droned on about joining lives together, before rambling on about something else, the importance of love, fidelity, and honor between husband and wife, or some such nonsense.

Connor stretched out his arm as it entwined with hers and then lost all rational thought as he traced his hand over her backside. He waited for a reaction, but saw none. Maél Muire stared past the priest at a dark opening in the back of the church, though her face still gleamed amidst her smile.

"Now face each other," the priest entreated. "Repeat these words I say." The priest then spoke aloud the vows for Connor.

When the priest finished, Connor repeated, "'I, Connor, now take you, Maél Muire, to be my wife. In the presence of God and before these witnesses, I promise to be a loving, faithful, and loyal husband to you, for as long as we both shall live'."

He watched Maél Muire smile. Her eyes glimmered in the light of the fire. Then the priest turned and spoke aloud the vows for Máire.

She began to repeat. "I, Maél Muire, now take you, Connor, to be my husband. In the presence of God and before these witnesses, I promise to be a loving, faithful, and loyal wife to you…" she intoned before trailing off and shaking her head. "I am sorry." She started laughing. "I forgot my name. I, Máire, do solemnly swear to see your corpse rot!" He then watched her eyes begin to glow with an inhuman, green light.

Connor felt his breath turn cold, for his new wife had turned into a goddess of judgment. Before he could say anything else, he felt a tug as she pulled him toward her with her right hand.

He then screamed in utter agony as her left hand plunged into his chest, accompanied by an echoing crunch of bone within the church. However, the intensity of pain seemed to fade. Soon, he could only feel freezing fear and cold shock as she withdrew her arm and held out his beating heart in her left hand. The world began to turn gray as her green eyes locked on his.

"This is for murdering my betrothed, you treacherous bastard!" she screamed, sounding like the banshees of his nightmares. The screaming did not stop as the gray ceased and became an all-consuming blackness.

Marcus watched Máire growl like a mortal caught between rage and victory. She raised the heart over her head, squeezed it, and then caught the blood draining from it in her open mouth. Immediately, Connor's body fell to the floor. Marcus sensed the pulse of rising power, and then darkness descended within the church. Every Deargh Du must have pulled down the darkness. The then door slammed open and shut, and he could hear someone rip open the hide that covered the opposite window. Soon, Máire's scent faded away.

Marcus watched a pair of arms reach out of the blackness, and he recognized a silver ring on Berti's hand. Marcus reached into the darkness, grabbed Berti, and tugged him out of the window.

"Did you see that?" Berti hissed.

"I could not miss it," Marcus admitted. "Go find Sáerlaith, Berti. I sense she's outside of the church. She will probably go to the third home on the left from the church." Caile's home offered a safe meeting place. He then turned to Mac Alpin. "Follow Máire, please. You–" A shout to the Lamia from within the building stopped his words.

Mac Alpin attempted a salute before running around the back of the church.

Berti began backing away from the church, creeping into the surrounding grove of oaks.

Marcus closed his eyes, hearing the yelling from within continued, but he could not remain, for the gathering troops awaited him. He then ducked around the back, surrounded himself in darkness, and then took to the sky.

Some mortals screamed in intoxicating fear, while others roared, enraged, their fury further intensified with drink. Then there stood Maél Muire, holding her gruesome trophy like an ancient warrior goddess of the old days. Mandubratius shook away his shock. Bloodlust raced through his bones as she raised Mac Turrlough's heart over her head, squeezed it, and drank what she could. A bizarre impulse to join her in that carnage grew, along with a sudden urge to throw her on the altar and tear her dress apart. He witnessed her look back at him with a strange grimace as the church turned black. He could hear footsteps, racing heartbeats, and deafening screams. Smells seemed to grow stronger, like that of blood. Then the door slammed open and shut, as if the wind slapped it back and forth. Mandubratius reached into the darkness but felt nothing.

"Get in here now!" he raged in Latin. "Cohort one!" He knew they hid within a farmer's barn nearby, close enough to hear his whistle blow. Mandubratius held the whistle to his lips and blew. Soon, the door opened again.

"Mandubratius," a voice whispered. "Where are you?" He heard the speaker stumbling as he raced through the doors. Then a loud series of screams and shouts echoed around the church.

"Use the pews to find your way. Block the doors and windows."

Another high-pitched cry interrupted his thoughts, and then the darkness disappeared as suddenly as it had arrived. He smelled blood as he witnessed one of his soldiers feeding on a mortal. He could see half of the wedding guests stare at the reddened horror as the other half turned back from seeing their chieftain still dead and the chieftain's bride missing.

A woman stabbed the feeding soldier, who pushed away his victim before ripping the annoying woman's throat out.

Mandubratius counted the death as only a mere distraction from his realization that his property still remained at large. "Sáerlaith and her party are gone!" he shouted, realizing he had been distracted. "Assemble the cohorts, search the village, and find that Deargh Du and the Phallus Maximus!" Then he barked more orders. "Round up the mortals and bring them here so we can interrogate them. If they resist, do not hesitate to kill them."

He heard a voice at the front of the church near the altar. "Call forth the warriors! Our chief is slain!" the priest yelled in Gaelic to the clansmen.

"Silence that man!" Mandubratius ordered. One of his soldiers beheaded the mortal priest without much ado.

Berti opened the door to the house, when the sound of swords being drawn caused him to jump.

"What are you doing here?" Sáerlaith asked.

"Mac Alpin went to find Maél Muire, and Marcus went to meet with the troops." He felt a weak smile move across his face and tried to give a more confident grin. "Marcus told me to meet you here. I suppose he believes I will be safer with you than with the Lamia outside."

Sáerlaith grabbed his arm and leaned toward him. "Berti, we are bait. They will probably be here any moment." He heard the door slam, and then the Deargh Du pushed him toward the shadows.

Berti turned around and watched as the Deargh Du moved into fighting stances. At that moment, the door flew inward, and then four Lamia marched into the room, followed by another figure who stood between the soldiers, smiling. As the Lamia grinned, he revealed his red eyes.

"Sáerlaith, I presume," he said in labored Gaelic. "I believe you have something of mine."

"You shall not have it, Mandubratius," Sáerlaith answered.

Mandubratius played with his golden sword for a moment. "I believe you are mistaken," he replied, before snapping his fingers.

Berti exhaled as the flurry of battle began. Heads rolled and bodies fell to the ground. The blurred onslaught paused, and he could see Mandubratius and one Lamia soldier facing Sáerlaith and Caoimhín.

"I will give you one opportunity to leave with your miserable lives if you give me what is mine," Mandubratius demanded, smiling. "Present it!" he shouted.

Berti watched Sáerlaith pull out a large piece of marble.

"You will never possess the Phallus Maximus!" Sáerlaith hissed.

Berti felt the air move around him as a fast, fluid motion blurred his sight again. Mandubratius knocked over Caoimhín with his left bracer. He then sliced at Sáerlaith's outstretched arm with his golden sword. Then an intense pain screamed as he felt a sword stab him in the stomach.

"Help me finish them," The Lamia leader shouted at his soldier.

Berti grew blind as darkness descended around him. He soon felt a pair of arms, one missing a hand and forearm, slide around him, and then they flew through the one window in the room. Berti looked on as Caoimhín followed them out.

"I wish we had known they could do that," Mandubratius lamented as he shook his head for a moment in consternation. At least his treasure remained.

He ignored the soldier and turned, picking up Sáerlaith's hand as it remained clasp around the Phallus Maximus. He then started impatiently pulling her fingers off it before tossing the long-fingered hand aside.

"I have it, Mars," he cried while holding it up, before kicking aside bodies to find the satchel Sáerlaith had used.

"Bring the rest of my armor," he told the soldier. The Lamia dutifully left.

He then managed to find the leather bag under one of the Deargh Du. He placed the treasure within the sack and closed it.

"Your armor, sir," said the Lamia soldier as soon as he returned.

Mandubratius dropped his cloak and then took the offered assistance with donning his remaining armor, before wrapping the bag around the underside of his shield for safekeeping.

Marcus landed in front of the Deargh Du army and looked over his gathered forces.

"Maon," he called as he gestured one of his Deargh Du over. "You are now the centurion of the third centuria." The other Deargh Du saluted him.

"Where is Mac Alpin?" Claudius asked in Latin. "Wasn't he to have led the third centuria? Or at least, isn't that what we had agreed upon during our battle plan discussions?"

"I have a newborn Deargh Du who has killed a chieftain by plucking out his heart, Claudius. I cannot let a mob kill her or her kill a mob," Marcus replied.

Marcus then turned to the gathered forces. "You have your missions. Let's accomplish them with stealth." He motioned for Centuria One to follow him. The third would serve as their backup. Claudius and the second would join them after ascertaining the needs of the innocent mortal population.

Claudius landed on the thatched roof of a home a few doors down from the church. The Deargh Du accompanying him clung to the branches of a few scattered oaks or on other buildings. Below, three groups of Lamia soldiers patrolled door to door, searching for other mortals. Claudius flew over to the roof of the church as three others came with him. He quickly motioned to the others to dispatch the patrols. He then signaled the other Deargh Du to take care of the guards positioned outside of the church.

The sounds of quick death echoed through the silence of the village. The rattle of falling armor and lifeless bodies seemed to break up the stillness. He then heard screaming within the church. He gestured for the Deargh Du to surround the church.

Claudius jumped to the ground and crouched, before creeping without a sound towards the door. The soft thrum of concentrated darkness surrounded the church, giving way to an extended period of silence, before voices tore away the quiet.

As the darkness held, he counted from three to one, hoping the others did the same. He then broke down the door. He could hear the Deargh Du flying in through the four windows. The sound of screams soon accompanied the thumps of dead bodies. Afterwards, the darkness melted into the floor, giving all a chance to see the carnage within.

The mortals started yelling and began pointing at him and the others.

"Wait! Wait!" he growled in Gaelic, hoping he would get this right. "These are the Lamia who attacked your clan."

"You are all Deargh Du!" A loud man yelled while waving a dagger. "You and that Maél Muire. She killed our chief." The dagger hovered closer to the blood-drinkers.

The Deargh Du started to explain in Gaelic what had happened, but the mortal's confusion seemed to grow. Claudius grumbled under his breath before blowing his whistle. The mortals covered their ears for a moment and then dropped their hands. He exhaled and concentrated on willing the mortals to hear his words.

"Listen," he began to explain. "Your chieftain deserved death. He not only took part in murdering a friend of Maél Muire's, he also raped her and lent assistance to these Lamia. I am certain that some sort of hearing will be held. Now, there are more pressing matters. We must protect you all from these Lamia. You will remain here with some of our warriors who will offer you protection."

"How can we tell you from the Lamia?" a woman shouted.

"Deargh Du will be in green and dressed as we are," Claudius answered. "Lamia are in red, as the soldiers of Rome were." He did not bother with further explanations about his race and the Ekimmu Cruitne, which would be too confusing. "However, there is another way to differentiate us. The Lamia's eyes turn red in bloodlust. Ours become green."

He then faced Fianait. "Remain here with a detachment of twenty five. The rest of the cohort will join the battle!" he shouted to the others.

Mac Alpin walked through the clearing on the path through the forested glens. "If I was a newly created Deargh Du and I had killed my betrothed during an extended moment of insanity, where would I go?" he queried the landscape. He then closed his eyes, upon hearing a raven's caw, and wondered whether the bird wished to speak and tell a secret. Utter rubbish.

"Cousin Caile," Mac Alpin answered himself, before clucking with his tongue. He then turned around and raced for the village. As he flew, he noticed a series of fast moving objects in flight, one of which flew headlong into a tree.

"Sáerlaith?" He could sense the elder Deargh Du, and the scent of her blood made her identity clearer. As he landed a few feet away, he saw Sáerlaith feeding from Caoimhín's wrist. Mac Alpin felt surprised to see that her right arm ended in a bloody stump. He also noticed a burn on Caoimhín's arm and that Berti held his stomach.

"Let me," he said to Caoimhín. "Your talents are needed on him, and you need to heal." He pulled back his sleeve, before sitting down next to the female Deargh Du, and smiled. "Drink," Mac Alpin murmured before feeling her pull in his arm and break the skin with her extended canines.

He closed his eyes as she fed. "I am searching for a bride, Sáerlaith. Have you seen Maél Muire?"

Sáerlaith's head remained low as she continued to feed. She then released him before pulling her léine sleeve over her mouth, leaving a bloody stain. "No, we have not," she answered while meeting his eyes.

Mac Alpin then looked over at Caoimhín and Berti, as the other Deargh Du wrapped up the mortal's wound and cupped his hands over it for a moment. "I have done all I can for now," Caoimhín whispered. "We need to get to the river Moy."

"I will be fine," Berti said, motioning the other Deargh Du away. "You need to find Maél Muire," he said to Mac Alpin while placing his left hand over his wound. "The Tuaths' mercy will be upon her if that crazed mob in the church or the Lamia find her."

Marcus watched his fellow warriors shift as the sounds of battle echoed through the forest. "Patience, have patience," Marcus whispered to himself as he raised his arms, before passing his shield to Ula. He tried to remember the words from his past that he would use to steady the mortal soldiers. "Wait until the signal," he ordered, though the Deargh Du still continued to fidget.

No other words came to mind. Other weighty matters presented themselves, like what would become of him after this battle?

Soon the sound of horns echoed in the distance. After he gestured to Ula and to the rest of his staff, they flew up to the canopy of trees to study the situation. At the sound of the horns, the Lamia ranks lined up in a tortoise formation with spears bristling over the interlocked shields, leaving little room for an overhead attack.

"It is time," he murmured. The wind rushed around him as he levitated above the troops. He then raised his two gladii. "Prepare to rise," he called, as his subordinates echoed his orders.

"Rise into formation," he heard the repeated phrase again, before swallowing a nervous, unnecessary breath as he moved up above the formation to direct it. Faces turned up to watch him as he motioned for the troops to move out.

He called out to his lieutenants to follow their attack plan as the Lamia loomed closer. He watched the Lamia ranks shift the top of the tortoise to allow for the first spear throwers to aim. He then heard a series of spears hit their shields as the aerial tortoise continued to hover closer. Marcus soon flew down and joined the others. The first series of spears hit several of the unguarded Lamia soldiers, pinning them to the ground. The Deargh Du tortoise then hovered lower, closer to the ground troops.

Marcus decided to fly higher again to get a better view of the battle, but he soon heard the whistles of spears as the Lamia began throwing volleys of spears towards him, now. He held no shield, so he brought up his arms to protect him, but he suddenly felt a burst of pain and a burning sensation through his body. He bit his lower lip, not wanting to reveal the fact the enemy had wounded him.

As the pain radiated through the break in his armor, Marcus felt himself slip a bit, unable to focus his concentration on flying. Marcus soon descended into the canopy of leaves of the tall oaks. Branches broke his fall as he finally met the ground, breaking his arm. As he attempted to assess his situation, Marcus could sense two Deargh Du racing towards him.

"General," Ula cried as she rolled Marcus to his side.

"Go back to the cohort," Marcus ordered Ula and the other warrior. "I can take care of this myself. You are needed in the battle. It will be a waste of time for you to stay here." He watched them stare at each other. "Go! That is an order and not a request!" he shouted in an attempt to sound authoritative. "You must take my place until Claudius or Mac Alpin arrives."

"Yes sir," she agreed, before she and their comrade took to the air.

He heard their swift movements as they pulled back, leaving a lingering moment of magic.

Marcus closed his eyes. "Heal, soldier," he ordered himself, before taking note of a good, strong oak about ten feet away that could help. He needed a few minutes to gather his fading strength.

Máire tripped over the root of a tree, before turning and kicking the tree in anger. She then pushed her hair away from her face, as the curled strands she had combed with a strange care and pride earlier now felt as if her hair had dried itself into bloody plaits. She took another few steps and then lost her footing, slamming into a rock. She rubbed her forehead as she considered that there seemed to be a big difference between the graceful and beautiful Deargh Du and herself. She then stared at the ground, upon sensing movement.

Did a Sidhe lord plan to walk by tonight?

"No, just Lamia," Máire whispered, upon hearing their footfalls and smelling their rank blood. She got to her knees and then rose up as they neared her. Rank or not, her hunger, a steadily growing force, whispered in her ear. She then remembered her dagger and pulled it out.

"Look what we have here. It's a little bride," one teased while leering at her.

"Congratulations, little bride," another one said.

How many stood before her? She found her mind abuzz with numbers.

"Where is your husband?" one of the five goaded as he took a step closer. "How do they manage to be so... lovely?" he chuckled. "We should play with her first. You have no protection, do you little bride?"

Máire soon felt movements of her arms and legs that she could not identify... movements not of her will. She also spoke words that seemed to appear from nowhere. "I deliver to you the same fate I that delivered to my husband," she growled, smiling at the soldier as her hand closed around his throat.

He squeaked a little, though he still grinned.

Why did they all have to smile?

"Hmmm? Trouble in the marriage bed? I bet your husband found fear in consummating that contract."

"Look at the hand that grips you," she murmured. "He died by this hand, as will you." Máire then tore out his throat in one quick movement. The blood spilled as she ripped that one's neck from his shoulder. The other soldier, who tried to flee, she caught, before draining and then beheading him. With both soldiers dead, she confiscated the steel sword one of them wore.

The warmth of Lamia blood felt like a healing fire. With the infusion of fresh blood, Máire could feel her senses increase. Now, she could sense a mass of Lamia nearby. Máire could feel her mouth open as a rage-filled scream echoed through the night. She then launched her body into the skies. The caws of flying ravens echoed in her ears as she landed in front of the gathered Lamia and mortal soldiers. She screamed again and watched the unkindness pulse and roar like a wild wave of blackness. An airborne assault overwhelmed what could be described as frightened children.

She witnessed one of the Lamia point at her and scream in terror, "Demon with bird's eyes, leave us in peace!"

She tipped her head, feeling no control over her movements, as her mouth formed into a strange smile.

Claudius stopped his cohort as he heard screams in a nearby clearing. He watched a lone figure flying above a disorganized pack of mortals and a few Lamia. Their reserves tried to stay in a tortoise formation, but the figure, a woman, would drop onto their shields, avoiding the spears, and slice her sword through as many bodies in the gap as possible. Ravens and crows fed from the dead and dying. He surmised fifty lay in their blood with limbs hewn, and a remaining force of nearly one hundred and fifty tried to fend off the... Maél Muire? Their golden spears did not seem to dissuade her tactics.

"Go help her!" he ordered his cohort as he joined them in the melee. As he flew towards the fight, he saw her cut down more soldiers.

Claudius lost himself in the battle and emerged feeling energized afterwards. How much time had passed? He wiped his sword against the tunic of mortal within the reserve Lamia ranks when he spied Maél Muire, naked and bloodied, staring up at the moon, but he felt startled to see a raven resting upon her shoulder. As Claudius strode closer, she turned to face him. Her face revealed a peaceful bliss. He inhaled as she locked her gaze on him. Her eyes reflected nothing back at him. They seemed all black, like the ravens that gorged on the bodies of both mortal and immortal.

Claudius took another step forward, wanting to make sure his eyes did not play tricks on him.

"Claudius," she called, though a different woman's voice moved past her lips. "Go to the east. That is where you are needed."

Patroclus removed the head of another Deargh Du, just before Wicus ran towards him yelling, "Sir, sir! We have received word that a woman is decimating the reserves. I have no idea of the numbers remaining."

Patroclus backed off, allowing others to take his spot. The unbelievable story Wicus relayed could be a Deargh Du ploy, so Patroclus thought he might take this opportunity to remove some dead weight. "Lucretia," he called. He watched her turn and gallop to his side like an eager dog. "Our reserves face a severe enemy," he told her. "Take Teá, her husband, and your child, along with thirty of the rest, and assist them." He smiled at her as she saluted him before gathering her guild of miscreants.

Claudius motioned for a halt and silence as he closed his eyes, knowing the Deargh Du could smell the new group of Lamia moving towards the field of dead reserves.

"Fan out," he whispered while watching the Lamia troops move into place. Maél Muire still stood in place with the raven on her shoulder as if lost in thought or between the mists of the mortal realm and the mists of the Gods.

"Halt!" a woman's voice shouted as he watched the enemy turn toward him. A volley of golden spears danced in the moonlight.

"Form up!" he yelled, furious with himself for not being prepared. Over twenty of his soldiers fell as spears penetrated their shields. He then signaled for a counterstrike. The two armies stared at each other and then roared before colliding in battle.

Teá took an uneasy cut at a Deargh Du, slicing off a hand. She already hating this battle, as well as fighting in general, but engaging in combat while wearing the heavy and confining golden armor did not help. Exhausted, she pushed her way past others to get away from the fighting, when she noted a figure staring off into space. The woman stood, clothed only in a thin sheen of blood. Teá crept closer before realizing that she beheld Maél Muire. Her niece's eyes appeared closed as she faced away from her, lost in ignorance or something equally repugnant.

"Insolent child," Teá hissed before charging at Maél Muire with her sword raised to strike, when a force knocked her away from Maél Muire. Her oblivious niece remained standing not twenty feet away.

"Woman, you will not kill my sister's child!" Cennedi yelled as he pushed Teá to the ground and then sat on her backside.

Teá growled as she clawed at the dirt in fury. "Get off me, you treacherous bastard!" She tried to shake her husband off herself, but soon Teá heard footsteps. She then heard the metallic song of a blade, before feeling her husband's dead weight fall aside and hearing his head tumble to the ground. Teá looked over and smiled at Mandubratius.

"I heard rumors of a madwoman killing my reserves," he stated as he pulled Teá to her feet. "I came to see this for myself, only to find your husband had turned traitor. I am sure you are quite glad to be rid of him. He was unfit to be Lamia. Next time, you will choose wisely."

She noticed Mandubratius faced away from Maél Muire, as the battle still continued around them.

"So, where is this supposed madwoman?" he asked while beaming at her.

Teá heard him suppress his chuckles.

"That madwoman is my niece, Maél Muire," she whispered, "and she is perhaps twenty feet behind you."

Mandubratius turned around and saw a blood-drenched, naked figure in front of him. The woman turned around, but her eyes remained closed. Mandubratius smiled, astonished she still wandered free. Then a sudden cold wind saddened him as he watched a raven land on her shoulder. His desire for her at the church soon ebbed.

"Maél Muire," he called to her, deciding to ignore the warnings in his head. "You look a little different."

He watched her eyelids open, and then he gasped as he saw black eyes, which promised to swallow him whole. She cocked her head to one side in the same manner that a bird might. Her body seemed to contort as she leaned forward, and then a loud scream from her made his body and soul feel as if they would collapse.

He noticed all of the Lamia and Deargh Du stop and stare at the banshee wailing her soul-stealing scream. The piercing cry grew in volume as his ears began to ring. He started to back away, covering the sides of his head with his hands. He noticed everyone else doing the same, as the unearthly shriek echoed through the glens. Mandubratius soon tripped over what felt like a body, but he managed to keep himself on his feet.

Suddenly, the unearthly noise stopped, and the Lamia turned to stare at him. Mandubratius inhaled, knowing the truth. If he hesitated, they would falter. The Deargh Du also stared at him, as if realizing who he might be. Their eyes then moved back to Maél Muire, as if revering her. The fools probably believed Morrigan stood in front of them.

Mandubratius pulled his blade from its scabbard and screamed back at the smiling Maél Muire. He then charged, running towards her at top speed with his sword poised to pierce her chest.

Time seemed to stand still as he approached. He watched her pull back her right fist and then strike him in the center of his chest. Pain radiated from that spot as he felt himself propelled backwards, into the air, before slamming to the ground several feet away. He squeaked as he tried to move, but he could not. He could feel that his armor was dented inward. Broken ribs and a shattered sternum made every attempt at movement painful. He tried to move his legs, but they would not obey. On top of his injuries, Mandubratius wondered where the fearsome warrior woman went.

He could see Lucretia and Teá move to his side as they struggled with something. He then witnessed Lucretia pick up a sword.

"Let's finish him," she said to Teá, while playing with his hair. Lucretia stood over Mandubratius, straddling him, before raising her sword. "I have been yearning to pay you back. Now I have an opportunity."

Her words accompanied a resounding ring in his ears. His confusion grew, until he witnessed his other child raise her sword.

"Perhaps not," he whispered. He then watched Lucretia's eyes grow large as Teá cleaved Lucretia's head from her neck.

Máire watched the Lamia's body fall to the side as her head rolled. Its brown eyes stared at Máire with a lifeless horror. Then from nowhere, feet began to block her view of the Lamia's face. She furrowed her brow in confusion as she noticed that eight Deargh Du now surrounded her. They then turned their backs toward her in a synchronized offer of protection. She watched in rage as her aunt and a few others dragged Mandubratius towards the woods. Fighting soon began again with a renewed zeal that made the air sing.

Máire soon felt an invisible force pull at her soul, and then she found herself bathed in daylight, face to face with three women... a young maiden with hair that gleamed like silver, a matron with hair the color of dried blood, and an elder crone with white hair and one eye stood before her. All were guises of Morrigan, and all three stared at her with black eyes gleaming of wisdom.

"I want to kill him," Máire said. "I deserve his blood on my hands. You started this. Let me finish it."

"No," the crone whispered. The hills echoed with the 'no's of the others.

Máire clasped her hands over her ears until the cacophonous replies died.

"He must stay alive," the matron stated as She touched Máire's hand. "For now, this is how the balance is to be in place and maintained."

Máire stared at the three women. "Very well, I will not kill him… now."

The three women smiled before touching hands. The maiden and the crone then disappeared in blinding light as Morrigan the matron stood in front of her.

"You are wise, my child, and show much promise. I will release you now to continue the battle on your own." The Goddess smiled as She stepped back.

"Thank you, grandmother," Máire whispered. The sun soon faded, causing her to blink.

Then the night skies, lit with thousands of stars, overwhelmed her senses as the aroma of sweat and blood awoke her own desire to slay the Lamia. She drew her captured sword and pushed her way past the Deargh Du and towards the fighting. Máire could hear the others follow behind as she yelled while striking down the first Lamia in her path.

Assim cowered in the darkness of the trees before running towards the west. He had left during the fight and the screaming, hoping he could escape. That woman and her raven would haunt him in his dreams.

When he arrived at his hiding place, he took off his armor and then slung it and his supplies over his shoulder. The cowl of his cloak hid his features. If he could reach Britannia, he could find a way home. He would leave behind the darkness and return to his civilized and cultured home.

chapter eighteen

eá gestured to the other Lamia around herself and Mandubratius after reaching the forest, motioning for them to stay still, before noticing Amata approach. They both then started to remove his armor. "All I hear is ringing," Teá said to him, hoping her voice did not carry.

His eyes seemed to draw her in closer, so she leaned in.

"I cannot move anything," he groaned. "I think she broke my spine."

Teá stared at the mass of bones jutting from his body and shook her head. She then noticed a satchel in his hand, which seemed frozen in place.

"Guard this with your life," he whispered.

She took the satchel and peeked inside at the piece of marble. Teá then pulled out the black phallus and stared at it in awe.

"Domina," a soldier said as he saluted Amata, "we need to leave."

"I will determine when it is time to leave," Amata snapped. Teá watched Amata's face soften as the prominent frown left her face. "However, you are right. It is time to head for our departure point."

"You six," ordered Amata while motioning soldiers over, "carry him with your capes." She then strode off ahead of them.

Teá followed her sponsor, wondering whether she would live to see another night.

Marcus struggled as he grasped a young elm tree and pulled himself up. He started taking painful steps towards the old oak tree, while clutching the spear that had entered him through a chink in his armor. Once he managed to get there, Marcus turned away from the tree and closed his eyes, willing himself to gather what remained of his strength. He growled before running backwards towards the oak. He grimaced in pain as the spearhead lodged itself into the tree. The pain blinded him, and then all became red.

Marcus stood on the tips of his toes, bent his knees, and then felt the gold head and wood begin to give. He tried it two more times before it gave way and popped as the spear broke away from the barbed head. He took a step from the gold and soon felt the burning begin to subside. He then clenched the wooden shaft and yanked the rest of the spear out of his body, yelling during the flourish of motion. After tossing aside the wooden staff, Marcus dropped to the ground.

Claudius wiped the blood-drenched sweat from his face, as the remaining Lamia ran for the woods, before noticing that Maél Muire stood away from the other Deargh Du. He watched as she stumbled towards the body of a beheaded Lamia, staring at the lifeless corpse.

Her eyes now emanated the color of emeralds. Claudius' earlier fear dissipated upon seeing Maél Muire hugging herself. She clasped a sword in her fist for a moment before resting it against her leg.

"Are you well, Maél Muire?" he asked, before touching a blood-drenched arm that felt sticky.

"Máire," she replied. "My name is Máire now. I am well, Claudius." She then met his eyes. "You are needed at the village."

"Do you need protection before I leave for the main battle?" he asked.

She smiled a bit before shaking her head, causing her bloody plaits to swing back and forth.

He nodded before heading towards the remainder of his cohort.

Máire stared at the circle of bodies that lay scattered at her feet. Ravens came to the dead and began to feed at the blood and flesh. She pushed the tip of her sword into the ground and walked away from the death, stepping around the maze of bodies. After escaping the labyrinth of fallen flesh, Máire fell to her knees and started to cry.

Soon gentle footsteps echoed. Had Marcus come to stroke her hair and whisper words of sweetness in her ears? No. At that moment, stench filled her nostrils, and the trees seemed to wither as she noticed Seosaimhín approach.

"The strong winds echoed in our ears that the soulless matron to be would be here," Seosaimhín muttered.

Máire sat up on her knees to look at the elder druid. "Your son deserved his fate," she answered while meeting the other woman's eyes. "He murdered my beloved. His allies probably murdered my father."

"It is only fitting that the daughter of a weakling and the niece of a misguided fool would lose everything dear to her, including love. You would have made an excellent mother for our grandchild, and perhaps a good pupil. However, because you rejected this chance by killing our son, we will take from you the last vestiges of love you've entertained for the soulless one of Rome and anyone else in your worthless immortal life."

Máire tried to duck as a piece of rotting fruit came her way, yet the apple hit her in the chest and splashed her with a viscous, black residue that smelled of the worst things she could ever imagine. She looked back up to see that Seosaimhín remained. Máire gagged at the stench, while the elder druid chuckled.

"Marcus?" she whispered, trying to dredge up feelings for him that seemed so endless and vibrant a few minutes ago. She tried to think of Uncle Fergus, father, poor Seanán, but only the pit of black nothingness grew clear. She remembered sex with Seanán and Marcus, yet a disjointed hollowness only remained. She could remember no tenderness, no sweet feelings, or emotions.

A chill traversed her being as the horrible reality remained. She grabbed a nearby sword and threw it at Seosaimhín, impaling her, and the old woman fell. Máire got to her feet and started to run, hoping the curse would break apart soon with that old crone's death.

Seosaimhín watched the young Deargh Du run away with perfect tears on that perfect face. Soon, nothing alive remained in the field of the dead and dying. She started to chuckle as she pulled out the sword that had pierced her abdomen. Seosaimhín then rose before licking the blood-laden blade.

"We will meet again some night, Maél Muire," she whispered.

Marcus wandered towards Mhuine Chonalláin, expecting the see the battle raging forth. His blurred vision lent little assistance to his senses as he leaned against a rowan tree. The burning from the gold remained in his system, yet he could still limp. He soon felt more distaste upon sensing more gold coming closer. As a figure in gilded armor moved toward him, Marcus drew one of his gladii. He then noticed that the Lamia raise his right hand.

"Please put that down, friend," said the figure in front of him.

"Patroclus? Why are you here?" Marcus asked.

"There is time for that answer later," the Lamia suggested as he started to pull off his armor and toss it aside. He then bit into his wrist and took a few steps closer.

Marcus fed from him and soon felt his strength begin to return. He closed his eyes and said, "Thank you."

"I am certain you would have done the same," Patroclus answered.

Marcus pulled back and wiped his mouth. "I… yes I can safely say I would have done the same. What happened to your troops?" he asked.

"Your soldiers bore down on us," Patroclus answered. "We were not prepared for an attack from the sky. We tried throwing spears, but we could not penetrate most of the shields. Then we heard whispers of our fallen leader. We heard he had found the Phallus Maximus. We are now leaving your home and returning to Rome."

Marcus chuckled as he wiped his brow.

"You do not believe me after all we have between us?" Patroclus asked.

Marcus watched the Lamia's brows rise.

"No, no, my friend, I will tell you the truth, because I trust you. Mandubratius does not possess the Phallus Maximus. What he has is a copy."

The Legate laughed. "That is indeed a well-played ruse. Mandubratius will not be pleased when he learns the truth. I must admit that I found your troops to be most difficult to fight. I have not seen such skill since the days of my commander, Trajan."

Marcus nodded. "The legion was at its prime then, Patroclus. Where are you going next?"

"I have thought about it long and hard. I believe that it is foolish for the Lamia to follow Mandubratius and Amata if we want to achieve a modicum of our former Roman greatness," he said with a sigh. "I hope that you and I can work together in stopping them." The legate paused in his voiced thoughts for a moment. "However, I do owe allegiance to Amata and Mandubratius. They are still better than what we have had in the past with Felician and the others. I am still what I am, a Lamia and a Roman, and I will not do anything to jeopardize my home."

Marcus nodded his head. "We are both sons of Rome, Patroclus. I hope Mars and Neptune will guide you safely home."

Patroclus smiled. "I hope one day that the Rome we remember will return." He then saluted Marcus.

Marcus saluted in return and turned towards the west.

Béal Átha an Fheadha

Sive tossed herbs onto the fire to clean out the dun. As the smoke spread, she closed her eyes. Then, with a sudden crash, the door slammed open, and a red figure ran in, pushing its way past Bearach. She finally recognized Maél Muire underneath a dried coat of blood.

"What hap–" Sive began, before she stopped talking and turned to Bearach. "Bring out the brass tub." She then pulled her niece toward the tub. As she did so, her niece stared at her with hungry eyes.

Sive stuck out her left arm. Maél Muire looked back at her with her lips moving, but she said nothing. However, her eyes revealed a growing fear and pain.

"You fear you might kill me in your present state?" she asked Maél Muire.

Maél Muire inclined her head in a motion that looked like a nod.

"I trust you that it will not happen. It will be dawn soon, and you need to rest after your bath."

Maél Muire took her arm and began to feed. After a few moments, she released Sive's arm.

"Good," Sive praised as she patted Maél Muire's back, trying to ignore the dried blood. "Now, you need to get clean."

Mac Alpin noticed Claudius heading towards the dun.

"Young Claudius, hold!" he shouted. "Have you seen Máire? My luck has been terrible. I witnessed her kill an ancient mortal and then run this way, but I could not catch up with her."

He watched Claudius snicker a moment before the laughter disappeared. "Mac Alpin, what I witnessed had to be seen to be believed. Maél... Máire, turned into a banshee. I found her alone, attacking a reserve cohort of mostly mortals and several Lamia. My cohort joined in, and it was a bloodbath. However, Mandubratius arrived, and during the fighting with the new group of Lamia, he said something to her. I did not hear exactly what, you see, I was a bit busy, but then I heard it..." They continued walking towards the dun. When they arrived, Bearach motioned them towards the door.

Mac Alpin frowned. "I had hoped that the sound was just my imagination. So that was the scream that froze my soul and rendered me into a quivering fool for a few moments."

"It took me some time to get my hearing back after that scream," Claudius admitted. "She hit Mandubratius once, and he could not move afterwards. That was the last I saw of him. I do not know what happened to him."

Once they stepped into the dun, Mac Alpin saw Sive standing in front of a fire, trying to dry her wet and reddened clothing.

"She sleeps now. Twenty-five cauldrons of water, and she is finally clean, though she did not speak to me at all."

"Maél Morrigan?" Claudius asked as he looked at Sive.

"Máire," Mac Alpin corrected him.

"'Máire'," Claudius acknowledged while shaking his head. "I may grow used to her new name, but in my mind she is 'Maél Morrigan'."

Mac Alpin watched him go towards one of the cauldrons to wash up. "I am happy your niece is safe and sound," he said to Sive. "That damned fool Marcus owes me a battle." He soon noticed Edward walk into the dun.

"Edwina! Where have you been?" he asked.

"You would not let me go, remember?" his servant whined.

"Oh, right. I thought I might have to chase you all night with a bucket of water," Mac Alpin teased, before rubbing his forehead.

At that moment, the door burst open, and he watched as Sáerlaith and Caoimhín carried in Berti. The mortal waved over at him, his blue eyes radiant against his colorless skin. "I should go get Sitara," Mac Alpin said.

"No Arwin, do not tell her just yet," Sáerlaith whispered. "Caoimhín, go find Ruarí."

The doors opened and more Deargh Du, as well as the other blood-drinkers, wandered into the dun.

"Edward, see if you can help Basala scrounge up proper sustenance," Mac Alpin started to say when he heard a scream echo in the dun.

Sitara stood in the doorway. Her eyes grew wide as she clung to a stranger.

"What happened?" she screamed as she galloped to her husband's side, pushing aside everyone who dared to step in her way.

"I am so sorry, Sitara," Berti murmured while giving her a weak grin. "I went to the wedding and ended up in a battle with Sáerlaith and Caoimhín. Mandubratius cut me, or some other Lamia did. I thought it would be alright, but I fear my wound festers."

"Nonsense," Sáerlaith challenged as she watched Caoimhín and Ruarí come in and start working on Berti. "Claudius, Arwin, how did we fair in battle?"

"The Lamia left all the battlefields," Claudius answered. "Their desire to fight seemed to disappear when the banshee screamed and revealed the weakness of their leaders."

"I see almost everyone here but Marcus..." Sáerlaith said as she looked around.

Then the door opened, and Mac Alpin saw a bloody Marcus wandered into the dun. "I fear any rumors of my demise are premature, Sáerlaith," Marcus announced.

"You are wounded?" Mac Alpin watched Sáerlaith study Marcus.

"Yes, but I had a chance to feed, and I escaped." He stopped talking and looked over at Sitara and Berti, studying them for a moment. "I came upon the battlefield at Mhuine Chonalláin, and I saw none there but dying Lamia. The Deargh Du protecting the church had escorted the mortals to their homes. I believe the Lamia left, carrying their spoils."

Mac Alpin watched Marcus give Sáerlaith a final exhausted smile before taking a seat near Berti.

Máire awoke, remembering the sound of the scream that had echoed through her soul and resounded with such fury. She stood on shaky feet before leaving her room, clad in a léine and a blanket. When she got to the great hall, she heard soft conversations in Latin and Gaelic. She then saw that the other Deargh Du had settled in for the day. Many of them had collapsed in weariness, still clad in battle armor.

The smell of mortal tears drew her towards several cloaked figures leaning over a prone Berti. Máire began to recognize faces and saw Sitara weeping into her hands. The stench of dying laced the air with illness and blood, revolting and entrancing her at the same time.

"About time you awoke," Berti said while staring into her face. "Come closer."

The other blood-drinkers moved aside as she came in and sat down next to him.

"Please take care of my wife and child, Chieftain," he requested as his face broke into a smile. "That was a very interesting wedding."

"I will. You have my word," she promised, before patting his arm. She then backed away, feeling that she could do no more for him, other than distract him further.

Berti motioned Sitara in closer and whispered something into her ear.

Sitara nodded and wiped away her tears before kissing her husband for what may have been the last time.

Berti then pointed at Marcus. She watched the Deargh Du kneel down and lean in close. She could hear Berti inhale and exhale before speaking again. The whispered words grew with strength in her ears.

"See you later, my brother." As Berti closed his eyes, she heard a raven caw outside on the winds.

"Our mortal friend flies free now," Ruarí said. "He will journey to the Otherworld and join in Dagda's feast. Berti can enjoy the hospitality of Dana and battles with our gods and goddesses. When he finds himself bored with that, he will return to us. Morrigan shall guide him in his ride to the Otherworld."

Máire wiped away a few tears, realizing she had little left to shed now.

"We will hold our wake here in two nights' time," Sáerlaith announced, "if that is alright?" she asked.

Máire nodded her head. "Please ask the warriors to strip the Lamia's bodies of their golden armor tomorrow. We will give it to those who lost loved ones during this tragedy. It will not ease the pain, but it will feed their clans."

"Of course, Chieftain," Sáerlaith replied.

Sive and Sáerlaith took Sitara's arms and lead her away from Berti's lifeless body. The other druids who remained began their preparations.

Máire then noticed Marcus watching her. He walked over to her and then wrapped is arm around her waist.

Máire looked at him, waiting for the normal pleasure, warmth, and love to grow as she stared into his eyes, but nothing happened.

"What, no kiss for your warrior and general?" he asked, before turning her lowered chin towards his eyes. "No sweet words of adoration and devotion? You wound me, Máire," he teased, smiling at her.

"I need to go to sleep," she said as she pulled away.

"And so do I," he replied. "I will join you and ease you into sleep." His words turned seductive.

"No," she answered, placing a firm hand on his chest, "I want to be alone."

She noticed the sad and hurt look in his eyes as they turned to the color of soft blue skies and then back to hardened steel.

He said nothing more before turning away.

She walked back to her lonely room before sitting on the bed that they had shared. She had gone so far to think of it as theirs and no longer just hers a few nights ago, but as fatigue threatened to wrap up her mind, Máire rolled under the covers and slept, dreaming of an eternity of loveless nights.

Mhuine Chonalláin

Máire walked across the battlefield and felt Marcus' hand on her left shoulder. She turned and smiled at him. "I forgot that the Lamia and Deargh Du are equal on some terms."

"How do you mean?" he asked.

She continued walking through the empty village of Mhuine Chonalláin. "We turn to dust, as do they, at sunrise. It is so silent here," she told him. "I cannot believe that no one looted the golden armor."

"Most of the village relocated to Béal Átha an Fheadha or other places. They seem to believe that this is hollowed or haunted ground," Marcus said. "You missed much of that, Maél... Máire."

Máire chuckled. "Claudius calls me 'Maél Morrigan'." As she walked around some empty golden armor, she heard the movement of the carts as mortals and blood-drinkers carted away armor and stuck Deargh Du swords in the ground where the dust of their owners remained. She then pulled up her cloak, as the wind gathered strength, and then found her way to the smaller field where many dead mortals lay. She covered her nose, finding the stench unbearable.

Marcus pulled her away from the bodies. "Many are calling you that now, Maél Morrigan, Morrigan's servant. Weakness grows in between the smell and the gold. Is this where Morrigan possessed you?"

She looked at him.

"I deduced that from what others said," Marcus commented.

Máire felt the surprise fade from her face. "Yes, but it happened earlier than here. It first started in the church."

Marcus took her arm, and they moved toward the small stone house of worship. "Do you think that Her taking you over is why you took Connor's heart?"

She slid her hand around Marcus' arm. "It was our mutual decision to end his life in that horrific way," she replied.

As they stepped through the open door of the church, she noticed some candles lit at the now clean altar. She smiled.

"So, why did you not kill him?" Marcus asked.

"Kill who?" Máire queried.

"Why did you not kill Mandubratius?" He met her eyes, and his stare grew impenetrable.

"You have met Her before," Máire said, instead of answering his question.

She did not clarify 'who', but she knew she didn't need to. She watched Marcus turn back to the altar and then saw the corners of his mouth turn up into a smile.

"Yes, I have," he answered.

"I know who you are," she whispered. "Morrigan shared her sight and memories with me. I can remember Adhamdh's birth as if I were there. How he infuriated her and inspired her all at once, just as she felt in creating you," she said while reaching for Marcus' hand. "Even though I cannot love you now, I appreciate the gift you gave me. You allowed me to become more than just Deargh Du. You need not fear, for our secret remains with us, Marcus."

"The transformation changes us all," he said, before bringing her hand to his lips, "but how did this change your feelings for me?"

"I am not sure," she admitted. "It could have been the transformation, or… Seosaimhín threw a viscous, slime-encased apple at me. She cursed me, and that was when my love for all things and people faded. I can feel concern for things and fondness," she admitted as she met his eyes, "yet maybe that will fade as the change strengthens." She felt a weak smile settle on her lips as he let her hand go. "I hope it is just an effect of the transformation," she added. "I am worried that if it is Seosaimhín's curse, there may be no druid who will have the strength to remove it."

"If that is the case, then we can work on it," he said.

She said nothing more, not wanting to deny the hope that it might fade over time.

Béal Átha an Fheadha

Smoke filled the dun and moved over the gathered guests, making some cough and others blink their tear-filled eyes. Máire rubbed the tip of her nose, hoping not to sneeze as the druids lit the other ceremonial fires to commemorate the spirits of the dead leaving this world through the mists to move to the next. Horns, harps, drums, and whistles played a soft, yet cheerful tune that everyone seemed to find happy and joyous. Máire sat down outside the circle of blood-drinkers and mortals, dressed in clothing befitting a glorious celebration. Even she found a new dress, yet she still felt confusion and malaise that would not lift.

Sáerlaith glided to the center of the dun, her flowing blue dress seemed to float over the common dirt. When she stopped, all the musicians paused but the harpists.

"We are gathered here this hollowed eve to reflect on those who have passed to the Otherworld. A great darkness threatened our Lady, Éire. Bloodthirsty armies from the south invaded our lands seeking conquest and treasure. We Deargh Du had isolated ourselves from the rest of the world, and we were unprepared for the onslaught of the Lamia armies. However, we found hope amongst our brethren and our newfound allies. Through the assistance of many, we found victory, yet this victory did not come without cost. The blood of Deargh Du, Ekimmu Cruitne, Sugnwr Gwaed, and mortal fell, and they have all made the journey. Tonight, we celebrate their lives and deeds and thank them for their sacrifices."

Sáerlaith then raised her cup. "To the travelers," she toasted, before drinking.

Those gathered echoed her words before quaffing their drinks and returning to the loud dance. Mortals ate the remnants of the wedding feast and danced blissfully, convinced of their safety.

"You should be done with the change now," Marcus suggested as he leaned in over her shoulder, before resting his face against the hollow between her neck and arm. "Please do not be glum. I feel sad every time I see your listless expression. Come and dance with me. We should be past the grief. We need to realize that we cannot be downcast for eternity."

"The curse gives me little but grief," Máire replied.

Marcus sat up before moving next to her. "Let us think through this, Máire. Granted, Seosaimhín knew a great deal about perverting nature to meet her needs, but do you honestly believe she had the strength to do this to you? I believe you feel guilt."

"Marcus, with our strengths, we can manipulate nature to forge a glamoury that makes love certain. Druids and others of a darker calling can corrupt such beauty to bring about darker results. Aunt Sive says Seosaimhín carried such gifts. I may be stuck in this position for quite some time." Máire slid an arm around him and leaned against him, hoping he would not see this as an opportunity.

"So, do you believe this magic will wear off, or can it be reversed?" Marcus asked.

"I will try to find a way," she answered.

Marcus pulled her up for a dance, and she resigned herself to try to find some pleasure in that.

Sitara sat down against the wall as the revelers spun around, drank, and ate. She wished to feel a great, morose sadness, yet a numb acceptance and a good deal of pleasure ate at her, making her feel a profound guilt.

"This is Berti's culture," she reminded herself. She could almost hear him whispering in her ear, demanding that she dance with the others. She watched the drunk stumble around a bit, with Mac Alpin apparently leading them in a song about women of loose virtue, which she found so funny. Sitara chuckled so loudly that she felt she had to cover her mouth.

Mac Alpin turned in her direction and squinted, as if unsure that she was there or not. "Sitara, how are you fairing this magical evening?" He sat down next to her, took the drink from her hand, and poured half of it into his mug.

"I am not sure, Arwin. I feel sorrow for the loss, yet I feel some joy that I loved my husband and will have his child. Berti died for a noble cause. I have cried, and I wish to cry more."

"You forgot something," the elder blood-drinker told her.

"What is that?" she asked.

"You forgot to dance," he bellowed as he pulled her up, despite her grumbling protests. He then started twirling her. "You are smiling. You must really try harder to hate this," he said.

Sitara said nothing more and closed her eyes as her guilt started to ebb away and the music grew louder.

As Seosaimhín moved past the revelers, the hood of her cloak covered her features. She soon exited the dun and then peeked through the slats and crevices, which seemed much easier than walking through the drunken sloth and the blood-drinkers. "Ah, two soulless lovers talking," she whispered, knowing Nagirrom would hear her words. "Maél Muire and Marcus, infinitely loveless and foolish, stand in the middle of the dancers, talking and drinking." Or rather Maél Muire spoke as Marcus drank from a bottle of wine.

Maél Muire ducked away from Marcus and meandered closer towards Seosaimhín's hiding place. She then sat down on the ground and propped a hand against her chin. Marcus walked off and started dancing with the others. The whistles and drums grew louder, causing Seosaimhín to wince. Then, the disjointed music became a mere cacophony.

"Silence the music," Seosaimhín hissed. A few moments later, the musicians obeyed. "Thanks be to Nagirrom for heeding our call." She then studied the figure a few feet away from her. All she could see now was a head of glossy, red curls. "The wretch alone is she. Alone, she will be, until the end of her eve. Perhaps we should send her to the Otherworld this eve. She is but a lonely wolf in an empty wood without the pack's protection. So close we could move, so silent." She neared the side door. "We could creep in, like an ancient snake. A quick grasp of the mouth and draw of our knife across her throat, and her screams would be silenced before they could be uttered. Though her body would try to heal, one twist and yank would pop her skull from her neck, and she would begin her journey to the Otherworld. Ah, how we desire this to be."

Seosaimhín began to open the door, thankful the music drowned out the noise.

However, a caw made her turn away from the door. She saw the white crow standing on the outer wall of the dun. The crow stared at her and shook its head a bit.

"Oh mighty Nagirrom, you wish for this to be so?" Seosaimhín asked, before moving in closer to the omniscient bird.

"She must live for now," a voice whispered. "Her trail will cross with yours once again. Your destiny is linked with hers. Abide by my wishes, druidess."

"As you command," Seosaimhín murmured.

The crow nodded again and cawed. Its voice echoed around the dun as it took to the air.

Seosaimhín sighed. Maél Muire still sat oblivious to her presence.

"Heart-ripper, our paths will cross again," Seosaimhín purred like a cat about to pounce on an unsuspecting mouse. She then turned away, took to the night skies, and began her flight towards home.

Sáerlaith looked over the newly born council of five. Emer and Finn had died during the battle with the Lamia, which left them with Ruarí, Nuadin, and Etain. The three of them waited with her and Marcus in peaceful silence.

"I am not late, am I?" Fianait asked as she walked into the room. "General, this is a pleasant surprise," she said while grinning at Marcus.

Another figure walked towards Sáerlaith.

"I am Donal. Finn was my father-in-darkness. I am taking his place," the new council member said to her with a bow of his head. She noticed him look over the other council members. He then began to study Marcus as he and Fianait spoke to each other.

"Finn," Sáerlaith said, before catching Donal's attention again. "We will all miss him. Well, let us begin. I call this meeting to order and wish to welcome our new council members tonight. They are succeeding our dearly departed friends who served us honorably in fighting against the Lamia a week ago."

Nuadin, Ruarí, and Etain nodded to the new members of the council. Everyone but Donal took their seats. Donal still stared at Marcus.

"Why is this bastard child here?" Donal asked as rage colored his words.

"I requested Marcus to be present for the issue of the business before us," Sáerlaith answered, while placing a hand on Marcus' knee to advise him that she would take care of this matter.

"What council business could possibly require him?" Donal asked. "Go back to Rome, you son of a whore," he added, after turning to address Marcus.

She watched Marcus' eyes focus on him ever so slightly. A green glow chilled his eyes.

"Please take your seat, Donal, and be civil," she said, while keeping her voice calm. She watched Donal sit in between Ruarí and Etain. "If Marcus had not helped our family, the Lamia would be sitting in our home now."

Donal rose from his seat. "That is an outrageous lie! If anything, this bastardized Deargh Du defied the warrior's code of our home! Our warriors had the right to their own glory. Instead, they were mere cogs to his megalomaniacal schemes of Romanization."

"Be silent!" Sáerlaith shouted, raising her voice, before willing herself to calm down.

"The warrior code has existed for over one thousand years," Donal said. "Who is he to come here and ignore our code? Our victory, as you call it Sáerlaith, was but a fluke."

"Excuse me, I have no knowledge of proper etiquette in this council," Fianait argued, interrupting Donal, "yet I know firsthand that if we fought the Lamia by traditional means, we would have been dead, by now."

Donal sneered at Fianait. "Utter cac," he said. "Because of these new so-called skills, we lost many Deargh Du, too many, I say. We also let many of the Lamia escape. If anyone else had been in control–"

"Like you, Donal?" Sáerlaith growled. "We are not here to talk over the past. We are here to discuss our future. We owe Marcus and his allies a great debt for saving Éire and us. They have shown us that our isolationism can exist no longer. We must make a concerted effort to learn about our enemies, and we must extend influence beyond Éire. We need to solidify relationships with our new allies."

"Savages you mean," Donal muttered. "I would sooner fornicate with pigs than call the Sugnwr Gwaed or Ekimmu Cruitne allies. Bastards of Morrigan have no business in Éire."

Sáerlaith sensed Marcus tense, before silently sliding back his chair. All the council members turned to watch Morrigan's brood grow infuriated. She placed her hand on his leg again, hoping she could convince him to remain calm.

"They are no more bastards of Morrigan than you and your ilk," Marcus said, before standing and meeting Donal's stare. He fingered a forgotten dagger, or at least she hoped it was forgotten. "The Sugnwr Gwaed and Ekimmu Cruitne shed Roman blood for us, and yet you repay their courage, generosity, and friendship with insults to their heritage? If we were not in the council chamber, I would make you eat your words."

She watched his eyes grow dark for a moment.

"Marcus, Donal, we will have no more of this," she said.

Marcus' eyes turned to a calm blue again as he faced her. "My apologies, Sáerlaith," he said.

"Now, if I may begin in proper fashion of this council, I propose that we formalize relations with our allies to the east and that we commission a council to conduct intelligence gathering, and if necessary, subversion against those who pose a threat to the balance. Our Creator gave us the mission to maintain the balance, and through this council, we shall do that. Gone are the days when we could sit idly by and contemplate the cycles of the moon and stars."

"I second this motion," Nuadin stated as he nodded to her.

"Let us put this motion to a vote," Ruarí said. "All in favor raise their hands."

Sáerlaith held up her hand and watched as all but Donal did so.

Ruarí smirked at her. "I would say this means we have a new council. What shall we name this council?"

"'Cothromaigh'," Marcus suggested.

"Balance," Ruarí repeated. "I like that."

The others agreed, except for Donal, who remained sullen and silent.

"Then let it be known to all Deargh Du, the Cothromaigh is born. Marcus, I would like you to be the head of this Cothromaigh."

Sáerlaith leaned back in the tub, allowing the water to caress her back and neck. Soon a soft knock echoed in her room.

"Enter," she called out.

Marcus came in.

She smiled at him for a moment, forgetting why she had called for him.

"You sent for me?" He looked over her with a certain boyish curiosity. Men were such funny beings. The transformation did little to quell certain appetites of theirs.

"We cannot have a dissenting voice on council, Marcus," she said, remembering her concerns after the meeting. "If we are to leave behind our isolationist past, we must toss aside some of our old prejudices like a worn out piece of clothing. Time changes perceptions, and so must we. We are destined to move into a new reality."

"I agree," he said.

She studied him again. "Well, I believe that you need to take care of it however you see fit. Let this be the first mission of the Cothromaigh."

"The balance will be maintained, Sáerlaith," Marcus said, before turning on his heel.

Before he could leave, Sáerlaith stood up from the tub and said, "Marcus, wait. Before you go…" She paused a bit, wondering how best to speak with him about delicate matters. "I was wondering whether I might have your companionship." Sáerlaith grinned in spite of her nervousness. It had been many months since she had felt enough at ease to allow for such niceties.

Marcus turned back towards her with a ready grin. "Only if you scrub my back," he said as he started to remove his clothing.

Máire sat at the tavern, playing with the mead in her cup, thinking over the week. She soon remembered holding Connor's heart in her hand as he collapsed to the ground, and then of her emotions draining away at the moment the rotten apple exploded against her chest. "Can I ever escape it?"

The revenge, except for the touchy matter of Mandubratius, had begun to wane, and as her father-in-darkness had predicted, little purpose to life seemed to remain. She soon heard the soft squeak of the door opening, which allowed the sounds of night into the inn.

"Marcus," she said. Every sensation thrummed as he came nearer. The sensation seemed pleasant.

He placed a hand on her right shoulder before leaning in for a kiss. His lips tasted of something somewhat familiar… Sáerlaith. She smirked as she arched a brow at him.

"You are late," she stated. "I heard the council meeting had ended several hours ago."

Her father-in-darkness sat down next to her. "I had a brief discussion with Sáerlaith after the meeting with the Council of Five. They agreed to my idea. They even called on me to lead this group.

She raised her cup. "Congratulations. I am most happy for you."

"Are you happy for me?" he asked.

She stared into his eyes for a moment. "Marcus, even though I cannot love you, I can still feel happiness for your good fortune. Oh yes, I am happy." She clasped his hand before taking her drink.

"Excellent," he said. "Then, as my first official act as the head of Cothromaigh, I will give you your first assignment."

She could not deny her curiosity. Marcus always managed to surprise her. "You are giving me an assignment?"

"Yes," he answered. "I need someone I trust by my side. I know of no one else I have more trust in than you."

After the innkeeper placed mead in front of him, he took the mug and drew a long swallow of the brew.

"What about Claudius and Arwin?" she asked.

"Of course I trust my lieutenant and that crazy Pict," Marcus replied. "Yet, they have their own politics that will call them back home after Berti and Sitara's child is born."

"If I am in such high esteem as your comrades, I will accept this assignment," she said, before attempting a Roman salute.

Marcus started to laugh. "Excellent. Now, let us discuss this first assignment."

Berti stood on unsteady feet as he dusted himself off while walking out of the verdant grove. He then heard soft whispers and could see a pair of beautiful eyes settle on him and then a wide smile, before the Sidhe ran away, gathering her skirts as her pale, shimmering blonde hair floated behind her, trailing flowers over the green grass.

He crossed through the fields of flowers and butterflies as he meandered toward the great dun in the distance.

Around him, the sounds of hunters and warriors regaling each other with tales of bravery echoed along with the peaceful plucking of harps.

Berti walked to the dun and took the stone stairs that led to the second level. He opened the first door and proceeded into the room. He then kneeled down on a soft pillow, keeping his face toward the floor, much like a monk at vespers.

Then the door opened and closed, and he could tell that She drew near. He could hear a sigh of relief as a swell of the sweetest smells settled over him.

"So, did you like this past life?" She asked, as Her melodious voice echoed in the small room.

"Yes I did," he replied, feeling a smile spread across his face. "I always find enjoyment and satisfaction during the times I go there, and soon I will return again."

She walked around him, before placing Her finger under his chin. He then rose to his feet, studying Her appearance, and saw that a scarlet cloak curled around Her armor-clad form.

Morrigan pursed Her lips. "Why do you choose to live this way? You live one mortal life and then another, then you die and find sustenance and rebirth in the great cauldron. Why, Adhamdh?"

Adhamdh sighed. "I am your first, Morrigan. My duty is to serve you to the best of my abilities. I feel that I serve you by living mortal lives to keep you informed of how they live and how they have grown. Besides, it is always good to see my brother through fresh eyes."

Morrigan's black eyes widened as a smile spread over Her features. "So, does he know? Have you told him?"

"Yes, he knows."

Morrigan looked to one side and smiled. "I am sure that he knew. Marcus is no fool. I knew that he would exceed my own expectations."

"Of course you did," he said, nodding. Morrigan never admitted it in words, but in Her deeds. Then again, actions bespoke one's heart better than words ever could.

She gestured for Adhamdh to move towards Her. "Well, my child, it is time. Your new life awaits you."

"Off on another journey I go," he replied.

"Have a good journey, Adhamdh. I will miss you. This visit between lives was too short." Morrigan kissed his lips and walked away. "If you need me, let me know. I will be there if you call."

Adhamdh closed his eyes. Soon pressure gripped his body as the transformation began.

He then opened his eyes, and the gray world shifted into focus. Hunger and exhaustion overwhelmed his being, and he started to wail.

The cold faded away as he looked into Sitara's eyes and stopped crying.

"He is a beautiful little boy. You should be proud," Sive's voice echoed in the room around him.

The scent of honey tickled his nose.

"He has his father's eyes," Mac Alpin's loud voice rang in his ears.

"He looks very much like his father," commented Claudius.

He could sense movement, and then he stared into his brother's face.

Silver eyes stared at him. He tried to smile as he grasped an outstretched index finger.

"Welcome, young Bertius, to this world," his brother whispered as he leaned in and kissed his forehead.

"Stop being so greedy, Marcus." Another face moved in close and smiled at him. "Already, he has a warrior's grip," Máire said as she touched his hand as if fearful she might break him.

The sensations grew overwhelming, and he started to cry.

"Alright, you four, let's give them time to rest," Sive said.

He heard the blood-drinkers walk away, preparing to go find food. He then yawned, drifting off into sleep, feeling the steady pulse of a heartbeat. Memories started to fade as they always did, until the time of revelation.

epilogue

y friend, Marcus,

It may be many cycles of the seasons before it will be safe to deliver this message to you. However, if I do not record these events, their clarity will fade and dull with the passage of time. I imagine that this happens for your kind as well as mine.

I hope that you will find these events humorous, yet they ring of foreboding future events that are not lighthearted. The Mandubratius I knew no longer exists. Only a shell remains... a twisted, maniacal, brooding shell of his former self.

It started with his possession of the copy of the *Phallus Maximus*. During our journey, he would carry it in a silken bag under his tunic, strapped to his shoulder. He slept with it, and even comforted it. I cannot deny that he grew obsessed with this inanimate object and the power he believed would be granted to him when he returned it to the statue of Mars in the temple.

I tell you, Marcus, it was difficult to restrain my laughter at seeing this fool. He grew distressed at our slow journey and drove us to go faster on our grueling trip. I wondered whether he would stop and decimate us for our lack of performance, but it never happened. He soon forgot to feed, and forgot our needs as well. The few of us who remained from our campaign to Éire did not resemble an army. We looked more like refugees evacuating a far-flung disaster. Only once have I been hungrier, the first night of my transformation to Lamia.

The shining promise to see the comprehension on Mandubratius' face when he discovered that this was not the treasured offering made the travel seem worthwhile.

We arrived in Rome a week ago. He had sent Amata ahead of us in order to prepare for the procession into the temple. I had not seen such pomp since my days as a mortal.

Mandubratius held it aloft so all Lamia could see that he alone possessed it. You should have seen his face. He looked like so many of the blissfully blind pilgrims who come to see a holy relic. What a fool.

I could see Amata's eyes as we walked by, and I could tell in her hurt eyes that she wished to share that moment of glory. Would it have been too much for him to allow her to assist him? I cannot help but have sympathy and respect for our Domina, much more for her than for that Briton.

This mockery of a religious procession coursed through the hallowed halls of the temple, down to the holy chamber with the statues of Mars and Venus. Mandubratius led the way as the catacombs echoed with the chants of the faithful. So loud were the chants that I felt the ground shake.

Our leader stood before the statue of Mars as we fanned out so we could see and behold the triumph of the Lamia, the rebirth of our power.

Marcus, you should have been there to see this strange celebration. When he mounted the relic onto the statue, the chanting stopped. Utter silence deafened my ears as we watched and waited with baited breath to see how Mars would grant Mandubratius and all Lamia with His gifts. Of course, I knew that no gifts would be granted this eve. I am not sure what I would have seen if this had been the real Phallus Maximus, yet I could tell Mandubratius expected a grand explosion of holy energy, for he seemed to stand dumbfounded when nothing happened.

For many seconds, the chamber remained still as everyone stared at the statue. Then, with a resounding creak, the false relic fell from its seat and shattered like glass on the cold marble. The halls remained quiet. Mandubratius fell to his knees and began mumbling prayers to Mars. The rest of us began to file from the room, returning to our duties. I left the temple after shaking my head, trying hard not to break down in fits of laughter at the folly and how low we have sunk under this Briton's leadership.

After sleeping at my home, I awoke to whispers that Mandubratius had kept vigil over the shattered remains of his prize. I returned to the temple and found him disheveled and gaunt. Amata had kept watch over him during the day.

He told me that he must be unworthy due to his defeat in Éire. Amata, for her part, tried to convince Mandubratius that the defeat could not be the reason for this rejection. After all, they had done their best.

He went wild-eyed, accusing her of attempting to decry the sacred relic as a fake. Amata backed away from him. Mandubratius crawled to the shattered remains, brushed some into his hands, and then brought his hands up to examine the fragments. Mandubratius stared at the broken pieces of treasure and then inhaled the dust.

His visage grew dark and almost frightening to behold. Mandubratius then screamed the word 'fake', before rising up from his hands and knees. He growled, and I swear to Lady Bellona, I thought he planned to run to Éire that very night. Amata went to restrain him, and I joined her.

Mandubratius resembled those overwhelmed by the falling sickness. He drooled and raged over the Deargh Du and that he would take care of that Maél Muire. He kept yelling that she must have something to do with this, and that the ancient druid would suffer at his hands as well. He further promised to raise another army to raze Éire to the four directions.

I did my best to keep him in the chamber and whispered to him that he did not have an army capable of defeating the Deargh Du now. I said I believed that the Phallus Maximus would remain hidden in Éire.

My words seemed to sooth him. He promised to have the army back up to its original strength, and then we would find it, even if it took a thousand years. He even complimented me for the wisdom of my words, before saying that he wished Maél Muire were still mortal so he could rip out her heart as she did to her husband-to-be. He looked blissful at that moment. I assume he meant this figuratively, since I know the chieftain is still a mortal, or at least, I have not heard different, and I doubt that I can take the words of our leader at this moment as truth.

I know over the next century, Mandubratius will not sit idle, though I am fairly confident that he will not take troops to Éire for many centuries, if not a millennia. However, I am certain that if he sees you, or any other Deargh Du, he will be uncontrollable. I look forward to the next time we meet. I hope before then, I may send you this letter. May our Rome return to its former glory.

- Patroclus Statilius Messalinus

continue the journey with...

Dark Alliance
Morrigan's Brood Book III

published september 2011

about the authors

Heather Poinsett Dunbar

Born in Houston, Texas, Heather began writing her first book at age eight. While her grammatical structure left much to be desired, she continued to hone her writing and storytelling skills. During a college internship in London, England, her curiosity about ancient cultures and mythology intensified. She backpacked through Europe, fell in love with Scotland, cried at the retelling of part of Ulster cycle, garnered ghost stories from the Beefeaters at the Tower, wandered the Roman ruins in Bath, and danced around the stones in Avebury.

After spending all her spare time studying these new interests in many libraries and on the road, she began working on her masters in Library and Information Science at the University of North Texas. She now resides in the Houston area with her husband and three cats. She loves exploring the local culture as well as the many Celtic festivals and events in Texas. She also works as a librarian for a local college, and her favorite authors include Morgan Llewellyn, Neil Gaiman, Terry Pratchett, Evelyn Vaughn, Alison Weir, and Randy Lee Eickhoff.

Christopher Dunbar

Chris Dunbar was born in Greenport, Long Island, New York and then moved to Texas as soon as he could, at least that is the story he tells to native Texans, such as his wife. Chris keeps searching for ways to leave Houston, like moving to Auburn, Alabama, Dallas, and even San Antonio, but Houston just keeps reeling him back. Chris' day job is performing Business Continuity and Disaster Recovery, but his night job is coming up with creative ways to wound and maim the characters he and his wife Heather created. For fun, Chris enjoys the occasional novel and video game, but he also likes to delve into his Scottish ancestry and tool leather. When he can find the time, Chris pretends to play the Bodhran and the didgeridoo, much to the chagrin of his cats Lucius, Ophelia, and Clyde, not to mention his wife Heather. Chris is also an avid wearer of the kilt.

published and future works

Title	Synopsis	Release
Morrigan's Brood Morrigan's Brood Book I	Éire is invaded by a race of blood-drinkers seeking an artifact they believe will restore them to power. Yet the Deargh Du, the protectors of Éire, are not prepared to defend the island. Only with the help of a Roman general from an earlier time can they hope to rise up against the invaders.	Dec. 2009 Re-print Jan. 2012
Crone of War Morrigan's Brood Book II	The Lamia expeditionary force has gained a foothold in Éire and has formed an alliance with a powerful Irish chieftain and his malevolent mother. To reinforce them, a massive Lamia army, which is departing Rome, will soon give them enough power to conquer Éire and find their lost treasure. Will the Deargh Du and their new-found friends be able to protect Éire from the invaders, or will the Deargh Du's suspicion of other blood-drinkers allow their enemies to be victorious?	July 2010 Re-print Aug. 2012
Madness & Reckoning Madness - Short-Story	Following the events of 564 CE, madness strikes one of the Lamia's most important personages. Can the Lamia march on, or will this insanity cast them into civil war?	eBook Apr. 2011 Print Feb. 2012
Madness & Reckoning Reckoning - Short-Story	Following the events of 564 CE, the Deargh Du must come to grips with change or see old strife resurface, which could tear the Deargh Du apart.	eBook June 2011 Print Feb. 2012
Dark Alliance Morrigan's Brood Book III	A new menace threatens the Balance within the Holy Roman Empire as vicious murders of both mortals and blood-drinkers spread throughout the empire like wildfire. Can a hastily formed alliance between archenemies thwart this new menace, or will festering hatred bring about the empire's doom?	Sept. 2011
Curse of Venus Morrigan's Brood Book IV	The Strigoi, the Cursed of Venus, have spread through the Holly Roman Empire and parts beyond like a plague. In response, Pope Leo III takes advantage of the scourge to settle an old score with the man he placed on the throne: Charlemagne. Will their bitter rivalry send the Empire further into chaos and destruction, or will their Deargh Du "angels" save them from themselves and from Venus' Cursed?	June 2013
Shards of Light Morrigan's Brood Book V	Many sets of eyes peer through the mist, watching events unfold as the dark alliance seeks out an ancient device that they hope will uncorrupt the menace that has nearly brought the Holy Roman Empire to its knees. However, not everyone beyond the mist is content merely to watch.	TBD 2013

Other Morrigan's Brood Series titles include <u>Odin's Chosen</u> (Book 6, in progress), <u>Hera's Wrath</u> (Book 7, in progress), and <u>Dynasties of Night</u> (Book 8, in progress).

Other works include <u>It's in the Cards</u> (a novella that will appear within an anthology with other authors, in queue for publication) and <u>A Year and a Day</u> (novel, on hold).